PASSION'S PRISONER

Archer's face was so close that, even by the subdued light of the moon, Margaret could see the smoldering expression in his eyes, feel the sensual heat of his flesh. Before she could stop him, his parted mouth angled across hers. He kissed her deeply, a lusty kiss involving his seductive lips, his questing tongue and animal sounds low in his throat. Her senses rioted on her. For a mindless moment, she experienced nothing but a molten heat that intensified when his hands skimmed along the sides of her breasts.

Was this what he had meant back on the river when he'd vowed that, before he was through with her, she would be begging? Recovering herself with an effort, she reminded him softly, "You agreed that we would wait."

"Aw, hell, that's right. Afterwards, when we're rested, huh?"

"Yes."

He caressed one of her hands before lifting it tenderly toward his mouth. "But you know what, sweetheart?"

"What?" she whispered.

Turning her hand, he planted a kiss against her palm, then looked directly into her eyes. "You are so full of bull."

Steel flashed in the moonlight as he whipped the handcuffs from his back pocket with his free hand. Before she could prevent it, the bracelet had been slapped over her wrist and snapped shut.

Other *Leisure* books by Jean Barrett:
DELANEY'S CROSSING

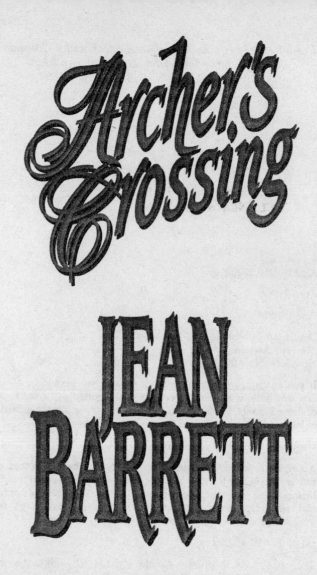

Archer's Crossing

JEAN BARRETT

LEISURE BOOKS NEW YORK CITY

To Kathy Chwedyk, Jackie Schauer, and Jennifer Coleman.
Nothing is more important than your friendship.
Except for chocolate cake, of course.

A LEISURE BOOK®

April 1999

Published by

Dorchester Publishing Co., Inc.
276 Fifth Avenue
New York, NY 10001

ISBN 0-8439-4502-8

Chapter One

Saint Joseph, Missouri, 1844

Margaret Sheridan shuddered over the sight of the gallows. There was no way to avoid the abominable thing. They were erecting it smack in the center of the wide street she had to cross on her way to the jail.

Making an effort to protect what she considered her well-bred sensibilities, she concentrated on the cloth-covered tray she carried. She regretted her inattention a moment later when a stream of tobacco juice narrowly missed the hem of her immaculate green plaid muslin skirts.

Disgusting! The street was already filthy enough. Didn't anyone in this awful town have a sense of propriety? Pausing, she glared at the offender, who proved to be the elder of the two workmen on the scaffold.

"Looks like supper on its way to the condemned," he hooted, in no way apologetic about his action.

Margaret was tempted to ignore his rude observation, but he would have considered her silence unfriendly. Most of Saint Joseph already thought she was a snob. She didn't mind what their opinions were, but she did care about her sister-in-law, who had to live among these people. For Hester's sake, she offered the grizzled bear on the platform a prim response.

"Even the damned have to eat, Mr. O'Hara."

He rumbled with laughter. "Not much longer, ma'am. This is just about ready for him." He tapped the sturdy gallows tree with the side of his hammer. "Soon as the sheriff is back from Sparta to officiate, Archer Owen'll swing from here."

The spotty-faced youth who was his assistant beamed at her. "He'll get hisself a fine view up here of the ol' Missouri River before the noose settles around his murdering neck."

They wanted her to admire their impressive creation. Wanted her to agree that Archer Owen should feel honored to be sent to his reward on such a grand structure. It was what the rest of the town was feeling. She had heard them smugly expressing it in the streets.

"Gonna be Saint Joseph's first official hanging, so we got to get it right. A quick rope and a handy tree might've been all right when the place started as a rough trading post in the twenties. Not now. Heck, this town's going places. Everybody knows that. Yesiree, got to show that upstart Independence and stuck-up St. Louis that Saint Joseph knows how to do things in a proper civilized fashion, even if it is perched on the raw frontier."

"You turnin' out for the hanging, miss?" the youth wanted to know. "Gonna be a real show."

Margaret couldn't imagine herself attending such a savage spectacle. Not that she had any sympathy for Archer Owen. He had been convicted by a conscientious jury and no doubt deserved to pay for his vile crime. Besides, though he didn't know it, the wretched man had seriously inconvenienced her. Still, she couldn't understand how anyone could take pride in an execution. But then what could you expect of a community inhabited by a lot of barbarians?

"It's not my definition of entertainment, gentlemen, but thank you for the invitation."

She left them to continue with their gruesome activity, and went on reluctantly to the jail. Floyd Petty, the paunchy deputy in charge of the prisoner, met her at the street door, regarding both her and the tray with exaggerated suspicion.

"You ain't the regular girl what brings the meals. Did Miz Sheridan go and hire herself a new serving maid?"

It was bad enough that she had been drafted into carrying a supper tray for a murderer, but to be mistaken for a servant was downright insulting. Margaret lifted her chin to a haughty angle and corrected him.

"I'm Mrs. Sheridan's sister-in-law. Her boarding-house is bedlam this evening. There was no one else available to deliver the tray."

"Is that a fact? Course, I can't say as how I'm surprised, what with the town already fillin' up with folks come to watch the excitement. It's good for business. Well now, ma'am, forgive me my caution. I did hear as how you was stayin' at your brother's place since the trial. Just that you can't be too careful with a desperado like the one we got locked up. Let's go feed him."

Margaret followed the deputy through a cluttered office and into the rear of the building, where the cell was located. The sun had just set, and the place was already thick with shadows. While the deputy fussed around lighting a pair of lanterns, she waited outside the bars with the supper tray.

Unlike the rest of Saint Joseph, she had been in no way curious about Archer Owen. She would have preferred never glimpsing him at all. That was not possible now.

There was an iron-framed cot in the cell. A long, lean figure was stretched out upon it, the visored cap of a river pilot tilted down over his eyes. The corner where the cot was situated was too gloomy to offer her more than a scant impression of its occupant. He wore a kind of nautical uniform that matched the flat-topped cap. It consisted of dark blue trousers, a coat with tarnished brass buttons, and a lawn shirt that had once been white but was now filthy. Margaret could almost smell the odor from it.

There was something else she could see. Hair the

color and thickness of a lion's mane. It reached to his shoulders in the style of a plainsman. His sideburns were wide and luxuriant, flowing into a full mustache.

Feeling her gaze on him, he looked up suddenly and discovered her there outside the cell. She couldn't tell his expression. It was hidden by the shadow of the visor. He must have been interested, however, either in her or in the food she had brought. Swinging his long legs to the floor, he rose and sauntered across the cell until his rangy figure was directly in front of her. There were just the bars separating them now.

Margaret found her gaze colliding with the most unusual pair of eyes she had ever seen. They were light amber in color, like the feral eyes of a lynx. She couldn't help herself. Mesmerized by their hot glow, she searched their depths, expecting to see the haunted, trapped look of a man facing death. All she found was pure insolence.

She shivered and drew back quickly from the bars, reminding herself that he was a dangerous animal. He chuckled over her reaction and went on staring at her brazenly, the amber eyes intimately appraising the swell of her bosom.

"Looks like the boardinghouse is hiring a better class of waitress," he drawled in a voice as low and rough as river gravel.

Her hands tightened on the tray, the only visible sign of the rigid self-control she exercised.

"You're in the presence of a lady," Floyd Petty warned him as he secured the lanterns to their hooks on the wall, "so watch that dirty tongue of yours."

"Or what? You'll hang me?"

"Always got to make it tougher on yourself, don-

11

cha, Owen? You just close that trap or you don't eat tonight. Now stand back there against the wall while I open up."

The prisoner was in no hurry. With a final impudent grin in Margaret's direction, he strolled to the rear of the cell and leaned negligently against the brick wall. Pushing his cap back, he revealed the strong, square face of a Celtic warrior. Probably the result of a Welsh ancestry, she thought, finding nothing appealing in features quite so hard and bold.

The deputy made a self-important little show of producing his keys and unlocking the cell door. He gripped a long-barreled Colt pistol in one hand and with his other hand took the tray from her. Entering the cell, he placed the tray on a small table equipped with a stool. Then he backed out and locked the door, never taking his eyes off the prisoner.

Archer Owen watched the elaborate ritual with his hands in his trouser pockets and amusement hovering around his wide mouth. Margaret didn't blame him. Floyd Petty was rather a fool.

The deputy turned to her with a throat-clearing air of authority. "No need for you to wait, ma'am. Tray can be collected in the mornin' when breakfast gets delivered."

Margaret would have liked nothing better than a fast retreat. It wasn't possible. "I promised Mrs. Sheridan I would return with the tray as soon as the prisoner is finished eating. Her house is so full this evening that she's obliged to feed her guests in two sittings and will need all of her dishes. Besides . . ." She hesitated, risking a glance toward the cell. "The small coffeepot came back dented last time."

12

Owen laughed as he ambled to the table and seated himself on the stool. "Got you mounting guard over the crockery, huh? Looks like I'm a menace to society in more ways than one. Well, hell," he said, whipping the cloth off the tray, "I don't mind the company. Not when it's good to look at."

He flashed another wicked grin at her, which she tried to ignore. She detested this situation, regretted that her sister-in-law had agreed to supply all meals for any prisoners in the jail. But it was necessary. Hester needed every penny she could earn.

The deputy nodded. "Your choice, ma'am." He ducked into the front office, and came back dragging a rush-bottomed chair for her. Margaret thanked him and seated herself well away from the bars. Satisfied by her caution, he returned to the office and the interrupted game of solitaire that was waiting for him on his desk.

Uncomfortable with her vigil, Margaret was prepared to remain silent as she perched there stiffly on the battered chair. Archer Owen tasted the beans on his plate, then made a face. "Cold," he grumbled.

She offered no response.

He leaned back on the stool and considered her. "Seems to me," he said with ease, "that if a lady invites herself to have supper with a man, the least he can expect is a little pleasant conversation. No? All right, then I'll provide it. See, when I complained the beans are cold, that was the perfect opportunity for you to cut me with a witty remark. Something like, 'Where you're going, Mr. Owen, you won't have to worry about anything being cold.' Now that's what I would have said."

13

She maintained her silence.

"So, what else have we got tonight?" He was in no hurry to eat his supper. He looked over the food on the tray, aggravating her with his deliberate slowness. "Yum, roast chicken."

Selecting a piece, he carried it to his mouth. But instead of sinking his teeth into the chicken, he sniffed at it while one of his fingers stroked the tender flesh.

"I'm just the man to appreciate a plump white breast when it's offered to him." His tongue appeared, licking at the meat with a sensuality almost painful to watch.

His brash allusion wasn't lost on Margaret. She could feel her cheeks flaming, but she refused to give him the satisfaction of looking away.

He bit into the chicken breast, chewing on it with pleasure, savoring its flavor. "Mmm, hot and sweet, just the way I like my breasts. Sure wish you were in here with me to share in this."

He was a devil, relishing his performance as he taunted her with his lewd analogies. She gazed at him with contempt.

"Let's see what's next on the menu." He poked around the tray, lifted a saucer that covered a small bowl, and smacked his lips over his discovery. "Cherries! Don't know when I've last had me a nice ripe cherry just begging to be sucked on." He popped one of the succulent fruits into his mouth and chewed with eyes closed in mock ecstasy. Juice trickled down his chin. "Luscious," he moaned, his tongue snaking from the corner of his mouth to lap at the dribbling juice.

She wasn't going to talk to him. She wasn't.

"Sweetheart," he coaxed in a silky growl, "why don't you come over here and let me feed you one of these through the bars? Then afterwards . . . well, afterwards you can clean off my fingers with that pink, wet tongue. Guarantee you'll enjoy it."

The chair clattered as Margaret surged to her feet. "You're disgusting, and I don't have to stay here and listen to your obscenities." She would wait for the tray in the office, or out in the street if she had to.

As she started to rush away, the saucer slipped from his fingers and shattered on the stone floor. "Oops," he said with casual innocence.

She rounded on him furiously. "You did that on purpose!"

He looked injured. "An accusation like that isn't very nice. It was an accident. See, I was just holding it like this . . ." He seized a cup from the tray and suspended it threateningly over the hard floor.

"Don't!"

Hooking his little finger through the handle, he swung the cup playfully back and forth above the stone flags. "Guess I could be persuaded to be more careful. With a little encouragment, that is."

He was blackmailing her! The cur was blackmailing her into staying! She had no choice. Hester couldn't afford to have more of her dishes broken. Fuming, she sank back on the chair.

"No more of your crude language then."

"Perfect gentleman," he promised solemnly.

He returned the cup to the tray with exaggerated care and began to eat the rest of his meal while she watched him with mistrust. He started to spear one of the small potatoes with his fork. It resisted penetration, bouncing around the plate like a ball. She grimaced, realizing it must be undercooked. Her sister-in-law had requested her help with the potatoes. Considering her history in the kitchen, Margaret should have known better than to comply.

"A little raw, isn't it?" he said thoughtfully. "Gonna need some gentle handling, then maybe one quick, hard thrust to get me inside. What?" he wondered when she frowned at him warningly. "I'm discussing a potato here. It's not like I'm doing some gutter talk about a virgin."

Margaret started to get to her feet.

"All right, relax. You want polite conversation, I'll give you polite conversation." Abandoning the potatoes, he worked on the chicken again. "Weather. Now that's a nice safe topic. How is the weather out there? A little hard to tell from in here."

She had to remain here and listen to him, but she didn't have to talk to him.

"Can't tell much of anything else either," he said. "Say, how is the work coming on my gallows? They got that up yet and tested? Hear I'm gonna be a real attraction."

It was a mistake. She knew it was a mistake before the words were even out of her mouth, but she couldn't stop herself from challenging him. "How can you? How can you sit there eating chicken and making vulgar jokes when you're facing your own hanging?"

"Suppose you think I ought to be down on my knees prayin' over my sins. Probably asking yourself, what kind of man is he? Well, now, I'll tell you. I'm a man who still has all his appetites even if he is looking at a noose. Which brings up an interesting possibility.''

What was he talking about now? She was afraid to know.

''The thing is . . .'' He paused to toss the rest of the chicken on the tray and to wipe his greasy hands on the cloth. ''The thing is, there's this tradition that on his last night a condemned man gets the meal of his choice. That's so, isn't it? Hell, I say that's all wrong. I say a man locked up all that time isn't hungry for roast beef. He's got another appetite that wants satisfying. So why not just go ahead and provide him a little sport in his cell with the female of his choice?''

Scraping back on the stool, he got to his feet and came to the bars. He pressed his craggy face against them, his teeth gleaming in a smile of invitation. ''What do you say?'' he whispered seductively. ''You interested? Maybe something could be arranged.''

Margaret came to her feet with such force that this time the chair overturned with a loud crash. Alarmed, the deputy came charging in from the office waving his Colt pistol.

''What in dad-blame is goin' on?''

She ignored him, directing her outrage at the tall figure lounging against the bars. ''What they say about you is true! You're worse than despicable! You're a brute without a shred of decency!''

''That's pretty strong language.'' He nodded toward the tray. ''You're forgetting the dishes?''

''Break them! Break every last one of them! I don't care because I'm leaving!''

She started to push past the startled deputy.

The prisoner called to her from the cell plaintively, "Do I take this to mean that you won't be accommodating me on my last night?"

Margaret swung around in the doorway. "Hanging is too good for you, Mr. Owen."

"Uh-huh. What would you suggest?"

"Something slow and agonizing. Like poison."

He issued a long whistle. "That's pretty vicious."

"Yes, and given the opportunity," she added for good measure, "I'd administer it myself."

His mocking laughter followed her as she stormed out of the jail. She passed the gallows in the gathering twilight. This time she viewed the structure without a qualm. If she'd had any modicum of compassion for Archer Owen, it was gone. Pausing for a moment in the street, she relished the image of him mounting the scaffold. Then, with a little smile of grim pleasure on her mouth, she hurried off in the direction of the boardinghouse.

The deputy snorted with disgust as he picked up the overturned chair. "You're your own worst enemy, Owen."

"Yeah, that's what they tell me."

"Put that broken saucer back on the tray, and then slide it over here by the door where I can reach it without comin' in all the way. After that little performance with the lady, I wouldn't put nothin' past you."

Arch decided it wasn't worth arguing about. He obliged the deputy.

All right, he thought sourly as he collected the

pieces and shoved the tray toward the bars, so he had entertained himself a bit at the expense of that bitch. But what did she have to be so insulted about? She wasn't the one who would have a rope dropped around her pretty neck. What did he have left anyway but sarcasm and a few leers? They'd stripped him of everything else, and if he lost those his pride would go, too, and he meant to keep that intact when they sent him to hell.

"Now back against the wall again while I open up here," the deputy ordered him.

Arch headed for the wall, wishing that the small, barred window in it offered more than a view of a dirty alleyway. He longed for a glimpse of the river and his lady. She was the only thing that mattered to him, the only female he trusted. Precious to him because she had been so hard won. But she had been taken from him along with the rest.

Feeling deflated by the hopelessness of his situation, he flopped down on the lumpy cot, hands locked behind his head as he stared up at the stained ceiling.

"Why did you have to go and behave that way with her?" the deputy demanded, bustling around like an old woman as he recovered the tray from the cell.

Arch ignored him.

The man was persistent, an irritation. "If you figured you was payin' her brother back by hurtin' *her,* you figured wrong. No way Trace Sheridan would even know. Hear he went off to try an' join a wagon train headed west."

His interest sharply aroused, Arch lifted his head to stare at him. "You telling me that woman is *his* sister?"

Trace Sheridan. The chief witness against him in that mockery of a trial. He'd heard the bastard had left town while the verdict was still warm.

"Got your attention now, have I?" Floyd Petty chuckled, leaning against the door he had just relocked. "So you didn't know that was Miss Margaret Sheridan. Got here the day the trial ended. Lot of good it did her with Trace already gone. Tell you somethin' else. She ain't just his sister. I hear she's his *twin* sister. Only, on her it looks good. Real eyeful, though folks say she's stuck up. St. Louis. What can you expect?"

Arch sat up on the edge of the cot, excited by the deputy's revelation, though not understanding why. Not yet, anyway.

Twin sister, huh? Yeah, he could see it now. They shared the same striking combination of black hair, cleft chin, and eyes as blue as a deep fjord. There'd been a Norwegian mother. He'd heard Trace mention that in the saloon. And the deputy was right. On Margaret Sheridan the combination was a winner, if you didn't mind that her eyes were also as frosty as a fjord.

Arch wondered. On some level had he already sensed she was Sheridan's sister, recognized that proud, arrogant face? Is that what had compelled him to try to torment her? Because he hated Trace and people like Trace who had looked down on him all his life?

The deputy, realizing he was getting too friendly with his prisoner, was suddenly impatient. "Ain't got time to gossip with you, Owen. None of this is gonna do you any good where you're goin', anyway."

He departed with the tray, leaving Arch to deal with his churning emotions. For the thirty-two years of his existence on this earth circumstances and individuals had been trying to break his spirit. They had failed. He had grown up learning to conceal all the wounds under careless laughter, a swaggering confidence, and a fiery temper. Even a sentence of death hadn't defeated that stubbornness. They wanted to see him suffer before the end. He wouldn't let them.

But underneath that cynical mask was fear and a bitter despair. The secret conviction that this time there was no way out. He was going to die. Only now . . .

Arch breathed deeply and slowly, ridding himself of the bleakness, filling his lungs with determination.

Margaret Sheridan. He ought to thank her. Her visit had shifted his black mood, reminded him of his need to survive.

Turning his head, he gazed again in the direction of the river, his frustration deepening until it was pure desperation. He wanted her. He wanted the *Missouri Belle* back in his possession. There was only one way to achieve that. He had to get out of here. Whatever it took, he promised himself fiercely.

And just what would it take?

Leaving the cot, he began to pace the cell, his mind attacking the problem. How? he wondered. *How?*

The alleyway outside his window was dark with night when his brain finally began to shape a plan. It was a real long shot, the success of it depending on a couple of chancy things. He had to hope that the sheriff wouldn't return from Sparta, where he was testifying at another trial, for at least one more day. The sheriff was canny, but his deputy was all dumb bluster. Given the opportunity, Arch knew he could manage him.

The other thing was getting Margaret Sheridan back here tomorrow night with his supper tray. That was not going to be so easy.

Margaret let herself into the kitchen of the frame house on Poulin Street. Her brother's wife was at the bake oven, removing a batch of biscuits while the hired girl, Agnes, loaded a platter with chicken. They were hurrying to serve the second sitting of lodgers.

Hester's plump cheeks were flushed from the heat. There was a smudge of soot on her chin, and her fine dark hair had escaped from her pins in damp, untidy strands.

Margaret gazed at her sister-in-law with a mixture of sympathy and scorn. She was fond of Hester. Or as fond as she could be of any woman her own age. She'd never had a real girlfriend, not one she could confide in. Probably because she'd always viewed other girls as rivals who were jealous of her looks. She'd told herself she didn't miss that kind of closeness, but sometimes . . .

She didn't pursue the thought. It made her uncomfortable. Anyway, she was too busy regarding Hester as a fool for loyally loving her brother. Trace had never been anything but a burden to her.

I could strangle him, Margaret thought, for running out on her like this.

"An opportunity that couldn't wait," Hester had explained to Margaret when she'd arrived in Saint Joseph to find Trace already gone. "I'm not clear about it. There was no time for him to explain, but Trace is positive it will make our fortune.''

Margaret knew better. Another wild dream. Her irresponsible brother was forever chasing them.

Hester, reading the disdain in her eyes, had defended Trace, murmuring. ''It's just as well business has removed him from the scene. Of course, he had to testify, but the trial was very hard on him. This Archer Owen is an awful man, and even if he can't touch Trace with anything but curses and threats . . .''

Poor Hester, Margaret thought. But under her pity was a grudging admiration for her sister-in-law. Hester didn't need Trace to survive. She had her boardinghouse now and the grit to make it succeed. She wasn't helpless without him. On some level, which Margaret was also afraid to examine, she envied her that kind of independence.

Yes, but Margaret had her own ambition to realize, didn't she? A much more enviable one, too, because it didn't involve the hated drudgery of housework and watching every penny that was spent. Enoch Rawlins was waiting for Margaret back in St. Louis, and she was eager to return to him. Enoch was very rich, and within a month she would be his wife. She was determined that nothing be allowed to interfere with their wedding. At the age of twenty-three and haunted by her father's ruin, she was convinced that Enoch was her last chance for the solid security she so desperately craved.

''Was there any difficulty?'' Hester asked.

Margaret realized that Hester had finished removing the biscuits and was staring at her a little anxiously. Did her face betray her encounter with that revolting man back at the jail?

"Not in the least," Margaret assured her, thankful that her sister-in-law was too distracted by her preparations to notice yet that she hadn't returned with the tray. She would make some excuse about it later. In the meantime, distasteful as it was, she felt she had to offer to help. "What else can I do?"

She didn't miss the swift glances Hester and Agnes exchanged, nor the way the hired girl's eyes rolled in the direction of the plates collected from the first sitting. They were piled near the sink, waiting to be scraped. The only food left on them were the potatoes cooked by Margaret and ridiculed by Archer Owen.

"I would be so grateful, dear, if you would sit with William," Hester said. "He went to sleep when I put him down for the evening, but he is teething and sometimes wakes up and starts to fuss. If that happens, a little soothing is all he needs."

The care of babies was as alien and unwelcome to Margaret as housekeeping. Given a choice, though, she preferred her nephew over duty in the kitchen. All the same, there was something a little disconcerting in the realization that even dull-witted Agnes was too valuable to spare, whereas *she* was considered next to useless.

William was peaceful in his crib when Margaret arrived with a fresh lamp in the small bedroom at the back of the house. She hoped he would go on sleeping. He was a good baby, but she felt awkward whenever she was around him.

The boardinghouse was so full that she was forced to share these tight quarters with both Hester and William. At least the air was pleasant with the window open to a mild spring evening.

Fearing how her appearance might have suffered in that visit to the jail, Margaret paused in front of the cheval glass to smooth her hair and to check the condition of her dress. She had no intention of lowering her standards just because she was trapped in this primitive outpost.

Satisfied with her repairs, she seated herself at the tiny desk to continue with the letter she had begun this afternoon. Enoch was a thorough man, and he expected a detailed account of the situation here in Saint Joseph.

It was Enoch who had insisted that Margaret make this visit to her brother's. A report of the brutal murder, along with Trace's involvement in it as a witness, had appeared in a St. Louis newspaper. As a prominent fixture of St. Louis society, Enoch wanted to be certain that his future wife's reputation would in no way be stained by association.

"Besides," he had added in his precise manner, "your brother and his wife are the only family you have. I do think, my dear, you should be there to offer them whatever support you can through this ordeal."

Duty was every bit as important to Enoch as reputation. He had left her with no choice. Irritated with Trace for threatening her careful plans, Margaret had reluctantly traveled to Saint Joseph.

Pen in hand, she finished the paragraph that assured Enoch the scandal could not possibly reflect against them. Then she began to describe her visit to the jail. When the image of Archer Owen's sardonic face intruded on her restless thoughts, she threw down the pen and made up her mind.

This was absurd. She was not going to complete this letter. She would leave Saint Joseph on the first boat she could get, tomorrow if possible. She would tell Enoch in person all he wanted to know. There was nothing more to keep her in this place.

The sound of the pen hitting the desk must have awakened William. He started to whimper in his crib. Margaret went to him. Leaning over the rail, she tried to pacify him with reassuring murmurs.

"Good baby, Will. Good baby."

No, that had to be all wrong. He wasn't a dog. She tried again.

"Now, now, what is this all about? Are those nasty gums sore?"

She felt like a fool. A helpless one. In any case, he didn't want words. He wanted to be picked up and held.

"William, please, I can't. You wouldn't like it. I don't know how."

His whimpering threatened to escalate into angry howls. No choice. She scooped him up from the crib, dangling him out in front of her like a package whose contents she didn't trust. He squirmed and kicked, terrifying her.

"What? What is it now?"

Frantic, she tried bouncing him up and down. He went on struggling in her hands, loud and red with rage.

"Oh, all right!"

She did what she had watched Hester do and had never tried herself. She nervously cradled Willian against her bosom and rocked him slowly. He was immediately comforted.

Then something unexpected happened to Margaret as she went on holding him, something completely unfamiliar. She experienced a sweet, pleasing sensation, a feeling of serenity evoked by his small, warm body snuggled against her and the baby smell that clung to him. It was very strange.

Her pleasure lasted until she put William back in his bed and discovered that he had drooled down the bodice of her dress, leaving a noticeable stain. Margaret sighed. There was a time when it wouldn't have mattered, when she had been spoiled with all the stylish, pretty gowns she had desired. Now her clothes were precious, and she had to be careful with them. At least until she married Enoch.

It was frustrating. Not just that, of course. It was the sudden realization that she couldn't leave Saint Joseph tomorrow after all. William had just reminded her that, however ineffective she might be, her sister-in-law still needed her. She would have to stay until after the hanging when the crowds were gone and the boardinghouse was manageable again. She owed Hester that much.

But one thing she would not do, Margaret promised herself emphatically, was to carry another meal to that appalling Archer Owen. She'd sooner empty the chamber pots.

Chapter Two

"Well, if this don't beat all," cackled Floyd Petty when he met her at the street door. "Way you fled this place the other night, ma'am, I figured wild horses wouldn't get you back here bearing another supper tray for Owen."

"Circumstances change," Margaret informed him brusquely. "Will you hold the door for me, please?"

What *am* I doing here? she asked herself. How did it happen? Hester, of course. When her sister-in-law put her mind to it, she could be very persuasive.

"You see, dear," she had implored, "it isn't just a matter of your carrying his evening meal to him again, though naturally it would be a great relief to me not to have to spare Agnes for that errand. It's different when she delivers the trays to the jail at breakfast and noon. Those are much less hectic hours here in the kitchen, and I don't need her so badly. But . . .'' She'd paused to give emphasis to her next words. "Agnes has brought a message from the prisoner. Margaret, he begs you to take his supper to him. It seems that Mr. Owen earnestly regrets his harshness with you and wishes to apologize in person. It's true, isn't it, Agnes? Well, I think he must be suffering remorse at last."

Archer Owen with a conscience? Margaret found that hard to believe of the man she had encountered last night.

"Really, dear, I don't see how we can deny him such a simple request. Not when he is facing . . . well, you know. Beside''—Hester lowered her voice to a confidential hush—"I have a feeling there is more to it. I think he wishes to forgive Trace for bearing witness against him. But since Trace isn't here, he will ask his sister to convey that forgiveness for him. The possibility isn't so far-fetched. They do say that the condemned try to atone for their sins just before the end."

Margaret must have finally agreed to the whole thing, though for the life of her she couldn't remember having done so. But here she was and regretting it already.

"Too bad the sheriff didn't get back," the deputy said as he led the way through the office. "If we'd had the hanging today, nobody would've had to bring a tray to anybody."

"Yes," Margaret agreed with a wry smile, "it was very inconsiderate of him."

She braced herself for another encounter with the prisoner as they arrived in the back room. He was pacing his cell with a nervous impatience. When she appeared, he was at the bars in an instant, clutching them so tensely that his thick knuckles whitened.

Margaret had promised herself beforehand that she was not going to lose her self-control this time, no matter what he said or did. But she already found her composure threatened when those amber eyes slammed into hers again, making her catch her breath.

"You're late," he said, his voice husky with an urgency that surprised her. "I was afraid you weren't coming."

It was difficult to believe her presence could be that important to him, that it should matter at all whether he apologized to her for yesterday. The deputy must have thought the same.

"If it's the grub you want that bad, Owen, then back away so's I can get it into you. You know the routine."

A moment later Margaret was alone again with the prisoner and seated on the same creaking chair outside the cell door. She regarded him gingerly. Maybe he had changed his mind about that apology. He did seem, after all, far more interested in the meal she had brought. He'd wasted no time in settling himself at the table, and was eating the baked fish with relish. Except for those first terse words, he hadn't spoken to her, though she was conscious of him eyeing her.

In the end it wasn't the silence she couldn't stand,

but the certainty that she had been a fool. "I'm flattered, Mr. Owen."

"Why is that?" he asked around a mouthful of fish.

"I'm flattered that—according to Agnes, anyway—you have this grave need to beg my forgiveness for your conduct of last evening. Flattered but deeply puzzled."

"How so?"

"I can't convince myself that all out of nowhere you've decided to be repentant. It doesn't fit with the man I'm convinced you are."

He chewed thoughtfully for a few seconds. When he swallowed, the Adam's apple in his strong, tanned throat bobbed noticeably. She found the action oddly and provocatively disturbing.

"Pretty cynical judgment for a lady, isn't it?"

"I happen to be a realist, Mr. Owen. And though you may deceive silly girls like Agnes and sentimental women like my sister-in-law, I don't for a moment—" She broke off to stare at him. "What is it?"

He had stopped eating. There was a strange expression on his face. A look of extreme discomfort.

"Don't feel so good," he muttered.

"The way you were gobbling that fish," she said, her tone sharply acerbic, "I'm not surprised."

He didn't answer her. He sat there on the stool without moving, as if he could make himself feel better by remaining perfectly still. Margaret decided that his color was definitely bad. She started to get to her feet.

"If you're feeling ill, then I ought to call—"

A sudden spasm must have seized him. Moaning deeply, he stumbled to his feet, knocking over the stool. He really was sick! Alarmed, she sprang to her feet and shouted for the deputy.

He trotted into the cell area annoyed. "What now?" he asked.

By this time the groaning prisoner was almost doubled over and clutching his belly in agony.

The deputy approached the bars with suspicion. "You tryin' to pull something, Owen?"

"Last night," Archer said with an effort, the words coming in strangled gasps. "You heard her, Petty. Threatened to poison me. She's gone and done it. Slipped it into my food."

"That's insane!" Margaret cried, hovering anxiously beside the deputy, who had turned to gaze at her speculatively. "The fish must have turned bad. Either that or he's just pretend—"

She was cut off by the sound of painful retching from inside the cell. Archer staggered across the floor, trying to reach the solace of his cot. Before he could drop across it, his knees buckled and he collapsed on the floor against the bed's iron frame. His body jerked, clenching into a tight mass. Face against the stone flags, he went on retching. There was the terrible noise of a violent battle going on inside him, and in the next second he had spewed a putrid green mess on the floor. This was no pretense! Oh, Lord, he looked ghastly!

"Why are you just standing there?" Margaret shouted at the deputy. "Help him! You can't let him die like this!"

"Right, all right. Hang on, I'm comin'."

Margaret watched with a frantic impatience as the deputy fumbled with his keys, taking too long to open the door. Colt pistol in hand, he crossed the cell.

"Any way you can manage to crawl up on the mattress on your own, Owen? I don't aim to let go of this here gun unless I have to. Once I see you settled on your bed, I'll fetch the doc. Owen, you hear me?"

Margaret waited, her tension mounting. But there was no answer from the man huddled on the floor. Had he slid into a state of unconsciousness? The deputy must have feared that he had. He leaned down over the prisoner to try to rouse him. When his hand closed on a hard shoulder, there was an explosive reaction.

Archer's powerful legs, which were drawn up against himself, shot out like the pistons in a high-pressure steamboat engine. The force of the double kick caught the deputy somewhere in the area of his groin. He went down with a roar that was silenced when his head cracked against one of the iron legs of the cot.

Margaret's shriek, wrenched from her throat in horror, was followed by the sight of Archer Owen launching himself toward the pistol. It had flown out of the deputy's grasp and landed with a clunk several feet away, where it was spinning on the flags. She didn't wait to see him pounce on it, raise it toward her. Whipping around, she fled toward the door. She had never been so terrified.

How could they have been such fools to fall for a trick that was probably as old as time? But he had been so convincing, even down to the vomit. Pea soup! She remembered now. There had been pea soup at lunch. He must have somehow saved a portion of it, managed to stow it out of sight under the cot.

Oh, what difference did it make? He was armed, and the cell door was open. She had to get out of here, find help! Dear God, maybe he had already killed the deputy!

Heart in her throat, she flew across the shadowy office and reached the outer door. Her trembling hand was on the latch, ready to tear open the door, when a gun barked behind her. The bullet from it bit into the frame beside her, splintering the wood. It passed so close to her head that she actually heard the whine of it, could swear she felt its heat.

It was a bullet that meant business, and Margaret knew better than to defy it. The next one would be more than a warning. She went very still. Obediently still.

"Smart," he said behind her.

In three swift strides he was across the room. Her flesh crawled when his hand grabbed her by the arm and swung her around. Before she could object, he had her pinned against the rough plaster of the wall, the pistol at her throat and his face shoved menacingly into hers.

He was so close that she could see the dark stubble on his craggy jaw and the dangerous glitter in his amber eyes, so close that she could smell the male odor of him, feel the heat of his savage virility. It was an effort for her just to breathe.

"Please," she managed to whisper.

His mouth curled in a little smile. "You begging me, precious? What are you begging me for?"

She was afraid to answer him.

His face leaned in another inch until it was almost

touching hers. When he spoke, his warm breath lashed her skin. "Tell you what we're gonna do. We're gonna take care of a few essentials in here. And if you're real cooperative about them, I won't have to use this." He squeezed the pistol against her throat, reminding her that he was a convicted murderer who wouldn't hesitate to kill again. "Then maybe afterwards, if there's time, we'll get around to what you're begging for. Providing it's interesting, that is. Understand?"

No choice. She jerked a quick nod. To her relief, he released her and stepped back.

"Now," he instructed, "lock the street door and close the shutter on that window."

Margaret obeyed him. Just before she drew the shutter across the glass, her gaze scanned the street, hoping to see figures in the twilight racing toward the jail. But the street was deserted. Apparently, no one had heard the shot or her shriek for help. The brick walls were too thick. And now that the door was locked and the shutter fastened, permitting no outside glimpse into the building, Archer Owen was free to do whatever he pleased.

Sick with dread, she turned to face him. He had moved out of the concealing shadows by the wall and into the glow of the lamplight.

"Back to the cell," he directed her, indicating with the barrel of the pistol that she was to precede him.

Not daring to argue with him, she returned to the cell area on legs that were so unsteady she feared they wouldn't support her. The cell door was still open. The deputy, sprawled on the floor, hadn't stirred. Margaret was convinced he was more than just unconscious. Otherwise, Owen wouldn't have risked leaving him behind to come after her.

"You've killed him!"

"Naw, just knocked him silly. No brains in that head to injure. Get inside. Not there. Go sit down on the cot where I can watch you."

She did as she was told, huddling in the corner on the bed, trying to keep as far out of his reach as she could. Taking the deputy by his feet, he dragged him away from the cot, blocking the route to the door in case she tried to bolt. Then he went to work, rapidly stripping the deputy of his suspenders and neck bandana.

In less than three minutes the thick-waisted deputy had his hands snugly trussed up behind him and his mouth firmly gagged. Archer got to his feet, the keys he had removed from the deputy jangling in his hand.

It would be her turn now, Margaret thought. He would bind and gag her like the deputy, then lock both of them in the cell while he made his escape. She prayed that was all he would do.

"Move," he said, the lethal pistol in his hand gesturing toward the office.

Her heart sank. "Why don't you just leave me here and go?" she implored him.

One of his thick eyebrows elevated. "You begging again? Pleading like that sounds damn appealing to a man when he hasn't had a woman in weeks."

She'd had enough of his filthy taunts. Dangerous or not, she dared to challenge him. "You don't stand a prayer. What do you think will happen when I fail to return to the boardinghouse? Hester has probably already raised the alarm. In no time at all there will be armed men swarming around this place.''

"Don't think so. See, little Agnes can be real talkative, especially with a bit of encouragement. And guess what I learned while she waited for the noon tray? Learned that supper time at the boardinghouse is so wild with two sittings that your sister-in-law hasn't time to notice anyone not there. And even if she does wonder about you being so late . . . well, Agnes will remind her that I wanted a nice long talk with you about your brother and my awful guilt. Real sympathetic about that, Agnes was. So, are you coming along, or do I have to use another form of persuasion?''

Seething with outrage, and unable to express it when her fear was greater than her anger, Margaret left the cell. He locked the door behind them for good measure, and then escorted her back to the office, where he commanded her to sit on a chair.

Tossing the keys on the battered desk, he helped himself to a supply of ammunition for the pistol. Then he quickly searched through the drawers of the desk.

"Well, lookee here," he said, holding up a pair of handcuffs. "Could be real useful, huh? Maybe even pleasant.''

He looked down thoughtfully at his own wrist. Then his gaze shifted to one of her wrists. Margaret could feel herself tensing.

"Oh, you wouldn't.''

"Relax. I don't have time to play games with you.''

She hoped that was true, but she didn't know what he was capable of. The possibilities were too loathsome to consider. She had to find some means of getting away from him before he—

"Let's go," he ordered, pocketing the handcuffs and their key.

Dear God, he *did* intend to drag her with him. She didn't know which was worse, him forcing himself on her here and now or taking her along on his mad flight out of here. Either way, she wasn't given the chance to argue about it. The gun was suddenly in her ribs, urging her along a gloomy passage to a back door she hadn't noticed before.

"Open it," he insisted from behind her.

Cool air met her when she unlocked the door and pulled it inward. Twilight had deepened into full night. She could make out the dim sight of a deserted alley off the back of the jail. There was no comforting sign of life. The area was still, silent except for the rollicking sounds that issued from a saloon far down the street.

Margaret knew it wasn't the chill of the spring evening that made her shiver as she hesitated there in the doorway. It was the sick fear that if she went out there with him she might never come back. She couldn't do it. Not willingly.

"You're a fool," she blurted out rashly.

The gun tightened against her ribs.

"It's true," she rushed on. "You'd do much better to leave me behind. I'll only be a handicap to you, delay you in getting away."

"Maybe I'll get lonesome out there," he drawled from the shadows behind her. "Want some company."

Her nerves were on fire. She could feel him close behind her.

"On the other hand," he whispered, his mouth against her ear now, his breath stirring her hair, "could be I've got other plans for you."

She swallowed, struggling for the desperate words. "I won't be of any use to you as a hostage."

"No," he agreed, mystifying her with his response, "you'll be something much better than that. See, precious, before it's all finished, you're gonna provide me with a ticket to permanent freedom."

"Give me a hairpin," he whispered from the shadows, making her jump with his sharp demand.

She was bewildered by his request. "Why do you need a hairpin? What are you going to do with it?"

He blew out his cheeks in exasperation. "Stop asking questions. Never mind, I'll help myself."

Before she could stop him, his hand was on her head, his nimble fingers sifting through her thick dark hair. Margaret shrank from his touch. There was something hot and intimate about those probing fingers, something that panicked her far more than his verbal threats. She was relieved when he found a pin and came away with it in his hand.

"Stand over here beside the door with your back against the wall. And remember, I've got the pistol handy in my belt."

She understood his intention now. He was going to use her hairpin to pick the lock on the back door of the building where they had stopped.

Since it seemed safer at the moment to obey him, she flattened herself against the wall and nervously watched him as he began to work at the lock by the light of a newly risen moon. Her mind churned with questions.

If his escape was so urgent to him, why was he risking it by this break-in and the delay it involved? And that other strange business behind the jail . . . his chilling assertion that she was going to be the means of his permanent freedom, what did that mean? He had refused to give her any further explanation.

"What is this place?" she hissed.

"Do you care?" he said, twisting the wire in the lock.

He was right. Her curiosity was unimportant. Nothing mattered but getting away from him, and so far there had been no opportunity to achieve that. They were several streets away from the jail by now. He had driven her ahead of him along alleys and across backyards, and nowhere on that dark route had they encountered any other life except for a startled cat. It seemed that all of Saint Joseph was behind closed doors tonight. There was no one to help her. And she didn't dare to cry out. Not if she wanted to survive.

Maybe he would be caught entering this place. That was a possibility. And if he was cornered—

"You waiting for an invitation, precious?"

He had succeeded with the lock and swung the door inward on a well of blackness. He meant for her to precede him into the building.

"What am I walking into?" she demanded anxiously.

"Trouble, unless you move. I'm allowing us maybe twenty minutes in there, and when we come out we're gonna be two different people."

She was afraid to wonder what he meant by that.

It wasn't until seconds later, after she had stumbled across the darkness of a storeroom at the rear of the building and emerged into the spacious area occupying the front, that Margaret realized where she was. The moonlight through the large window on the wall facing the street revealed crowded counters and shelves and barrels on the floor. She had been here twice before with Hester. The Sweetwater Emporium. What did he want in a general store?

"Think it'll be safer if I hitch you to a rail while I shop."

Before she could prevent it, he captured her hand and snapped one of the handcuff bracelets around her wrist. The other bracelet he secured to an iron handle on a massive cupboard. She was trapped. Furious, she started to object.

"Do it," he warned her softly, "and you get a gag along with those handcuffs."

She closed her mouth. He left her no choice but to hate him in silence.

Leaving her, he vanished into the storeroom. When he reappeared, he was armed with a pair of empty flour sacks and Margaret was ready with a plan to free herself from the cupboard. If he could pick locks, why couldn't she do the same?

She waited, making sure he was too busy to watch her. Aided by nothing but the moonlight, he had begun to move swiftly around the store, peering at items and then dropping them into one of the flour sacks.

With furtive care, she located another pin in her hair. That was the easy part. What proved difficult was trying to spread it open when one of her hands was chained to the cupboard. The pin kept resisting her efforts, which were made doubly awkward by her need to conceal her activity from him. Fearing she would drop the pin, she checked again on her captor.

It was difficult to tell in the feeble light, but it seemed that he was collecting, along with such small necessities as matches, food that could be eaten easily on the run. Dried fruit, hardtack, beef jerky, cheese and crackers. He was ignoring her. It was safe to renew her secret attack on the hairpin.

Frustrating. It refused to stay parted, kept slipping in her fingers.

He was like a cat. She never knew he was beside her until he'd snatched the hairpin away from her. In one quick, simple movement he popped the pin into a straight wire and slapped it back into her hand.

"There, entertain yourself," he said and strolled away.

Margaret threw the thing on the floor in disgust. The cur! He had known all along what she was trying to do and that she'd never manage to open handcuffs with a hairpin.

By the time she had her anger under control, he had returned with a stack of garments he'd selected from the open shelves. She watched in dismay as he began to casually peel away his clothes right there in front of her.

The dark blue nautical-style coat dropped to the floor along with his cap. Then he stripped off his shirt. Faint though the moonlight was in the recesses of the store, she could see the gleam of hard, sleek muscle on a broad chest and a pair of brawny arms. The sight was unsettling, generating a strange weakness at the bottom of her stomach.

He was aware of her worried gaze. His teeth flashed whitely from the gloom in a lusty grin. "Be happy to remove the handcuffs if you'd care to help me with the rest. A little hard to get totally naked on my own. Got a hand here that's giving me trouble from when I took that tumble in the cell. *This* hand."

He demonstrated by stroking it down over his chest, his fingers trailing through a shadowy expanse of dark hair. The hand descended slowly until it reached his lean belly, where it teased the exposed flesh.

Margaret's mouth felt dry, her head light.

"It's gonna get interesting now," he promised her on the heels of a low, seductive chuckle as his hand went to his wide belt. "Something memorable for you to see."

When he started to undo his trousers, she quickly lowered her gaze. She heard the whisper of his trousers slithering to the floor. He kicked them away. Then he must have shucked his drawers. She caught a glimpse of them on the boards and knew that he had to be completely naked now.

Fearing his intention, she was sick with alarm. She couldn't bring herself to lift her gaze, but when she heard him starting toward her a moment later she panicked and yanked uselessly at the handcuffs restraining her. Her body went rigid when he stopped in front of her. This time she raised her eyes defiantly.

He was dressed. Denim trousers, a dark flannel shirt, and a wide-brimmed felt hat. Clothing he had taken from the shelves. She drooped with relief. It was a temporary relief. Releasing her from the handcuffs, he thrust another set of garments at her. Male garments.

"Here. Not gonna be easy with all those sweet little curves, but do your best to turn yourself into a boy. And make it fast."

Refusing to move, Margaret glared at him.

"Want me to do it for you? Take you right down to the skin?"

Hugging the folded trousers and shirt to her breasts, she uttered fiercely, "They're going to hunt you down and shoot you like a mad dog, and when they do—"

"You'll celebrate, won't you, precious? But you're gonna do it wearing pants and a shirt. Get busy."

The pistol waving in his hand again left her with no alternative. She would have to change her clothes. Even worse, she would have to undress in front of him. She knew he would refuse her any form of privacy.

"You might at least turn around while I disrobe."

He lounged against a counter and eyed her disarmingly. "I might, but I won't. A position like that could give you ideas."

She shouldn't have expected otherwise. He had absolutely no sense of decency. Fuming, she turned her back on him and began to unfasten her gown with hands that shook. She could feel his gaze lingering on her, hot and familiar, as she shed her dress, petticoats, and pantalettes. But her humiliation was nothing compared to her ongoing fear that he would try something.

She was down to her unmentionables now and determined to remove nothing else. It had been necessary to place the shirt and trousers on the floor while she undressed, forcing her at this point to bend over to recover them. Her only defenses were a corset and a thin chemise. They weren't enough.

"Makes a man's breath quicken to look at a bottom like that."

Margaret clenched her teeth in silence, knowing that a response would only encourage him. As swiftly as possible, she donned the male garments, stuffing the skirt of the chemise inside the waistband of the trousers. As strange as she felt in the masculine garb, she was relieved to be clothed again when she faced him.

He grunted his approval and tossed her a hat similar to his own. "Do something about hiding that hair."

"You don't really believe these outfits will prevent you from being caught, do you?" she challenged him as she did her best to cram her thick hair under the hat.

"They'll do their part," he said confidently as he collected their discarded clothing and stuffed it into the second flour sack, which he made her carry. "And if the storekeeper doesn't notice for a while that he's got missing articles, they're going to be looking for something else out there."

His hand closed on her arm like a steel band. The brute had the strength of an ox. "Let's go," he said. He hauled her through the storeroom and out into the alley again, where he paused to lock the door behind them, leaving no obvious sign of a break-in.

Margaret didn't know where he was taking her this time, but seconds later they had emerged on the street at the edge of town. When she looked back, she saw in the moonlight the shadowy outlines of the gallows in the distance. She gazed at it longingly.

"Disappointed, aren't you?" he whispered, chuckling softly. "There won't be any crowds tomorrow to watch a hanging." His hand gripped her forcefully by the elbow, reminding her of just how scared she was. "Looks like it's just you and me now, precious."

Chapter Three

Margaret trudged beside him as they passed a field of newly planted hemp. Resistance was useless. Whenever she tried to delay him by slowing her steps, he would nudge her with the hateful pistol or drag cruelly at her arm.

She asked him where they were going. He told her to be quiet.

The field of hemp was behind them now. She could see the gleam of the river below in the moonlight. She realized they had circled the town from its back side to avoid possible encounters, and were descending the bluffs toward the bottomland.

Jean Barrett

She asked him what he intended to do when they reached the river. Again he told her to be silent, only this time he was less polite about it.

She couldn't do what he ordered. There had to be some way of reaching him, some argument that would convince him to release her from this intensifying nightmare.

"I'm to be married next month," she informed him recklessly. "Enoch Rawlins is a powerful man in St. Louis. I promise you he'll move heaven and earth to get me back, and once he gets his hands on the man who abducted me . . . well, Enoch can be very unforgiving."

Archer wasn't impressed with her warning. He remained silent.

A dog barked somewhere off in the distance, and Margaret's desperation deepened. She tried a softer plea.

"There's something else you should know about Enoch. He's sinfully rich. If you let me go now, unharmed, he would be very grateful, very generous. I'm sure something could be arranged."

What she didn't tell him about Enoch was how much he abhorred scandal and that this infuriating situation endangered the marriage she craved. Owen wouldn't have been interested in that. Nor, apparently, was he foolish enough to trust the bribe she offered. There was no reaction from him. His continuing silence as they followed a rough path to the narrow flood plain was maddening. Margaret went back to threatening him.

"I've been gone too long. Hester must be worried by now. She'll send someone to the jail. Maybe they've already learned what happened. They'll be out after you with guns and dogs. But on your own you could still make it.''

He went on ignoring her. They had nearly reached the river. She was frantic, ready to appeal to a side of him that probably didn't exist.

''Perhaps,'' she said breathlessly, ''you had a good reason for killing that man. It is just possible you did. But I'm an innocent victim, and if you have a conscience . . . well, I'm sure you must . . . I mean, I assume that you do, in which case I beg of you to consider—''

It happened so swiftly that Margaret had no chance to prevent it, much less anticipate it. In one second she was rushing along beside him, trying to match his impatient stride. In the next second the loaded flour sack flew from her grasp as he swung her around on the path. Two great hands trapped her startled face between them. Before she could issue a gasp, his mouth came crashing down upon her mouth.

God help her, he was kissing her! Kissing her deeply, his sinful tongue forcing a warm, wet entry into the recesses of her mouth, which he plundered without mercy. Both shocked and shamefully aroused by the potency of his wicked assault, Margaret went limp. It was mindless, intoxicating, and her head was so light she was convinced she would faint if he didn't stop.

When he finally released her, she staggered back on the path, too stunned to voice the outrage his performance deserved.

''Looks like I finally managed to shut you up,'' he observed casually. He retrieved their bundles from the ground, thrusting the second flour sack back into her shaking hand. "No more objections out of you. You do exactly what I tell you from now on, and I might just let you survive."

Furious, but too shaken to argue with him, Margaret accompanied him the rest of the way to the riverbank. He paused there and gazed upstream. They were standing below the elbow of the river where the steamboats landed to collect the furs and buffalo hides that reached Saint Joseph from the upper reaches of the Missouri.

What now? she wondered.

He was silent. She stared at him nervously. He was paying no attention to her. His mind and vision were focused on a small steamboat several hundred yards off to their right.

Margaret remembered something her sister-in-law had told her about Archer Owen. He was the master of a rather sorry-looking stern-wheeler, which explained the outfit stuffed into the flour sack she carried. That must be his boat. The *Missouri Belle*.

An alarming possibility occurred to her. Despite his warning, she dared to express it. "You can't mean for us to steam out of here on that. The boat was impounded. I heard them say so in town. If you try to fire up the engine, they'll hear and start shooting at anyone on board."

"You think that would stop me from grabbing the *Belle*? I'd do it if I could. But they've lashed her with chains to the bank, and even if I was able to break the locks, there's no place she's going with a damaged wheel and a busted driving rod."

She couldn't see the expression on his face in the

shadows. She didn't have to. She could read the bitterness in his voice and the longing that accompanied it. It was the first honest emotion she'd heard from him, and it surprised and disturbed her.

He must have immediately regretted revealing that emotion, probably regarding it as a weakness, because the next thing Margaret knew he'd handcuffed her again. This time to a sturdy sapling on shore.

"Where are you going?" she demanded as he started away through the willow thickets.

"Wherever it is," he muttered, "you'll be in range of this Colt if you get any ideas about exercising your lungs."

Then he was gone, leaving her alone with her dismay and the muted sounds of the flowing river and the nighttime insects. She stared after him where he had disappeared downstream. Her mind was still in a whirl from his kiss, unable to forget the power and danger of it. Even now she could feel the surprising softness of his mustache, scent the virile odor of him, taste his warm breath mingling with hers. His mouth had captured hers with the force of a primitive brute, and she ought to be nothing but disgusted by the episode. She was disgusted. Wasn't she?

Oh, she had to get away from him! She just had to.

With a renewed determination, she shifted her attention in the direction opposite the one he had taken. There was another steamboat berthed just beyond the *Missouri Belle*. A much larger vessel with a hurricane deck that was higher than the *Belle*'s pilothouse. Excitement stirred in her when she caught a movement on that deck. A second later she was able to make out the figure of a crewman sauntering to the rail. She could see him in the moonlight as he leaned there, smoking a pipe and idly gazing at the water.

This might be her chance, but how could she attract his attention? She was too far for him to detect her down here in the thick shadows, and whatever the temptation, she didn't dare risk a shout.

In mounting frustration, she struggled with the problem, fearing that at any moment he would turn away and go back inside. Then the answer came to her. Matches. Owen had added matches to the food he'd snatched from the Sweetwater Emporium. And he'd left the flour sack containing those essentials right here on the ground along with the other sack.

Straining at the handcuffs binding her to the sapling, Margaret fought to reach the sack. Maddening. She couldn't get low enough for her fingers to grasp her target. The steel bracelet would slide down no more than a few inches before it was blocked by the thickness of the trunk. If only the sack were a little closer to the tree . . .

In the end, by stretching out a leg as far as she could, she was able to work the sack toward her with her foot. Success! Now she could lean down far enough to capture and lift the bundle with her free hand. When she had raised it as high as her waist, both of her hands could deal with it, even though one of them was restrained by the cuffs.

Hampered by the awkwardness of her situation, it took her a moment of searching through the contents before she found the tin of matches. Clutching her prize, she dropped the flour sack and glanced swiftly in the direction of the boat, fearing the crewman might have left the deck. He was still there, but if she didn't hurry and signal his attention with the flare of the matches, she would lose what might be her only opportunity to be rescued.

The first of the matches she tried refused to light. She seized another from the tin and struck it carefully. Just as it leaped into flame, a hand snatched it away and extinguished it with a snarled curse.

"Try something like that again and you'll find yourself at the bottom of the river."

He had reappeared silently out of nowhere, and even in the darkness cast by the trees she could read his rage. She remembered something else Hester had told her about Archer Owen. How the witnesses who'd helped to convict him at his trial had testifed he had a murderous temper. And that temper was now directed at her.

Margaret's mouth was dry with fear as he unlocked her from the sapling, almost jerking her arm out of her socket in the process.

"You're hurting me," she croaked.

"I ought to break both of your arms. I would if I didn't need them. Since those hands of yours are itching for activity, I'm going to put you to work. You can start by lugging both sacks this time. That should keep you occupied. Come on, this way."

He motioned for her to precede him through the willow thicket. She couldn't imagine where they were going. If he'd no intentions of snatching the *Belle,* why had the river been his destination?

The answer appeared on the other side of the thicket. As she cleared the willows, she could make out the form of someone's fishing skiff dragged up on the bank. Owen must have remembered spotting it along there when he'd steamed into Saint Joseph on the *Belle* and had gone to relocate it. Then he *was* planning to make his escape by water. But in a stolen skiff?

Margaret approached the craft with misgiving. It was difficult to tell in the moonlight, but it looked about as dependable as a washtub and not much bigger than one: What was her chance now of persuading him to leave her behind?

He gave her no opportunity to test the possibility. He was already barking a new order at her. "Put the sacks in there with the oars and help me to float her."

"Must you forever—"

"Do it!"

She wanted to fling the sacks at him. She also wanted to live. Dropping the sacks in the boat, she began to tug at the skiff.

"Not like that. Put your shoulder to it up here."

Margaret joined him at the bow and shoved from her side. The skiff refused to move.

"That what you call an effort?" he complained.

Since it was safer to direct her anger at the skiff, she strained fiercely against the bow. The boat suddenly slid toward the water. It was so sudden that, before she could let go, she was dragged down with it through the mud of the soft bank. When she picked herself up, she was plastered with the stuff. She didn't know which she detested more, the mud smelling of dead fish or her captor's odious laughter. Could this nightmare get any worse? Apparently, it could.

"Get into the boat," he commanded.

"But I need to clean off—"

54

"*Now.*"

Muttering invectives under her breath, Margaret clambered aboard the rocking skiff. In the dark she almost stumbled over a large object on the floorboards. It proved to be a rock. What was a rock doing here? she wondered as she started to settle herself on the bow seat.

"Not there," he said. "Take the middle seat."

"But that's where the oars are and . . . Oh, no! You *wouldn't*!"

"You'll have to row. My hand, remember? Told you back at the store I hurt it when I went down in the cell."

Good. She hoped it was killing him. "I don't know how to row." Why should he imagine that she might? She'd been in small boats like this only a few times in her life, and always with gentlemen who, of course, had handled the oars themselves.

"Well, I beg your pardon. Forgot you were a refined lady under that mud. No rowing, huh? Too bad, precious, because it looks like you're about to get a lesson in reality."

By now Margaret's jaw ached from her frequent needs to clench her teeth. She hated it when he called her "precious," implying she was some spoiled belle. And she wasn't. She wasn't.

"We're waiting," he said, patting the pistol in his belt.

What was the use? He had the gun, and she had nothing but her resentment. Stepping over the rock again, she seated herself at the oars. He freed the skiff from the bank with a shove and hopped aboard. Once settled on the stern seat facing her, he instructed her briefly in the use of the oars.

"All you have to do is pull us out into the center, and then the current will take over and do most of the work."

Margaret grasped an oar handle in either hand and thrust the paddles simultaneously into the water as he had directed. She tried. She really did try. At first she made a clumsy progress, drawing the skiff several yards away from shore. Then it all went wrong. She couldn't seem to maintain an even rhythm of dipping and dragging. When she unconsciously applied more pressure to one oar than the other, she lost control. The boat swung in an endless circle. In a panic, she struggled to correct the balance. All she succeeded in doing was spinning the skiff in the opposite direction.

"Jeeezus Keeerist," he bellowed, "you're making me dizzy!"

She released the oar handles and glared at him.

"I should have known not to expect something useful out of a pampered darling."

Even coming from him, the words stung.

"This hand is just gonna have to suffer," he grumbled. "Change places with me. That is, if you can manage to do it without overturning us."

Margaret wondered what her chances were for walloping him with one of the oars. She managed to resist that temptation, concentrating instead on squeezing past his bulk with a minimum of contact. The memory of the hard body she had glimpsed back in the store was still fresh and unsettling. She didn't need any treacherous collision with it.

Once they were installed in their new positions, he

seized the oars and drove the skiff toward the middle of the river with aggravating ease and accuracy. Now that they were clear of the concealing willow thickets, the steamboat just beyond the *Belle* came back into view. But any hope Margaret might have had that the crewman at its rail would be alerted by either the sight or sound of them was defeated. This time the deck was deserted.

Equally discouraging was the chill mist that was beginning to collect above the surface of the river. The stuff veiled the skiff, and within minutes the town was lost to sight. Huddled there on the seat, cold and muddy and miserable, she knew there was no one now to help her.

Though she did consider it, throwing herself into the river was out of the question. She was no better at swimming than at rowing. Besides, he was too quick and strong for her. He demonstrated that by the force with which he propelled the skiff. Nothing wrong with his hand at all, she grumbled to herself. He'd just been making a fool of her.

She had to revise that decision a few moments later when he rested on the oars. They were out in the main current by now, drifting slowly but steadily downstream. She could see him in the hazy moonlight, flexing the fingers of his bruised hand in an effort to ease the ache. She offered him no word of sympathy. There was silence except for the water lapping softly against the boat.

"This is as good a spot as any to do it."

It wasn't his low voice abruptly cutting through the stillness that startled her. It was the intention behind it. She gripped the sides of the boat, ready to risk a

57

leap into the water if he made a move toward her.

Her body tensed when he leaned forward. Nor did she relax when he reached for the rock instead of her. She had a horrible certainty, as he hefted the stone, that he was going to kill her, weigh her body down, and send her to the bottom of the river.

"Don't just sit there," he said. "Hand me that flour sack with the clothes."

"Why?" she asked nervously.

"Why do you suppose? I'm gonna get rid of it, of course."

Margaret found she could breathe normally again. It was all right. He was simply eliminating the evidence that they were wearing other outfits now.

"Hurry up," he urged. "What are you doing? Put that back in the sack."

"I'm just getting the handkerchief that was tucked into my bodice. I need it to wash off this mud."

He grunted something, but he permitted her to rescue the handkerchief before she thrust the sack at him. Clutching the handkerchief, she watched him stuff the rock into the sack and knot the top. He hesitated for just a second before he dropped the weighted bundle into the river. She could sense the regret in him. Had he been so proud of that river pilot's uniform?

Margaret experienced her own regret when the loaded flour sack went into the dark waters with a soft splash and sank out of sight. She had been very fond of that blue foulard dress, not to mention the lace-edged petticoats that went down with it. On the other hand, she was still alive.

She tried to appreciate that fact as Archer Owen took up the oars again, but her concern increased with every yard of distance he put between the skiff and Saint Joseph.

They must have traveled miles downstream from the town before he stopped to rest himself again in a quiet stretch of the river. In most places the spring current had been fairly swift, requiring more guidance with the oars than physical effort. Even so, she knew the injured hand had to be bothering him a great deal. The moon was high and brilliant now. She could see the grim expression on his mouth.

Margaret wondered. Was his discomfort enough to make him reconsider her abduction? If she could just convince him that she was a mistake, nothing but an added burden in his flight downriver . . .

"Why don't you put me ashore?" she appealed to him. "I'm no longer of any use to you as a hostage, and long before I can walk back to Saint Joseph and tell them, they'll have discovered you're gone."

"Give me that handkerchief of yours. Maybe that'll help with this hand."

She passed the handkerchief to him. It was still damp from her effort to clean the mud off her clothes. She watched him as he bound his hand, creating a cushion to relieve the pressure against the oar.

"You'll make much better time on your own," she persisted.

"Thought I made it clear to you back in town that I've got plans for you."

"This is about Enoch after all, isn't it? You're going to demand a ransom for me."

"I don't want your bridegroom's damn money," he growled. "All I want is the return of my steamboat and my freedom."

"You should have thought of that before you knifed that poor man in cold blood."

"Yeah? Well, you're gonna help me prove I didn't kill him."

"How?" she cried. "Even if it's true, and I don't believe it is, what can *I* possibly do?"

"I'll let you know when we get to Independence."

Margaret gasped. "Independence must be fifty miles from Saint Joseph, probably a good deal more than that by water."

"Think that's gonna stop me?"

"But what is so vital in Independence?"

"It's where the wagons leave for the overland trails, even if Saint Joseph is forever blathering how one day they'll take that trade away. But right now Independence is still where the emigrants gather to connect with trains heading west."

Margaret suddenly realized his intention. He was going after Trace, who had left for Independence after the trial to find a train bound for Oregon. It was in Oregon where Trace expected to realize some insane dream he hadn't shared even with Hester.

"You want revenge against Trace," she accused him.

"You don't listen very well, do you? Told you I'm gonna see my name cleared, and that means Trace Sheridan hauling his ass back to Saint Joseph where this time he'll tell the truth."

He sounded so convincing that for a moment Margaret actually wondered whether Archer Owen was innocent of murder. No, he had to be guilty. There would have been no reason for Trace to lie about what he had seen and heard. Besides, there had been other witnesses and the evidence of Owen's character and reputation. Revenge must be his motive for this wild flight downriver. Unless . . .

"You got it figured out yet, precious?"

All at once she did understand. He wanted Trace to perjure his testimony, swear now that he'd been mistaken about the accused. "You're going to use me to force him to go back to Saint Joseph!"

"Yeah, it did occur to me he could be persuaded to cooperate when he hears about the little surprise I've got with me."

"That's impossible!"

"You're his sister, aren't you? His *twin* sister. I know about twins and how close they are. There were these twins I once worked with back on the keelboats. Hell, it was nothing for them to share thoughts and feelings even when they were apart. Maybe you know what's on your brother's mind right now. Huh?"

"That isn't true of Trace and me. We were never close like that. *Never*. Most of the time we didn't even like each other, so if you imagine anything I might say or do would influence him in any way . . ."

She went on with with her pleas, striving to convince Owen that he was mad if he expected to reach Trace through her. But he couldn't be shaken in his stubborn conviction that all twins shared some magical bond.

"And what if Trace has already left Independence?" she argued desperately. "What then?"

"Then we go after him. Whatever it takes."

"But if he won't listen, if he doesn't care that you're holding me—"

"He will when his devoted sister begs him to agree

to my terms. Because before I'm through with you,'' he promised with a rough-voiced certainty that sent a shiver down her spine, ''you are going to be begging.''

It must have been close to midnight, perhaps even later than that, when Archer beached the skiff on a narrow stretch of sandy shore that hugged a limestone bluff.

She watched him as he slumped over the oars, broad shoulders sagging, head down. She knew he had to be exhausted. For a moment he was silent, and then he lifted his head, drawing a tired breath.

''Gotta catch an hour of sleep before we move on.'' He looked around, judging their situation. ''Should be safe enough here.''

It was a deserted spot. But every place along the river had been that, Margaret thought. They had seen no one since leaving Saint Joseph. If the authorities were aware yet of his escape, either they were trying to track him on land, or else they were waiting for daylight. She was beginning to lose hope that anyone would catch up with them and rescue her.

''Help me drag the boat up on shore.''

She was too emotionally weary to argue with him. By the time they had secured the skiff against the bluff, both of them were slapping at hungry insects.

''Damn bugs'll eat us alive down here. We'll go up on top. Should be clear of them up there in the open.''

The bluff was too sheer at this point for climbing, but the moonlight guided them to a nearby gully. There was an animal trail there that took them to a level clearing directly above the skiff on the shore.

"Hasn't rained in a while," he said, peering around the clearing to make certain it was empty. "Grass should be dry enough to offer us a bed if the dew hasn't settled on it."

Margaret struggled with her fear as she watched him hunker down to inspect the ground. It was a fear that had altered since early evening, leaving her less scared now of the man who held her captive than of her own emotions. This was what really worried her. She wasn't supposed to have feelings that had become disturbingly confused. She wasn't supposed to have to remind herself repeatedly that he was a killer who was only keeping her alive because he considered her useful.

There was one certainty, anyway. On any level the situation was dangerous to her. It was more imperative than ever that she get away from him. And this, she realized, could be her opportunity to escape. *If* she could manage to be convincing.

Kneeling beside him, she tried to sound casually concerned. "If the ground is damp, it isn't going to benefit that hand of yours."

He turned his head, trying to read her expression in the moonlight. "You suddenly worried about my health?"

Her shoulders lifted in a small shrug. "Just being helpful."

"Yeah? Well, you can stop being helpful. The hand is gonna be just fine. I've had parts of me survive a lot worse than a few hours of punishment at a pair of oars. Where rivers are concerned, I never had a choice but to stay tough. Not when I had an old man who, drunk or sober, wouldn't tolerate any weakness and had a heavy fist to enforce it. But I guess you wouldn't know about things like that, precious."

"You don't have to be unfriendly about it."

"Oh, we're getting friendly now?" He leaned toward her. "This oughta be interesting. How friendly?"

Margaret felt her insides tighten, and prayed she could control the situation. "Look, I'm just trying to endure my circumstances, since you've made it clear I have no choice about them."

"That all?"

"Yes. Well, there is the matter of the handcuffs. I'm as tired as you are. How am I supposed to rest handcuffed to another tree while you sleep?"

"Like that one there, you mean?" He nodded toward a slender birch growing nearby at the edge of the bluff.

"I imagine it might be your choice since the spot would let us keep an eye on the skiff."

"That's right. Only you're saying the cuffs aren't necessary this time, huh?"

"That's for you to decide, of course. But . . ."

"What?"

She shook her head. "Nothing. There's no purpose in my pointing out what you already realize yourself."

"Which is?"

"Just that, cuffed or uncuffed, I couldn't hope to get away. You know I can't manage the skiff, and I'm too exhausted to try to walk off on my own. Anyway, we're miles into the wilderness now. Where could I possibly run to, even if I wanted to run?"

"Let me get this straight. You tellin' me you're no

longer eager to put distance between us? That maybe I've, uh, convinced you I'm not a fiend, after all?''

He had shifted his solid body so that he was directly facing her, and dropped to his knees to match her position. There were mere inches now separating them. She was vulnerable. She had to be careful to neither encourage him nor antagonize him.

"I won't lie to you. I'm not ready to believe you're innocent. But I am prepared to question your guilt.''

"Not sure what that means, but it sounds good. Real good.''

His face was so close that, even by the subdued light of the moon, she could see the smoldering expression in his eyes, feel the sensual heat of his flesh.

"So,'' he purred, his voice deep and tantalizing, "just how grateful will you be if I don't cuff you?''

"I don't think this is an appropriate time to demonstrate that.''

"No?''

His hand was on her cheek, fingers stroking her slowly. Margaret fought for self-control, managing an answer that was full of promise. That it was also suitably breathy required no pretense. "Wouldn't it be much nicer to wait until after we're rested?''

"Sure, but how about a little foretaste?''

Before she could stop him, his parted mouth angled across hers. He kissed her deeply, a lusty kiss involving his seductive lips, his questing tongue, and animal sounds low in his throat. Her senses rioted on her. For a mindless moment, she experienced nothing but a molten heat that intensified when his hands skimmed along the sides of her breasts.

Was this what he had meant back on the river when

he'd vowed that, before he was through with her, she would be begging?

His mouth was so busy with hers that she was scarcely aware of his hands descending now to her waist. It was only when those hands slid behind her, cupping her backside and dragging her tightly against his granite hardness, that she was jolted back to reality.

Margaret had had little experience with sex. There had been Enoch's chaste kisses and gentle embraces and that single messy episode back East, a horrible mistake she had made every effort to wipe from her memory. But she knew enough to realize she'd just made a serious error in judgment. Her coyness had backfired on her because now Archer Owen was blatantly aroused.

As he squeezed against her lasciviously, she flattened her hands on the hard wall of his chest, pushing against him in a panic. To her relief, he let her go.

Recovering herself with an effort, she reminded him softly, "You agreed that we would wait."

"Aw, hell, that's right. Afterwards, when we're rested, huh?"

"Yes."

He caressed one of her hands before lifting it tenderly toward his mouth. "But you know what, sweetheart?"

"What?" she whispered.

Turning her hand, he planted a kiss against the palm, then looked directly into her eyes. "You are so full of bull."

Steel flashed in the moonlight as he whipped the handcuffs from his back pocket with his free hand. Before she could prevent it, the bracelet had been slapped over her wrist and snapped shut.

Chapter Four

There were three simple facts that determined Margaret's decision. The first was the vulnerable position of the skiff. The slender birch to which she was handcuffed was so close to the edge of the bluff that, by leaning forward from where she was huddled on the ground, she could see the craft resting below her in the moonlight.

The second was the boulder. It was a fair-sized chunk of rock within reach of her foot and poised on the lip of the bluff directly above the skiff.

Lastly, and most importantly, was her state of mind. She didn't think it would be an exaggeration to say she was absolutely seething. Archer Owen had encouraged her to humiliate herself with that seductive performance, knowing all along it was nothing but another of her bids to escape. He had laughed when he'd dragged her over to the rim of the bluff and secured her to the birch. Margaret wanted revenge.

Emotion aside, there was, of course, a much more useful motive in her intention. By putting a hole in the skiff, she would be delaying her captor, making it that much more possible for any pursuers to overtake them.

Resolution confirmed, she undertook her objective. Careful not to disturb her snoring enemy sprawled on the grass several yards away, Margaret stretched out her left foot and made contact with the boulder. It seemed so precariously balanced on the crumbling edge of the bluff that a mere nudge would send it on its way. But that proved to be an illusion.

The thing, though loose, was stubbornly lodged in a hollow. Margaret found she had to work at it with both feet, rocking it back and forth and praying the whole while that the soft scraping sound of her effort wouldn't waken the man on the ground. It didn't, though she checked on him with quick, nervous glances.

She was determined, and she was persistent. Straining and struggling, she finally succeeded in sliding the boulder out of the depression. It hung there for a second in indecision. Then, with a small grunt of triumph, she smacked it with both feet. The boulder plummeted toward its target.

A missile launched from a siege catapult couldn't

have been more accurate. Or more effective. Margaret had the supreme satisfaction of hearing rock smashing into wood.

There was another explosion directly behind her as Archer leaped to his feet with the roar of a warrior alert for battle. In three rapid strides he was at the edge of the bluff and gazing down at the destroyed skiff.

He understood the situation almost immediately. When he rounded on Margaret there was such a livid expression on his face that she cowered against the birch, which offered no protection whatever.

"Go ahead and strike me," she challenged him, though she didn't know how she dared when she was trembling with fear. "You're just the sort of brute who would hit a woman."

"You deserve more than that!" he thundered. "What I ought to do is pick you up and throw you down there on top of what's left of the skiff!" Producing the key, he unlocked her from the birch. Then, grasping her by the wrist, he jerked her cruelly to her feet. "You know what you've gone and done with your clever little cannonball, don't you?"

"Yes," she defied him. "Made it impossible for you to reach Independence."

"Think again. Because all you've succeeded in doing is making the whole trip harder on yourself. No more comfy boat for you to park your backside in. From now on you walk. And know what, precious?" He shoved his face down toward hers, his teeth flashing in the moonlight in a diabolical grin. "It's a long way yet to Independence. You're gonna wish you never saw that boulder by the time you get there."

Margaret's heart sank. How could she have been so foolish to think her impulsive action would stop him? He was right. She had only made the ordeal more difficult for herself.

"Come on." Snatching her by the arm, he pulled her in the direction of the trail that descended the bluff.

"Now?" she objected. "Shouldn't we at least wait for daylight to find our way?"

"You'd like that, wouldn't you?" he said, retrieving the flour sack with its essentials. "Me sitting here waiting for the sheriff and his men to arrive on the scene."

She didn't answer him. There was nothing more she could say. Not then. But there was plenty she could, and did, say throughout the next hour and a half. Their trek along the riverbank, on a path that often lost itself in tangles of vegetation through which they had to squirm and squeeze, was a nightmare. There was mud, there were brambles that snagged and scratched, there were voracious insects, and there was more mud. At times Margaret found herself wallowing through it.

"Why must you set such a killing pace?" she grumbled.

"Keep moving," he ordered, driving her ahead of him. "Unless you want to find yourself handcuffed to me and dragged every step of the way."

"I'm tired," she complained. "I didn't have any sleep."

"I did," he said, reminding her it was her own fault she had occupied herself with a boulder instead of resting.

71

"I've got blisters on my heels," she groaned.

"They hurt?"

"Of course, they hurt. My shoes weren't made for this kind of punishment."

"Too bad. And stop slapping those branches back in my face."

"I can't help it. They're here." She sniffed, sighed, then complained again. "I'm thirsty, and I'm hungry."

"What's the matter, precious?" he snarled. "Life never been mean to you before? No, I guess not."

"You're nasty! And stop calling me that!"

"It fits, doesn't it?" he taunted her. "That's what you are, a precious, self-centered, pampered little darling. Fit for nothing outside of a man's bed. And maybe not even there. You look the type to be squeamish."

"You'll regret that filthy tongue of yours! When Enoch learns of—"

"Enoch? Oh, yeah, the pompous ass waiting for you back in St. Louis. He should hear you now sniveling about a few mosquitoes and a little mud. Hell, he wouldn't want you back."

For the first time since they had left the bluff Margaret was silent, stung by his sarcastic assessment of her. How dare he judge her? How dare he assume that she had never suffered a day in her life when over the course of the last few years her existence had been nothing but a series of hardships?

And before that? Well, was it her fault she had been born to an affluent St. Louis investor? An indulgent man who had provided Trace and her with every advantage, including her expensive education at a female academy in New York.

It was during her last year of school that she had become betrothed to Jonah Cuddeback, the irresistible brother of the girl who shared a room with her. She had given herself to Jonah one warm spring evening because, after all, he was as good as her husband and he adored her.

Margaret hadn't enjoyed the experience, but she hadn't considered it a grave mistake. Not, anyway, until almost overnight her life had fallen apart. The financial panic of '37 had claimed her father as one of its victims. The Sheridan fortune had vanished and with it Jonah Cuddeback, who no longer adored her now that she was penniless.

With her connection to the female academy and its privileged society abruptly severed, Margaret returned to St. Louis. She came back to a mean little cottage in an unfashionable neighborhood, a father who had to be nursed following a severe stroke, and a weak, impractical brother who was of no use to them whatever in their crisis.

It was during those long, depressing months, while they managed to survive on the meager funds rescued from the disaster, that Margaret learned that though her careful education had prepared her for every aspect of ladyhood, it had taught her nothing about poverty: not how to cook meals, clean a house, or wash clothes. She had struggled with each of these tasks despising them, missing the servants who had once performed them for her and the carriage that had driven her everywhere and the pretty clothes that had filled her wardrobe. She had never stopped regretting their loss, never entertained a moment's guilt because she still valued these luxuries.

That was when Margaret had determined that someday, somehow, she would be what her upbringing intended her to be—the wife of a wealthy gentleman. But no rich gentleman appeared in her life, at least none who was interested in marrying her. All that did happen was that her father eventually died and was buried, Trace married Hester and went off to Saint Joseph, and Margaret, alone and with the last of the funds spent, found she had to go to work or starve.

She accepted a position in a girls' school, where she was no more successful as a teacher than she'd been as a housekeeper. The place was hateful, the girls nothing but trouble, and her lack of security more terrifying with each passing day. And then one night something wonderful happened. The school burned down.

Enoch Rawlins, returning from a late engagement, had stopped his carriage to help lead the girls from the fearful blaze. That was how Margaret met him. Enoch had been very gallant, very solicitous about her welfare. Naturally, the fire was a tragedy, he'd argued, but Margaret was much too refined to waste herself in a girls' school. She must depend on him to find her something more suitable. And he had. Three months later they were engaged to be married.

But now the union Margaret so fiercely needed—because, face it, she was fit for nothing else—was threatened by this brutal man who had abducted her. A ruffian who had the audacity to suggest she might not be worth even that much.

Well, he was wrong. She would make Enoch a conscientious, caring wife. Why should she care anyway what Archer Owen's opinion of her was? Why should she permit herself to be hurt by it when he was nothing better than a savage running from the law that had condemned him? But strangely, she was hurt, and that was as frustrating as all the rest.

There were lights, there were voices! To Margaret they meant only one thing! Rescue! In her reckless excitement, she opened her mouth to call out a plea for help. Her cry was silenced by a rough hand from behind clapped over her mouth.

"You've got a short memory," Archer hissed, his hot breath fanning her ear. "Guess you need a reminder."

She stiffened as she felt the muzzle of the Colt pressed against her ribs. "Back away," he ordered, "and not a sound out of you."

She was too scared to do anything but obey him. They retreated slowly and silently into the alder grove from which they had been about to emerge.

"Far enough," he whispered after a few paces, satisfied that the alders now adequately concealed them.

He came up beside her on the narrow path to reconnoiter the situation. Through an opening in the trees they had a view of a clearing at the side of the river a few hundred feet in front of them. Margaret now had an opportunity to sort out the lights and the voices.

A steamboat had tied up to the bank for the night. Lanterns mounted on its deck revealed its cargo, which had been temporarily unloaded to the clearing where a makeshift corral had been erected with stakes and ropes. Horses bound for upriver. She could see the animals cropping the lush spring grass, a measure no doubt intended to conserve the necessary feed carried on board the vessel.

One of the crew was leaning over the rail, talking to an officer who paced along the side of the corral. Their voices carried in the still air, reaching the alder grove.

"You sure two of 'em horses is gone?"

"I can count, can't I?" growled the lanky officer. "And a couple of saddles as well."

"That's it then. That pair of good-for-nothing deckhands helped themselves to mounts and deserted. Probably miles away by now. You want me to wake the captain and tell him?"

"Not yet. He'll go off like a Chinese rocket if it's true, but I ain't so certain those boys are up to anything more than a moonlit ride. They're rascals, but I don't figure them for thieves."

"Well, it's your funeral if you're wrong."

The crewman sauntered away from the rail. The officer went on pacing. Margaret watched him, longing to hail him but knowing she didn't dare to open her mouth. The pistol was still very much in evidence in her captor's hand.

And what, she wondered anxiously, was he waiting for? She would have expected him by now to be leading them in a wide circle around the back side of the clearing. Surely he wanted to avoid any possible contact with that boat. Of course, though the whole thing did make her nervous, the longer they remained there, the better were her chances of alerting someone on that boat. But how, without getting herself shot?

Margaret was struggling with the problem when the tension was suddenly relieved by the sound of hooves from the direction away from the river. A few seconds later the two truant deckhands cantered into the clearing and dismounted just outside the corral.

They were looping the reins of their horses over the stakes when the angry officer reached them. "Captain is gonna skin you alive when he hears you two helped yourselves to the valuable cargo!"

"No, he ain't," promised one of the youths, gleefully holding up a bulging sack. "Not when he sees what we brought back with us and how little it cost."

His grinning companion held up another sack. "Found us a farm a few miles inland."

"What you got in them sacks?" demanded the officer.

"Eggs and butter and cream."

"And in mine some early vegetables. *Fresh* vegetables. Captain's gonna pin medals on us."

"Yeah, and then he's gonna keelhaul you. Hey, where you two going? Get back here and unsaddle these horses."

"Aw, they can wait a bit. We got to get this stuff on ice in the galley before it spoils."

The deckhands went on board the steamboat, the officer still uttering threats as he followed them up the ramp. The second the door of the galley closed behind the three of them, Archer acted.

"Looks like we've got us some new transportation, precious," he said, seizing her by the arm and hurrying her forward into the clearing.

Margaret, understanding his intention, gasped. "If

you think I'm going to turn into a horse thief in addition to everything else, you're mistaken.''

"There's no time to argue with you about it. You either do what I say, or I'll offend those dainty senses of yours in a manner you won't like.''

He had dropped her arm and was nudging her with the gun. Again, she had no choice but to obey him. She was terrified of being shot as they approached the horses, if not by Archer Owen, then by one of the outraged crew aboard the steamboat.

"You take the sorrel, and I'll grab the roan," he whispered. When she hesitated, glancing fearfully in the direction of the boat, he hissed impatiently, "*Now*, before one of them comes back on deck.''

Margaret released the sorrel from the stake and tugged her in the direction Archer silently indicated, toward the path that continued downriver on the other side of the clearing. Much to her relief, the gentle little mare followed her obediently. Or was she relieved? A successful theft of the horses meant she would be losing another opportunity to gain her freedom.

Archer, leading the larger roan by its reins, brought up the rear. Margaret tensely waited to hear a shout from behind them, but the clearing remained silent. Within seconds, the trees and shrubbery swallowed them.

She could almost feel her captor breathing down her neck as he said impatiently, "Can't you move any faster than that?''

With a last regretful glance toward the clearing behind her, she dragged the mare along the path. Archer waited until they were several hundred feet into the thick growth, well out of sight and hearing, before he stopped her.

"Can you ride?" he demanded. "Because if you can't, you're about to learn fast."

She hesitated. "Yes, a little, but—"

"Then climb on that horse, and don't give me any back talk about ladyhood and side saddles. You're wearing britches now, so ride like they mean something."

He never lost an opportunity to insult her, did he? She promised herself all over again that when he was recaptured she was going to be right there under the gallows cheering while they hanged him. But until then . . .

Turning away, she managed to awkwardly mount the horse while her companion swung with maddening ease into his own saddle. Without wasting another second, he urged them swiftly along the path. To her relief, she found that straddling a horse was unfamiliar but much easier than riding side saddle.

There were difficulties, however. Although the undergrowth was thinner here, allowing them to make rapid progress, the low boughs of trees presented hazards. In order to avoid being smacked by a limb, she flattened herself over the mare's neck, desperately hugging its thick mane.

There was also the threat of pursuit. When the crew on the steamboat learned that two of its precious cargo were gone, they were bound to come after them. This could be to her advantage, if they were willing to listen to her. If not, she might be facing an ugly reprisal. The same thing had to be on Archer's mind. He kept scanning the river that paralleled their route, though she didn't understand why until he finally ordered a halt on a gravel bank.

"This is the place," he said, gazing out over the moonlit waters.

She was afraid to wonder what he intended now.

"We're going over to the other side," he said, as casual as though he proposed crossing a country lane on foot.

"You can't mean it! The spring currents are treacherous!"

"Not along this stretch. It runs easy and shallow. The horses can wade most of it, except for the main channel, which is narrow enough for them to swim without a problem. You forget, precious. I know the Missouri better than I know myself."

"But why must we risk a crossing?"

He scowled at her without comment because of course it was obvious. They would be safer on the other side. Pursuers would either not realize they had crossed the river, or if they did consider this possibility probably fail to learn exactly where they had crossed.

"Let's have your reins," he ordered.

Before she could object, he crowded his horse close to her side and removed the reins from her hands.

"What are you doing?"

"Leading you across. I'm going to be busy out there. I don't have time to worry about you trying to make a break for it or losing your head and getting swept away."

She was left nothing to hold onto but the pommel of the saddle, which she clutched with both hands. "What if I fall off?"

"Then I hope you can swim. Or are you as bad at that as you are at riding a horse?"

Without waiting for her indignant response, he took the lead, plunging them down the bank and into the river. The horses went willingly. Margaret didn't. Feeling giddy, she clung to the mare's back and prayed she wouldn't lose her grip on the pommel.

Archer had chosen wisely. The river bottom was mostly firm gravel in this area, a rarity for the Missouri, whose bed was largely sand or mud. The horses were able to splash with ease through the wide shallows.

But then the water deepened. When it reached the bellies of the horses, they resisted. Archer had to goad them into the current of the channel. As the cold water rose around her legs, Margaret closed her eyes, unable to look.

The two animals were buoyant now, swimming furiously against the current with Archer coaxing and coaching them. It seemed forever before they found their footing again, struggling up out of the depths as they gained the shallows on the far side.

She opened her eyes and discovered that there was no solid bank waiting for them. The shallows here stretched away into a broad, marshy floodplain. It was a dangerous place to be, capable of trapping them in mire if they lingered. Archer didn't. He directed them as quickly as possible across the expanse.

By the time they reached higher, dry ground, the river itself was no longer in sight. The moon was still high and bright. She gazed around at the endless, undulating prairie and shivered. This was a much wilder shore. She knew from the talk in Saint Joseph that there were no permanent settlements on this side and few, if any, farms. They were alone in the vastness.

Without the river as a guidepost, she was lost. She hoped her companion's inner compass was more reliable. Perhaps it was. He seemed in no way confused as he turned them to the left.

Margaret didn't know how many miles they rode across the monotonous terrain. She forgot to be worried about their direction. All she cared about now was how sore she felt after what seemed like hours of cruel jolting. She finally said as much.

"I'm not surprised," Archer sneered. "Didn't that fancy education of yours teach you anything about riding in rhythm with a horse, instead of bouncing against it? You're all over the place on that saddle."

As useless as it was, she lashed out at him resentfully. "I'm doing the best I can."

He grunted and made no further comment. She was too weary to offer another complaint. So exhausted that, in spite of the conditions or her position on the horse, her eyes finally closed. She dozed where she sat, and by some miracle she stayed in the saddle.

She didn't know how long she napped, but when she opened her eyes again daylight was breaking over the empty prairies. "Where are we?" she mumbled. "I can't see the river."

"It's out there," he answered. "We're still avoiding the floodplain."

Twisting around, she gazed hopefully behind her.

"Sorry, precious, if anyone is following us, we lost them."

As disappointing as that was, other, more immediate needs concerned her. She was cold in the chill dawn, her legs still damp from their soaking in the river. But mostly she was hungry.

"If I don't have something to eat and drink soon," she informed him miserably, "you won't have anything left to bargain with when and if we do catch up with Trace."

She must have finally succeeded in impressing him, because he agreed with her. "All right, we'll stop for a little."

But the sun had cleared the horizon before he found a spot that satisfied him. They rode down into a sheltered hollow where there were trees. Oaks and ashes, she thought. They drew rein inside the grove.

Margaret was so stiff when she dismounted that she feared her legs wouldn't support her. But she had to be able to walk in order to accommodate a pressing need. The problem of explaining this to her captor was humiliating.

"I need to, uh, go off by myself."

She expected some mortifying remark out of him, but to her relief he merely nodded. "All right, but don't get any ideas about sneaking out of here."

She found a thick oak a safe distance away behind which she hastily relieved herself. A pool of rainwater had collected at the bottom of the hollow where she was able to rinse her hands and face afterwards. She even risked a drink from the clean end of the pool.

By the time she returned to the horses, who had lowered their heads and were browsing on the grasses, Archer had unpacked the flour sack he had tied to his saddle. She was eager to sample its contents as they settled on a wide, flat boulder.

"Better have a nip of this first," he said, uncorking

a small, squat bottle and passing it to her.

Margaret regarded it suspiciously. "What is it?"

"Something to warm you. Or are you too much of a lady to drink brandy?"

She snatched the bottle from him and defiantly swallowed a healthy measure of the liquor. It went down like fire, taking her breath away. He grinned at the startled expression on her face. She didn't care. As promised, it warmed her.

They ate in silence, munching on dried fruit, cheese, and hard biscuits. It was fare that Margaret would have considered inferior on any other occasion, but this morning she relished it.

She eyed him as she chewed. What were her chances this time of convincing him that their trek was a madness, that even if they managed to overtake her brother, she had no influence whatever over Trace? But she knew this course was hopeless. Archer Owen was relentless in his stubborn, single-minded determination to find Trace and force him to return to Saint Joseph. She would have to discover some other method for outwitting him.

She did have one vital skill in her favor, if and when she could find an opportunity to take advantage of it. It was something she had managed to conceal from him. But the circumstances had to be right for her to make use of it. Until then, she had no choice but to wait.

He finished his simple meal and helped himself to a swig of the brandy. Then, while he waited for her to eat the rest of her own breakfast, he began to exercise the hand he had injured back in the jail cell. It must be troubling him again, she thought as she watched him slowly flex his fingers to rid them of stiffness.

His action made Margaret think of her own hands. She examined them, grieving over their condition. She had always prided herself on her carefully manicured hands. And look at them now! Two of her fingernails broken, traces of mud under the rest, and a blister beginning to swell on one palm. As for her dark hair and ivory complexion . . . well, without a mirror she couldn't tell, but she was certain they had suffered too.

Archer must have become aware of her preoccupation with her hands. He suddenly laughed. It was another of his detestable sardonic laughs. "Is that all you ever think about?" he challenged her. "Your looks?"

"If I do, it's none of your business."

"That's right. It's whatshisname's business. The poor fool you're going to marry. He have any idea what kind of a wife you're going to make? How you'll pass your days gazing into a mirror—that is, when you're not out spending his money on clothes?"

He was accusing her of being vain and shallow. "You know nothing about the kind of wife I'll make. I intend to be very useful, a credit to my husband."

"Yeah? Like what?"

"I—I'm not sure. Probably helping others who are less fortunate. Yes, I'll be involved in charity work. All sorts of charities."

He hooted with laughter. "Sure you will, precious. You can spend even more of your husband's money. Bet he'll love that. You probably already have him panting to please you."

"I have no intention of discussing Enoch with you. A man like you wouldn't begin to understand someone with his sensibilities."

"A real gentleman, huh? Knows how to treat a lady."

"That's right."

"Well, I'll tell you something, sweetheart." He leaned toward her on the boulder they shared, his voice lazy and mellow with promise. "If you were my woman, I certainly wouldn't be any restrained gentleman about it. I'd be all over you. I'd be doing things to you that wouldn't be gallant, but you wouldn't care because you'd be too busy begging for more."

She found it difficult to breathe. It was his eyes. She didn't like the way he was devouring her with those hot, amber eyes. Uneasy, she tried to move away from him on the rock. He was too quick for her. Catching her around the waist, he hauled her up against the hard wall of his chest.

Margaret struggled against his embrace, but she was no match for him. The man had a powerful build, probably from all those years he had spent working on the rivers before he acquired his own steamboat. There was something primitive about his strength. Primitive and, at the same time, strangely compelling.

Oh, why did she keep experiencing all these unwanted emotions whenever he touched her? It was shameful. He was a dangerous brute. She had to keep reminding herself of that.

"Let me go!" she demanded.

His only response was a slow, seductive smile. She could smell the masculine aroma of his body, feel the searing heat from him. It was a potent combination. And a fearful one.

"You wouldn't!" she whispered as his mouth moved toward hers.

"Wouldn't what?" he teased her, his mouth now a mere fraction of an inch from hers.

"Force yourself on me."

"Is that what you think I want? To take you right here on the grass?"

She began to tremble, certain now that was just what he intended. "Please, if you have a morsel of honor in you at all, you won't do this."

For a moment his intense gaze held hers. Then, in a kind of disgust, he abruptly flung her away. "You can stop swooning," he growled. "I'm not going to ravish you. You're not worth the trouble."

Margaret didn't know whether to be incensed or relieved. Sliding away on the boulder, she watched him with wary eyes as he stuffed their unused food back into the sack. He got to his feet, stretched, and yawned. Then he was thoughtful for a few seconds as he looked around the hollow where they had stopped.

"We both of us need to catch a couple of hours of sleep before we move on," he decided. "Should be safe enough in here."

He was all business again as he jerked his thumb in the direction of a sapling on the other side of the boulder. "That's going to be your bed over there. Let's get you secured to it."

Like last night, he meant to handcuff her to a tree to prevent her escape. Margaret offered no objection this time. There would have been no use in that. Besides, she had just recognized the chance she'd been waiting for!

Feigning reluctance, she stood and followed him to the sapling, which was tall and tough-looking but no more than a few inches in diameter at its base.

"You know the routine," he said, facing her with the handcuffs ready.

Fighting to keep her nerves steady as she flicked a glance at the Colt pistol stuck in his belt, she held out her left wrist to be manacled. She was ready when he bent toward her, both of his hands occupied with the cuffs. Before he could clamp the open bracelet around her wrist, she moved with the swiftness of a coiled snake. Her right hand struck, whipping the Colt from his belt.

With a shout of rage, he lunged toward her. But he was too late. Margaret had already dropped back out of his reach and was covering him with the raised pistol.

"Don't come any closer," she warned him. "I'll shoot you if you try."

His face was livid with fury. "Why, you little—"

"I mean it."

He glowered at her in silence for a few seconds. But she refused to be intimidated by the threat in his blazing eyes, though she knew if he ever got his hands on her he would make her regret she had tricked him. She didn't mean for that to happen. She kept the gun leveled at him.

He must have decided she was capable of drilling him where he stood. "What now?"

"Take the key for the handcuffs out of your pocket

and throw it over here by my feet,'' she instructed him.

Extracting the key from his pocket, he tossed it at her feet. Margaret was careful to keep her gaze on him as she felt for the key with the tip of her shoe. Once she'd located it, she kicked it off into the grass, making sure it was well out of reach.

"Now," she continued, "lock one of those bracelets over your wrist." He hesitated, and she waved the pistol at him. "I either keep you here this way, or I do it with a bullet."

He angrily slapped the bracelet over his wrist. She listened carefully to be sure she heard the click that told her it was locked in place.

"I assume you know what comes next," she said.

He did, and though he was still seething, he snapped the other bracelet around the sapling. Now that he was tethered to the tree, Margaret felt it was safe to lower the pistol. She went and got the food sack, removed the knife he'd taken from the general store, and shoved the rest within his reach.

"I wouldn't want you to cheat the gallows by starving to death before I send the law back here to rescue you."

"You little fool," he shouted as she turned around and started toward the horses, "you'll never survive out there without me! You can barely keep your seat on a horse, never mind trying all alone to find your way back to civilization!"

Reaching the horses where they still grazed, she seized the reins of the sorrel, holding on to them tightly so that the little mare wouldn't escape. Then, lifting the pistol into the air, she fired it. The sound of it discharging had the desired effect of spooking the roan. Turning tail, it bolted, racing up the slope of the hollow and out of sight.

Only after she had quieted the sorrel in her grip did she turn around and smile sweetly at the man restrained by the sapling. "Oh, I shall manage very well, Mr. Owen," she informed him triumphantly. "You see," she went on, lifting herself with the ease of long experience into the saddle, "there's one little truth you neglected to discover about me. I happen to be a very capable actress, which is precisely why you never guessed just how skilled a horsewoman I am."

She proved her boast by efficiently swinging her mount around and spurring it into a gallop up and out of the hollow. She left Archer behind bellowing obscenities that would have shocked a pirate.

Chapter Five

When Archer got tired of cursing her for running out on him and leaving him stranded, he cursed himself. He was the biggest fool in the territory.

He had underestimated her. Badly underestimated her. Margaret Sheridan might be a spoiled, self-centered belle, but she wasn't as empty-headed as circumstances had led him to believe. There was a brain behind that pretty face, and she had used it to outwit him in a careless moment.

And damn it, she certainly knew how to handle a horse! She had proven that by riding out of here like the wind. But she would regret her deceit. When he got his hands on her again—and he would, he promised himself—he was going to have her pleading for mercy. But until then . . .

Arch twisted and tugged at the handcuffs binding him to the ash, grinding his teeth in frustration. Useless. All he managed to do was make his wrist raw. The chain was too strong to break.

He thought about picking the lock, but he had no pin this time. Anyway, the handcuffs had been built to resist that kind of maneuver. What about smashing the chain? No good. He would need a rock for that, and there were none within his reach.

Refusing to be defeated, he considered the problem. There was only one possible solution. If he couldn't break the handcuffs, then he would break what they were attached to. After all, it was just a sapling. How strong could it be?

Stronger than he'd realized, Arch discovered within seconds of attacking the tree. It was deeply rooted, its trunk slim but tough. He put his whole weight against it at shoulder height, bending it back and forth to weaken it. The drag against his captured hand was a punishment he tried to ignore.

When the stubborn ash refused to snap, he rested a moment, wondering if he was wasting his time. Then he thought of Margaret riding smugly off toward the horizon, and with a fierce resolve he heaved himself against the tree again. The crown of twigs and leaves whipped around over his head as he strained against the trunk.

He was sweating with exertion when it finally happened. There was a sharp crack as the upper half of the tree toppled from the lower half. A few strands of wood and bark had to be ripped away with his free hand before the separation was complete and he could slide the bracelet up and over the remaining stub. He was free!

Well, all but the bracelet still pinned around his left wrist. He'd need the key for that. On hands and knees he crawled through the grass where she had kicked it. He couldn't find it, and he was wasting precious time. The dangling handcuffs would just have to stay on him. He'd find a way out of them after he recaptured Margaret Sheridan.

That this was a remote possibility, when she had a good twenty minutes start on him and was mounted on a horse while he was on foot, was something Archer refused to consider. He was going after her, and that was that. Slinging the flour sack over his shoulder, he climbed out of the hollow.

There had been a heavy rain in the area sometime within the last twenty-four hours. The earth was still soft, revealing the impressions of the mare's hooves. And where the ground wasn't exposed, the grass was disturbed by the passing of the sorrel. Both betrayed Margaret's direction. Archer, following the signs, strode off across the prairie, a grim expression on his face.

Five minutes later he sighted the roan peacefully grazing at the edge of a copse of wild cherry trees. It took some patient and careful maneuvering, but he finally succeeded in reclaiming the horse. Luck was with him, he thought as he mounted the roan and headed after his quarry. He hadn't counted on the weather.

Arch had been so occupied recovering his horse,

he hadn't noticed the sun vanishing under a rapidly thickening cloud cover. There was no way to ignore the change when it began to drizzle. The thin rain persisted, escalating finally into a downpour.

He was soaked within seconds. That didn't worry him. The problem was, the rain washed away any trace of the sorrel's hoof prints. The only signpost that kept him on track was a pile of fresh manure. After that he had to rely on the roan. His horse seemed to sense the path of the mare, and followed without urging.

At some point Arch became conscious that his objective had picked up a kind of defined trail across the prairies. Its route alarmed him.

The little fool, he thought sourly. She might now be a capable horsewoman, but she had absolutely no sense of direction. Either that or the weather was confusing her.

Margaret was headed not back toward the Missouri, but away from the river. She was moving southwest, taking herself deeper into unoccupied country.

Where the hell did she think she was going? But that was the whole point. She obviously didn't know where she was going, probably figured if she stuck to this trail that sooner or later she would reach a settlement. She wouldn't. This was Kansas country, belonging to the Indians. The trail here was probably one of their hunting routes.

Arch had heard that sometimes the local tribes were friendly, and sometimes they weren't. It was a dangerous situation for a woman out here on her own. He drove his horse into a faster pace.

The morning wore on with the long miles he covered. He judged it had to be nearly noon, and still he hadn't overtaken her. There was no sign of life, nothing but the rolling prairies with their low hills and occasional gullies.

The endless grasslands bordering the track were thick with wildflowers of every description. But Arch wasn't interested in nature, particularly when the weather remained foul.

The rain continued to slash at him, dripping from the brim of his felt hat, coursing down his long, golden brown hair and drooping mustache. He was a sodden, miserable mess.

None of it helped his explosive Welsh temper. When he wasn't cursing the rain, he went back to cursing Margaret. She deserved to be abandoned out here. That was what he ought to do, except he still needed her to reach her brother. But he promised himself that when he caught up with her he was going to make her suffer.

The vengeful scenes he entertained himself with ranged from his hands closing joyfully around her throat to his booted foot delivering several well-aimed kicks to her backside. And that was all before he dragged her like a log behind his horse.

The primary reason for Archer's vile mood was something he refused to admit, because such a conscious confession would have been a weakness. But the truth was, he was deeply worried about her. When it came to survival in a place like this, she hadn't the sense of a prairie chicken. Useless woman.

None of his anger was enough, though. In the end he was still defeated by the desire he had been struggling with since his first encounter with the woman.

Enemy or not, he'd found himself overwhelmed by his desire for her. And even now, in spite of swearing to punish her, the treacherous images crowded into his brain. A full mouth designed for kissing, a pair of sweet breasts, that luscious little bottom. Oh, hell, he was making himself hard just thinking about her!

Enough!

She was trouble. His longing for her was trouble. Forget it. Concentrate on the only lady that mattered to him in the end. The *Missouri Belle*, his motive for needing to clear himself. His reason for wanting Margaret Sheridan back in his control.

But there was no Margaret. There was only the rain and the empty prairies. Could he have somehow lost her trail?

The hours passed. The rain finally eased off and then quit altogether. It must have been late afternoon, and the skies were beginning to clear, when Arch saw them. Buzzards in the distance circling overhead.

Something was either dead or dying. Probably just an animal. All the same, his heart leaped into his throat. The roan was tired, but he spurred it into a trot.

Minutes later, he crested a rise. There was an unexpected, sharp descent on the other side into a deep gully. The ground was rough and uneven. That had to be the explanation for what Arch saw at the bottom of the gully.

She must have been pitched from her horse. The little sorrel, grazing placidly on the lush turf on the floor of the gully, was apparently uninjured. Its rider hadn't been so fortunate.

There was no movement from the woman sprawled

on the ground. She had lost her hat in the fall. He could see her dark tumbled hair spilling out over the grass.

Fearing the worst, and sick about it, he dismounted and scrambled down the slope. The roan followed him and happily joined the mare.

Reaching Margaret, Arch hunkered down beside her. Her face looked like death, pale and still, and there was a trickle of blood from an ugly swelling on her temple. She must have struck her head on one of the rocks scattered around the gully when she landed.

He checked for breathing and a pulse. He found both of them, though they were thin. He tried to rouse her, shaking her gently by the shoulders.

"Precious, can you hear me?"

She couldn't. She remained unconscious. He didn't know how hurt she was, but he feared she was in a bad way. Sinking back on his heels, he considered their dilemma. Should he make camp here, try to nurse her? It didn't seem like a smart choice. She needed a shelter, somewhere warm and dry.

Damn her for getting them into this fix!

Coming to his feet, he climbed back out of the gully. He went and stood on the highest point of the rise, searching the horizon in all directions. The sun was finally out, giving him a clear view. There was no visible hint of the Missouri River, and he didn't expect one. It lay far to the northeast now, almost a day away. Too great a distance to go back with an injured woman. He looked in the other direction.

Was it his imagination, or was that a column of smoke off to the southwest? He thought it was smoke from a fire. Miles away yet, maybe from an Indian encampment. That might not be so good, but right now it seemed like his only option.

His mind made up, Arch got busy. He had already determined that it would be a mistake to try to carry Margaret on either of the horses. He needed to provide her with a transport that would keep her flat and at the same time not jar her too much during the ride. And he knew how to get what he wanted. He had once watched a plains Indian construct one.

Back at the bottom of the gully, he caught the sorrel without difficulty. He searched the saddlebags and found the Colt pistol Margaret had taken from him. The bowie knife was there too, and that was what he sought.

Removing the knife from its sheath, he went to a cottonwood tree at the other end of the gully and hacked off several of the straightest branches. Then, using the sharp blade, he stripped away twigs and leaves. What remained was a pile of slender, but strong, poles. These he carried back to the horses.

Using the mare's saddle blanket, which he sliced up into strips, he bound the poles into a framework covered with a webbing of blanket. When he was finished, he had a light platform to hitch to the mare. He had fashioned a travois that would be dragged behind the horse bearing its injured load.

That load was still unconscious when he went to get her. There was no further sign of bleeding, but the lump on her head wasn't encouraging. He tried to be as gentle as possible as he transferred her from the ground to the travois, but she stirred with his action.

"Hurt," she complained.

"Yeah, I know," he said gruffly as he bent over

her. "I'm trying to do something about that."

Her eyes opened. She searched his face, and he could see that she was striving to understand what had happened to her. Apparently she lost the struggle. Her eyes closed again. She drifted back into unconsciousness.

Using the last of the strips, Archer lashed her securely to the travois, then connected the shafts of the raised platform to the mare. He worked rapidly, trying not to worry about Margaret, telling himself that his concern was only because he needed her to clear himself. He didn't care otherwise. But he feared his argument wasn't a very convincing one.

There was still an hour or two before sunset when he mounted the roan and led the sorrel by its reins out of the gully. But the lengthening shadows bothered him as he headed them toward the pillar of smoke still visible on the horizon. He didn't want to get caught out here after dark with an injured woman.

They had to travel slowly and carefully in order to protect the travois and its load, but the pace frustrated Archer. The woman on the upended platform, riding like a silent papoose, remained unconscious.

When they finally neared their destination, two interesting things revealed themselves. The first was the gleam of water in the lowering sun. A stream, Arch realized, and a fairly wide one. He knew his rivers, and there could only be one in this location. They had reached the Kaw.

On its banks was the source of the smoke. Not an Indian encampment. It was a fairly substantial outpost of some kind. He could recognize a huddle of buildings constructed mostly out of slabs of stacked sod.

Smoke issued from the chimney of what he figured was the house. There was a corral with some kind of animals in it, and a covered wagon behind what could be a barn.

A farm? He thought so until he noticed the large, flat craft staked to the riverside. A ferry station then. But why? Who would be crossing the Kaw River here in sufficient numbers to support a ferry operation? It was a mystery.

Never mind, he told himself. Just be relieved that it isn't a band of hostile Indians, though maybe a good medicine man might be more useful now than an unwilling ferryman.

There was another mystery as Archer and his burden crossed the prairie toward the frontier outpost. They passed two fresh, rock-covered mounds with crude crosses planted in each. Obviously they were graves. What was going on, and how worried should he be about it?

Their approach must have been observed. A lone figure emerged from the main building and moved toward them cautiously. He was carrying a rifle, and he looked ready to use it if the suspicious arrivals proved to be a threat.

"State your business!" he shouted, lifting the weapon to his shoulder.

Obeying the challenge, Arch drew rein and dismounted. Hands raised to show he was unarmed, he started forward at a friendly saunter, forgetting that the telltale handcuffs were still dangling from his left wrist.

"I don't hear any explanations from you, mister," he was warned, "but I sure see me something I don't like hangin' there from your arm. That's far enough. I got a trigger finger here that's real nervous.''

Archer stopped. That voice! He could swear that voice was familiar!

The two men were still separated by a good twenty yards, but even at this distance and in the failing light he couldn't mistake the shock of red hair behind the rifle. He knew of only one head of hair as fiery as that one. It couldn't be, but it was!

"Hey," he yelled, "get your face out from behind that rifle and treat me to a big fat grin! Should be a hole in it where the insulting Orangeman knocked out your tooth that night at the Sweeter 'n Sin Saloon. I sure saved your ass that time, boy.''

The rifle was lowered, revealing a startled expression on a freckled Irish face. "Archer Owen, is that you?''

He didn't wait for an answer. Flinging the rifle to the ground, he raced forward. The two men met in a bear hug that consisted of smacks on each other's backs and whoops of joy. When they finally parted, the redhead favored him with the gap-toothed smile Arch had demanded.

"Mike O'Malley, what in the name of all that's holy are you doing way out here in the middle of nothing? Last I heard, you and that brother of yours were running some leaky old scow on the Arkansas.''

"Sure, but you know how restless Buck and me always was. 'Sides, this is a much more profitable operation we got goin' for ourselves.''

"A ferry service in the wilderness? How can that be?''

Mike laughed. "Don't you know?''

"What?"

"This here is where the Oregon Trail meets the Kaw. There's wagon trains comin' through here all the time, and they're willing to pay to cross the river. We got us a store, too. Last chance for them to buy provisions they might have overlooked in Independence before they head out for the rough country."

"I'll be damned! So Buck is with you?"

"Well, not this week. He's got hisself a girl in Independence. Went down there to spend some time with her and to haul us back a load of fresh supplies for the store."

Mike fingered the handcuffs hanging from his friend's wrist, his good-natured face turning sober. "What's this, Arch? You in trouble?"

"You could say that."

The riverman angled his head to one side, staring at the two horses and the travois behind him. "And what's that all about?"

Arch would trust Mike O'Malley with his life. As a matter of fact, he had on several occasions in those brutal days when they had worked the keelboats together and it had been necessary to battle the competition for survival. He was prepared to tell Mike everything, but this wasn't the time for an explanation.

"It's a long story, boy, but it'll have to wait. Right now I need your help. I've got a woman back there, and she wants attention."

"I expect she ought to be gotten out of those muddy clothes," Mike observed.

"Yeah," Arch agreed.

There was a long silence. Neither of the men moved. They went on standing there at the side of the bed, solemnly gazing down at the still figure of Margaret.

"Reckon one of us ought to get busy and do it."

"Guess so." Arch paused, cleared his throat, and wondered hopefully, "How about you doing it, Mike?"

"Don't think so. She's your burden, ain't she?"

"Uh, yeah, looks like it."

He didn't know why he was so reluctant. He had undressed plenty of women in his time. Of course, none of them had been unconscious. And none of them had been Margaret Sheridan, though why that should make any difference was beyond him.

"You figure she should be stripped down to the skin, Mike?"

"Seems like a good idea, Arch. Make sure nothin' is broken underneath."

"Uh-huh."

"Well, then."

There was another pause. Then Mike turned and went out into the main room. When he returned a few minutes later, he was bearing a ball of soap and a tin basin of warm water with a cloth swimming in it. Over his arm was a lady's flannel nightdress. Where he had gotten such a garment Arch couldn't imagine. He didn't ask. He was still standing beside the bed, trying to work up the nerve to expose his patient.

"Thought you'd want to clean that wound, maybe give her a quick wash while you're at it," he said, laying the articles on a chest next to the bed.

" 'Preciate that."

103

"Got enough light in here?" Mike asked, glancing at the glowing oil lamp on a shelf over the bed.

"Think so."

"I'll leave you to get on with it then. Got to see to the stock before it gets full dark."

The riverman retreated, closing the door behind him. Arch found himself alone with Margaret. He had no more excuses. Then why was he delaying? Maybe because she was so damned vulnerable like this, and that made him uneasy. Or could it be he was afraid of his own vulnerability?

The hell with this!

Bending over the bed, he got busy. He didn't have any trouble removing her shoes, dragging off her trousers, easing her out of the shirt. Well, not enough trouble to count, anyway. The problem came with what lay underneath.

She would be wearing a corset. That meant laces to deal with. Why they should confound him, when there wasn't a sailor's knot he couldn't untie, he couldn't imagine. But his fingers were as awkward as sausages as he fumbled with the laces. He ran out of cuss words, which for him was pretty incredible, before he got the thing off her and tossed it on the floor in disgust.

The worst was still to come.

There was a chemise. There were lace-trimmed underdrawers. There were stockings. The stockings were held up by garters. Pink garters. Arch had a terrible weakness when it came to female garters. They did things to him. They were doing things to him now.

Fighting for self-control, he managed to get rid of the garters. Then he peeled away the stockings, exposing a pair of legs that were long, smooth, and shapely. He stared at them for a moment, swallowing past the lump in his throat.

Bastard.

What kind of man was he to entertain himself with an image like that when the woman was injured and unconscious? He had pictured those long legs wrapped around him. That was what he'd gone and done.

Forget it, boy.

The chemise was waiting for him. It was a struggle, but he got it off over her head. It was probably a mistake to remove it. No, it definitely was a mistake. He found himself gazing at the sweetest, most tantalizing pair of breasts he had ever had the pleasure to behold.

You could destroy a man with those, precious.

She *was* destroying him. After that, he didn't have the courage to strip away her drawers. The way the blood was pounding in his ears, never mind a certain other aroused area, he would have exploded.

How he achieved all the rest, examining her, bathing her, getting her into the night dress, was a mystery. It involved several silent prayers for restraint, a pair of shaking hands that were seared whenever they came in contact with soft, fragrant flesh, and a patience that was exhausted.

Mercifully, Margaret never stirred throughout his whole clumsy performance. She remained unconscious and that concerned him, though he found no evidence of another injury. None that he could detect, anyway.

Arch was weak, but relieved, when he finally covered her with a quilt and staggered out into the main room. Mike had yet to return from his evening chores outside. There was a pot of something simmering above the hot coals in the fireplace.

Stew, Arch thought. Drawn by its savory odor, he drifted toward the fireplace. He realized how hungry he was. He had eaten nothing since that meager breakfast in the hollow.

He was about to examine the contents of the pot when he was startled by a mewling sound. He swung his head in the direction of the noise. It came from an oblong wicker basket to one side of the hearth.

An animal? Was Mike keeping some kind of animal in that basket? Sure sounded like one. He approached the open basket with caution, peering down at its contents. What he saw made him jump back with horror.

Couldn't be.

The mewling got more insistent. Arch went back to the basket and looked again to make sure he wasn't mistaken.

It was.

The outer door opened and Mike came into the house carrying a pail. It contained milk he had gotten from the cow Arch had noticed earlier in one of the pens. The riverman saw his friend gazing into the basket.

"See you've met Molly," he said cheerfully.

Arch turned his head and stared at him. "It's a baby!"

"Close enough." He chuckled at the expression on Arch's face. "No, not mine, but I've got the care of her for a bit. Well, I had no choice, did I? Not when her ma and pa up and died on me."

Arch looked toward the window, suddenly understanding. "The graves out there?"

Mike, who had never forgotten his Catholic upbringing, crossed himself and nodded. "Deke and Meg Carver."

"What happened?"

Before Mike could explain, the baby started whimpering again. "She's hungry. I better get her fed."

Arch wasn't particularly interested as he watched his friend warm a portion of the fresh milk in the pail. But his detachment turned into amused disbelief when Mike began funneling the milk into a glass container.

"Hell, Mike, that's a whiskey bottle!"

"Been real handy, too," he said, proud of his resourcefulness. "Even made a supply of nipples for the bottle." He held up a small square of rubber whose center had been pricked with tiny holes. "Stripped the rubber layer off an old rain poncho and cut it into pieces. Well, without a mother's teat being handy, I had to get inventive, or Molly would have starved."

Securing the makeshift nipple to the bottle with a length of yarn, he collected the baby from her nest in the basket. "You wanna feed her, Arch?"

Arch backed away, hands raised in protest. "Not me. The only thing I know about babies is how to make 'em, and I aim to keep it that way. How come you're such an expert?"

"Can't help knowing. Seems like Ma was having a baby every year and the rest of us expected to pitch in with the care." He settled on a stool, cradling

Molly, who began to suckle eagerly the instant the nipple was guided into her mouth. "Ain't been so bad having her here, except when it comes to dealing with her diapers. Never was partial to that duty. Arch, don't wait on me. Help yourself to some of that stew. Bread's over there in the box."

Arch didn't wait for a second invitation. He found a plate, ladled himself a generous helping of the stew, and settled at the plank table to eat.

"Yeah, she's a good baby," Mike said. "Healthy, too. Not like her folks."

Arch swallowed a mouthful of the stew. It tasted as good as it smelled. "They were both sick, huh?"

"Had some kind of fever when they turned up here. Dunno what it was. Maybe the typhoid. Wasn't much I could do for them, except to give them a Christian burial in the end. I was worried maybe me and the kid here might get it, but we've been fine."

"What was this couple—what did you say their names were?—doing way out here all on their own?"

"Carver. Deke and Meg Carver. Said he was a preacher, and they sure acted real devout. Dressed as sober as Quakers, too. You know what they was aimin' to do?"

"You got my attention."

"Travel out to Oregon to spread the gospel to the Indians. Damn fools actually thought they could make it without the benefit of other wagons traveling with them. Well, this is as far as they got." He looked down at Molly Carver nestled in his arms. "She's asleep. Guess she got her fill. Didn't even wait for me to burp her."

Coming carefully to his feet, Mike placed the baby

back in the basket that served as a cradle. Then he dished up his own supper and joined Arch at the table.

"So what happens to their daughter?" Arch asked.

"Now that's a problem." Mike shoveled a spoonful of stew into his mouth and chewed before continuing. "There ain't no family I can send her to, because I asked when I saw neither one of 'em was gonna make it. These Carvers were all alone in the world. Or so they said."

"So the kid gets left with you."

"Along with their wagon, their oxen, all their provisions, even the cow out there."

Which explained the ladies' nightdress Margaret Sheridan was now wearing, Arch thought. "Mike, you're not planning on keeping this baby?"

"Do I look like I'm that noodle-headed? What I'm hopin' to do is hand her over to the Delaneys."

"Yeah? And who would they be?"

"This couple, see, Agatha and Cooper Delaney, they been bringing wagon trains out to Oregon to settle in the Willamette Valley. Most of 'em on these trains is women with troubled pasts looking to start new lives. The Delaneys are due any day now to pass through here from Independence with this year's bunch."

"Full of charity for needy souls, huh?" Arch asked dryly.

"Enough that I figure they'll take Molly with them and see her settled in a good home in Oregon."

The two men were silent as they finished their supper. Then Mike, pushing back from the table, jerked his head in the direction of the bedroom.

"Looks like I'm not the only one who ended up

109

getting hisself saddled with a female needing care. You ready to tell me now what's going on?''

"Be happy to, Mike." He held up his left arm where the handcuffs were still attached. "But I'd be even happier if you'd work on getting me out of this thing while we talk.''

"Think I could manage that.''

Mike produced a hacksaw from his supply of tools, and while Arch propped his arm on the table, he began to cut through the steel of the bracelet.

"So what happened, Arch?''

"That half-witted engineer of mine hung us up on a sandbar at Saint Joseph. That's how it all started, anyway.''

Mike shook his head sympathetically. "Sorry to hear it.''

"Thanks, Mike.''

"I wasn't being sorry for you, Arch. I was pitying the poor engineer. He survive after you got through with him?''

"How should I know? The last I saw of him after I heaved him overboard, he was swimming downriver like an anxious beaver.''

"Not surprised. You sure know how to roar when that Welsh temper gets heated up. Hold your wrist steady, Arch.''

"I had a good reason to roar. Even if she is a sorry excuse for a steamboat, the *Missouri Belle* means everything to me. Hell, Mike, you know better than anyone the miserable existence I came from and how much I had to sacrifice to buy her.''

"Guess I do. Was she badly damaged, Arch?''

"Bad enough. A busted driving rod and a cracked

wheel. And me without enough funds for repairs. I was desperate. That's why I sat in on a card game at the local saloon. Thought if my luck changed, I could win the price of repairs for the *Belle*. Only, my luck didn't change. I got cleaned out. All of us at that table did, except for this Willis Hadley, who was another stranger in town.''

"Hadley didn't know how to lose, huh?''

"Not then.'' Arch's voice sobered. "But he lost big that night at his hotel. Someone put a knife in his back and grabbed his winnings.''

Mike issued a long whistle of surprise.

"That's not the worst of it,'' Arch continued. "The worst is they put me on trial for his murder and condemned me to be hanged. This bastard, Trace Sheridan, who was the chief witness against me, testified that he saw me do it. Don't look at me like that, Mike, because I didn't do it.''

Mike, who had paused in his sawing, was staring at him. "Trace Sheridan?''

"Yeah, the brother of the woman in the next room.''

Mike lowered his gaze and continued working at the bracelet. He was silent now.

"Come on, Mike, we all know that I broke a few jaws in my keelboat days. Well, like you say, I have a hot temper. And the men at that card table, including Trace Sheridan, saw it. They knew I wasn't happy losing to someone I think might have been cheating. But knifing a man in the back and robbing him isn't my style.''

"I wouldn't be sawing this cuff off of you if I thought it was, Arch. Guess the reason you're sitting here wearing it means you somehow got away."

Arch quickly told him the rest, how he had grabbed Margaret and escaped. How he intended to catch up with Trace Sheridan in Independence, where he would use Margaret to force her brother to return to Saint Joseph and clear him.

"Looks like that plan went a little wrong, Arch."

"You could say that, but I plan to remedy it."

The hacksaw bit through the last of the steel. The bracelet fell away from his wrist. He was free of the handcuffs and feeling hopeful again—until he saw Mike's unhappy face.

"Maybe more than just a little wrong, Arch. See, there's something you don't know. Something I sure hate to tell you, but I guess you gotta hear it."

Chapter Six

"You're too late, Arch," Mike informed him solemnly. "This Trace Sheridan and his friend are already gone. They passed through here with a train of freighters bound for Oregon country."

"Sonofabitch!" Arch slammed the palms of his hands down on the table. "When?"

"Yesterday about midday. They didn't linger either. Well, you know how it is with freighters. Always on the move."

"You're sure it was Sheridan?"

"For certain. I heard one of 'em call him by name when I was delivering them to the other side of the river. 'Sides, he had that same black hair as his sister. Same elegant looks, too." He frowned. "Arch?"

Archer, dealing with his immense frustration while trying to figure out what he was going to do next, mumbled distractedly, "Huh?"

"I been thinking. Why would this Trace Sheridan lie to a jury that you killed Hadley? What'd he have to gain by that?"

Arch shook his head.

"You think maybe he killed Hadley for his winnings?"

"If so, he didn't keep them. They were planted in my room where the sheriff found them. That evidence, along with Sheridan's testimony, was all it took to convict me." A realization struck him. "A *friend*! That's what you said, isn't it? I don't remember hearing about any friend traveling with him."

"Sure seemed like they was together. A meek-looking little fellow. Dressed like he was headed for town instead of the Oregon Trail. I never got his name. You think he's involved?"

"Maybe. All I know is that Sheridan is supposed to have business out West, something he claimed is going to make his fortune. He can have it, after he goes back to Saint Joseph and clears me."

"How you figure to manage that now?"

"I know what I'd like to do. Climb back on that roan out there as soon as it's daylight and ride after him. But"—he swung his head, scowling at the closed door to the bedroom—"I need that little cargo I grabbed to bargain with, and that's laid up in there for who knows how long."

"Maybe," Mike said softly, lowering his eyes and playing with the hacksaw in his lap so he wouldn't have to meet Arch's angry gaze, "maybe what you ought to do is forget about going after her brother. It's a real big risk, Arch. And what with the law out looking for you . . . well, I'd get away from here fast and far. Head south. Lose myself in some big place like New Orleans. There's always plenty of river work down there."

Archer's reaction was a thunderous one. "And do what about the *Belle*? Just go and abandon her? I'd rather face the noose again than do that! She's all I have, and I won't lose her! I'm going to do whatever it takes to get her back!"

Mike nodded. "Figured that's how you'd see it, but I did have to try. So . . ." He glanced in the direction of the bedroom. "You think your cargo will be all right?"

"I won't let her die," Arch promised fiercely. "Whatever it takes, prayers, a bolt of lightning, or a pact with the Devil, I'll see to it she recovers."

He was alert for any indication to assure him Margaret was recovering. That was why he slept on the floor beside her bed rolled in a blanket. And that was why he came awake in the middle of the night. She was restless, stirring.

He was on his feet in an instant. Turning up the lamp, he leaned over her.

"Thirsty," she whispered hoarsely.

Mike had left him a mug of water sitting on the chest next to the bed. He supported her head and held the mug to her mouth while she drank. Her head fell back against the pillow when she was finished.

"Head aches," she complained.

"You'll feel better by morning."

He believed that. It had to be an encouraging sign that she was no longer unconscious, that she had taken water. He believed it until he looked down into her wide, deep blue eyes. What he saw there scared the hell out of him. Or more precisely, what he *didn't* see.

He might have expected the expression of a woman who was dazed, disoriented. That would probably have been normal after her accident. But there was nothing, *absolutely* nothing. No trace of her arrogance remained, no gleam of rebelliousness. It was as though she had shed all character, all personality. Been wiped clean. Margaret Sheridan was a blank canvas.

His suspicion was confirmed when he asked her, "Do you know what happened to you?"

"Yes, of course," she murmured. "I've been sick." Her brow furrowed. "That's right, isn't it?"

"Close enough."

She was silent for a few seconds, and he could see she was trying to understand. "Are you a doctor?"

"Don't you remember?"

She made another effort, and then shook her head slowly. "I'm sorry, I can't. But if I could ask . . ."

"What? Something you want to know?"

"Yes. I want to know that you won't go away. That you'll stay with me. Will you, please?"

A knot twisted inside Arch's gut. She was frightened. As frightened and guileless as a child. He felt helpless and awkward in the face of her appeal. He wasn't used to anyone needing him. In fact, he didn't think it had ever happened before.

"I'm right here," he promised her gruffly.

She summoned a feeble smile. "Thank you. I'll go back to sleep now. I'm tired."

That was exactly what she did. Arch envied her. Though he stretched out again on the floor, he was awake dealing with this newest blow to his plans. Just how serious was her condition, and what was he supposed to do with her like this? He had half a mind to abandon her and head for the Deep South, as Mike had urged him to do. Damn it, why couldn't anything ever work out?

He was in a low mood the next morning when he joined Mike in the main room. His friend was feeding the baby from her bottle.

"You decide yet just what you're gonna do?" Mike asked him as he helped himself to coffee and settled at the plank table.

"No," he said, not bothering to explain the latest complication.

"How's your cargo doing this morning?"

"She was still asleep when I left."

Mike finished with the baby and placed her back in the basket. "Well, maybe she's awake by now. Think she might like some breakfast? I got oatmeal there by the fire. I could bring her a bowl."

Arch considered his offer, and decided he could use Mike's opinion. Maybe he was exaggerating what had happened last night. Or maybe by this morning she would be all right, and Mike would verify that for him. And yeah, maybe he was still too scared to find out for himself what the truth was.

"That would be good, Mike."

The ferryman filled a bowl with oatmeal and disappeared into the bedroom. Arch sat there tensely at the table and waited. He could hear the murmur of their voices behind the closed door, but he couldn't tell what they were saying.

When Mike reappeared moments later, shutting the door behind him, the expression on his freckled face told Arch everything he needed to know. And feared to hear.

"Heck Arch, she ain't got no memory. I mean, *nothing*. She don't know where she's at, what happened to her, or even who she is. I never seen anybody like that, though I heard tell of 'em. There's a name for it, ain't there?"

"Yeah, I think so. I think they call it amnesia. What did you tell her, Mike?"

"Nothing. I didn't know what to say. I just said she should rest and get well and everything'd be fine."

"Didn't she ask you anything?"

"She wanted to know if the doctor had gone. I told her yeah, and she looked like she was gonna cry. Hell, Arch, what are you gonna do about her?"

Archer didn't know then, and he didn't know later as he paced anxiously outside the front of the sod house. Mike had gone off to see to the stock and to make a repair on his ferry so that it would be ready when the Delaney caravan arrived, which could happen by sundown.

He had a real dilemma here, Arch thought. Trace Sheridan was on the Oregon Trail, getting farther out of his reach with every hour. How was he supposed to go after him with a woman who no longer even knew she had a brother? But if he didn't somehow find a way to resolve this whole mess, he would be on the run forever. And that was an unbearable prospect.

Damn it all to hell, how had Margaret Sheridan ended up getting to be his responsibility instead of his solution?

Sleep was soothing, healing. She preferred it to her conscious moments. When she was awake, and she was now for longer intervals, she had to deal with the void inside her throbbing head. It was very unsettling not to recognize yourself or your surroundings.

It must have been the illness that had robbed her of her identity, she thought. Perhaps she would remember everything when she fully recovered. She already felt stronger.

She did wish, though, that he was with her. His presence had kept her from panicking last night when she had awakened to find her memory gone. She didn't know who he was, but somehow she had felt a connection with him. But perhaps, like her past, he didn't really exist. Perhaps she had dreamed him in the night. She couldn't recall what he had looked like.

She frowned. Although the doctor in the night, or whoever she had imagined him to be, might not be a reality, what she was hearing now *did* exist. A baby was crying in the house. Not a loud, wailing sound, but demanding all the same. It was somewhere on the other side of the closed bedroom door.

She lifted her head from the pillow and listened, waiting for someone to answer its need. But the frustrated crying persisted. Where was its mother? she wondered anxiously. Why didn't she come? She couldn't stand the child being ignored like this.

And then suddenly a vague memory stirred. It was the image of a teething infant, and it had been her responsibility to pacify it. There was no other recollection, just that solitary image, but it was very insistent.

She thought she understood what was happening. Maternal instinct was very powerful, and though everything else in her mind remained shut down, this urge had surfaced by necessity. The baby was *hers*, and it wanted her. She was convinced of it.

Though she was still weak and had to hold onto things to support herself, she managed to get out of the bed and across the room to the door.

"Hold on," she called to her baby. "Mama is coming."

Her gait was slow and unsteady, but determined, as she opened the door and headed directly to the basket at the side of the hearth. Bending over, she scooped the baby up into her arms and rocked it lovingly.

"Don't fuss, sweetheart. Mama is here for you. She's sorry she doesn't remember your name, but that's not important now."

She was feeling a little light-headed, and still wobbly on her legs. Better get back to bed.

"Come on, sweetheart. We'll lie down together."

With her attention focused entirely on the baby in her arms, she returned to the small room and climbed back into bed. She gathered the child close to her on the pillow and crooned to it softly. It was quiet now, content to be with its mother. She had determined it was a girl.

I'll be damned.

Arch had witnessed the whole scene from where he stood at the window outside, and he was astonished. He had been on his way down to the river to talk to Mike again when he heard Molly howling in the house. Turning back, he'd started for the door and was passing the window. It was then that a glimpse of Margaret through the glass captured his attention.

Like a sleepwalker, she'd remained completely unaware of him watching her. Her only interest had been in reaching the baby, claiming it, reassuring it. He realized almost at once what had just occurred. Margaret Sheridan thought she was Molly Carver's mother!

Sweet Jesus, not another problem! This was getting too complicated. He had to set her straight.

He strode to the front door and across the main room of the house. But when he reached the open doorway to the bedroom, he stopped. Both the woman and the baby were sleeping soundly again. Arch didn't have the heart to rouse them. It could wait until she was awake again.

He was softly closing the bedroom door on them when inspiration rocked him like an earthquake. The solution to his dilemma!

Wait a minute. Was he actually going to undertake what his brain had just gone and proposed to him? It was improbable, maybe even impossible, and certainly outrageous. But hell, he was desperate!

Arch was fully aware that he would be taking advantage of her amnesia. So, all right, maybe it was a rotten thing to do. But he refused to examine the morality of his intended masquerade. Why should he, with a death sentence hanging over his head? And Margaret Sheridan's brother had put it there.

Smothering any threatening guilt before it was fanned into a blaze, he got busy. Mike had unloaded the Carvers' personal belongings from their covered wagon and stacked the boxes against the wall behind the table, meaning to sort through them at the first opportunity. Arch had just decided for Mike what was going to happen to those possessions.

He found the articles he needed and removed them from the boxes. Scissors, a razor, clothes. There was a sink against another wall with a mirror fixed above it. Arch carried the essentials to it, casting glances at the closed bedroom door as he worked. He'd need to hurry. He had to be finished before she was awake again and maybe this time asking lots of questions. They were bound to come, and he had to be ready for them.

Mike stared at him, his mouth working like a fish before he found his voice explosively. "Are you out of your friggin' mind? You'll never get away with it!"

"Yeah, I will, Mike. Look at me. Archer Owen is gone. Brother Deke is alive and well."

The mirror had assured him of that. He'd transformed himself into the preacher by cropping his golden brown lion's mane into the short, severe style of a devout missionary. Gone also were the luxuriant side whiskers and the full mustache. He was clean-shaven now, his angular features fully exposed.

"I didn't even recognize myself when I looked into the glass afterwards," he insisted.

The clothes helped. He was wearing stout brogans, an unbleached homespun shirt, and black trousers held up by wide suspenders hooked over his broad shoulders. There was no color in his outfit. Everything was plain and unadorned, including the low-crowned, wide-brimmed hat of plaited straw crammed on his head. Of course, the clothes were almost a full size too small for him. He was kind of squeezed into them, but he'd have to get used to that.

"You've been a sinner all your life, Archer Owen, not a saint. How you planning on disguising that?"

"I don't have to convince them I'm a saint, just that I'm Brother Deke Carver traveling to Oregon with his wife, Sister Meg, and his daughter, Molly. I'll manage it," he stubbornly maintained. "I have to, Mike. I need to go after Trace Sheridan, and that means hiding myself under another identity on this Delaney wagon train. Not just because of the law looking for me, either. I'm a riverman. What do I know about finding my way on land across the continent, or surviving alone out there on the trail? But don't you see, if this wagon train will take us on as a family—"

"I'll tell you what I see," Mike interrupted him caustically. "I see a man willing to trade his soul for an old steamboat."

"Don't preach to me, Mike."

"Yeah, that's right. You're the preacher now, ain't you? And what about little Molly? What becomes of her?"

"You were going to send her west with the Delaneys, anyway. I'll take good care of her, Mike. And I'll make sure she ends up with some loving family who wants her."

"Got it all figured out, huh? Only, there's a little problem here. That woman in the next room. Even supposin' she does accept you as her husband, what happens when, and if, she gets her memory back?"

Arch had already considered that, but he had no answers. It was a real issue all right, but he refused to let it stop him. "Maybe by then I'll have caught up to her brother."

Mike considered him for a moment in silence, and then he shook his head. "It's wrong, Arch. It's all wrong. You'll end up hurting her, and maybe yourself in the bargain."

Her daughter was still peacefully asleep at her side. She herself, however, was awake again, admiring the baby's tiny, perfect features, when the tall man entered the bedroom.

He was a stranger, though not the same one who had brought her a dish of oatmeal earlier. He had a craggy face, but it wasn't a displeasing one. He carried a straw hat in his hand, the kind with a low crown and flat brim.

"How are you feeling now?" he asked her. His voice was deep, rough around the edges, though not unkind.

How was she feeling? It was difficult to know with her memory stripped from her. "I—I'm sure I'm better, thank you."

"You had an awful headache."

"Yes, I recollect that much. It's gone, I think."

"That's good." He pulled a stool up beside the bed and perched on it, leaning toward her. "Do you know who I am?"

"No, I'm sorry, I don't."

"I'm Deke Carver." He cleared his throat before adding huskily, "I'm your husband."

She stared at him. She had absolutely no recognition of him. It seemed strange to hear him tell her he was her husband, that they were something as intimate as man and wife. But she didn't fear him, and she could think of no reason not to believe him. On the other hand, she didn't know how to answer him. She was reluctant to just simply accept him.

"Will you trust me?" he asked her.

He seemed so anxious for her to believe him. He kept twisting the hat nervously in his hands. She felt sorry for him. "I'll try," she promised him.

"You're Meg Carver," he said.

"Meg?" She tested the name on her lips. It wasn't familiar. She glanced quickly at the baby. "And my— our daughter?"

"Molly."

Molly. Yes, that much, anyway, sounded right.

"You've been ill with a fever. We were both ill. That's how you got that lump." He gently touched the swelling on the side of her head. "You were delirious and fell. Afterwards, you didn't have any memory."

His explanation did make sense.

"I'm sorry I wasn't here for you when you woke up this morning," he apologized. "I had to be out taking care of our oxen. Now that I'm recovered, I couldn't expect Mike to go on taking care of them.''

He went on to tell her that Mike O'Malley had brought her the oatmeal and that this was his ferry station. They were stopped here waiting for the wagon train they were going to join. It would take them to Oregon where they would be missionaries.

She listened to him without comment. It was all very bewildering, an existence to which she was unable to relate.

When he was finished, he asked her if she had any questions.

''Only one,'' she told him. ''When I woke up last night and was so frightened . . . was that you there with me?''

''Yes.''

She relaxed. If he was the man who had comforted her in the middle of the night, then everything was going to be all right. The rest didn't matter. She would find a way to deal with it.

Mike was waiting for him when he emerged from the bedroom. The disapproval was still evident in his manner when he asked curtly, ''Well?''

Arch was damned if he would avoid his gaze. Looking him directly in the eye, he answered Mike defiantly, ''She's accepted it. It's done, so let's not chew over it again.''

''I hope you know what you're doing.'' Turning away, Mike went and got his rifle down from the chimney breast.

''Where are you going?'' Arch challenged him.

''Up along the river to see if I can bring me back some fresh meat for when the Delaney party arrives.

126

I'll probably be gone for an hour or so.''

Hunting wasn't his motive in leaving the station, and they both knew that. It was Mike's way of washing his hands of Archer's scheme.

Arch panicked when his friend got to the door and opened it. "Hey, wait! What happens when the baby wakes up and wants to be fed?''

Mike looked at him over his shoulder. "You feed her. There's plenty of milk left from this morning, and you know where the bottle is.'' His mouth curled in a crooked Irish grin. "Your chance to play father. Better get used to it, *Deke*.''

What did Mike know about it, anyway? he thought sourly when the door had closed behind him. Mike wasn't a hunted man desperate to keep his head out of a noose. Conscience wasn't something you could afford when you were on the run with everything you valued stripped from you.

Then why did Arch feel like vermin when he went back into the bedroom a minute later, bringing her the box of clothes she had asked for? Why did he find it so hard to watch her as she removed Meg Carver's belongings from the box, slowly and solemnly examining each one? As if to convince herself that these articles were hers, that they established her identity.

He was grateful when Molly gave him an excuse to escape from the scene. She had awakened and started to whimper.

"I'll take her,'' he said, hastily gathering up the baby from the bed. "It's time for her feeding. I'll see to it.''

Margaret—Meg now, he reminded himself—

looked up with an odd expression on her face, but she said nothing.

Molly was back in her basket, and he was hurrying to ready her bottle and making clumsy mistakes it shouldn't have been possible to make with so simple a procedure, including scalding his hand as he warmed the milk, when Meg came out of the bedroom. He was surprised to see her fully dressed.

"You're supposed to be resting."

"I was tired of that nightdress and tired of resting."

"Then sit down. You're still a bit shaky on your feet." And still slightly dazed, too, he thought.

She didn't argue with him. She perched on a stool and looked around the room, trying to remember her surroundings. But he knew none of it was familiar to her. He sneaked worried glances at her as he filled the bottle and struggled to attach the nipple to it. It had seemed so easy when he'd watched Mike do it.

Meg Carver's clothes were a little too big for her. He waited for her to ask him about that, and he was ready with an explanation of how she'd lost weight during her illness. But she said nothing.

What she was wearing probably in no way resembled anything Margaret Sheridan would have chosen for her elegant wardrobe. It was a simple gray dress with white cuffs and collar and a full white apron. It made her look demure and innocent, nothing like the haughty Miss Sheridan.

But no matter how modest the outfit, it couldn't hide her feminine charms. Her allure was as strong as ever, and he was as hot as ever thinking about her in those terms. He'd have to watch that. Aside from all the complications involved, which he wasn't ready yet to confront, lust probably wasn't in character. He was playing a preacher, and that meant restraint, didn't it? But it was going to be one wicked devil of a problem. Hell, the woman was supposed to be his wife and he, her husband, was entitled to her bed.

He was relieved when he finally had the bottle prepared and Molly in his lap, eager for her feeding. But something was wrong. Seconds after he inserted the nipple into her mouth, she spat it out. When he tried again, she pulled away and began to cry.

Were the pin holes in the nipple clogged? He examined them. No, there were beads of milk there. Then what was the problem?

"Come on, Molly," he coaxed. "Take your bottle."

This time when he attempted to squeeze the nipple into her mouth, she set up an angry squalling.

"I could swear she was hungry," he said. "Maybe she's ill. Maybe she caught our fever."

Meg rose to her feet, crossed the room, and took the bottle out of his hand. She sniffed at its contents and quietly informed him, "I don't blame her for refusing it. This milk has gone sour."

Arch blew out his cheeks in exasperation. What had made him think this masquerade was going to be easy? Oh, hell. Coming to his feet, he placed the baby in Meg's arms. Then he went to the wall and lifted a tin bucket off its hook.

When he started for the door, she called out to him. "Where are you going?"

"Out to milk the cow." He had no choice. The kid had to eat. And he had to learn how to milk a cow. Unless he wanted Molly to starve, the animal would need to accompany them on the trail. Which meant he would have to be the one to regularly milk it, because it sure wouldn't be a skill Margaret Sheridan had picked up in that snooty female academy she'd attended.

"But that's ridiculous." She was wearing that odd expression on her face again. "The solution is—"

"Now, Meg, you just let me handle it." If he sounded confident, maybe he would be confident.

The cow wasn't deceived by his act. She gave him trouble the minute he approached her with bucket and stool where Mike had staked her out to graze. Rolling her eyes at him, she seemed to sense he was in no way familiar with the process of emptying her bag.

Arch had seen cows milked before. Trouble is, he'd never paid much attention to the operation. He had a vague impression that you grabbed the teats and pulled them. But this cow didn't appreciate his method of handling her teats. She kept sidling away from him.

It didn't help that Meg had followed him out to the pasture. She was sitting there on a stump, rocking Molly in her arms and watching his failure with that faraway look in her eyes. She had to wonder why the cow was being so obstinate with him, though she didn't ask. What she did want to know, however, was: "What's her name? I don't remember that, either."

Name? Yeah, he supposed cows did have names. He couldn't remember Mike mentioning it. Meg would think it funny if he didn't know. He searched his mind for a name. Anything would do. Penelope. It came out of nowhere. No, that wasn't true. He had once known a temperamental, redheaded whore called

Penelope. Well, the cow was red, and she definitely was temperamental. So from now on, she was Penelope.

"Penelope," he said. Maybe giving her an identity would make her more cooperative. "Come on, Penelope, don't be so difficult."

It didn't work. He managed to get a few squirts into the bucket before she started to dance and pull away from him.

The noise behind him didn't help. Molly had started to yowl again. In a mother's attempt to soothe her, Meg sang to her. She was the worst singer Arch had ever heard, jarringly out of tune. Her voice offended his Welsh appreciation for rich music.

The cow didn't like it, either. This time when he tried to yank her teats, she kicked him. Losing the last of his self-control, he slapped her on the side and roared blisteringly, "You low-down, ornery sonof"—he caught himself just in time, ending his curse feebly—"daughter of Satan!"

A close one. He'd have to be careful from now on. If Meg heard him bellowing obscenities, when he was supposed to be a God-fearing preacher, this whole illusion would start to come apart.

"Sorry," he mumbled. "Penelope has never been a problem like this before, and—" He turned his head to finish his apology, and stopped himself, shocked. "*What are you doing?*"

Meg had unbuttoned her bodice, exposing a breast. The captivating sight of that naked plump flesh and pink nipple paralyzed him!

"I'm going to nurse Molly," she explained calmly.

"I don't know why we've been bothering with the cow."

No wonder she'd been wearing those puzzled expressions whenever the subject of feeding the baby was mentioned. "You can't!" he said in a panic.

She hesitated. "Why not?"

He thought fast. "You don't have any milk. Your milk dried up when you were sick."

"Are you sure?"

"Positive."

"Oh, that explains it then."

To his relief, she tucked herself back in and buttoned her bodice. She had almost stopped his heart with the vision of that firm, fulsome breast, never mind what it had done to another portion of his anatomy. Sweet mother, he was never going to survive this masquerade!

Meanwhile, the kid was still hungry, and the cow was still fighting him. In the end, he remembered something he had once heard a farmer say. "Cows object to cold hands on their teats." Were his hands cold? Yeah, they were, probably from being so nervous.

Arch warmed his palms and fingers by briskly rubbing them together. Then he tried again. What do you know! It worked! Well enough, anyway, that Penelope delivered sufficient milk into the bucket. He discovered that a firm pumping rhythm on her teats also helped.

The only bad moment occurred when Meg, gazing across the prairie as he finished with the cow, asked him, "Are those graves out there?"

The real Deke and Meg Carver's graves. He had

forgotten about them. "Uh, it looks like it."

"I wonder who's buried there. I suppose Mr. O'Malley could tell us."

"Better not ask. If it was loved ones he lost, he wouldn't want to be reminded."

"Yes, I suppose you're right."

Another victory. If she went on accepting what he told her without seriously challenging him, everything would work out just fine. There was always the possibility, of course, that sooner or later the defiant nature of Margaret Sheridan would surface, but why cross that bridge before he came to it?

Back inside the house, with Molly suckling happily on a fresh bottle of milk, he congratulated himself that he'd gotten through the ordeal of the cow with his impersonation still intact. The real test, however, was still to come when he faced the Delaneys. Could he convince the couple to let his family join their wagon train?

That opportunity arrived less than two hours later when Mike rode back to the station. He brought with him the rabbits and prairie chickens he'd shot and his annoucement of: "Covered wagons on the horizon! They're here!"

Chapter Seven

They were a remarkable pair, Archer decided. And as unalike as any husband and wife could be.

Agatha Delaney, a good six feet at least, was probably the tallest woman he had ever encountered. And certainly the most regal. But there was an innate gentleness behind those sedate features, and he was counting on it to help him win his case.

Her husband was another story. Cooper Delaney, a mountain of a man, was as rugged as the trail over which he piloted his wagon trains. And probably just as unforgiving to any man who crossed him. It wasn't going to be so easy deceiving him.

But Delaney's obvious devotion to his wife could be in Archer's favor, he thought. If she ended up siding with him, then maybe her husband would go along with her decision. Hell, a man in love could be an awful fool. Arch had seen that happen before, though he'd never understood or appreciated it. He'd always regarded the emotion as a kind of silly weakness and himself as immune to it. He planned to keep it that way.

On the other hand, Delaney's adoration of his wife might be explained by her condition. She was wrapped in a voluminous shawl, but Arch had glimpsed a swelling that told him she was pregnant. He couldn't imagine a woman choosing to deliver her baby out on the trail, but that wasn't his problem. His concern was to sound as pious and earnest as he could as he made his appeal to them.

There was a long silence after he finished explaining his need to join their caravan. The three of them were standing behind the Delaney wagon. The other wagons were parked in the customary circle, and all around them was the bustle of a train making camp for the night. Arch could smell the smoke from the cooking fires as he waited tensely for the couple's response. He could see them trading glances.

Cooper Delaney finally replied gruffly. "I can appreciate your intention, impractical though it strikes me, and the fact that you've already got your oxen and a sound wagon loaded with the essentials, but the thing is, Mr. Carver—"

"Brother Deke," Arch corrected him brightly. "We are Brother Deke and Sister Meg."

"Uh-huh," he said dryly. "The thing is, Brother

135

Deke, this wagon train is already much larger than it should be, and to add another wagon . . . well, you can see my problem.''

"There is another consideration," his wife said quietly. "Although there are men here to aid us with the crossing, the caravan, like all of our previous ventures, is composed primarily of disadvantaged single women in search of better lives. It has never been our purpose to transport families. If we included you, Brother Deke, it would be a departure for us.''

Arch, desperate for their acceptance, went out on a dangerous limb. "Just think, ma'am, of the spiritual comfort I can offer your ladies on this difficult crossing.''

"Real tempting, Brother Deke," Delaney said with a wry smile, "but I think we're going to have to give you—''

"Our decision after we have the opportunity to confer with each other," his wife said swiftly, placing her hand on Delaney's arm to forestall him. "We will inform you of it directly after the evening meal.''

Arch had done all he could to convince them, except pray. And since he was supposed to be a preacher, maybe that wasn't such a bad thing to try. But hell, with his luck, the Almighty would probably answer by striking him down for being such a monumental fraud.

Thanking the Delaneys, he walked away, hoping for the best and expecting the worst.

Cooper, after making sure Brother Deke was out of earshot, rounded on his wife. "Damn it, Aggie, why did you go and stop me like that? I was about to tell him he couldn't join us.''

''Yes, I realized you were, my love. Why do you wish to exclude him?''

''Not sure. I have the feeling there's something not right about the man.''

''You are too suspicious, my love.''

''And you're too trusting.''

They smiled at each other with the familiarity of two people who had engaged in this argument many times before.

''You telling me you actually like the man, Aggie?''

She was thoughtful for a moment, then nodded. ''Yes, all things considered, I believe I do. I spoke to his wife earlier. She seems a pure soul.''

Cooper rolled his eyes. ''I think your judgment is slipping, Aggie. I think this time you've gotten just plain soft. It's because of this.'' He placed his hand lovingly against the place where she carried their child. ''It's got you forgiving the whole world.''

She covered his hand with her own. ''Perhaps you are right. Perhaps the Carvers are not all they pretend to be, but . . .''

''What, Aggie?''

''Underneath,'' she said wisely, ''I sense something very deserving in both of them. It just needs the opportunity for them to demonstrate it.''

''And we're supposed to give them that opportunity. All right,'' he relented, ''we'll let them join us. But I won't pretend I like it, anymore than I like you being here instead of safe at home in Oregon.''

''Cooper—''

"I know, we've had that battle, and I lost it. But it's crazy your having the baby on the trail. Something tells me this crossing is gonna be trouble enough. I can already smell it. . . ."

Enoch Rawlins, whose slight, dark-haired figure was conservatively dressed in the best materials that his St. Louis clothier could provide, confronted the sheriff at the jail in Saint Joseph.

"I haven't traveled all this distance, Sheriff," he said coldly, "not to have satisfaction. I demand to know what's being done to recover my bride."

Sheriff Sykes, a sober man with a long face and a reputation for patience, answered him calmly. "Everything that's possible, Mr. Rawlins. Countryside's been scoured for miles in all directions."

"Without result, I understand."

The sheriff spread his hands in a gesture of helplessness. "Problem is, Owen was able to snatch a pair of horses. They could be a long way off by now."

"And meanwhile you sit here doing nothing."

"Owen ain't the only lawbreaker I got to attend to, Mr. Rawlins. I can't be off personally chasing him more than I have already. That doesn't mean I've given up, because I want to see his head in a noose same as you. I've got people up and down the river looking and asking questions, and wanted posters going up in every settlement."

"It's not enough."

"What more do you suggest, Mr. Rawlins?"

"They can't have just disappeared into nowhere. Have you offered a reward?"

"A substantial one."

"It's an outrage, the whole thing! When I think of Margaret being abducted like that, carried off by that murdering devil . . ." The thought of what Archer Owen might be doing to Margaret made Enoch tremble with fury and frustration.

The sheriff, aware of his agitation, tried to pacify him. "We'll do everything we can to get Miss Sheridan back to you unharmed. Meanwhile, best for you to go home and try not to worry, and we'll get word to you as soon as something develops."

Enoch was convinced of it. Sheriff Sykes was incompetent. Did he think he would accept his recommendation and meekly return to St. Louis? He hadn't gotten to be rich without action or by failing to obey a simple, ruthless code: No man took what was his and got away with it. Margaret was his, and he wanted her back. He also wanted Archer Owen to pay for taking her.

He was determined to achieve both aims when he stormed out of the jail. The paunchy deputy, Floyd Petty, who had listened to the exchange between the sheriff and Enoch and recognized his fierce resolve, followed him from the building and stopped him in the street.

"Just how far you willin' to go, Mr. Rawlins, to catch up with Owen and your intended?"

Enoch regarded him suspiciously. "I am prepared to do whatever is necessary to find them. I assume you have a purpose in asking?"

"I do. That include spending money, Mr. Rawlins? Maybe a lot of money?"

"It does." He regarded the deputy with contempt. Floyd Petty didn't look like he had the wits to catch a cold. "I hope that doesn't mean you plan to offer your services to me, Deputy."

"Not me, Mr. Rawlins. I got someone else in mind. Someone who'll hunt your man to the ends of the earth, if that's what it takes. But he don't come cheap. Probably cost you a big sum—that is, if he's interested at all."

"Who?" Enoch demanded.

"Name of Hank Shaw. Used to be sheriff here. But the town didn't like his methods. Hank can be mean, real mean. I've seen him handle prisoners in ways that'd make a man shudder just thinking of 'em. Lawbreakers that nobody thought could be caught, but he caught 'em. Always caught 'em and brought 'em back."

"Your Mr. Shaw sounds perfect. Now, before you tell me where I go to find him, I'll ask you to explain why you're doing me the favor of recommending him."

Floyd went pink with embarrassment. "Owen," he mumbled. "He made a fool of me when he escaped. Figure I owe him something."

There was no humor in Enoch's smile. "I'll be happy to repay him for you, Deputy. Now oblige me with those directions."

Ten minutes later Enoch reached the destination Floyd Petty had described, a sorry-looking, unpainted cottage at the farthest end of Messanie Street. The man who inhabited it was seated on the sagging front porch, his booted feet propped up on the rail as he smoked a cigar.

Enoch could appreciate the deputy's opinion as he joined Hank Shaw on the porch. The retired lawman was a brawny figure with a brutal mouth and a pair of crafty eyes that said the man behind them could be dangerous.

Those eyes sized him up for a moment before he demanded in a hard-bitten voice, "You got business with me, mister?"

"If you're Hank Shaw, I do."

"State it."

He didn't stand or ask Enoch to join him on one of the chairs cut from barrels. He went on lounging there, smoking his cigar and listening without comment to his visitor's proposition.

When Enoch had finished, Shaw turned his head and spat over the rail before reacting easily. "For the right price, I can be persuaded to go after this bastard." Then he peered at Enoch shrewdly through a cloud of smoke. "You got the right price, Rawlins?"

They haggled for several minutes before they came to terms. Enoch agreed to cover all expenses, and when Owen was behind bars again, Hank would receive five hundred dollars in gold.

"There is one further condition, Mr. Shaw. I will be traveling with you."

Hank scowled at him. "I work alone."

"Not this time," Enoch insisted. "Miss Sheridan means a great deal to me. I mean to be there for her when she's rescued. More than that, I want to see the expression on Archer Owen's face when we capture him."

Hank Shaw smiled at him, a gleam of respect in his dark eyes. "Looks like we think alike about a few things." He flipped the cigar over the railing and looked Enoch up and down. "But that's on the inside.

On the outside you don't look built for the rough country where we'll probably be going to pick up his trail.''

"I'm tougher than I look, I promise you."

"That so?'' Shaw's eyes narrowed, his broad face hardening. "Well, I got a promise of my own. If you give out along the way, I don't stop to play nurse-maid. You'll be on your own, Rawlins, because I'll go on without you."

"Fair enough."

They settled the final details of the search that would begin at first light in the morning. Then Enoch left and walked back to the other end of Messanie Street. He found a place that looked down on the river where the steamboats were docked. Among them was the *Missouri Belle*.

Margaret's sister-in-law had told him about Archer Owen's cherished stern-wheeler when he had called at her boardinghouse immediately after his arrival in town.

Enoch gazed at the craft for a long moment, a vindictive expression in his eyes. Then he turned away and went to look for the officials he was confident, for enough money, would be happy to accommodate him. It was his last piece of business in Saint Joseph, and it involved the *Missouri Belle*.

Clutching the faded brown calico dress against her breasts, Meg summoned the courage to speak to the two women who were approaching her wagon from the other side of the encampment. They were carrying bulging sacks. She knew they intended to do their laundry on the the nearby banks of the South Platte

River where many of the others were already gathered.

One of the two women, the taller one with red hair, was called Violet. Meg didn't know the name of her companion. Violet talked all the time. She was chattering now. Meg hoped it was a good sign and that Violet would be sociable enough to talk to her.

She stopped them as they started to pass by the wagon, offering a nervous smile as she held out the calico dress. "I wonder if either of you ladies could help me."

They traded quick glances with each other. The short one, who bounced when she walked, replied impatiently, "We're on our way to do our wash."

"I won't keep you. I just need your advice. It's this dress. I'm trying to take it in, but I'm helpless with a needle and thread. Where do I start? If you could just show me—"

Violet cut her off brusquely. "Oh, just take a few tucks in the waistline. You can manage that much."

Giving her no further opportunity to delay them, they moved on toward the river. Meg, watching them go, saw Violet poke her friend in the side. They both laughed.

Their rejection hurt, and not because of the dress, either. It was their friendship she had been looking for. All the women seemed so close, and she had been left out since joining the train. She was lonely.

"Give them time," a voice behind her urged gently.

Meg turned around to find Agatha Delaney standing there. The tall, robust woman had arrived on the scene with her usual quiet dignity.

143

"The women have been together for a long time," she continued. "They have had the opportunity to get to know one another, whereas you are a relative newcomer."

Meg heaved a sigh of regret. "I'm afraid it wouldn't matter. I'd still be an outcast. They think I'm strange because of my amnesia."

"Perhaps, but I believe it is more than that. I believe they are uncomfortable because of your manners."

"But I've been careful to be courteous to all of them."

"Yes, that is precisely the problem. Your manners are those of a refined lady. Which, of course, is what you must have been."

Meg was shocked. "But I couldn't have come from that kind of background!"

"I think you did. I think your past must have been very unlike those of the other women, and they sense that."

"You mean they resent me?"

Agatha shook her head. "Not resentment exactly. More like suspicion. Many of our women suffered abuse from people of wealth and refinement. They left those lives behind them, but the memories remain."

"Yes, but you're a lady, and they always treat you with warmth and affection."

"Ah, that is different. I am helping them to find better lives. Also, I have worked hard to earn their trust." She tipped her handsome head to one side and smiled. "I can see, Sister Meg, that you still doubt me. You still believe that your amnesia is why they avoid you, because your ladyhood cannot possibly exist. But why not ask your husband? He must know all about your past."

Meg shook her head. "I do ask him all the time. He gives me answers, but they're never very satisfactory ones. To tell you the truth, I think he'd be content for me not to remember the past. He said we left our old lives behind, so we should forget about them and concentrate on our new lives."

"Perhaps he is right." But Meg had the feeling Agatha wasn't convinced of that. "And where *is* Brother Deke, by the way?"

"Oh, one of the men took him to fish in a pool he knows up the river. He says fish will be a welcome change from beans and bacon." She glanced down at the calico dress she was still clutching. "Uh, I don't suppose you . . ."

Agatha laughed. "I fear I am just as helpless with a needle and thread."

"It looks like I'll have to go on wearing oversized clothing. I don't understand it. I lost all that weight when I had the fever. But Deke was ill, too, only he gained weight because his clothes are too tight."

"Yes, that is odd."

Meg frowned. "I wonder if I knew how to manage things like sewing and cooking before I lost my memory."

"Possibly you did. I imagine amnesia is an unpredictable condition."

"I feel so useless. Deke tries to help out, but he's every bit as hopeless with domestic skills. And then, with all those awful storms that never quit, he was too busy with the wagon and oxen to—"

They were interrupted by a burbling sound from

the basket resting on the lowered tailboard of the covered wagon.

"Molly is awake."

Agatha joined her as Meg went to check on her daughter. Molly was babbling incoherently and kicking her legs in the air.

"Is she happy like this all the time?"

Meg grinned proudly. "As long as we don't forget her bottle. Deke handles the food for her. He's on good terms with Penelope, for which I'm thankful. I'm afraid the cow isn't my friend, either."

"May I?"

"Yes, of course."

Agatha picked the baby up from the basket and talked to her softly. Molly seemed fascinated.

Agatha's interest in her daughter reminded Meg of the woman's pregnancy, which was growing more evident with each day. She asked her about it. "Deke says it will be autumn before we arrive at the Willamette. That has to mean . . ."

Agatha understood her. "Yes, I will deliver long before then."

"Doesn't that worry you, having a baby out on the trail?" The mere thought of it scared Meg. But then everything about this journey frightened her, much as she tried to hide it.

"I refuse to let myself be concerned about it. I suppose that is because I have already known the worst. On our first trek to Oregon we were all women except for Cooper."

Meg was amazed. She couldn't imagine that kind of courage.

"I survived that challenge," Agatha said. "I will

survive this one. It is my husband who is anxious, perhaps because we already lost a child.''

Meg stared at her, not knowing what to say.

Agatha, who must have read her sympathetic expression, chuckled. "No, not like that. Callie was a little girl who came west with us on that first crossing and lived with us after we were married. We thought her an orphan, until her father turned up one day and claimed her. We still miss Callie, Cooper especially, but I remind myself that she found the father she lost. What is going on over there?''

Meg could see that Agatha was annoyed by a sudden commotion several wagons away. Three of the burly men hired to accompany the train had accosted a gangly figure returning to the camp from the river. The young man held his fresh laundry protectively against his thin chest and nervously eyed his grinning assailants.

"Hey, sister boy, you been doin' your own wash?''

"That's women's work, sister boy. Not what a man is supposed to be doin'.''

"But then he ain't a real man, is he?''

Overhearing the scene, Agatha muttered angrily, "I have warned them repeatedly not to bait Toby, and still they persist.''

Meg knew his full name was Toby Snow and that he was . . . well, different. His mannerisms were decidedly unmasculine, and he wore outfits that would have challenged a rainbow. She hadn't spoken to him yet and didn't know why he was with the emigrants, but she did recognize him.

Toby, being so unique, was easy to recognize. Meg was still struggling to learn the identities of all the others on the caravan. There had been no opportunity to sort them out before this. The weather had made everything a blur to her since leaving the ferry station weeks ago. The rain had never quit, creating conditions so harsh and miserable that no one had had time to notice anything but how to struggle through each day.

But then, one merciful morning, the clouds rolled away, and the caravan found itself no longer in prairie country. It was mid-June now, almost summer, and there were buffalo wallows along the trail, coarse grass, and a sandy terrain broken by low, treeless ridges. They had reached the vastness of the plains.

Cooper had called for a much-deserved two-day rest stop when they arrived at the place where they would cross the mile-wide South Platte River. It was the chance to do laundry, catch up with chores like sewing, and to cook their first decent meals.

And for Meg it meant that the company began to emerge as invididuals. People like Toby Snow. She felt sorry for him, maybe even understood what he must be undergoing. He's like me, she thought. He doesn't fit in.

"I will not tolerate such cruelty," Agatha said. "They must be made to understand Mr. Snow is not to be ridiculed. Excuse me, Sister Meg."

Meg regretted it when the tall woman marched away from her wagon to do battle on behalf of Toby Snow. She admired Agatha Delaney, would have enjoyed pursuing a friendship with her. But in all fairness she couldn't expect Agatha, kind though she'd been just now, to devote more time to her. There were a lot of other women on the train who demanded her attention, and problems like Toby's to settle, and a husband who was concerned about her pregnancy and expected her to rest as much as possible.

Meg understood, all right. But she was still lonely for the female companionship the others enjoyed.

"I should be the one to cook them since you cleaned them," she had said.

"I don't need to ask one of the other women to help me," she had said.

"I can do it myself," she had said.

Meg seemed to remember a couple of other things she had said about the bass Deke had been so proud of catching, and which he'd been so reluctant to entrust to her care. Arguments like. "How can I ever have confidence in myself unless you have confidence in me as well?"

All of those assertions came back to torment her. Why hadn't she guessed that her effort with the fillets and the frying pan would be a colossal disaster? Why had she refused any suggestion from Deke and sent him away to entertain Molly? Why had she been so idiotically self-assured?

The trouble had begun with the batter.

You coated fish with a batter before you fried it, didn't you? Yes, she was sure of that much. But what did the batter consist of? Flour, eggs, and milk, right? Yes, she was certain of that, too. Well, fairly certain.

She had no eggs, but she had plenty of flour, and there was the milk from Penelope. She mixed up a gooey mess in a bowl and flopped the slabs of fish around in it. The batter stuck, but it didn't seem

149

enough. She used a knife to slather on more of the paste, as much as the fish would take.

She was about to consign the fillets to the pan over the fire, where the melted lard was already bubbling nicely, when she remembered something she'd overlooked. Salt. The bass would benefit from salt, wouldn't it? She got the tin from the traveling pantry at the back of the wagon, scooped out a handful of salt, and smeared it over the fish, tossing on another pinch or two for good measure.

By this time the fillets were looking a bit on the heavy side. Oh, well, it was how they were going to taste that counted, not how they looked. She popped them into the pan, and they began to sizzle. Chunks of the coating came off and floated around in the melted fat, but that didn't seem to be a serious problem.

She watched the fillets intently, ready to turn them in the pan when she judged their bottom sides cooked. So far, so good. And then the mosquitoes arrived.

They won't stay, Meg thought. The smoke from the fire will drive them away. She was wrong. They whined around her head, hungry and insistent. She swatted at them. Her wildly waving hands fanned the smoke up into her face, where it stung her eyes.

She was so busy fighting smoke and mosquitoes that she failed to concentrate on the fillets. Couldn't see them anyway when her eyes were tearing so badly from the smoke. But she could smell them when they began to burn.

In a panic Meg went to snatch the pan off the tripod, forgetting what someone on the wagon train had said about cooking fires on the plains fueled with buffalo chips. They created an intense heat. She learned just how true that was when her fingers came in brief contact with the long handle of the pan.

Though she managed to save her hand from a severe burn by leaping back with a little yelp, she didn't save the precious fillets. The assaulted pan slid off the tripod, spilling the strips of fish onto the ground.

"Everything all right?" Deke called from the other end of the wagon where he had been singing softly to Molly in his deep, rich voice.

Meg cast a guilty look in his direction, praying that if he decided to poke his head around the side of the wagon he would be unable to make out what was happening in the thickening twilight.

"Uh-huh," she assured him.

"I'm hungry. Will it be ready soon?"

"Soon."

Meg contemplated the fillets on the ground. He'd be so disappointed if he didn't get to eat his bass. Should she? Why not? He'd probably never know the difference.

This time she was careful and used a towel wrapped around the handle. Ignoring smoke and mosquitoes, she rescued the pan, dusted off the fillets, and flipped them back into the pan, adding more lard when she returned it to the tripod over the fire.

The fish was looking rather pathetic by this time, lumpy with blackened batter in some spots and naked in others. It also bore a distinctly scorched odor. But Meg was still hopeful that it would taste just fine.

That hope wilted and expired minutes later when, seated near the fire, their plates loaded with fish and squares of cornmeal bread Agatha Delaney had sent over to them earlier, Meg tensely watched Deke shovel the first forkful of bass into his mouth. He chewed for a second, paused, and in the flickering firelight she saw a peculiar expression cross his face.

"No?" she said in a little voice.

He didn't immediately answer her. Maybe he couldn't. The sight of his Adam's apple bobbing noticeably indicated he was involved in a struggle. When he had finally swallowed and cleared his throat, his verdict was charitable. "Interesting."

It couldn't be that bad, Meg thought. She tasted her own fish. It was worse than bad. It was an impossible, nasty mixture of something charred on the outside, raw on the inside, too much batter, far too much salt, and—yes, grit. The grit that was fine Nebraska sand. She hadn't gotten off all the dirt.

Meg spit out the mess and stared at him mournfully. "Oh, Deke, I've ruined your wonderful bass!"

He gazed back at her, not knowing what to say.

"What's the matter with me?" she wailed. "I can't even do a simple thing like fry fish. I can't cook, I can't sew, I—I can't—"

"What?"

"I don't know," she blubbered. "Everything. The other women not only cook and sew, they know how to manage the stock and drive a wagon and—and shoot a rifle. I don't know anything!"

She was weeping in earnest now, hating her tears but unable to control them. She couldn't stand it. Maybe Deke couldn't stand it either. He looked awkward and embarrassed.

And then something wonderful happened. He put his plate down on the ground, shifted over to her side, took her own plate away from her, and gathered her into his arms. She went limp against the solid wall of his chest.

He hadn't held her like this before. Not since her illness, anyway. There hadn't been time for anything but the exhausting hardships of the trail. Had this been what she'd been missing, what she'd needed? She thought so. She found it very reassuring; the security of her husband's strong arms around her, his husky voice soothing away her misery.

"It's going to be all right, precious. Everything is going to be just fine, you'll see."

She was far from convinced of that, but in this moment it didn't matter. All that counted was his comforting presence. Lifting her head from his chest, she confided shyly, "I like it when you call me precious."

There was a surprised look on his face. "You do?"

"Yes, it makes me feel"—she searched for the right word—"safe."

"Oh, Lord," he muttered.

"What is it, Deke? Did I say something wrong?"

He hesitated before replying quickly, "No, of course not."

She had a sudden desire to touch him. Maybe the longing had something to do with Agatha and Cooper Delaney. She had watched the couple when they were together, noticing how they communicated as husband and wife. Sometimes it was with spoken endearments, and on other occasions they traded loving caresses that seemed to need no words.

Meg had found herself envying the Delaneys. But why should she when she had her own husband to share the same kind of closeness? Giving into her urge, she reached up with one hand and began to stroke Deke's angular features.

"Uh, maybe you'd better not do that," he said, his voice sounding thick and hoarse.

"Why not?" she asked him innocently.

This time he had no reply, so she went on touching him. At first she felt self-conscious about her action. But that was silly. The Delaneys were never self-conscious with each other. And anyway, she must have touched Deke like this many times before. It was just that she had no memory of it. That was why it felt as if her fingertips were learning his face for the first time.

"Meg," he warned her.

She ignored him, whispering playfully, "There's a little bit of the lobe of your left ear missing. I suppose there's a story that explains it, and you must have told me. You'll have to tell me again. It's right here along the bottom."

Her finger lightly traced the contours of his ear. He made a sound, something between a groan and a choke. Then, as though recklessly shedding all self-restraint, he caught her face between his hands and began to kiss her feverishly.

In the first seconds of his siege on her mouth Meg was shocked, resistant. As though this, too, were happening for the first time. But perversely, there was also something familiar about it. A kind of magical belonging.

She didn't understand it, and after a brief moment she didn't try. She simply surrendered to the sensations of his breath mingling with hers, of his tongue performing a sensual dance with hers, of the yearning sounds deep in his throat. It was an intimacy that had been denied to her until now, and she welcomed it.

Not until his hands dropped to the sides of her breasts, not until he felt their incredibly soft fullness, did an alarm go off inside Arch's head. He remembered Mike O'Malley warning him: *You'll end up hurting her*.

Oh, God, he thought, he was in trouble. If he went on kissing her like this, it wouldn't stop here. They'd wind up in bed together. And a woman with her breeding and background was bound to be a virgin. How would he ever explain that after he'd made love to her?

Well, he couldn't make love to her, even if he was already hard as a stone and burning for it.

Hell and damnation, why couldn't he catch up with Trace Sheridan and end this whole masquerade before he was no longer able to control it? But he was trapped on this maddeningly slow wagon train, and Sheridan was still somewhere ahead of him on the trail.

It was with a massive effort that Arch ended their tantalizing kiss and pulled away from her. Though it was totally dark by now, the glow from the fire showed him the bewilderment on her face.

"What is it?" she asked. "What's wrong?"

He thought fast. "Molly," he said. "I heard Molly."

"Are you sure?"

"Think so. Isn't it about time for her last feeding?"

She nodded and got reluctantly to her feet. "I'll give her her bottle."

"And I'll clean up here. Then I think we should turn in. We'll be on the move again tomorrow, and that means getting up at first light."

She agreed with him, and went to take care of the baby. He'd be safe now. By the time she was ready for bed he'd be alone inside the tent, and she and Molly would be in the wagon. Sleeping in the wagon wasn't customary, but the weather had been so wet since leaving the ferry station that it was the only reliably dry place to spend the night. There was no room in there for two adults, what with all their gear and provisions. That had left him regularly using the tent, and though damp ground was no longer a risk, the pattern had been established for them.

But tonight was to be an exception.

Arch was stretched out on the bedroll, staring up into the gloom and wondering how he was going to keep from touching Meg in the weeks ahead, when he was startled by the rustle of the tent flap being lifted aside.

Jerking his head up from the pillow, he saw her silhouetted in the opening against the starry night. There was just enough light outside to show him she was wearing nothing but a thin nightdress. Before he could stop her, she was inside the tent and setting the baby's basket she carried down in the corner.

Finding his voice, Arch started to challenge her. "What are you—"

She cut him off with a whisper. "Molly is fast asleep. I hope you don't mind our joining you."

"Well, I—"

"Now that the skies are clear, there's no longer a reason for us to sleep apart, is there?"

No reason at all, he thought, except to preserve his sanity.

The next thing he knew she had lifted the cover and was sliding in beside him. He was suddenly aware of her alluring warmth, of the fact that he had stripped off his shirt and trousers and was wearing nothing but a pair of underdrawers. Her nightdress must have hiked up. He felt the silken skin of her bare thigh brush against his hair-roughened leg.

The contact was like a charge of electricity. His heart began to thud against his ribs. It threatened to explode out of his chest when she squirmed against him.

"Sorry," she murmured. "Just trying to get settled."

She was finally still, but by then it was too late. He was throbbing painfully. There was silence in the tent. But he knew she wasn't asleep. He could sense her tension. It matched his own.

"Deke?"

"Yes?"

"Don't be upset with me. I—I needed to be close tonight."

She was breathless when she said it, nervous. He didn't blame her. He was perspiring freely himself. Well, it must have required a considerable effort for her to come to him like this. A woman like her would regard such an action as shamelessly bold, even with her own husband. What could he do to keep from hurting her and still save the situation?

She didn't give him the chance to find out. Restless

again with her longing, she turned into him. Her magnificent breasts pressed against his naked chest. There was nothing between them but the thin material of her nightdress. He could smell her fragrant flesh, almost taste it.

This couldn't go on. In another minute she would be touching him in more intimate places. If that happened he would lose the last shreds of his self-control, would tear the nightdress from her body and lose himself inside her. It would be unbelievable. He knew it would. A wild session of hot, writhing sex. And afterwards there would be his enormous regret.

Sweet mother, when did he start having a conscience where a willing woman was concerned?

But it was true. And this time it had nothing to do with the risk of his exposure if she lost a virginity she must not even know she had. For the first time in his life he wanted to do what was right and decent. All right, he was using her, but the least he could do when this masquerade was ended was to send her back to her St. Louis bridegroom untouched.

He almost laughed out loud. Archer Owen protecting someone other than himself? Looked like it.

"Deke," she whispered.

He could hear the urgency in her voice. There was just no way not to hurt her, but in the long run . . .

"No, Meg, we can't."

"Why? I don't understand."

"Your illness. You're not strong enough. You're still recovering." It was a lame excuse, but it was the best he could produce. "You need your rest. Try to go to sleep now."

Shifting away as far as the bedroll would allow, he

turned on his side facing away from her. I won't touch her, he promised himself fiercely. Whatever it takes, I won't touch her.

Margaret Sheridan didn't know it, but her purity was being bought at the cost of his enormous frustration.

Meg, on her side of the bed, ached with her own unfulfilled longing. And a misery she found unbearable. First the women had rejected her, and now her husband. Why didn't he want her? What was wrong with her?

Chapter Eight

Buffalo had been sighted. That was why the wagon train had made camp at mid-afternoon, allowing the men sufficient daylight hours to go after the herd. If they could bring down a few buffalo, the caravan would have plenty of fresh meat.

Everyone had buffalo steaks on their minds. Except Meg. She was too busy fretting about an antelope. Or more precisely, the portion of it that was to be their supper this evening. That is, if she didn't ruin it.

"It's simple," Deke had advised her before riding out with the other hunters. "One of the women told me how to fix it."

Yes, Meg thought sourly, the women were more than willing to speak to him. She had watched them eyeing her brawny husband.

The antelope, which one of the other men had shot earlier and shared with them, was an old one. "Meat's too tough for roasting, or anything like that," Deke had explained. "You make a stew by dicing it into small chunks, slicing up a few of the potatoes we got left, and tossing all of it into a pot with a little water. Go easy with the salt, keep the fire low, and let it simmer all afternoon. You can't go wrong."

Oh, yes, she could, and they both knew that. But Meg was willing to give it a try. She was just as weary as Deke was of the endless beans and bacon, which seemed to be the only meal either of them could capably manage.

It was quiet in the camp as she worked. Many of the women were down along the Platte River, the north branch this time. Others were out collecting buffalo chips, and Molly was asleep in her basket. Meg had managed to dice the meat and potatoes and get them into the pot over the fire—all without error, she hoped—when the serenity of the camp was ruptured.

A clamor of voices directly across the circle from her own wagon caught her attention. She looked up to discover a nasty scene in progress. It was similar to the one she had witnessed several days ago, only worse.

Toby Snow's tormentors were at him again. They had him cornered from three sides and backed up against a wagon.

"Whooee, lookit what sister boy is wearin' today!"

"Ain't it just too pretty for words?"

Meg had to admit it was an outrageous outfit that consisted of yellow pantaloons, a patchwork tunic that hadn't missed a color in the spectrum, a rope of beads he had traded for from a Kansas brave, and a hat with iridescent feathers in its band. But that didn't give these three brutes the right to taunt him.

They were left behind to protect us, not harass us, she thought angrily. She found herself drifting toward the scene, anxious about what would happen to the rawboned young man. He seemed too frightened to do anything more than roll his eyes at them. Their fingers were plucking at his tunic.

"Bet he's the envy of all the other sister boys at their sister boy parties."

"Yeah, this is a mighty nice whatyacallit, but it sure hurts the eye to look at it. All 'em colors."

"Know a way to tone 'em down, though."

Someone ought to put a stop to this, Meg thought, gazing around for a source of rescue. But Agatha was nowhere in sight this time. No one was.

When she looked back, the three devils had Toby down on the ground. They were laughing as they rolled him around in the dust. She couldn't stand this. Racing to the wagon, she made an effort to stop them.

"Let him alone! You have no right to touch him!"

Paying her no attention, they went on treating the hapless Toby like a log. She tried to snatch at one of them, but he shoved her back against a wagon wheel.

Recovering herself, she searched for a weapon and found it in the shape of a long cattle prod used to drive the oxen to pasture. It was propped against the tailboard. Seizing the pole, surprising herself as much as Toby and his attackers, Meg came fiercely to the young man's defense.

Fury giving her strength, she whacked at arms, legs, and whatever else came in contact with the swinging prod.

"Ouch, that hurt!"

"Lady, are you crazy?"

"All right, all right, we're backin' off! See?"

Not until they had moved away in the direction of the river was Meg satisfied. Dropping the pole, she knelt on the ground beside the huddled figure, who was staring at her in amazement.

"Are you hurt?"

"No more than usual, love."

"You mean this sort of thing happens to you often?"

"Oh, all the time. Fancied it might be different when I left London and came to New York. Silly me. Then I thought, why not try out here?" He grinned cheerfully and shrugged his bony shoulders. "Wrong again. Well, perhaps in Oregon."

"But why do you let them go after you like that?"

"It's worse if I attempt to fight back. Learned that long ago. But you, love . . . a regular whirlwind, you were."

"Yes, I don't know what got into me. It's the strangest thing."

"I shan't forget it. Now could you lend an arm?" Meg helped him to get to his feet. "Lovely. Thank you."

He stood there like a gangly scarecrow, inspecting his clothes for damage. It was hard to tell what they had suffered when they were so covered with dust.

"If it's so bad," she pointed out, "why do you make a target of yourself by dressing the way you do?"

He looked at her in surprise, as if the answer was obvious. "Well, I have no choice about it, do I? It's just who I am. Besides, I'd still be a sister boy to them whatever I wore."

His philosophy was certainly an unusual one, Meg thought. But she decided she liked him. He was amiable, easy to talk to. "Look," she said, reluctant to part from him, "I have to get back to my fire. I need to watch the supper I'm cooking, and my daughter may want me. But if you'd like to join me, I'll help you to clean up those clothes."

"You are a heroine," he said, falling in beside her.

Reaching her wagon, Meg checked both the contents of the pot and the basket. Neither the stew nor Molly seemed to have missed her. She stirred the first and made sure the second was still sleeping peacefully. Then she found a stiff brush and applied it briskly to Toby's garments as he pivoted slowly, long arms outstretched. The powdery dust came off easily in little puffs.

"As good as new," she reported. "All but the elbow here. I'm afraid there's a tear in it."

He turned the sleeve of the patchwork tunic, fingering the spot. "Not to weep. It's just a parted seam. I can repair it."

"But will it match the other stitches? They're so tiny and perfect."

"Should do so, love, since they're my stitches."

She stared at him in wonder. "You made the tunic yourself?"

"I sew all of my clothes." He giggled at the expression on her face. "You didn't imagine it was possible to *buy* apparel like this, did you?"

I may have just struck gold, Meg thought with budding excitement. "Do you think you could teach me how to sew? Just enough to, say, alter this?"

She indicated the shapeless gray dress she wore. Toby eyed it critically. "It does want something, doesn't it? Don't mean to be unkind, love, but are all of your dresses sacks like this?"

"I'm afraid so. I was ill back at the ferry station on the Kaw, and apparently I lost weight. Now nothing fits, and I seem to be hopeless with a needle and thread."

He looked at her, his long face solemn. "Not all you lost back there, is it?"

She realized he was referring to her amnesia. There was probably no one on the wagon train who didn't know about it.

"Makes both of us just a little different, doesn't it?" he said gently. "Kindred souls, I think the expression is. Or is it spirits?"

Of course, he understands, she thought. He knows what it's like not to fit in.

Meg felt she had just found the sympathetic friend she had been looking for. And though he wasn't exactly the gender she'd had in mind, it didn't matter. He seemed to possess all the best qualities of her sex, though at this moment a skill with thread and needle was the one she valued most.

They started with her brown calico dress and a pair of scissors. He showed her how to measure and pull stitches, what material to trim away and what to save.

Molly woke up and demanded attention. Toby insisted on holding her so that Meg could continue with the alterations. He was as good with babies as he was at directing her sewing efforts. Molly played happily in his arms, pulling at his long, rather comic nose. Toby didn't mind.

Meg and Toby chatted like longtime companions. He told her how Agatha Delaney had understood that life had become intolerable for him in the East and had permitted him to join the wagon train. Toby had no idea what he was going to find in Oregon or what he was going to do once he got there, but he was hopeful. Life was an adventure, an optimistic search for eventual acceptance of the man he was.

He asked her about her amnesia. "It must feel strange," he said wisely. "As though you'd been born again."

"It is," she agreed, and went on to explain how difficult it could be. "I know it's awful of me," she confided, "but sometimes I find myself wishing that my husband and baby would just go away, so that there would be no one I'd have to take care of or think about but me. Do you suppose I was terribly self-centered before I lost my memory? I must have been to feel like that."

Toby shook his head. "It doesn't quite fit with your circumstances, does it, love? Nor would a truly selfish person have bothered to rescue me from those thugs. You've just been overwhelmed by everything, that's all."

Meg wasn't sure. She suddenly remembered the stew. "I'd better stir the pot again."

"No excuses now. Just keep stitching. I'll mind the pot for you."

He put Molly back in her basket and went to the fire, where he added a few buffalo chips to maintain the low heat. Then he peered suspiciously into the pot suspended from the tripod.

"What is this?"

"Antelope stew."

"Hmm." Dipping the wooden spoon into the deep iron pot, he tasted the contents.

Meg watched him anxiously, and was disappointed when he made a face.

"You don't cook, either, do you, love?"

Not another failure, she thought in discouragment. "Is it beyond hope?"

"Actually, it isn't. It's just flat. It wants a bit of seasoning." He glanced toward the wagon. "Uh, I don't suppose . . ."

"Yes, there's a little chest with herbs and spices in it. I just didn't remember how to use them."

She put down her sewing and found the chest in the wagon, bringing it to him. Fascinated, she watched him as he added to the pot a sprinkle of this and a pinch of that, stirring them into the simmering stew.

"I might have guessed," she said with a sigh. "You know how to cook as well as how to sew."

"Not to mind. I'll teach you that, too, and before we're through you'll be a chef as well as a seamstress. Ah, that should do it. Now taste." He held the spoon toward her.

She sampled what was in its bowl and smiled in relief. "Why, it's very good."

He tried it for himself. "Yes, that's perked it up, though actually I think a simple hash would have been better than a stew."

"*Pytt i panne* served with fresh *lefse*," Meg said dreamily.

Toby stared at her. "What did you say?"

"It's a Norwegian hash with a special bread. A recipe my mother used to—" She broke off as she suddenly realized what she was telling him. Her hand covered her mouth, and she stared back at him in wonder. "I had a Norwegian mother?" she whispered.

"Must have. With that pale skin of yours and those eyes, it wouldn't be surprising. What else do you remember?"

She shook her head, shaken by the experience. "Only that little scrap out of nowhere. I don't even have an image of my mother to go with it. Nothing like that. The recollection, if that's what it was, was just there and then gone."

"Have you had other flashes before this?"

She frowned, trying to recall. "Just once, and it couldn't have meant anything. Deke was sitting by the fire flexing the fingers of one hand, as if it was bothering him. It seemed so familiar, but nothing I could grasp. Anyway, it's the real things that give me trouble. Things that I can touch but don't understand."

"Like the spice chest here, you mean?"

"More personal than that." She gave him an example. "I found a wedding band in the wagon, and since I wasn't wearing one I thought it had to be mine. But when I tried it on, it didn't fit. Deke said it *was* mine and that it didn't fit because it had been his mother's before me and that I'd wanted no other so I always wore it on a chain around my neck.''

''And you found that peculiar.''

''I don't know. There was a chain in the box.'' She didn't tell Toby that there were occasions when she wondered if her husband might be lying to her. It was something she didn't want to acknowledge even to herself, not just because it was disloyal, but because there was no reason why Deke should lie to her.

''Frustrating,'' Toby sympathized. ''But be patient with yourself. It will all come back to you one day.''

People were forever telling her that, Meg thought. It was because they didn't know what else to say to her. They were as helpless about her condition as she was. Toby even admitted as much.

''Well, I can't sew a cure for you or cook one, I'm afraid. But if you have any other dilemmas, love, I'm willing to look into my bag of magic tricks.''

There wouldn't be a solution there, Meg thought dismally. Not for the problem that troubled her most these days. Missing domestic skills, loss of memory—they both mattered, but they weren't as important as her lack of intimacy with her husband. Deke still refused to touch her in *that* way, and she didn't know why or what to do about it.

It was curious there could be those moments when she wished her husband would just go away or when she suspected him of lying to her, and yet at the same time she had this wanton longing for him. But why should she feel any shame about that? After all, he was her husband, and it was only natural.

Then something else occurred to her. Did she love

169

him? She hadn't thought about that until now. She supposed she must have loved him, but the memory of it had gone with all the rest. Now she wasn't sure how she felt about him. Her emotions on that subject were definitely confused.

All of it was disturbing, maddening, and Deke wouldn't talk about it.

"Brother Deke," Toby said.

"What?" Startled out of her reverie, Meg stared at him.

"You were drifting, love. I was telling you it was time I got back to my own wagon, but I'll see you tomorrow at the service when Brother Deke preaches."

"There's to be a service?"

Toby was surprised by her bewilderment. "Tomorrow is Sunday," he reminded her. "The first Sunday when all of us won't be either trapped in our wagons by foul weather or on the move at daybreak to make up for lost time. I heard some of them talking about it, how this will be the opportunity for a proper observance before we roll out again and that with Brother Deke here we can expect an inspirational sermon." He rolled his eyes toward the heavens. "Not too inspirational, I trust. My sinful soul wouldn't know what to do with it."

Meg shook her head. "He didn't tell me."

"Must have slipped his mind. Well, I shall be very respectful tomorrow morning and make every effort to address you as Sister Meg."

Gutting a dead buffalo was not the most pleasant job Arch had ever performed. And he sure as hell knew it wasn't the cleanest. He was a mess, and a rank one at that, by the time he got back to camp. He was grateful for the ball of soap and the basin of hot water that Meg provided for him.

While he washed up, she told him about her success with the stew and her first efforts with sewing under Toby Snow's direction. "When I'm good enough, I should be able to let out all your trousers."

She sounded happy for the first time. He was glad about that. He let her talk, only half-listening because he was thinking about his own satisfaction with the buffalo hunt. It was while he was toweling himself dry that her one-sided conversation took a wrong turn.

"I'm the one who's supposed to have amnesia, Deke. Why didn't you remember to tell me they'd asked you to preach tomorrow at the Sunday service?"

At first he wasn't sure he understood her. Then the full significance of what she was telling him penetrated his dazed brain. He slowly lowered the towel from his face, managing somehow to hide his shock. "Uh, they haven't asked me."

"Well, they're planning to. We'll have to get your frock coat out of the wagon." She left him to dish up their supper.

Arch stood there, panic seizing his belly like savage bear claws. No way out of it. They were already a little suspicious of him, and if he tried to beg off with some invented excuse, they'd see through it and he'd be exposed for sure. He'd have to stand up in front of them tomorrow morning in a black frock coat that threatened to split down the back and deliver a rousing, God-fearing sermon. Archer Owen, whose

171

only acquaintance with his Maker had been the curses he'd bellowed when his fiery Welsh temper had gotten the best of him.

He should have guessed that, sooner or later, they would ask him to conduct a service. He was supposed to be Brother Deke, a devout preacher. So why hadn't he anticipated this situation, prepared for it?

Too busy surviving each harsh day on the trail, he hadn't even bothered to open Deke Carver's wellworn bible in the wagon. He could have armed himself with a few impressive passages from it. Now there was no time for that. It was already too dark to read the small print, even by firelight.

Feeling his legs could no longer support him, Arch sank down on a camp stool, his head in his hands.

This was all much harder than he'd planned. Every day brought a new complication. Things like keeping his anger in check when there were occasions he wanted to punch offenders, not piously forgive them. The worst was Meg and the baby. He had never had to worry about anyone before but himself. Now he was responsible for a wife and a helpless child.

The really terrible thing was that sometimes he felt he might actually be starting to care about his adopted family. It scared the heck out of him. He couldn't let them matter. He couldn't tear himself up that way when, sooner or later, he'd have to let them go. They had their lives, and he had his. Anything else wasn't possible.

All of which was not helping him to answer this latest problem. Sweet mother, what was he going to do?

*   *   *

Arch didn't have an answer, not then and not after he spent a restless night hoping for a bolt of lightning to deliver him from his misery. Nor did he have any miraculous solution in the morning when he stood there in that infernal woolen frock coat, which was hot and itchy, and faced a sea of expectant faces.

He was sick to his stomach, his mind was a blank, and they were waiting for him to lead them along a righteous path to salvation. Lord, was he going to throw up? No, he couldn't throw up! He had to tell them something, anything! Think, *think*! His mind burned, but no words came out of his mouth.

Then he saw Meg. She was holding the baby, and she was smiling at him. There was trust and confidence in her pure blue eyes. And he knew that, hellfire or not, he couldn't let her down.

"Sin!"

In his nervousness, the pronouncement blasted out of him like a heavy charge of black powder. The congregation gaped at him with startled expressions.

"Why, it's a terrible thing, brothers and sisters. Makes us stumble and fall. So we, uh—we've got to avoid it. Trouble is, sin comes in so many diabolical forms. Oh, yes, all of them just lurking out there ready to fall on us if we fail to know them. Looks like we'd better know them, wouldn't you say?

"Now you've got your sin of cussing. That's a bad one. You shouldn't do it." He hesitated, considering this command. "Course there's always bound to be exceptions. Sometimes a man just has to let it out, doesn't he? Well, it's probably all right if he's not too blasphemous about it.

"Then you've got your sin of liquor. That's a ter-

173

rible one, brothers and sisters. Can destroy us for sure. Unless we take it as medicine. That should be all right. If we're real careful about not enjoying it.

"Uh, what else? Well, gambling. Some people don't hold that as a sin. But then again others say it ought to be forbidden. Guess you'll have to decide for yourselves on that one."

There were murmurs among the gathering. They had to be outraged. They were going to lynch him. He must be violating every sacred doctrine in the Bible.

"What about fornication, Brother Deke?" someone in the crowd challenged him. "Where do you stand on fornication?"

Arch tugged at his collar and cleared his throat. "That's a tough one for sure, isn't it? I say that if a man is willing and a woman is willing—"

They all leaned forward, waiting to hear his verdict on the subject of carnal sin.

"—then they'd better hunt up a preacher."

What did he say after that? He would never know. Whatever it was, it had to be a tangle of absurdities. Somehow he bluffed his way to the end with a loud and impressive "Hallelujah and amen!" And then he found it wasn't the end.

Some blasted woman down in front piped up. "What about a prayer, Brother Deke? Aren't you going to lead us in prayer?"

He swallowed. He tugged at his collar again. He had an inspiration. "I suggest, brothers and sisters, that on this occasion we all pray in silence."

They bowed their heads and prayed. Arch prayed

that it was finally over with and he would be punished no more. His prayer wasn't answered.

"We can't end the meeting without a hymn," that same aggravating woman objected when they had raised their heads. "You'll surely lead us in a hymn, Brother Deke."

Hymn? He didn't know any hymns. Not a single one. What should he do now? They were all waiting again. If there was a Divinity, then he badly needed His help. It came. Sort of.

Lifting his head high, Arch opened his mouth and began to sing in his rich, true baritone. "Silent night, holy night! All is calm, all is bright. . . ."

They filed past him with shining eyes, shaking his hand, expressing their gratitude.

"So fresh, so original!"

"Best Sunday-go-to-meetin' ever!"

"Words to live by, Brother Deke!"

Arch couldn't believe his ears. Were they crazy, or just plain desperate after so many weeks on the trail?

Meg was there, linking her arm through his. Meg, whose singing voice had made him grit his teeth when, with spirit if not harmony, she had joined the others in his desperate version of a hymn.

"I'm so proud of you, Deke." And she stood on tiptoe and kissed his cheek.

There was a man who introduced himself as Walter Something-or-other. He kept pumping Arch's hand as he praised him. "I'm with the party of emigrants who arrived in camp late last night. We're headed back to Independence. I was feeling pretty low about that. You know, giving up and turning back like we're doing. But your sermon has sure lifted me.''

It wasn't until the man walked away that a possibility occurred to Arch. Here was an opportunity too good to overlook. He was in a fever of impatience to escape from the crowd of well-wishers so that he could go after the fellow. When he'd finally dealt with the last of his enthusiastic congregation, he went looking for the man.

Arch found him hitching his team to his wagon, preparing to head down the trail in the direction the Delaney party had already come from. Knowing he had to be careful not to let any member of his own caravan overhear him, Arch drew the man aside.

"Can I ask you something, Walter?''

"Well, sure.''

"You were ahead of us on the trail, maybe by a week or two. Did you happen to run into a party of freighters bound for Oregon?''

Walter nodded. "We passed them on our way back. Shared a camp with them one night, same as we did you. You got a friend in that party, Brother Deke?''

"You might say so. Goes by the name of Trace Sheridan.'' Arch described him.

"Yep, he was there. Traveling with this other fella. Meek little guy who didn't have much to say and wore the strangest pants I ever seen. All checkered they was. About all I can tell you, Brother Deke, except if you was hopin' to catch up with your friend, you probaby won't before Oregon. These freighters had mule teams and was travelin' fast. Must be well past Laramie by now.''

Arch thanked him and walked away, his mind seething with frustration. The distance between him and his objective seemed to be growing wider with each passing day, and there was nothing he could do about it.

He went down to the Platte and stared at the waters, thinking about it. Wondering, as he had already wondered over and over, why Trace Sheridan had lied in court about his having murdered Willis Hadley. Who had killed Hadley that night? The stranger traveling with Trace?

Arch thought he could identify the man now. One of the players at that card game in the saloon had been a farm implement salesman. The kind of quiet little mouse you didn't pay much attention to. Arch wouldn't have remembered him at all, except for those checkered pants. He sure as hell wasn't the type to be a killer, but still . . .

Another party of freighters, this one bound only as far as Laramie with supplies for the fort there, was camped for the evening on the Little Blue River. Enoch Rawlins and Hank Shaw were with them.

"My best estimate," Shaw said, puffing on one of his cigars as he stared into the flames of their campfire, "is that we're a week or so behind this Delaney wagon train."

Enoch nodded, too exhausted to do more than droop where he sat. The rigors of the trail were proving harder than he'd anticipated. He still couldn't imagine what Margaret and Archer Owen were doing with that Delaney caravan, but at least he and Shaw had picked up their trail.

For a long while their search had been a hopeless one. They'd made inquiries everywhere, but no one had provided a clue. No one had seen the woman in the daguerreotype of Margaret that Enoch carried with him. No one had recognized their description of Owen.

Shaw had been relentless in their pursuit, and in the end his persistence had paid off. A Kansas Indian they'd questioned in Independence had identified the woman in the daguerreotype with her hair like sable fur. The Indian had seen her with an Oregon-bound wagon train crossing the Kaw River.

Enoch had learned just how ruthless Hank Shaw could be when they hastened to the ferry crossing. The man operating the station had denied any knowledge of Margaret or her captor. Not until Shaw submitted the poor fellow to his brutal variety of persuasion did he admit that Margaret might be on the Delaney train. It was good enough for Shaw. He had wasted no time in joining with a caravan of freighters passing through.

"Gonna be an interesting chase from this point on," Shaw said, a note of satisfaction in his rough voice.

He's like a vicious animal who's got the scent of blood in his nostrils, Enoch thought with a shudder.

Shaw tossed his cigar into the fire and looked at Enoch. There was no sympathy in his hard gaze. "You don't look so good, Rawlins."

"I'm all right. I'm just tired."

"Hope that's all it is. Because if it ain't—" His heavy shoulders lifted in a shrug. "—Well, like I told you back in Saint Joseph, if you give out along the way, I go on without you. Figure I owe this Archer Owen something special for all the trouble he's given me catching up with him.''

There was a savage promise in his voice.

Chapter Nine

"What's wrong, love?"

"Nothing," Meg insisted, concentrating on her task. She and Deke had run out of their ground coffee, and Toby had been showing her how to furnish a new supply by slowly roasting the beans in a Dutch oven and then passing them through a mill.

They were stopped again for the night farther along the North Platte River, which would parallel their route all the way to Ft. Laramie and beyond. The country was changing daily. There were outcroppings of rock now along the trail and a vegetation that was no longer familiar.

Meg could feel Toby eyeing her suspiciously. She avoided his gaze and continued to crank the handle on the coffee mill.

"Then why," he wondered, tapping his chin with a long, bony forefinger, "do I have this annoying impression that all is not well with Mistress Carver? H'm?"

"I can't imagine. I have every reason to be happy."

And it was true, she thought. Every day she was proving herself as a wife and mother, growing more secure with her cooking and sewing skills, even learning how to drive the oxen and handle a rifle. And as for her daughter . . .

Meg glanced down lovingly into the basket where the baby was playing contentedly with her bare feet.

Molly was both a joy and a fascination to her. She was eating some soft solids now, like porridge, and sitting up without support. Soon she would be crawling. Yes, her daughter was a delight.

As for Meg's amnesia . . . well, of course, that was still a problem. She'd had no more memory flashes, but she tried not to think about it. Tried to be confident that in time her memory would return.

So, all things considered, she had nothing to be troubled about. Nothing except the one thing that was making her increasingly unhappy. But she couldn't talk to Toby about it. She had confided everything else to him since they'd found each other, but not *that*.

"If you turn that handle any slower," he pointed out, "your coffeepot will be empty for another week."

She had been dreaming. He watched her for a moment as she accelerated the operation. Then he put down the cunning little bonnet he was sewing for Molly, got to his feet, and climbed into his wagon, which was parked next to theirs in the circle. She could hear him rummaging around inside.

Toby had painted a slogan on the canvas cover of his wagon inside a border of flowers. YOU'RE IN LUCK, OREGON. TOBY SNOW IS ON HIS WAY. It never failed to make her smile when she read it.

A minute later he returned to the campfire bearing a corked bottle and a pair of tin cups.

"What's this?"

"An experiment, love." He held up the bottle, squinting at its contents. "What do you think wine made from buffaloberries will taste like?"

"Like you should have used grapes."

"No doubt, but when in Rome . . ." He uncorked the bottle and splashed liquid into the two cups.

Meg shook her head. "I can't. It's spirits. What would Deke say?"

"Why should he even know when he's off watering the stock and milking that wretched Penelope? He'll be forever." He pressed one of the cups on her.

Meg hesitated. "I shouldn't."

"None of us should be in this flaming wilderness either, but here we are. Come on, love, think of it as Dr. Snow's Restorative Remedy."

She accepted the cup. He toasted her, and they both drank.

"Mmm, packs a nice little punch, doesn't it?" he observed. Leaning forward, he added more wine to her cup.

Meg gazed at him sternly. "You wouldn't be trying to loosen my tongue, would you?"

"What are friends for?"

Several minutes later, after emptying her cup and having it promptly refilled, Meg felt pleasantly mellow. And definitely in a mood to share secrets.

"All right, love," he urged, "tell Uncle Toby what's been making you so miserable."

"It's Deke," she whispered recklessly. "He—that is, he and I—well, we don't."

"Yes?" he encouraged, mystified.

She squirmed in embarrassment. "When we're alone together at night, we don't have—you know, that which is between a man and a woman."

His eyes widened in sudden understanding. "Ah, *that* that."

"Yes."

"Never?"

She shook her head. "What could be wrong with him, Toby? You're a man."

"There are those who would differ with you on that subject. But why ask me? Why not ask your husband?"

"I've tried. He makes all kinds of excuses."

"This is a bit of a situation, isn't it? Brother Deke chooses not to be intimate, whereas you . . . Well, love," he said gently, "you clearly want him."

Meg could feel her cheeks flaming. Yes, she supposed it was obvious just how much she wanted Deke. Every time he was near her she could feel herself go all soft inside. Positively yearning for his touch.

She punished herself thinking of all the things

183

about him that excited her. His eyes glowing like amber when he rocked Molly in his arms. And when he was impatient, the way he raked a strong hand through his head of thick hair that was like a lion's mane . . . His rugged face was so appealing at night in the firelight, all sharp angles and planes.

There was another image that made her feel like warm honey. Deke stripped to the waist as he washed himself from the basin, rivulets of water trickling through the whorls of hair shadowing his deep, powerful chest. She had entertained herself with some very wicked possibilities around that image. Things that involved both her tongue and her teeth.

The fantasies had almost become a reality the night he'd kissed her so urgently. They had almost made love, and then for some mysterious reason he had held back.

I can feel him watching me when he thinks I'm not looking, Meg thought. Imagining us together. Then why, *why*?

"You look light-headed, love. Is it the buffaloberry wine or Brother Deke?"

"Both."

"Then let's do something about them." Lifting the bottle with a flourish, he topped their cups. Meg didn't object this time. She sipped more of the wine and watched him do the same as he pondered her problem.

"Think," he said after a long, silent moment, "that I have the answer. Blatant seduction. I'll coach you, of course."

She stared at him. "You're asking me to seduce my husband?"

"Starting with your clothes."

"What's wrong with what I wear? Now that I've altered most of my dresses so that they fit me, they—"

"Are as alluring as potato bags."

"Toby, I can't be fascinating in silks and laces when I'm tramping through the dust of the trail every day."

"You don't have to be. All that's needed to restore Brother Deke's interest is one special gown, one special evening. The Fourth of July dance four nights from now. What are you wearing?"

"I don't know. I suppose my blue muslin. It's the only thing that resembles a party dress."

"Show me," he commanded.

Meg went into the wagon and got the dress. By the time she returned, Toby had fetched a box from his own wagon. He eyed the blue muslin critically as she held it up for his inspection. His judgment was a snort of disgust.

"Just like all the others. As plain as mourning, sleeves down to the wrist, and a neckline up to the ears. Not to weep, though. We have time to fix it. We shorten the sleeves almost to the shoulders. Use the material we cut away to make double scalloped ruffles here where the new sleeves end. Then, uh—yes, I think a flounce around the hem of the skirts, if we can manage it."

"Toby—"

"The neckline is what matters, though. We'll lower it into a scoop that gives a tantalizing glimpse of your bosom."

Meg was shocked. "I couldn't possibly appear in a neckline like that!"

185

He paid no attention to her. "The blue is very good. Matches your eyes. But it wants something."

He opened the box, revealing a trove of ribbons, plumes, fancy buttons, and an assortment of other treasures.

"This," he said, producing a yellow satin sash. "Ooo, and look what we have to go with it!" He held a wreath of yellow artificial flowers against the side of her head. "We'll get rid of that prim bun and dress your hair for the evening with the flowers in it. Good? You'd better have this, too." Removing a painted fan from the box, he placed it in her hand.

"What am I supposed to do with this?"

"Flirt with it, love. You'll have to practice. I'll instruct you."

"Toby, I—"

"What else? What have we forgotten?"

"Toby, *please*!"

"All right, love, I'm listening."

"I think we've had too much wine. I think I should take these beans I've just ground and make a strong pot of coffee for us."

He gazed at her severely. "Yes, I understand. You feel that you'd be crazy to trust me. That I'm a man and what could a man, even this one, possibly know about the art of a woman being mysterious and irresistible. P'rhaps you're right, but you can never be certain of that unless you have the courage to try my little technique. And if you do as I say . . ."

"What?"

"I can promise you Brother Deke will be howling for you. What's your decision, love?"

Meg tensely held his gaze for a moment, then dissolved into helpless laughter. "I'll do it!"

"Stop fidgeting," Toby commanded.

"Sorry," Meg murmured.

She tried to hold herself still on the stool while he finished arranging her hair. It wasn't easy. She was anxious about her approaching performance, which made her restless. She was also a little breathless, like a girl anticipating her first party.

In a way it was her first party. She had no memory of attending any other, although she experienced a queer feeling of having primped like this many times before, of readying herself for elegant occasions in an expensive gown and with a delicate perfume. Or was it all just a fairy-tale fantasy?

On the other side of the blankets Toby had draped across a line to provide an area for them screened from view, Meg could hear the sounds of the Fourth of July celebration. It had been in progress since the wagon train had halted at mid-afternoon.

The men had fired their rifles and marched around the camp bearing the flag while the women cheered and lifted their voices in patriotic songs. There had been impassioned speeches, some of them slurred by rum, and food. Far too much food. The boards placed across trestles to form tables, and decorated with bunting and bouquets of wildflowers, sagged with platters of roasted meats, bowls of pickles and relishes, plates of breads and cakes and pies.

It was after sundown now, and fires blazed around the perimeter of the open circle while a pair of fiddlers tested their instruments.

Deke approached her dressing area and spoke to her through the blankets. "What's keeping you in there? They're just about to call the first dance."

Meg and Toby exchanged swift, understanding glances. They had agreed that she wouldn't reveal her appearance to her husband until the right moment. This was not that moment.

"I'm not ready yet," she called out to him. "You go on ahead. I'll join you in a few minutes."

He muttered something, but to her relief he went away.

"Steady now," Toby cautioned her as he carefully wove the yellow blossoms in her hair.

"Am I—"

"One last strand and we're there."

"Are you sure that—"

"Yes, love, it's all in place. Now stand and look."

She got slowly to her feet and nervously faced the mirror he indicated. He had propped it on the lowered tailboard of the wagon next to the softly glowing oil lamp. Though it was a modest-sized looking glass, Meg was able to adequately view herself. What she saw both pleased and worried her.

Toby had piled her long dark hair in a glossy crown of ringlets spangled with the flowers that matched the sassy yellow bow of the sash snugged around her waist. He had achieved a miracle with the blue muslin dress, whose skirts seemed much fuller now that the bodice had been tightened and lowered.

It was that lowered neckline that worried her. It seemed to expose acres of smooth flesh in the slopes of her shoulders and in the prominent swelling of her breasts, whose ivory tops were in plain view.

Toby read her concern. "Yes, love, Brother Deke will be shocked. He will think it indecent, an outrage, and it will drive him into a frenzy of desire. Now kiss me and go to the ball."

She leaned over and planted a kiss on his cheek. "You are a love, love."

"I know." He handed her the fan. "I have only one request. Don't tell them out there what magic I performed, or there will be all kinds of nasty remarks about a fairy godmother."

Meg started to turn away, then remembered her daughter. "Molly—"

"Will be safe in my care." He picked up the baby and held her. "Remember, we agreed I'm keeping her all night so that you and Brother Deke will have"— he paused to clear his throat meaningfully—"ahem, no interruptions. See, she's cooing at you in approval. Now go forth and conquer."

Toby had shaped her, advised her, rehearsed her for four days. He could do no more. She was on her own. Meg lifted her head, seized a deep, steadying breath, and went off to the dance to bring her husband to his knees.

Deke behaved exactly as Toby had predicted he would when she joined him at the party where the fiddlers were already sawing a lively "Arkansas Traveler." He took one look at her dress, or more precisely its tantalizing neckline, and his eyes widened in thunderous disbelief.

Looking around to see who else might be staring at her, and half the males present already were, he leaned down and growled at her, "Are you out of

189

your mind? You can't wear that dress!''

"What's wrong with it?" she said with absolute innocence.

"You know what's wrong with it! You're practically"—almost strangling, he struggled for the rest—"practically spilling out of it!''

"You're exaggerating. Anyway, this is a fashionable neckline for evening wear."

"Not for a preacher's wife! This is Toby Snow's work, isn't it? I might have known that sister b—''

"Don't you dare call him that! Toby has been nothing but kind to me, a friend to our whole family, and I won't have you treating him cruelly like some of the others!''

He glared at her, but he said no more. He stood next to her in rigid silence, pretending she wasn't there while they watched the dancers forming for the next set. But she was aware of him sneaking repeated glances at her breasts. A moment later she caught him using his bandana to mop at his steaming brow.

"Feeling all right?" she inquired nonchalantly. "It's not particularly warm this evening. But maybe you'd like me to cool you."

Snapping open her fan, she started to wave it gently in front of his face. He angrily pushed it away.

"Try that again," he warned her, "and you've seen the last of your silly fan. I'm feeling just fine. There isn't a thing bothering me. Not a blessed thing. All right?''

"Whatever you say."

"I do say. And I'll tell you something else. You can forget about me dancing with you anytime tonight. I'm not going to be seen with you out on that floor.''

She was calm about it. She was indifferent about it. Exactly as Toby had taught her to be. ''No? I'm sorry about that. Perhaps someone else will take pity on me and invite me to dance.''

She didn't have long to wait for her first partner. When the other men realized that Brother Deke had no intention of stepping out with his wife, they began what nearly amounted to a stampede to claim her.

The first, not much more than a cherub-faced youth, was so polite in his request, asking Deke's permission first, that Deke could scarcely refuse. Not without causing a scene that would make him look like a jealous fool. Fuming, he watched his wife being led away for a cotillion.

After that, Deke never had an opportunity to raise an objection. How could he when Meg failed to return to his side as a stream of partners surrendered her to one another without interruption. She danced a polka, another cotillion, a waltz.

She swayed provocatively in her crinolined skirts, tossed her head like a French coquette, teased with her fan. Sometimes she was subtle in her playful flirting, at other times just short of brazen. Always obeying Toby's lesson.

''You don't entice *him,* love. You entice all the other men, and let him do the rest.''

How could Toby be so wise about feminine strategies? He certainly was; the men swarmed around her, were eager to demonstrate their interest. Except for the one male whose interest she longed for. Deke never came anywhere near her. He stayed on the side, gulping punch and glowering in every direction but hers.

Perhaps Toby was wrong after all. Perhaps this whole effort was a waste, a foolish mistake. She was starting to think so when an amused Cooper Delaney claimed her for a waltz and restored her faith.

"Don't worry," he assured her as he glided with her around the floor. "You've definitely got his attention."

"Am I that obvious?"

He chuckled. "Only to me because I recognize the method. Aggie once did something similar with me."

"Did it work?"

"She's having my baby, isn't she?"

Meg wondered if Agatha, unable to dance herself in her advanced pregnancy, could have understood her intention and sent her husband to support her. Cooper Delaney, except for Deke, of course, was the most attractive male on the wagon train. It couldn't hurt for Meg to be in his arms.

"But it isn't working for me," she said with a sigh. "Deke has been nowhere near me."

Cooper winked at her. "Maybe he just needs a little nudge. Let's see if this will do it."

He tightened his hold on her, gathering her close. Seconds later there was a hard tap on his shoulder. When Cooper released her to turn around, she discovered Deke standing there. He was wearing a dangerous scowl.

"All right, Delaney, you've had enough of her. I'll take over from here."

Cooper parted from her with a quick, knowing grin and shouldered his way through the dancers. Before

Meg could react to her husband's sudden arrival, she was hauled into his arms. Dragged up so tightly against his solid length that she could scarcely breathe as they began to weave through the other couples on the floor.

He was silent as they danced, but she could feel tension in every muscle of his body. When she dared to lift her gaze to his face, she met a stony expression and a grim jawline.

The pleasant-faced young man tried to cut in a few seconds later. Deke rounded on him severely. "My wife is no longer available tonight. Understand?"

"Y-yes, sir." The youth swiftly retreated.

Meg didn't think Deke could hold her any closer than she already was, but he seemed to gather her even more possessively against his chest, daring any man to come near his territory again. When he finally spoke to her, his gruff voice sent a shiver of excitement through her body.

"I've got a few suggestions for you, and you'd better listen to them."

"Oh?"

"You let another man see you in a dress like that again after tonight, never mind let him hold you, and a few necks are going to get broken. Starting with yours."

"Those sound to me more like commands than suggestions."

"Define them any way you want. Just don't forget them."

She smiled up at him archly, head tipped to one side. "I can't decide, Brother Deke, whether I'm angry or flattered."

His eyes narrowed warningly. "Don't you try that game on me. I'm not one of these other bumpkins panting like a dog every time you flutter those blue eyes at him."

"No, of course not. You have absolute control over your urges."

"That's right."

The hell he did, Arch thought. And what's more, the little witch knew it. He had spent all evening on the side suffering the frustration of the damned as he watched every man on the caravan handle her with his hot hands and leer at her spectacular breasts with an eager grin on his mouth. He'd wanted to pound those bastards with his fists, throw Meg over his shoulder, and stride away with her into the darkness where he would—

But the images had stopped there, always with an enormous amount of restraint. If he crossed that line, there would be no holding back. Every promise he had made to himself about preserving her virtue would be vaporized in one raw, searing eruption of passion.

The barriers had held, just barely held, until he saw her with Delaney. It wasn't the wagon master that worried him. It was the way Meg looked, had looked all evening actually, that finally got to him. Radiant with her shining hair piled on her head, cheeks flushed, and wearing something she hadn't worn before tonight. An infuriating self-assurance as she gazed up into Delaney's face with an expression of pleasure that should have belonged to *him* and no one else.

That was when Arch could no longer stand it. When he had to go to her, and damn the consequences. Oh, he had known full well what she was doing from the second she'd appeared at his side in that breath-robbing dress. Knew what she was deliberately doing to him now as they danced under the stars by the soft, flickering light of the campfires and to the strains of a plaintive ballad. He no longer cared. He let her do it.

Let her fill his nostrils with her tempting scent. Let her press those sweet, lush breasts against his chest where his heart was hammering like a piston. Let her mold her hips and thighs against him until he knew she couldn't mistake his raging arousal. If he didn't do something about that arousal, and do it now, he'd explode.

Abruptly releasing her from their waltz position, he seized her by the hand and drew her through the dancers. The last shreds of his resistance had fled.

"The waltz isn't ended," she protested.

"It is for us. As far as we're concerned, the whole party is finished."

"But where are we going?"

"To have our own Fourth of July celebration."

"Oh." Then she understood. *"Oh."*

She raised no further objection. She let him lead her away from the crowd, away from the music. The still shadows swallowed them. He took her where it was dark and where they could be alone, around the blanket and behind their wagon. The tent was waiting there. He held her against the side of the wagon and whispered a husky, "And now, Sister Meg . . ."

"Yes, Brother Deke?"

"Happy Independence Day."

Leaning into her, Arch angled his mouth across hers in a slow, gently probing kiss. His tongue leisurely traced the contours of her lips, tasting her, savoring the flavor that was uniquely hers. Then, knowing it was impossible to hold back, he intensified the kiss, his tongue finding a willing entry into the sweetness of her mouth.

When she matched his strokes with her own tongue, straining against him as their kiss deepened, he could no longer keep himself from possessing what had been driving him mad all evening. His hands struggled up between them, managing somehow not to break their kiss as he closed around the heavy fullness of her breasts, carefully squeezing and caressing. It felt wonderful! It felt even better when his fingers slipped inside her neckline and met swollen flesh. So hot, so incredibly soft!

He'd never know how he ended up releasing her breasts from that tight neckline without removing her dress or tearing it. Probably a combination of ingenuity and pure desperation. But he managed that, too. Then his mouth was no longer on hers. It was down on the rigid buds of her breasts where he laved, suckled, and groaned.

Her hands clenched his shoulders so fiercely that they would probably leave bruises, which didn't worry him in the least. But the complete loss of his self-control, before he was ready to lose it, did concern him. If he went on recklessly devouring her breasts like this, it would happen. Reluctantly abandoning them, he raised his head and planted a kiss in the hollow of her throat.

She laughed. It was a shaky laugh. "We made our own fireworks here, didn't we?"

"Sweetheart," he said, his voice deep and ragged, "we haven't begun to set off the rockets."

And with that promise, he swung her up into his arms, turned, and carried her into the tent. He was going to make it happen for them, the magic he had been anticipating since he'd first laid eyes on her in that Missouri jail.

But when they were alone together in the intimate darkness, the tent flap lowered, she stopped him cold.

"There's a problem," she whispered.

Her virginity, he thought with a silent curse of frustration. *Why would I have ever supposed a woman wouldn't be aware of her own virginity? She's going to want an explanation for it, as well as for Molly, and I don't have one for her.*

"My amnesia," she said solemnly. "I'm afraid that I don't remember just what we're supposed to do."

Arch exhaled in relief, ready to play her game. "That so? Guess I'll have to show you the steps."

"What comes first?"

"I'd recommend getting out of our clothes."

"That shouldn't be too difficult."

For her maybe, he thought. In his eagerness he had a hell of a time fumbling for buttons, groping for hooks. Sometimes they were his, and sometimes they were hers when she asked him to assist her. He got all tangled up in ribbons and drawers and garments he couldn't even identify in the dark. But somehow their clothing got shed and ended up in a pile, and happily, miraculously, he had her naked body in his arms.

Lord, she was beautiful! Even without the light, he knew she was beautiful. He could feel her sleekness, the feminine perfection of her. His hardness yearned for her.

"What now?" she murmured.

"This," he said, kissing her again. "And this." He guided her hands to touch him. Her fingers traveled over his length, across the flat nipples on his chest, sifting down through the hair feathering his belly, then closing, at first hesitantly and finally boldly, around his shaft. If she went on handling him this way, he would explode like a steamboat boiler!

"Any—of it—coming back—to you yet?" He could hardly get the words out.

"I-I'm afraid not." Her own words were breathless, choked with longing.

"Maybe this will help."

His hand slid between her thighs, into the soft nest of curls where his fingers tenderly explored, encountering a wetness around the vessel that he could scarcely wait to fill. Clutching at him, moaning, she collapsed against him, weak with need.

"Think," he said hoarsely, "that from here on we can let instinct guide us."

Dragging her down on the bedding, his hands and mouth branded every portion of her body until she was writhing under him, pleading for their joining.

Arch complied. There was a tightness when he slowly entered her. He'd expected that, and was prepared for the rest. It never happened. There was no subsequent resistance, no barrier. He found himself fully, deliriously inside her. She wasn't a virgin!

His relief was enormous. And brief. Whatever the

explanation, he didn't care. He had another matter to concentrate on, and he gave it his full attention. His movements were intentionally lazy at first, no more than a slight stirring, then a pronounced squirming as he rubbed his body across hers.

She responded with her own slow, measured rhythms, bringing him to a dangerous edge. Out of necessity, he rested, mouthing pleasurably, playfully at her ear, "Wonderful! Fantastic! You've remembered the technique after all."

"Then there's no reason for a further delay."

"Absolutely none."

Obliging her, he gripped her hips and drew back, then surged forward in a series of long, forceful strokes that left her gasping.

Meg exulted in her husband. His lovemaking, expressed both with his hard body and his whispered endearments, was everything she'd dreamed about, wished for, even more. Had it been like this between them when they'd conceived Molly? This all-consuming, supreme joy? It must have been there. How could she have forgotten something so wondrous?

But they were making another memory now. A precious, blinding one as he lifted her higher, ever higher. Meg hung on tightly, clasping him with arms and legs. They were nearing the pinnacle now, rushing toward it with cries of celebration.

With one wild, final upheaval, Meg found her release. Before her own shock waves subsided, Deke plunged after her. In the long, mellow aftermath, he held her close, cherishing her.

When he finally spoke, there was a smile in his

voice. "Know something? I'm no longer in a bad mood."

"I noticed that."

There was another contented silence between them. Then Meg also murmured, "Know something?"

"What?"

"I understand now what they mean by the Glorious Fourth."

Chapter Ten

The rest of the caravan was so overjoyed to reach Ft. Laramie on its hill above Laramie Creek that they paid no attention to Arch when he slipped away from the crowd after securing his wagon. He wandered through the post, searching for someone to answer the question burning in his mind.

It was a bustling place, a welcome outpost of civilization nearly halfway along the Oregon Trail. Sioux Indians camped outside its adobe walls, and in the spacious quadrangle Arch saw people of every rank and description. Emigrants, freighters, rough American mountain men, French-Canadian fur trappers.

He found who he was looking for in the shape of a bearded mountain man cleaning his long rifle in a shady, quiet corner of the quadrangle. The dust coating the fellow's buckskins was evidence that he was fresh off the trail.

"You just in from the west?" Arch asked him.

The man spat tobacco juice and eyed him suspiciously. "You got a reason for asking or just makin' conversation?"

It took some coaxing, but Arch finally learned what he was seeking. He came away from the mountain man with another assurance that Trace Sheridan and his traveling companion were still ahead of him, still bound for the end of the trail at Ft. Vancouver near the Oregon coast.

The knowledge that his objective was so far out of his reach was maddening. He wanted to hurry, race ahead to catch up with him. Instead, there were all these delays he was helpless to combat.

He tried not to think about Meg and the baby in his urgency. The guilt over them that had been eating away at him all this past week would drive him crazy if he let it. But he had the terrible feeling that, slowly and one by one, they were wrapping a web of lines around his heart, and that when the time came he might not be able to cast off and sail away.

He'd made a huge mistake in crossing that barrier and sleeping with Meg. But Lord, she was magnificent!

Agatha Delaney, with an indulgent smile on her mouth, watched the women from the wagon train as they streamed behind her into the long room where she had led them.

It never changed, she thought. The post store was always the first place the parties in her care wanted to visit when they arrived at Ft. Laramie. And she never failed to be pleased by their exclamations of delight as they examined shelves crowded with merchandise they hadn't seen since leaving Independence.

She chose a quiet corner to observe the scene, enjoying the chatter and squeals as the women chased from one end of the room to the other in their discovery of new treasures. Meg Carver was there, Molly in her arms, as she bent over a roll of flower-sprigged India cotton that Toby Snow was excited about. Agatha was glad that the two of them had become such close friends.

Agatha was still in her corner when Cooper came searching for her several minutes later. He wore a slight frown that told her he was concerned about something.

"It's bedlam in here," he complained. "Let's go outside to talk."

Placing a solicitous hand under her elbow, he led her carefully through the crowd. Once away from the store, they found a shaded bench against the wall of the quadrangle. Agatha was relieved to be able to ease her bulk down on it. Her burden had grown so heavy lately that her back ached with any amount of standing. Her time was very near, probably just a matter of days.

She turned to her husband, who had settled beside

her. "There's a problem?" she said, knowing there had to be one. "How serious?"

"Serious enough. I've just had a talk with Obidiah Randolph."

Obidiah Randolph, Agatha knew, was the factor at Ft. Laramie, a little man with big side whiskers and a special fondness for the Delaneys. They had trusted him on more than one occasion.

"He says," Cooper continued, "that the grasslands west of here have been under a real stress all along the trail. Reports coming into the post are that the drought is worse this year."

Agatha wasn't surprised. The plains through which they had already traveled, though always drier than the prairies to the east, had seemed even more parched on this journey. She understood the situation at once.

"You think the grazing will not be sufficient for our stock."

"Not when our train is as long as it is this time. I've made a decision, Aggie. I'm dividing us into two sections. The first section will head out as soon as wagons are repaired and fresh provisions loaded. The second section can follow in a couple of weeks. The grass should have recovered by then, hopefully with some rain to help it."

It was a sensible plan. She had always known that their train was longer than it should have been for an efficient crossing. But she hated to think of any of her charges under someone else's protection, necessary though it was.

There was something else Agatha understood.

"And you do not intend for either one of us to be on that first section, do you?"

"I'm sending it out under Frank Parker. He's a good man. He'll get them safely through. Damn it, Aggie, don't look at me like that. You know I'm right. You're due any day now. I want you delivering here at the post, not out on the trail. And you know I won't leave you either. Besides, Gentle Wind is at the fort."

"Gentle Wind is here?" She was pleased about that. The Lakota medicine woman was another old friend, as well as a famous midwife. Agatha was comforted in hearing that Gentle Wind would be at her side when she went into labor.

"Very well," she agreed. "How will we choose who will join the first section and who will remain with the second one?"

Cooper shrugged. "Draw lots, I suppose. Unless they'd like to volunteer. I've already had one volunteer who overheard me discussing the plan with the factor. Don't know why he's pleading to take his family on the first section, but he is."

Agatha realized her husband could only be referring to Deke Carver. "Perhaps he is eager to undertake his missionary work in Oregon as soon as possible."

Cooper slid a sideways glance in her direction, a wry look on his face. "Come on, Aggie, you and I both know Brother Deke is no preacher. He doesn't behave like one, and he doesn't have the character of one, even if his ridiculous sermons are popular."

Agatha sighed. "Yes, I have suspected for sometime that he is not legitimate."

"I don't know what his game is, but I'm asking Frank Parker to keep a sharp eye on him."

"You have never cared for our Brother Deke, have you?"

"I haven't made up my mind yet whether I do or I don't. I'll tell you something else you don't want to hear, Aggie. I'm not sure he and his Mrs. Carver are man and wife."

Agatha thought that perhaps her husband might be right about that, too. She didn't let it trouble her, however, because she knew in her heart that, whether Sister Meg and Brother Deke were married or not, they belonged together. She just wasn't sure *they* knew it.

Meg was distraught when she sneaked into the factor's private quarters where Agatha Delaney was reported to be resting. She was convinced that Agatha was the only one who could offer her the solace she needed. Otherwise, she would never have disturbed Agatha in the tiny sitting room that had been provided for her by the cordial Obidiah Randolph.

Meg promised herself that, if she found Agatha asleep or entertaining another visitor, she would quietly retreat. The tall woman was reclining on a couch when Meg entered the dim room, but her eyes weren't closed and she was alone. She lifted her regal head from the pillow with a smile of welcome.

"Come and join me."

Meg crossed to the couch, pulling up a straight-back chair and perching on it. "I oughtn't to bother you when I know you're supposed to be resting," she apologized.

"I am not tired. It is only my legs that are resting.

I have cramps in them sometimes with this load I am carrying.'' She patted the shawl that covered the mound of her pregnancy.

"Will it be soon?"

Agatha nodded. "Any day now, if Gentle Wind is correct."

"I don't remember my own labor with Molly, which I suppose is why the thought of childbirth for anyone makes me anxious."

There was an insightful look in Agatha's eyes as she gazed at her with turned head. "It is not that sort of concern, though, that brings you here. Something to do with your amnesia?"

"No."

"But has none of your memory returned yet?"

"Not really. Just quick images now and again that mean nothing."

"Then what is troubling you?"

Meg clasped the other woman's hand, needing a physical link. "We're leaving tomorrow with the first section. They say the trail ahead is much harder than the one we've put behind us, and you won't be there to share it."

"But you will have Brother Deke, and I understand Toby insists on accompanying you."

Meg shook her head. "It isn't the same. They're not women." She thought of how Agatha preserved her dignity in the face of adversity and how much she admired that. She tried to explain it to her. "You were an example to me, to all of the women on the train. Whatever the hardships were, you never complained, you never thought only of yourself, and you always had courage. All the things that I wasn't but needed to be. And as long as you were there, I could try to be them, but without you . . .''

"I am flattered, Sister Meg, but—" She broke off, struggling to raise herself. Meg helped her to sit up against the side of the couch, legs stretched out in front of her. "There, this is a much better position. It permits me to speak to you eye to eye so I can tell you what I have told all the women before you that I have tried to help. You do not need me for courage or self-reliance or strength. You need no one. You have only to reach inside yourself to find them.''

"That sounds too simple.''

"It is simple, though never easy. But think. Have you not already begun to discover these qualities in yourself? Is that not what rescuing Toby was all about, as well as all the other difficulties you faced and solved?''

"I suppose.'' But Meg suspected those problems were nothing compared to what waited for her on the trail ahead. "Anyway, I shouldn't have worried you with this. It's selfish of me to be afraid.''

"It is not selfish. It is natural. And you will overcome it.'' Agatha smiled at her. "Of course, you believe none of this. Never mind. In time you will.''

Meg tried to hold on to Agatha's wisdom in the days ahead, but bravery was an elusive state with the ordeals their shortened wagon train encountered.

There were the parched grasslands that made sparse grazing for their stock. There was the relentless sun that scorched the emigrants as well as the earth. There were the clouds of alakali dust raised by a wind that never seemed to quit. There were wagons that broke down and had to be repaired under harsh conditions. There was a new wagon master, capable enough but lacking the personal care and compassion of the Delaneys.

Tempers suffered. The men quarreled with one another over nothing, the women snapped at the slightest provocation, Molly fussed, the cow was more ornery than usual, and even the eternally optimistic Toby snarled. No one was immune. No one, that is, but Brother Deke Carver.

He, alone, was cheerful. *Exasperatingly* cheerful. He sang in his deep pure baritone and encouraged Meg to sing along with him, even though she knew her voice gave him nightmares. He relieved her of the care of Molly whenever he could, feeding her, changing her diapers, entertaining her when she was fretful. It was a marvel to watch him with his daughter.

He offered encouraging sermons to the rest of the caravan, and didn't seem to mind that they were received more frequently now by grunts than enthusiasm. He grinned a lot, and when he wasn't singing he whistled. It unnerved them. One of the women, a tough former prostitute, finally confronted him.

"What you got to be so all-fired happy about when the rest of us is spittin' dust?"

"I'm a preacher, Sister Hattie. It's my duty to remain in good spirits."

"Seems to me," she grumbled, "you wasn't in that big a mood back before Laramie. You sure you ain't sinnin' behind our backs with a secret bottle o' likker?"

"Why, Sister Hattie, you shock me!"

Meg could have explained the mystery of her husband's exuberance, though her cheeks flamed with embarrassment at the mere thought of attempting it. Deke's perpetual grin had nothing to do with liquor or faith. It was because of what happened between them each night in the intimate darkness of their tent, and had been happening since the Fourth of July celebration.

She didn't really understand it, but it was as though a floodgate had burst that evening. Before then he wouldn't touch her, and now he couldn't seem to get enough of her. Lusty, insatiable, he introduced her to every variety and technique of lovemaking. Positions that Meg had hardly dared to fantasize about, and others she hadn't imagined could be possible. He proved to her all of them were not only attainable but pleasurable beyond description.

Amazing, she would think. No matter how exhausting the demands of their trek, Deke seemed to have no shortage of energy for those blissful sessions in the tent. She didn't complain. As bone-weary as the days could be, the nights were always exhilarating. She felt as though she had been put in touch with her womanhood for the first time in her life. She had Deke to thank for that. Deke and his pure joy in her body.

It was this, the rapture she shared with her husband, that permitted Meg to survive the rigors of a journey that had become a torment.

Ft. Laramie was nothing but a dim memory on the morning when their leader called them all together. Frank Parker, barrel-chested, bandy-legged, and never wearing an expression that was anything but grim, spoke to them in a decisive voice.

"We're in a fix here, folks, and you all know it. Grass has been overgrazed by the emigrants that've gone before us, and with the drought so severe it ain't had a chance to recover. Our stock needs feed."

"You're not suggesting we turn back?" Deke challenged him.

"No, we ain't givin' up. I'm proposin' we leave the regular trail and head south a bit before we turn west again. With any luck we'll be on grass that ain't been touched yet. We can return to the main trail when things look greener."

Meg, eyeing the mountain ranges that were now in sight, had to agree it was a sensible plan. Their peaks, which had water in the form of snow but were far out of reach, seemed to mock them down here on the drought-ridden plains.

One of the other women offered the only objection. "What happens when the second section comes through? What if they want to know where we went? How they gonna follow us?"

"Thought of that," Frank said. "We'll leave a note in a bottle under a pile of rocks to mark our turning. Set up other markers along the way. Anyway, a wagon train can't help but leave signs of where it's passed through, and Cooper knows how to read 'em."

It was reassuring, but Meg still couldn't help a sense of forlorness when their train separated from the trail and struck south. This departure from the familiar route felt as though she were severing a last link with the Delaneys. They were venturing now into the unknown.

The new grasslands they crossed were no less arid, but the grazing conditions were considerably better. The travelers were encouraged—until the second day out when a band of Indians rode toward them on horseback.

The train halted, but there was no time to form a defensive circle. The cry went back along the line: "Rifles ready, but hold your fire!"

Meg tried to contain her fear as she clutched Molly to her breasts and watched the oncoming Indians. Deke stood protectively beside her, rifle in hand.

What worried all of them, Meg realized, was that the band was headed swiftly and directly toward them, as if its members had a purpose in mind. Was there a serious threat here? Had the wagon train trespassed on sacred lands?

They waited tensely, and when the party was close enough that some details about them could be distinguished, a trail-hardened veteran standing close to the Carvers offered his opinion.

"They're Cheyenne braves. This is pretty far west for them. Probably followed the buffalo looking for new pastures in this drought. Ain't so good they're Cheyennes. Cheyennes is war-like and don't appreciate the white man on the plains."

His words made Meg feel weak in the knees. Toby, she could see, was looking positively green.

"Wait, though," the veteran said a few seconds later. "They ain't bearing their sacred medicine arrows. Always carry them when they go into battle, so maybe this is a friendly visit after all."

Meg was reassured but far from ready to relax, even when the band abruptly drew rein a hundred feet or so away from the train. Its seven members lifted their hands in a gesture of peace and waited. The rifles on the caravan were lowered but not released. Frank Parker went out to speak to the Cheyenne.

They were a fierce-looking people, Meg thought. But they were also proud and handsome. The leader, who dismounted when he met with the wagon master, was exceptionally tall. What could he possibly want from them?

The explanation came a moment later when Frank Parker returned to the wagons, and it dismayed Meg.

"Carver," the wagon master said, approaching Deke, "it's you they've come for."

Her husband was astonished. "You sure about that?"

Parker nodded. "They heard there's a white man's holy man on the train. That's you. And don't ask me how they learned it. These people seem to know everything about the wagon trains crossing their lands. For all I know, the wind carries it to them."

"All right. What am I supposed to do for them?"

The wagon master shrugged. "Wouldn't tell me. They're bein' polite enough about it, but they ain't gonna leave until you go out there and powwow with them. Leader's name is Lone Wolf, and he speaks enough English to get by. You want company?"

"I can handle it."

Meg wanted to stop him when he put down his rifle and strode out to meet with the band that waited for him patiently. But she knew that their safety might depend on Deke's acquiescence. When he reached Lone Wolf, there was an earnest exchange. She prayed it wouldn't result in something dire.

The Cheyenne remained ominously in place when Deke parted from them and came back to the wagons. There was a grave look on his face when he spoke to them as they all gathered around.

"Lone Wolf is the son of a chief. His name is Gray Eagle, and the old man is dying back in their village. Far as I can make out, Gray Eagle once upon a time embraced the faith of the white man. Don't know how serious he was about it, but he did agree to be baptized by a missionary, and *now* . . ."

He didn't have to say it. Meg understood. "Gray Eagle is asking for the blessing of a preacher before he dies."

"Something like that. They want me to go with them to their village."

"Deke, you can't!"

"Have to, precious. It's my duty. I'm a holy man, remember? Hey, don't look like that. They'll bring me back. I think their word is good in a matter like this. You folks go on, and I'll catch up with you down the trail."

Minutes later he was riding off with the band on a horse borrowed from the wagon train's scout. Meg, watching him leave, tried not to be worried. But her effort was no good. She was worried sick.

I must be crazy, Arch thought as he headed for the horizon beside the silent Cheyenne braves.

It was one thing for him to play preacher on the wagon train. That was essentially harmless. All right, maybe it wasn't so harmless, though he hadn't really hurt anyone. But to attend a dying Cheyenne chief as a man of the cloth . . . that seemed a pretty heavy violation, even for him.

On the other hand, what was so wrong about providing comfort for an old man on his death bed? Nothing, right? Yeah? Who was he fooling? He was misrepresenting himself seriously this time, and his Maker wasn't going to like that at all. But since he must have already lied his way into Hell, anyway, what difference did it make?

The truth was, he had been afraid to refuse Lone Wolf's urgent request. What if the Cheyenne made trouble for the wagon train? A denial could have endangered Meg and Molly. He cared about them. And wished he didn't care.

The wagon train was long out of sight behind them, and Arch starting to get worried about the distance they'd covered, when they topped a rise and arrived suddenly at the Cheyenne village. It consisted of a number of tepees that were the familiar dwellings of the plains Indians.

Dogs barked and children stared solemnly at Arch as the party dismounted. The adults, after a few glances, paid no attention to them when Lone Wolf led him toward a tepee from which a mournful chanting issued.

The Cheyenne brave was about to conduct him into the tepee when something occurred to Arch. He hung back, thinking about it. Gray Eagle was dying. Of what, though? He hadn't considered that before, other than assuming the man was old and his time had come. But what if he had a contagious disease? Arch had to be concerned about that. He didn't want to bring something lethal back to the wagon train.

215

The tall brave was gazing at him, puzzled by his hesitation.

"Lone Wolf, your chief is ill and dying. Does anyone else in the village have his sickness? Have there been other deaths here?"

Lone Wolf shook his head. "No sickness, no death," he insisted. "Just Gray Eagle."

Was the brave telling him the truth? He hoped so. He nodded, and Lone Wolf took him into the tepee.

The place was dim and, though there was no fire, it smelled of old smoke fumes. The chanting stopped with their entrance. A number of men and women of various ages were grouped cross-legged on the ground around a pallet where Gray Eagle was stretched on a buffalo robe. They stared at Arch, respectful but silent. The chief's family and friends, he guessed.

Arch had never thought about death before. Not in terms of family, anyway. How could he when he'd never really belonged to a family and, therefore, was unable to relate to its special connections? But these people gathered here for Gray Eagle made him decide that having family and friends near had meaning when the end came for you. You weren't alone, others cared. It made him yearn for something he wasn't prepared to name.

Lone Wolf crouched down beside the pallet, gesturing for Arch to join him. The chief had a face as seamed and parched as the land that had nourished him. His eyes were closed, and he breathed with difficulty.

Arch had no knowledge of medicine, but the old man's wheezing reminded him of a serious pneumonia case he had once seen on a riverboat. The sufferer hadn't survived.

The Cheyenne brave leaned close to his father and spoke to him in the Algonquian language of their people. The chief's eyes opened, struggling to focus first on his son, then shifting his gaze to search Arch's face. Lone Wolf nudged Arch, indicating he should address Gray Eagle.

Arch had no idea how much, if anything, the old chief would understand of his English. But taking a deep breath, he began.

"Greetings, Gray Eagle. I have come to bring you the word of the Great Father above." He'd remembered to bring Deke Carver's bible with him, and by now had an acquaintance with some of its more familiar passages. Opening the book to the place he had marked, hoping he was doing the right thing, he began to read in his musical voice.

" 'The Lord is my shepherd; I shall not want. He maketh me to lie down in green pastures: he leadeth me beside the still waters. . . .' "

Meg, who had been imagining every variety of horror, from her husband serving as a target for Cheyenne arrows to a lovely bronze maiden capturing his heart and refusing to release him, was weak with relief when Deke finally rejoined the wagon train.

He told them the Cheyenne had treated him like an honored guest, that Gray Eagle had died peacefully, and he teased Meg about her needless anxiety.

"You can poke fun at me all you want," she said, hugging him fiercely, "but I've had all the stress I can take. I demand this wagon train proceed without any further surprises.''

''You do, huh? I'll see what I can do about arranging that.''

To her satisfaction, they *did* continue without a problem. The stock was able to feed off the grasslands, even though they remained dry, the wagons were cooperative and didn't break down, and there were no more unexpected visitors. It was an uneventful, smooth progress. It lasted for two days.

Disaster struck on the afternoon of the second day after Deke's return to the caravan. It began in innocence.

''There's a rare sight for you, love,'' Toby said to Meg.

They were collecting buffalo chips while the wagons rolled along. Looking up from her task, she gazed in the direction her friend indicated. An antelope raced without pause straight through the middle of the caravan and continued on its way north. Meg was bemused. As a rule the antelope, sensing they were targets, avoided the trains. This one had swept by as though the wagons didn't exist. Curious, but not particularly remarkable.

Meg bent to her work again. The chips were plentiful in this area. Her sack was beginning to fill.

''Look,'' Toby said, interrupting her again, ''there's another one!''

He was right. A second antelope, followed shortly by a third, cut fearlessly through the train. Behind them was a coyote. For a moment she wondered if the coyote was pursuing the antelope. Then she decided it wasn't interested in the antelope at all, though it rushed off in the same direction.

"It's odd," Meg said. "What do you suppose has gotten into them?"

Toby had no answer for her, and the other members of the wagon train were too busy driving the oxen teams to care about the antics of the wildlife.

A few minutes later, when a half-dozen jackrabbits fled past the rear of the train and a pack of wolves ignored the rabbits in their own flight to the north, Toby could no longer stand it. "What *is* going on here?"

Meg had decided herself that something was definitely wrong. "They're in a panic, running from some danger." Stripping off her gloves, she gazed in the direction from which the animals had come. There was a strange haze along the flat southern horizon. Toby noticed it, too.

"A dust storm?" he wondered.

It was possible, she thought. The wind from the south, hot and dry, was much stronger than usual. But the wildlife wouldn't try to escape from a dust storm. Surely they'd take shelter and wait it out. Buffalo? Could it be a buffalo stampede? If so, the wagon train was right in its path. She had heard terrible stories at Ft. Laramie about huge buffalo herds stampeding. But there was no trembling of the earth. Then another fearsome possibility occurred to her.

"You don't suppose . . ."

She and Toby exchanged looks of alarm, both of them recogonizing the threat at the same time. Oh, dear God! Abandoning their sacks of buffalo chips, they sped toward the train. The shouts of warning they raised weren't necessary. By this time the others were aware of the trouble and fighting to control the snorting oxen in their yokes.

There was no question now of what menace was on its way from the south. The odor of smoke was suddenly in the air, the haze on the horizon thickening into visible clouds. The terror of the prairies and plains was about to be experienced by the emigrants.

Meg, reaching Deke's side, panicked when she didn't see her daughter. "Molly! Where's Molly? I left her—"

"It's all right," he said, calming her. "She's right here."

One of the other women had been caring for the baby while he handled the bawling stock. He took Molly from her and put her safely into Meg's arms.

Pandemonium gripped the caravan, which had come to a standstill. Frank Parker and the other men, Deke among them, worked to restore order.

"Keep your heads, folks, and we'll get through this!" he yelled down the line. "There's water straight ahead of us! We just have to reach it and—"

"What water and how far?"

"A river wide enough to hold the fire on this side. I sent Gus ahead to reckon the exact distance to it," he explained, referring to the young advance scout who traveled with them.

"These oxen is slow! What if it's too far to make afore the fire gets here?"

"Then we cut our stock loose," the wagon master said, "and run for it on foot."

"Leave our wagons behind for the blaze? All our gear, all our provisions?"

"I ain't gonna do it! How'd we ever survive out here without our wagons and supplies?"

"If we don't get moving again," he thundered at them, "there won't be anything to save, wagons or us!"

Realizing he was right, they stopped arguing and urged their teams forward again. There was silence now in the caravan. Even the stock seemed to realize the necessity of pushing forward without confusion as swiftly as possible.

Meg, walking beside Deke as he hurried the oxen, cradled Molly and kept a nervous eye on the south where billows of dark, ominous smoke rolled into the sky the whole length of the horizon. There were no flames visible yet. The blaze was still some distance away, but she knew, with the grass so dry and the wind so powerful, it had to be traveling fast.

Deke, sounding grim, suddenly spoke to her. "I want you to promise me something."

"What?"

"When the scout comes back with his report, I want you to run with Molly to the river. You can take Toby and the cow with you."

"And leave you behind with the wagons? No, Deke, no!"

"You have to think of Molly."

That was true. "All right, but you have to promise *me* to abandon the wagons and follow us before the fire gets so near it traps you."

He nodded. She stared at him. He looked more than just grim. He was deeply flushed.

"Are you unwell?" she asked him.

He grinned at her reassuringly. "Me? I'm never sick."

It must be the heat, she thought. I feel baked by it myself. Her attention turned again in the direction of the rapidly advancing fire. It was possible now to make out flames beneath the clouds of smoke. Those twisting orange tongues stirred something that was buried deep inside her.

I've been through this before, she realized with a sudden jolt of recognition. Where? When?

There was no time for her to reach into her mind and search for answers. The scout came flying back on his sturdy mustang with the cry of, "River's about a mile off!"

Frank Parker shouted for the women to leave the wagons to the men and hurry to the stream. When Meg hesitated, Deke reminded her of her promise emphatically. "Go! Toby, see that she and Molly get there! We'll bring your wagon! And try to take Penelope with you!"

Toby untied the cow from the rear of the Carver wagon and dragged her forward by her lead rope. "Come on, love," he urged Meg.

In a state of bewilderment now, as the past started to clash with the present in her mind, she blindly followed Toby toward the scout who was waiting to lead them to the stream. The other women were also rushing forward. When Meg looked over her shoulder, hating to leave her husband, hoping for some last expression of encouragement from him that would calm her fears, Deke had already turned away. He and the other men were moving from wagon to wagon, doing their best to keep the unnerved oxen teams on course.

The women were in no better a state than the oxen. The air around Meg was filled with their cries of terror and excitement as they charged behind Gus toward the river. Molly, bouncing in her arms, was also shrieking, while the cow bawled and Toby cursed it for its obstinacy. The smoke fumes had thickened, so acrid now that they stung Meg's eyes, bringing tears. Was it her imagination, or could she already hear the crackle of the terrible blaze?

I've been through *this* before, too, she thought. Fleeing from a hellfire with a lot of other females. *Young* females. Not out on a raging grassland. A building in a large city. We were escaping from a burning building.

Someone was yelling in her ear. Back in that city, or here and now? For a moment she wasn't sure.

"Are you listening to me, love? We're there! We're going to be safe!"

It was Toby. He was telling her they had reached the river. It was a wide stream with a sandy bottom, but shallow enough after the drought that they could easily wade it. The women were already splashing through its welcome waters, the scout on his mustang guiding them.

"Shall I take Molly?" Toby wanted to know.

Meg shook her head. Making sure she had a firm hold on the baby, she followed Toby and the cow across the river. Hands were waiting on the other side to help her scramble up the slope.

There was silence now as the women, strung out along the riverbank, turned their anxious gazes in the direction from which they had fled. Their desperation this time was for the men they had left behind.

Had the conflagration overtaken the wagons? It was impossible to tell. Although the wind was carrying everything northward, and mercifully bringing no sparks to this western shore, the eastern side was buried by now in a fog of streaming smoke. The inferno itself couldn't be far behind, consuming everything in its path.

"You don't look so good, love. Sure you don't want me to hold Molly?"

It was Toby beside her. She didn't answer him. She rocked Molly in her arms, soothing her. It was an automatic action, as was her concern for the man somewhere on the other side. Her mind was no longer in this place. It was busy with other images triggered by the fire.

St. Louis. The school where she had taught. Leading the girls to safety when the building had burned. Enoch had been there. That was how she'd met Enoch.

It all came back. Everything came rushing to the surface.

Cheers went up all along the riverbank. The shapes of the first wagons were emerging from the rolling smoke. They were followed by the other wagons. One by one they descended the banks and crossed the river ahead of the wall of flames.

There was a celebration on the western shore when the men were reunited with the women. Hugs, kisses, whoops of joy and relief. Deke fought his way through the commotion and joined his family. He looked tired, and his face was streaked with windborn ashes.

"Are you all right?" she asked him.

"Fine, if you don't count the smoke we choked our way through."

"Good."

"Happy to see me, precious?" He held out his arms.

"Toby," she said, "will you take Molly now?"

Calmly placing the baby in Toby's arms, she went to the man who called himself her husband, drew her hand back, and struck him across the mouth with all the force she could deliver.

Chapter Eleven

"If they don't hang you in the end, Archer Owen, I'll do it myself!"

He rubbed his jaw where she had smacked him. "Ah," he said with a wry little smile, "you've remembered."

"Everything!" she spat at him. "*Everything,* you low-down, nasty excuse for a human be—"

"Don't, love," Toby whispered, his bony face wearing an expression of total shock. "He's your husband."

"He isn't my husband! He's an escaped murderer who abducted me back in Missouri and connived somehow to put us on this wagon train! All these long, miserable weeks he let me believe I was someone else! Let me cook and sew until my hands were raw! Manage filthy livestock and risk myself with a rifle and—and—'' She broke off, feeling she would explode with fury.

"Seems to me," Arch said casually, "you ought to be thanking me. For the first time in your life you were doing something useful."

"Thank you? *Thank* you, when you must have been laughing yourself sick at my silly efforts?"

"I never laughed at you, Meg," he said gently.

"Stop calling me that! I was never Meg anybody! I'm Margaret Sheridan!"

"You'll always be Meg to me."

"I'm nothing to you! You made a fool of me!" Then another memory occurred to her. The recollection of countless sessions of wanton lovemaking. She could feel her cheeks blaze with mortification. "We weren't husband and wife, and knowing that you still took advantage of me!"

One of his dark eyebrows elevated sardonically. "I don't recall any complaints."

She clapped her hands over her ears. "Stop reminding me! I don't want to remember how you— you seduced me!"

"Is that how it was? Funny, but I seem to have a recollection of a certain low-cut dress at a Fourth of July party, along with a few other, uh, feminine techniques."

He was right, and she suffered an agony of shame over the memory of that night and all the others that had followed. How could she? How could she have

227

thrown herself at this man? Archer Owen, a sinful devil!

"I thought we were married!" she raged at him. "You made me believe we were married! You deceived all of us on the train with that wicked performance as a preacher! And just where, Brother Deke Carver, did you get the clothes, the wagon, and—" Her glance fell on the baby still in Toby's arms. "Molly," she gasped. "Who does Molly belong to?"

He didn't answer her. There was a sheen of perspiration on his brow and a weary droop to his shoulders. But he didn't have to answer her. She suddenly remembered a scene back at the ferry station on the Kaw River.

"Those graves on the prairie," she said. "The real Meg and Deke Carver are buried there, aren't they? That's who everything, including Molly, belonged to. Did you kill them?"

He roused himself for the first time. "Are you crazy? I never killed anyone!"

"That isn't what a jury back in Saint Joseph said."

By now, the others along the riverbank were aware that something was happening. They drifted toward the scene in progress, gathering around Margaret, Arch, and Toby holding the baby. They had expressions of curiosity, exchanged looks of puzzlement.

Frank Parker shouldered his way through the crowd, frowning, demanding an explanation. "What's going on here?"

Seeing she had an interested audience, Margaret seized the opportunity to denounce Archer Owen.

"Listen, everyone. You all know I had amnesia. I

don't anymore. The fire brought back my memory, and I have something vital to tell you.''

She went on to give them the whole story, stressing Arch's guilt. When she was finished, the wagon master scratched his ear.

''I dunno, ma'am. All seems a bit farfetched to me.''

''But it's true!'' she insisted.

The wagon master scowled at Arch, who was leaning now against one of the big wheels of a wagon, thumbs hooked under his suspenders. ''What do you have to say for yourself, Carver? If that is who you are.''

Arch lifted his broad shoulders in a little shrug, as if even this small action was too much of an effort. ''I'm guilty,'' he admitted. There was a ripple of excitement in the crowd before he added nonchalantly, ''Guilty of having a wife with too much imagination.''

''He's lying!'' Margaret cried. ''I'm not his wife! He admitted as much to me a moment ago! Toby heard him! Didn't you, Toby?''

But Toby was too distressed to do anything except stare at Arch in disbelief. The others in the crowd were also eyeing him with a mixture of uncertainty and suspicion. Margaret pressed her argument.

''He used me, and he cheated all of you by posing as a missionary! None of his actions or words were those of a genuine preacher!''

''Come to think of it,'' someone muttered, ''those *were* mighty peculiar sermons.''

Another added in outrage, ''If he did trick us, then he is vile.''

"But a murderer condemned to hang?"

"It's looking like it. Hell, there *was* a trial in Saint Joseph exactly like the one she describes. They was talking about it back in Independence just afore we left, don't you remember?"

"And time we got to New Santa Fe, they was sayin' the killer escaped and took a woman with him. It's him, all right. Got guilt written all over him."

One of the men, who had disliked Arch ever since he'd taken the side of a Sioux in a dispute he'd had with the Indian at Ft. Laramie, snatched up a rifle and leveled it at him. "Wouldn't think about making a break for it, if I were you."

Arch, sounding amused, looked across the river at the charred, blackened remains of the grasslands. The fire had already swept by and was out of sight. "Doesn't look like much of anywhere for a man to run to, does it?"

"Just don't try it."

Frank Parker had a grave expression on his broad face. "Seems like we got us a case here that needs deciding."

Arch tried to defend himself. "This isn't a courtroom, wagon master."

"It is in the wilderness, where each wagon train has to make its own law." He turned to Margaret. "You ready to solemnly swear this here man is a convicted killer who escaped justice?"

"Is she going to be your only evidence?" Arch asked him before Margaret could answer.

"I got another," a woman called breathlessly, waving a newspaper she had run back to her wagon to fetch. "Bought it in Independence to line my chest.

It has a full report of that trial in Saint Joseph. Even describes the accused. This ought to settle it.''

The crowd parted for her, allowing her to come forward and offer the wrinkled newspaper to Frank Parker. The wagon master accepted it, scanning its contents while those closest to him read over his shoulder with a growing rumble of indignation.

When Parker had finished, he pinned his cold gaze on Arch. ''This don't leave much doubt about you, mister. Time we had us a parley on the matter.'' He summoned several of his men to join him. They moved off along the riverbank to confer, well away from the others. The guard kept his rifle on Arch.

''You're looking smug, precious. Pleased with yourself?''

She refused to answer him. He was still leaning against the wheel. There was a mocking smile on his wide mouth, which didn't match the dull look in his eyes.

''I think you are. I think I ought to offer you my congratulations. You've dug my grave, precious. Now all they have to do is push me into it.''

They didn't have long to wait for a decision. Within minutes, Frank Parker came back to where they stood.

''With the testimony of the lady here,'' he announced, ''and the detailed account in this paper, along with what we already know about you, the whole thing seems pretty conclusive. You're Archer Owen, and you're guilty of murder. Do your duty, boys.''

Two of the men sprang forward and seized Arch. He struggled, but before he could free himself they had him turned around and pinned against the wagon. A third man came forward with a length of cord to bind his wrists behind him.

"That's right," Margaret said, "tie him up. He ought to be made to walk like that behind a wagon all the way to Oregon."

Arch, with his head twisted around, spoke to her over his shoulder, all the while holding her gaze. "I don't think they plan for me to walk that far, precious."

The guard poked him in the back with the muzzle of the rifle. "Shut up, Owen, and move!"

With the other two men still holding him from either side, he was dragged forward. Frank Parker led the way up along the riverbank, the whole caravan trooping after them.

For a moment Margaret was baffled by their destination. Then she realized they were headed toward the only tree in sight, or what was left of it. The lone cottonwood several hundred feet away near the edge of the stream was still standing, though it had died long ago, its leafless branches plucking at the sky like the fingers of a skeleton.

At the same time she noticed that one of the men in the eager crowd carried a coil of rope. Appalled, she ran after them. How could she have been so stupid not to understand their intention?

Arch had understood from the start. His head turned, the cynical little smile still on his mouth as he was pulled along, he told her as much. "Satisfied, precious? They're going to provide you with the lynching you said I deserved back in Missouri. Remember?"

Margaret caught up with the wagon master and snatched at his arm. "You can't do this! You *musn't* do it!"

"He's a condemned murderer, ain't he? You said so yourself. What did you expect us to do?"

"I thought you'd confine him, keep him under guard until we reached Ft. Vancouver where he could be turned over to the proper authorities!"

"Don't talk nonsense, woman. How'd we manage something like that with Ft. Vancouver weeks away?" Without so much as glancing at her, or breaking stride, he continued on toward the cottonwood.

Margaret kept up with him. "Then send him back to Ft. Laramie!"

"I ain't sparing any of my men to do that. Need all of them right here. No one's turning back."

"But you have no right to hang him!"

"Sure we do. He's already been sentenced, ain't he? What's the difference if he's strung up back east or here and now?"

Arch stumbled, and was jerked up with a curse. He looked strangely drawn, ready to collapse, but he chuckled in her direction. "They're not listening to you, precious. Not this time. You did your work too well."

They had reached the cottonwood. The wagon master instructed the man with the rope to toss it over the highest, strongest limb. The guard laid down his rifle to help him.

Margaret gazed at the faces of the mob gathered around the tree, seeking support. But none of them, except for Toby, indicated the slightest interest in saving Archer. And Toby looked helpless. As helpless as she was.

They had the rope suspended now from the tree and were fixing a noose in the end of it. Margaret shuddered at the gruesome sight, and in desperation pulled again at Frank Parker's sleeve.

"You're not the law! This is wrong! It—it's evil!"

"Told you, we are the law out here." He pushed her away. "All right, boys, let's see how high he'll swing."

The men holding Arch hauled him toward the rope. Margaret was frantic. No one would listen, but somehow she had to prevent the hanging. Maybe it didn't make sense, her wanting to save this man after all he had done, but that didn't matter. She just knew she couldn't let him die like this.

The solution was obvious and available. No one was looking at her. They were all watching the noose being dropped over the prisoner's head. She edged toward the rifle on the ground. Before anyone could stop her, she grabbed up the weapon and swung it in the direction of the men who were about to stretch Archer Owen's neck.

"Back away from him!"

Everyone froze, gaping at her.

"Do it!" she ordered them.

"Now, ma'am, put down that gun," the wagon master said, trying to reason with her. He started to move toward her.

"I wouldn't try it," she warned him, her grip tightening on the rifle. "Remember, I know how to use this rifle. There were a lot of you who helped to teach me. I'd hate to repay any of you with a bullet, but I will if you won't do as I say. Now take that knife out of your belt, wagon master, and cut his bonds. Then all of you step out of the way."

Parker nodded at the men restraining Arch. There were resentful mutters and angry curses, but they released him and retreated. The wagon master joined them after sawing through the cord to free Archer's hands. Keeping the rifle ready and alert for any sudden move from the crowd, Margaret went to Archer.

"You don't deserve it, but you can take off that noose now."

He gazed at her for a few seconds, as if he was trying to decide whether to be surprised by her rescue. Then he slowly removed the rope from around his neck. The simple action seemed to cause him another considerable effort.

"That was some performance, precious. I'm proud of you."

He started to offer her a grateful little bow. Instead, with his eyes rolling back in his head, he crumpled to the ground. There was a moment of silence. They all stared at his motionless figure.

"Why, he's passed out cold."

"Swooned like a woman. Man's a coward."

"Probably fainted in relief."

Margaret, still clutching the rifle, dropped to the ground beside him. With one hand on the gun, she pressed the palm of her free hand against the forehead of Arch's inert figure.

"He's burning up with fever!" she cried.

That's why he passed out, she realized. Why he looked and behaved as he did. He was seriously ill. All the signs had been there since before the fire, and they had been too preoccupied to notice them.

Alarmed by his condition, Margaret looked up. The onlookers had been closing in on them, but now they went very still. "Why are you just standing there?" she pleaded. "He's sick. Isn't anyone going to help me?"

"Cholera," one of the women whispered. "He's got the cholera. This is how it starts."

"Bastard brought it back with him from that Indian village. Had to be what killed the old chief he went to pray over."

Frightened and angry exchanges went through the ranks of the gathering as they backed quickly away from the unconscious man and the woman kneeling beside him. Cholera was the highly contagious scourge of the Oregon Trail, more dreaded and loathed than any other threat in the wilderness.

"Lord help us," someone moaned.

"I say we get our wagons and move off from here as fast as we can."

"And anyone who touched Owen there . . . well, better pray none of the rest of us caught it."

Margaret, understanding what they meant to do, was horrified. "You can't just abandon him here! He'll die without attention!"

"Probably will anyway from the looks of him," the wagon master pointed out. "Seems as though Providence is gonna execute him for us. Come away from him, ma'am, before you catch it yourself."

"I'm not leaving him here! It's inhuman! We have to take him with us!"

"No, ma'am, we ain't, and there will be no argument over that."

Margaret didn't hesitate. "Then I'll—I'll stay here with him. You can leave our oxen and wagon with me. There are enough supplies and ammunition in it to provide for our needs, and in a few weeks the second section of the train will be here from Ft. Laramie. He won't be contagious by then."

"If he ain't dead, which he's more than likely to be, and you along with him. You're a fool, ma'am. First you accuse him, and then you want to save him."

He was right, though she didn't dare to examine her motives around that issue. She only knew that, just as she had been unable to stand by and watch the life choked out of him at the end of a rope, she was unable to desert him in this forbidding place. But the sudden realization that she was about to be left entirely on her own with his stricken body seized her with panic.

Getting to her feet, Margaret was prepared to beg again for assistance. "Look, won't any of you at least consider—"

"Keep your distance!" Frank Parker put up a warning hand as she started toward him. "You've made your choice. Now you bear with it."

The wagon master, along with the others, hastily left the infected area, mumbling scornfully about her. Only Toby, still carrying Molly, who in spite all the commotion had fallen asleep in his arms, remained.

"I'll stay with you, love," he offered earnestly. "We'll nurse him together."

He stood several yards away and was ready to join her. She had only to nod her assent, and he would cross the invisible barrier that now separated them.

She'd give anything to have him with her, but she had to resist the temptation. She had to refuse.

"Whatever they say about you, you're the bravest man on the wagon train. But Toby, you can't stay with me."

He looked down at the baby in his arms. "Molly?"

"Yes, Molly. I won't risk exposing her to cholera. I want her safe, and that means she has to go on without me."

"One of the other women would care for her, love."

"Not like you. I don't trust her with anyone but you. Toby, take her on to Oregon. God willing, I'll join you there, and if—if I can't—"

"I know. Don't worry, I'll see to it she has a good home."

Margaret looked down the river to where the departure preparations for the caravan were already under way. "You'd better go."

He bobbed his head with reluctance. "I'll bring your wagon and oxen up to you."

He left then, taking Molly with him. She knelt again beside Archer's prone figure. His eyes remained closed. He hadn't stirred. He must be desperately ill, and she had no idea what to do for him.

Turning her head, she watched the feverish activity of the wagon train, heard the exchange of shouts. They were about to pull out. They were going to leave her. She fought the despair that urged her to run and join them.

A breathless Toby returned minutes later with the Carver wagon and team. "I've moved Molly's things into my own rig," he reported from a secure distance.

She got to her feet. "The cow—"

"Yes, I have the wretched Penelope on her lead line behind my wagon, though how I shall ever manage to milk her—Well, not to worry. Listen, love, I spoke to Violet. She once worked in a hospital, saw all kinds of illnesses. She thinks it might not be cholera at all, that the signs are more like a severe influenza."

Margaret glanced hopefully in the direction of Archer. "But if that's true—"

"I know," he said. "I tried to convince the others it was influenza and to let you take him with us, but they won't hear of it. And with Violet not certain . . . Anyway, she did provide me with a few nursing instructions."

He quickly repeated them for her, and before he was through she heard Molly. Toby had placed her inside the wagon while he readied them to leave. She was awake now and demanding attention. He went and got her, carrying her around the side of the wagon.

Molly, who couldn't understand anything that was happening, whimpered when she saw Margaret and held out her arms to be taken. It broke Margaret's heart not to go to her, but she couldn't risk it. They had to part from each other without any contact.

It was silly for her to grieve like this. She wasn't a mother. Molly Carver wasn't her daughter. But her emotions wouldn't accept that. Her emotions made this good-bye something wrenching, something that had her eyes wet and her voice hoarse.

"Be a good girl for Toby, sweetheart. I love you. I—I'll miss you." *I might never see her again,* she

239

thought. "Toby, they're leaving. You have to go."

"We'll wait for you in Oregon, love. You will be there," he promised fiercely.

He and Molly were gone then. She watched him catch up with the others. The wagon train pulled away from the river and turned to the west again. The last sight she saw was Toby's lovably awkward figure, the only splash of bright color in the drab landscape, as he turned and lifted his hand in a forlorn wave. Then the wagon train vanished in its own cloud of dust.

Margaret found herself on her own in the vastness of the plain. Except for the murmur of the river, there was silence. A deep, lonely silence.

Dear God, what have I done?

She must have taken leave of her senses. What else could explain her impulsive decision to stay behind with a man she despised. A man who was unconscious and might be dying.

She was Margaret Sheridan, who knew all about fashion and manners and catching a rich husband. What did that Margaret Sheridan know about surviving in the wilderness?

It was more like a monk's cell than a sickroom. It contained a narrow bed, a single, hard chair, and a crude table bearing a pitcher and basin. There were no other furnishings, nothing to relieve the beaten earth floor or the rough adobe walls. It was the best that Ft. Laramie had to offer. Not counting the factor's own quarters, of course.

Hank Shaw stood in the open doorway, smoking one of his perpetual cigars, as he watched the Lakota medicine woman examine the man stretched out on the bed. There was no sympathy on his brutal face, even though Enoch Rawlins was in a bad way.

They'd reached the post less than half an hour ago. The frail Rawlins, ill and exhausted from their arduous trek, had had to be helped off his horse and carried into the tiny sickroom.

Well, Hank thought, he'd warned him not to come, hadn't he? Told him to go back to St. Louis and let *him* handle it.

In a gesture of contempt, Hank tossed the stub of his cigar out into the dust of the quadrangle. The medicine woman, graceful and solemn-faced, left the bed and came to speak to him. Her name was Gentle Wind, and her English was excellent.

"His white man's skin has been poisoned by the sun, and his strength is gone. It will be many days before he rides again."

"Just how many days?"

She shook her head. "Perhaps a moon's worth. Perhaps not that long."

Hank paid her, left Rawlins in a fitful sleep on the bed, and went off to collect some answers. He'd already learned there was a wagon train camped outside the fort's walls. He would start there.

A celebration was in progress when he reached the wagons. The men were already half-drunk. He managed to corner one of them who was still reasonably sober.

"What's the occasion?" he asked.

The skinny pup beamed at him. "We're drinking to the health and long life of Matthew Delaney, who came into this world two hours ago."

Hank was immediately alert. "What's that name?"

"Matthew Delaney, firstborn son of our wagon master, Cooper, and his wife, Agatha."

Then this *was* the Delaney train he and Rawlins were chasing! Why was it still here? By Hanks's reckoning, it should be ahead of them on the trail. Not that it mattered. It looked as though he was about to get lucky.

He had Rawlins's daguerreotype of Margaret Sheridan. He showed it to the pup. "You know this woman and where I can find her? She's traveling with you in the company of a man." He described Archer Owen.

The pup looked at the daguerreotype and scratched his head, perplexed. "That's Sister Meg Carver, except she sure has changed some from that. But she and her husband, Brother Deke, aren't here. They've gone ahead with the first section."

When Hank received all the explanation he knew he was going to get, he went on another search. The freighters he and Rawlins had accompanied weren't traveling beyond Ft. Laramie. He would need a guide for the next portion of his journey.

He knew just what he was looking for, and he found him in the person of a half-breed renegade. Black Feather had a scarred face, a nasty smile, and a willingness to do anything for the right price. When Hank had struck a bargain with him, he went back to the sickroom.

Rawlins was bewildered. "Margaret posing as that devil's wife? I don't understand!"

"You don't have to. All you gotta know is I'm going after them. Pulling out as soon as me and this Black Feather can get ready."

Enoch's face contorted in pain as he struggled to sit up. Any movement was agony for him. "What about me?"

"You can wait here until I get back with them or try to catch up when you can. Warned you I wouldn't play nursemaid for you."

"All right. You can do what you want about Owen. I no longer care. Just make sure Margaret is returned to me safely."

"Oh, I'll take care of Owen, all right," he promised with a hard-bitten laugh. "Told you, didn't I, that I wouldn't give up until he's in hell."

Chapter Twelve

The answer came to her from the bleak terrain that stretched around her on all sides. *Nothing. Margaret Sheridan knows absolutely nothing about surviving in the wilderness.*

What am I doing here? I don't belong. How did it happen?

Desperation clawed at her, and for one terrible moment hysteria threatened to defeat her. It was Agatha Delaney who saved her. She remembered what Agatha had told her at Ft. Laramie.

"You need no one. You have only to reach inside

yourself to find courage and strength and self-reliance.''

Margaret hadn't believed it back then, and she wasn't sure she was ready to believe it now. But it was all she had. Anyway, she no longer knew just who or what she was.

There was one certainty. Margaret Sheridan might be helpless in the wilderness, but Meg Carver was not. And it was time that Meg asserted herself and took charge.

Obeying this stubborn, angry self-command, she swiftly assessed the situation and went to work. Archer needed attention. He was lying there uncovered, exposed to the sun beating down on him. No shelter was available, unless she could get him up inside the wagon. He was still unconscious, though, and far too heavy for her to lift.

The best she could do was to move the wagon so that its bulk shaded her patient. Then she released the six oxen from their yokes, which was a struggle, but the animals were patient about it. There was a risk in turning them loose to graze, but they couldn't remain attached to the wagon. She figured, too, that if they did wander off, they would always return to the stream to drink and that somehow she'd manage to recover them.

This accomplished, she crouched down beside Archer, examining him. He hadn't stirred, and he was still very hot to the touch.

''Why don't you wake up and tell me what you have? Is it cholera, or is it influenza?''

If it was influenza, she determined, then it had to

be a particularly virulent form of the disease. An ordinary grippe wouldn't have struck him with such force.

"But you wouldn't give in to it, would you? You were sick during the fire, sick while they tried to hang you, and all you could do was smile and make jokes. No wonder your body has shut down on you completely, you obstinate lout."

Well, she had to do something for him. What were the instructions Toby had related to her? Keep the patient warm. Give him plenty of fluids. Sponge him with cool water to bring down the fever. The treatment was the same for both diseases. There was little else to be done.

Bringing the feather mattress and blankets from the wagon, she made a bed for him on the ground. She tried to rouse him just long enough to have him crawl onto the bed. He did mumble something when she shook him, but he didn't waken.

"You're going to make it as difficult for me as you can, aren't you? All right, we'll do it your way."

It took all of her strength, and most of her wind, to roll him over until he was on the feather bed. He groaned during the procedure.

"I'm not going to apologize. It's for your own good."

Keep him warm. What did that mean, when he was already warm from a fever that was probably much too high? She didn't cover him with the blanket. She went to the river, found a clean pool, and brought a supply of water back to the camp. When she raised his head and tried to get him to drink, he growled and pushed the cup away, spilling water on both of them.

"Why didn't I just let them hang you?"

At least he didn't fight her when she sponged his face with a wet cloth. She checked his pulse, listened to his breathing, and worried that neither was as strong as it should be. But she wasn't sure. She simply didn't know, and wasn't confident that any of her efforts were helping at all.

The sun was going down by the time she finished. The long shadows made her realize again how alone she was. How much she missed Toby and Molly, even the troublesome Penelope.

Don't give in to it. Keep busy.

She thought about putting up the tent, but decided it was too difficult to manage on her own. Instead, she made a fire, boiled water for coffee, and found something to eat. She wasn't the old Margaret Sheridan. She had skills now, useful skills that meant she wasn't helpless.

But despite everything she had learned, every piece of wisdom that people like Toby Snow and Agatha Delaney had shared with her, she was strained to the limit of her endurance by the ordeal of the long, horrendous night that followed.

The dry air cooled rapidly after sundown, and that was when Arch worsened. He began to shiver, seized with a bout of chills. She covered him with all the blankets and quilts the wagon could provide, but nothing seemed to warm him, even though he still carried a fever.

"Liquid. We've got to try to get some liquid into you."

This time, while she held his head, he drank greedily from the cup of water she offered him. She was encouraged. Minutes later she regretted her relief.

She was adding wood to the fire from the dead cottonwood tree when he started to moan in pain. Hurrying to his side, she found him clutching himself as a series of severe cramps gripped him. Then, turning his head to one side, he began to retch violently. Everything came up, fluids and all.

When he had stopped heaving, she stripped the blankets away and cleaned him up. Then she covered him again and waited. He was quiet again. She went back to the fire.

Full darkness settled on the camp. It was a lonesome night filled with terrifying sounds. There were strange rustles off in the blackness that might have been anything. Possibly they were only the oxen wanting to be close to a familiar human for comfort, or they could have been wild animals prowling on the plain.

Once there was a howl that made her jump. Another time there was a shrill scream like a woman in pain. For all she knew, there were unfriendly Indians out there in the stillness sneaking up on her.

Margaret was too scared to investigate any of the noises. She kept the fire going and the rifle within reach as she huddled on the ground, wondering if she would ever see the dawn.

From time to time, she went to her patient. She tried repeatedly to give him water, but he couldn't keep anything down. In the end, she had no choice but to give up.

It must have been long after midnight, and she was nodding where she sat beside the fire, when she was jerked awake. He was calling out in hurt and anger.

"Stop it! Stop clubbing me with that damn thing!"

Alarmed, she scooted over to his side. "What is it? What's wrong?"

"You don't stop, I'll make your head split like mine!"

Another ache added to the rest, she thought. She went and got the water and cloth and bathed his forehead again. "Is that better?"

He didn't answer her. She could only hope that her treatment soothed him. He sank back into his stupor, and she returned to the fire.

The hours crawled by with agonizing slowness. The night was unending. She dozed, but never managed any deep, restful sleep. The situation was too tense for that.

A cold daybreak found her stiff and sore, her eyes burning from lack of sleep. Rousing herself, she washed her face and hands in the river and returned to her patient.

His looks in the harsh light of morning worried her. He was not better. If anything, he was worse. The fever was still with him, and his face was hollow and drawn, as if the illness was shriveling him. He would soon be dehydrated if she didn't manage to get fluid into him and keep it down.

The plain water hadn't worked. Maybe some warm tea. Stirring up the fire, she heated water and brewed a tin of weak tea. She was careful when she settled beside him to merely wet his lips with the tea. Then she waited for any sign of revulsion. None. After that, she induced the tiniest of sips into his mouth. Again she waited. When he didn't retch, she had him swallow just a bit more.

"I think we're going to be successful this time, Mr. Owen. What do you think?"

He didn't answer her, of course. He wasn't aware of her presence. His responses to the tea, as with everything else, were involuntary ones. But she felt less alone talking to him.

When he had taken and kept down as much of the tea as it seemed safe to give him at one time, Margaret went and scouted up some breakfast for herself. It wasn't much. She had some of the tea and munched on a chunk of stale bread. But she felt better afterwards, refreshed enough to make a decision as she gazed out over the flat country.

This was a desolate spot, depressing with the burned wasteland on the other side of the river and nothing on this shore but the gaunt cottonwood. She felt they were exposed here, far too vulnerable. What were her chances of moving them to a more protected area?

There was a possibility. Up the river, a mile or so to the north, lay a range of hills. They angled out from the stream, climbing toward the mountains in the distance. Those hills offered the hope of shelter.

Her attention shifted to her patient. Did she dare to leave him long enough to investigate? No choice. It was either that or remain in this wretched place. Her mind made up, she went to the mattress and made sure he was covered and resting.

"I won't be long," she promised him, and then added with grim humor, "And no visitors while I'm gone."

Taking the rifle, she followed the river northward. She didn't have to trouble herself about the oxen.

They were in sight, grazing placidly on the meager grass. Whatever had been hunting in the night had sought another prey.

When she reached the hills, she was pleased to find a creek coursing through them. It would provide a source of water. She turned to the left where the creek joined the larger stream and followed it up into the hills.

Another mile brought her into a canyon carved by the creek as it tumbled its way toward the plain. It was the kind of spot she had been seeking. The banks were wide and flat before sloping up to meet the sheer rock walls of the canyon. The grass was more plentiful, and there were pine trees. The place was sheltered, and it was just green enough to be cheerful.

There was only one problem. How was she going to get her patient up here? She thought about that on her way back to the camp at the cottonwood tree. A possible solution had occurred to her by the time she arrived at the wagon, where, to her horror, she discovered that Archer was not alone.

In her absence, a large and deadly rattlesnake had appeared. It was coiled near the foot of the mattress within striking distance of her patient. Margaret caught her breath and prayed that Archer remained still. If he grew restless, started to move about—

She crept toward the head of the mattress, trying to position herself for a clean shot at the snake. It buzzed a warning at her as she slowly raised the rifle. If she missed, it could mean Archer's life, because the snake might strike before she could get off a second shot. She was shaking as she brought the rifle to her shoulder.

Then, to her vast relief, the snake decided it didn't like the odds and rapidly slithered away in the direction of the river. Lowering the rifle, Margaret dropped weakly to her knees beside the mattress.

"Thought I told you no visitors. Why are you so stubborn?"

No answer. He looked as though he hadn't stirred once in all the time she'd been gone. He was still hot to her touch. She made fresh tea, and he swallowed some of it. Then she tried to rouse him. If she could persuade him to scramble into the wagon, she wouldn't have to resort to another measure to transport him to the canyon.

Hopeless. He remained unconscious, and since she couldn't possibly lift him into the high wagon, she was left without a choice. Her method for moving him to the new site was complicated, time-consuming, and exhausting.

The sun was high by the time she had him and the bedding lashed to a platform that rested flat on the ground. She'd fashioned the sledge-like affair by shifting all of the supplies out of the wagon, prying up the floorboards, and knocking them together with hammer and nails from the toolbox.

It hadn't been easy rolling Arch onto the platform and tying him down. Equally difficult was recovering a pair of oxen, which she managed by coaxing them with a handful of salt. But they were yoked now to the sledge.

Dare she be pleased with her resourcefulness? Not until she tested it. But the platform held, and the oxen dragged it willingly up into the canyon, where she deposited Archer and the bedding beside the creek.

"All right, so I'm only halfway there. This time I mean it. *No visitors.*"

Back to the cottonwood tree she trudged, where the platform had to be dismantled, the floorboards restored to the wagon, and the provisions reloaded. She was able to catch and yoke another pair of oxen, but the last two beasts eluded her. Not a concern. The teams she had were sufficient for pulling the wagon the short distance to the canyon.

Before leaving, she checked the site. Everything was on board, but there was one last job to perform. Collecting a supply of stones, she arranged them underneath the cottonwood in the shape of an arrow pointing in the direction of the canyon. It was a message telling the Delaneys where they were when they arrived at the river. Margaret didn't let herself wonder what would happen if that second wagon train failed to appear.

It was late afternoon as she huddled beside Archer in the canyon, idly watching the grazing oxen she had released after positioning the covered wagon next to the creek. She was satisfied with their new camp, but so weary from her efforts that she couldn't bring herself to stir.

She prayed her collapse was no more than fatigue and not a sign that she was ill herself. What if she caught his disease? What would happen to them if they were both sick? *No, don't think about it. You're just tired.*

She glanced at her patient. He had survived the trip up here and seemed no worse. But he was no better either. It worried her that he hadn't revived in all this time.

"You're a strong man. That has to be in your favor. Tell me it's in your favor, Archer Owen."

He told her nothing. He was quiet, and had been for hours. She wanted to believe this was hopeful, that he was merely getting the rest he needed. But his unchanged condition frustrated her.

There was no strength left in her to make a fire or cook something for herself. She had another cold meal of hard biscuits, cheese, and raisins. Then she warmed the leftover tea above one of the oil lanterns, and succeeded in getting most of it down her patient's throat in a series of slow, tiny swallows.

The last light of day was fading on the heels of a flaming sunset when she piled covers over Archer. against the chill of the evening and crawled onto the hasty bed she'd made for herself next to him.

"Good night," she wished him softly. "And I hope this one is for both of us."

It was her second night on her own, and she was too worn out to stay awake and mount another watch over him. Checking the rifle to make sure it was still properly loaded and within her reach, she drew the quilt over her and was promptly asleep.

"What?" she cried out. *"What?"*

For a moment she was too disoriented to understand where she was or what was happening. Then, as the fog of sleep receded, she realized she was sitting up on her bed and staring into the blackness of the night.

Something had abruptly awakened her. Something

fearful. As it came again from off in the darkness, she identified it. That shrill cry, like a woman's shriek! She'd heard it last night down by the river. Now it was up here in the canyon. What could it be?

Straining her senses, she listened for the chilling sound. Nothing. Whatever had made it was silent again. But her patient was not. He was coughing, a deep and painful cough. How long had this new stage of his illness been going on?

Fully alert now, Margaret realized she was clutching the rifle. She thrust it aside and fumbled for the matches and lantern, struggling to light it. When she had it glowing, she scrambled off her bed and went to Archer.

He had thrown up again, maybe more than once. Damning herself for failing to hear him, she tried to answer his latest need by propping him up, supporting his weight against her body. Maybe that would ease his cough. It didn't. He went on hacking, a prolonged, terrible thing.

She brought the lantern close and saw blood. It alarmed her. How much more could his poor body take? Or hers? He was heavy and hot against her, but she went on holding him. Mercifully, his coughing eased, and somehow, still huddled there, they both drifted off again.

It was morning when Margaret awakened, her body numb from hanging on to him all night. She laid him back down and staggered to her feet. Relieving herself behind a thicket, she went to the creek and washed her face and hands in the cold waters that originated somewhere in the mountains.

There was an encouraging sight waiting for her

when she returned to Archer. His eyes were open. They focused on her in actual recognition, and a feeble smile hovered around the corners of his mouth.

"You look like hell," he whispered hoarsely. "What have you been doing to yourself?"

"Trying to keep you alive and wondering every minute why I should bother. I haven't found any reasonable answer."

"Sorry, precious. Wish I could help."

"Are you feeling any better?"

"Sure, I feel great."

He didn't, and they both knew it. He managed to get down more tea when she fixed it for him, but even this small effort drained him. After that, he was no longer lucid. He sank into another delirium, complaining of a head that wouldn't stop swelling. Whatever his aches, he finally settled into a long, unconscious stillness.

"I can't sit here all day and just watch you fading. I have to do something, *anything,* whether it helps or not. Because if I don't—" Her voice broke. The rest she said to herself in silence. *I'll start raving, and it won't be because I'm delirious with your fever.*

She made a fire, had breakfast, heated water. Then, with soap, a cloth, and a basin of water, she went to work cleaning him up. He reeked. He needed a bath and fresh clothes, and that meant stripping him down to his skin. *All* of him.

He was ill, and she was his nurse. There was no reason to be anything but impersonal about the entire undertaking. Which was why Margaret cursed her traitorous senses for finding every portion of his hard, exposed anatomy so appealing.

It made no sense at all. There was a stubble of beard on his jaw, and his face was looking gaunt by now. His body, wracked by illness, was limp and helpless. None of this should have been attractive, none of it should have accounted for her admiration or, even worse, the shameful yearning deep inside her. Not when he was her enemy.

And why, anyway, when she'd already been repeatedly intimate with this man, should the sight of him make her breathless? But somehow, now that she knew they weren't husband and wife, it was different. As if she were discovering him all over again.

There was another treachery involved. A memory that had never stopped haunting her. The memory of needing him when she'd been unwell herself back at the ferry station. He'd been a stranger to her in her amnesia, no more than a shadow in the night, but she hadn't been able to shake the feeling of somehow being connected to him. The soothing sensation that, as long as he was close, everything would be all right.

Nonsense, she told herself angrily. You're thinking a lot of nonsense. Don't forget how this man lied to you, used you, carried you off into the wilderness against your will.

Insisting that she keep her mind on her work, she finished bathing him, dealt with the difficult job of getting him into fresh clothes. Then she busied herself with a long day of necessary chores.

Taking advantage of the cooking skills Toby had shared with her, she made a nourishing broth out of dried beef. It would be ready for her patient when he was well enough for something besides tea. For herself she made a flavored dish of rice and beans. It would serve her for more than one meal.

The neglected laundry also demanded her attention. Gathering up garments and soiled bedclothes, she went to the creek and spent an hour scrubbing and rinsing. It was a lonely occupation. She missed Molly and Toby, wondered where they were now and how they were faring.

It was no good thinking about them, though. It only depressed her. In an effort to keep herself company and lift her spirits, she sang all the songs she could remember. It was a safe amusement. There was no one to hear her and make fun of her voice.

Throughout the day, she checked on her patient. He didn't awaken again, nor did his condition seem to improve in other respects. Sometimes his fever was down, and at other moments it was high. But at least he was hanging on.

She experienced a personal jolt in the late afternoon when she went back to the creek to collect her laundry, which she had spread over bushes to dry at the edge of a quiet pool. One of her undergarments had slid down and was threatening to trail into the water. She was bending over to rescue it when she caught her reflection in the glassy surface of the pool.

There had been no opportunity to look into a mirror since regaining her memory. Her discovery was a shock.

Who is that woman staring back at you? It can't be Margaret Sheridan.

Margaret Sheridan was a radiant beauty. A belle who spent her days caring for her appearance, whose skin and hair and gowns were always immaculate. She would have been horrified at this creature with her wild, unkempt hair, a face wet with perspiration, a stained dress, and red, work-roughened hands.

But then, she reminded herself, that Margaret Sheridan had pampered herself not just because she'd had the leisure to do so but because she hadn't known how to do anything else. Not how to cook or wash clothes. Not how to drive oxen or defend herself with a rifle. Not how to confront the wilderness and refuse to let it defeat her.

As satisfying as all that was, however, she still didn't appreciate the reflection in the pool. She spent the last hour of the afternoon correcting it with a bath, a change of clothes, and repairs to her hair.

When darkness fell, she dropped on her bed in exhaustion. It was her third night of struggling to survive on her own.

It must have been sometime after midnight when he woke her with the sound of his wheezing. She was up in a flash, knowing even before she bent over him that this was a new and frightening stage in his illness.

For a helpless moment she listened to him fighting to breathe with short, painful gasps. His lungs were filling up. Dear God, what could she do for him?

"Sit him up!" she commanded herself aloud.

That might help. Pray that it would.

But this time she wouldn't wear herself out by holding him through the rest of the night. Lighting the lantern, she swiftly gathered boxes from the wagon and every pillow and spare quilt she could lay her hands on. She made piles that would support his back and sides.

She was lifting him, using all the strength she could

muster to prop him up in the enclosure, when he suddenly turned aggressive on her. Heaven only knows what enemy he thought he was battling in his delirium, but he struck out with his fist, landing a blow on her jaw that stunned her.

"I'll sink you in the river yet, Mickey O'Hara!" he shouted between pants for air. "You see if I don't!"

Recovering herself, Margaret made an attempt to restrain him before he seriously injured either himself or her. "It's all right," she said, trying to pin down his wildly flailing arms. "You're all right."

He fought her, hitting her again, this time on the shoulder. "Come on, O'Hara! Come and get another taste of my knuckles!"

"Stop it!" she commanded him sharply. "Stop it before I tie you down with ropes!"

It was ended then. Suddenly drained of his crazed burst of strength, he sagged in her arms. She held him, calming him. His breathing was noisy and rapid as he struggled for air. He shivered, even though his body was on fire with fever.

The illness is peaking, she thought with a terrified little whimper. She knew it instinctively. Tonight would be the crisis for him. Tonight he would either live or die. And there was nothing she could do for him.

Nothing, she told herself resolutely, but be here for him.

And that was exactly where she was through the long, agonizing hours that followed. She had thought the first night a horror, the second almost as bad, but they were nothing compared to this nightmare of listening to him straining for each breath as he clutched his chest in pain.

That shrill cry came again somewhere out in the darkness. Whatever it was, she paid it no attention this time. It was nothing compared to the anguish of a man at war with his own body.

At one point he grew agitated again, muttering dazed threats and trying to swing at an enemy who wasn't there. Margaret held him down with her full weight, ordering him to be quiet, pleading with him to be still.

She bathed him repeatedly with cool water, trying to lower his fever. She kept sitting him up whenever he threatened to slide down. And over and over, like a desperate litany, she chanted Agatha Delaney's words to her.

"You need no one. You have only to reach inside yourself to find courage and strength and self-reliance."

Those words gave her the spirit and the determination she needed not to give up on him. Not to permit him to give up on himself. He almost did. There was a terrible moment when his labored breathing faded, when he started to sink into oblivion.

"No!" she ranted at him. "You will not die! Do you hear me, Archer Owen? *You will not die!*"

She refused to lose him. She shook him, blew rapid little puffs of air into his mouth with her lips locked over his. She fought the battle with him and for him, ignoring the tears of frustration streaming down her cheeks.

Whether it was this endeavor, or simply her stubborn anger, that willed him to live was of no importance. All that mattered was his response. With a shudder and an effort that must have been enormous, he started to breathe again. A breathing that somehow seemed less difficult.

"Thank you, God," she whispered, impatiently wiping the tears from her face with the back of her hand.

The pale glow of daybreak was in the sky when his fever broke at last. Within seconds, he was drenched in sweat. She washed it away, feeling his skin. For the first time since he'd sickened, it wasn't hot to her touch. And he was actually breathing normally. The worst was behind him. She lowered him flat on the bedding, covered him, and left him sleeping peacefully.

As weary as she was, her relief was too sweet to permit her to rest. She sat with knees hugged up to her breasts and watched the sunrise. It was a glorious spectacle as a golden light filled the canyon, bathing the rocks in ruddy hues.

The old Margaret Sheridan had never had any interest in nature. Her admiration had been spent on clothes, fine houses, sleek carriages. A simple sunrise would have bored her. But this Margaret Sheridan had a deep appreciation for the rugged beauty of this vast land.

With a little smile of wonder on her mouth, she curled up next to Archer and went to sleep.

"Where are we? What is this place? What's been happening to me?"

His eyes were open. His face was no longer flushed. He was fully aware of the world again, interested in his surroundings, demanding explanations.

She told him everything. He stared at her in a mixture of awe and disbelief. "You did all that? You stayed behind while the others abandoned us? You took care of me?"

"Yes," she said briskly, "you should be impressed."

"I am," he said, his voice still raspy. "Looks like I owe you my life, precious. Can you tell me something else?"

"What?"

"Why did you do it? Why did you save me?"

"Don't ask foolish questions." She pressed him down as he struggled to sit up. "And don't waste all my hard work with a relapse. You're far too weak to get up. You're going to lie there and rest until I tell you you're ready for something more strenuous. And you're going to drink and eat whatever I give you, starting with some broth."

He didn't argue with her. He was uncharacteristically meek about her orders. But she could feel his gaze following her as she gathered fuel, built up the fire, and warmed the broth. His rapt attention made her uneasy.

Nor did those compelling amber eyes leave her face as she fed him the broth. There was a glow in them that worried her. Finally, she could no longer stand it.

"I would be obliged, Archer Owen, if you'd tell me why you keep watching me like that."

His smile was the familiar wicked one. "Do I bother you?"

Yes, you bother me, and in ways I don't want to

admit even to myself. "Your health bothers me," she told him brusquely. "Now finish your broth and go back to sleep. The sooner you get well, the sooner we can be ready to leave this place."

She was relieved when he obeyed her. She couldn't have stood much more of his eager scrutiny, nor her fear of what might be responsible for it.

Busying herself with chores while he slept, she thought about their situation. The worst was behind them now. He would recover. They had only to wait for the arrival of the second wagon train, and then—

A distant rumble cut through her thoughts. Dragging her attention away from the pot she was scouring, she looked toward the north. The sky there was like an angry bruise. Dark clouds were massing over the mountains, spreading toward the range of hills where their canyon lay.

It's going to rain, she realized. It would end the long drought. The plains would turn green again, providing sufficient grass for the stock. Something else to be thankful for.

She was deciding what she had to get under cover before the storm broke when she was alarmed by a sudden recollection. One of the experienced men on the wagon train had warned them about western storms and how wild and intense they could be. The floors of ravines and canyons were traps for the unwary. Walls of water could rush through them in seconds, drowning everything in their paths.

We have to get out of the bottom of the canyon, Margaret thought. We have to move to higher ground.

Turning her head, she gazed up the steep slope that ended a few hundred feet above her in the wall of the canyon. There was an overhang there that would offer them a shelter. It might even be deep enough to qualify as a cave.

Deciding she needed to investigate the possibility, she snatched up the rifle and left the camp. Archer was still sleeping and the sky continued to growl ominously as she climbed the slope. But the storm was not yet a reality. She had time, as long as she didn't waste it.

At the top of the rise, where the ground leveled again, she stopped to catch her breath and to peer into the dim depths of the overhang. Why hadn't she remembered to bring one of the lanterns? She was chiefly concerned that some dangerous animal might inhabit the cavern. But as she ventured into the yawning cavity, the rifle ready, she saw no signs of occupation. Within a few yards, where the daylight still penetrated, the cavern ended in solid rock. Perfect, she thought. They would be snug and dry here.

Or maybe not so perfect, she discovered as she turned around to start back. There was a very large and very powerful mountain lion just outside the mouth of the overhang. Woman and beast froze, staring.

Something has to happen, she thought frantically. We can't go on standing here looking at each other.

Surprised at her self-control, she found herself speaking calmly to the creature. "I'm not stealing your den because there's no evidence you were ever here, and since I found it first, you have to leave. Do we understand one another?"

The lion wasn't impressed, and when she raised the rifle to her shoulder, it opened its mouth and issued a bloodcurdling screech. The cry was a familiar one.

"Oh, so you were the one shrieking in the night. Well, it isn't night now, and I don't have time to argue with you. You're a magnificent animal, so don't make me shoot you. Just go away."

To her amazement, the mountain lion respected her challenge. It turned and bounded away, and when she emerged from the overhang it was already out of sight.

It would have been tempting to spare a moment to gloat over her latest bravery, but the menace to the north was growing more imminent. Scrambling down the slope, Margaret woke her patient and explained their danger.

"There's no way the wagon could make it up there. Do you think you can manage it on foot if I help you?"

"Damn it, I'm not that helpless."

But he was helpless in his weakness, or close to it, as they fought their way up the incline, slipping and sliding on the rocky rubble in their slow ascent. He collapsed on the ground when they reached the safety of the overhang. The climb had exhausted him. She hovered over him, fearing a relapse.

"Don't fuss," he snarled when he'd recovered his wind. "I'm still here."

She understood. His male pride was suffering as much as his body. He felt useless. "I have to go back," she said. "I have to bring up as many of our supplies as I can."

She left the rifle with him and returned to the camp. In the next half hour she made several trips up the high slope, lugging as much as she could carry stuffed into a pair of flour sacks. Food, utensils, bedding, lanterns, ammunition, essential clothing. She brought it all and feared it wasn't enough. So much remained in the wagon.

The first raindrops were beginning to pelt her on her final climb. The oxen were nowhere in sight. Maybe they had wandered back down to the plain. She could only hope that their animal instinct would protect them.

By the time she reached the overhang the rain was falling in earnest. Archer staggered to his feet and tried to take the last load from her. She held the sacks away from him.

"What are you doing up? If you won't lie down, then at least sit down."

"No wonder that mountain lion ran away from you," he grumbled.

But he obeyed her, sinking back to the ground. After adding the sacks to the mound of their other stores, she joined him. They huddled at the mouth of the cavern, watching the storm. There was thunder and lightning off in the mountains, but here in the canyon there was just the rain. Sheets of it that fell in an uninterrupted downpour, soaking the hills, pouring down their flanks into the low areas.

The creek rose rapidly, flooding over its banks, becoming a savage torrent. Minutes later, there was a cracking sound below them. Archer leaned forward, peering through the driving rain.

"Look," he said grimly.

Margaret saw it, too. The wagon had tipped over on its side in the onslaught, and within seconds the wild waters had swept it away down the canyon.

Lost, she thought dismally. And without it, and all that it still contained, along with the vanished oxen, their chances for getting out of here weren't very favorable.

What if the second section of the wagon train failed to arrive? What if Cooper Delaney, now that they had ample grass again for the stock, decided not to leave the main trail to follow the first section? And if the Delaney caravan never turned up, how would she and Archer ever find their way out of this wilderness?

Chapter Thirteen

"You're squirming."

"Sorry," he apologized.

He made an effort to remain still while she finished lathering his face. Morning sunlight warmed the entrance to the cavern where they sat. After two days of dreary rain, the skies had finally cleared. It was a welcome change.

"I don't know why you can't do this for yourself," she said.

"I'm not well enough yet."

It was a poor excuse, and they both knew it. Even though he was convalescing slowly, and at night suffered bouts of a residual cough, which was probably to be expected, he certainly was capable of shaving himself. He had strength enough to defy her in other areas, an exasperating patient who was forever over-exerting himself in his impatience. She would be glad when he was fully recovered.

"Well, I'm no barber, and if you—"

"I know. If I wasn't scratching my whiskers all the time, you wouldn't bother. Can't help it. I told you, when a man's beard is new it itches."

His eternal scratching was an annoying habit, along with his grumbled complaints, which were another evidence of his restlessness. His mood this morning was much better, though. Actually cheerful. She appreciated that—until she picked up the razor and began to carefully scrape away his whiskers.

"Good of you to do this for me, Meg."

"Yes, isn't it?" She had given up reminding him she was Margaret.

"Guess I got all kinds of attention from you when I was sick, things I can't even remember."

"That's right."

"Like when I was chilled and shivering. How did you keep me warm? The heat of your own body next to mine? I'd like to think that's how you managed it."

She lifted the razor from his chin and stared at him. He wasn't in a cheerful mood. He was in a playful mood. *Sensually* playful. No wonder he had wanted her to shave him. "I gave you blankets and a fire," she informed him severely, "and that's all."

"Oh. Too bad."

She resumed shaving him. He was silent for a few seconds, and then he struck again.

"I had to be cleaned up, huh?"

"Of course I kept you clean."

"Did you wash me all over? I mean, did you strip me and wash everything?"

This was getting dangerous. She evaded his question with a crisp, "You're squirming again. If you don't hold still, I may slip with this razor. You may lose something."

"Like what?"

Her finger flicked the lobe of his left ear where the bottom was missing. "Like the rest of this. How did you lose it?"

"That's not very interesting. Couldn't we discuss—"

"No, we will not discuss any other areas of your body. We will either talk about this ear or you can finish shaving yourself. Now tell me what happened to the lobe."

If he was disappointed, he refrained from saying so. He responded blithely, "Mickey O'Hara happened to it."

She remembered the name. He had shouted it in his delirium. "And who is Mickey O'Hara?" she asked.

"The meanest sonofabitch on the Mississippi River. Or, for that matter, its tributaries."

"Mean enough to do what?"

"Bite off a chunk of my ear during this little dispute we were engaged in."

She held the razor away from his face and stared at him. "Oh, you can't mean it! That's horrible!"

271

"Huh, that was nothing. I once knew a fellow whose nose got chewed off by the bastard. A fair fighter Mickey was not. Hell, none of us were. Couldn't afford to be."

Margaret shuddered. "Just what kind of world did you come from?"

"A hard one, precious. And if you wanted to survive in it, you had to be tough. Running keelboats on the rivers was a dirty business. You always had to be alert for the competition. Rival gangs like Mickey's, who wouldn't hesitate to attack you in the night and burn your boats if they could."

"Is that where you acquired that fiery temper of yours?"

He chuckled. "Hell, no. Got it from a Welsh father, along with my knowledge of the rivers. He had me running the keelboats with him from the time I can remember."

"And where was your mother?"

"Don't know. Ran out on us when I was still a baby."

Margaret's heart ached for him. Nor could she help a sudden feeling of guilt. His upbringing had been harsh and brutal, probably lonely as well. Her own childhood had been entirely different. She had known every advantage, including loving parents.

The sympathy she felt must have been evident on her face, and his pride couldn't stand it. "Hey, don't you be feeling sorry for me. My old man wasn't so bad. Not when he was sober, anyway. When he was sober, he would talk to me about his dream. How he wanted to get away from the keelboats, have his own steamboat one day." Arch paused, a faraway look in his eyes. "Only, he never got his dream. The drink killed him first."

"But you went and realized his ambition for him," she said softly.

"That's right, because by the time he died it was my dream, too. The *Missouri Belle* may not be much as steamboats go, but she's all mine. Took me years of saving from every job I could get, every keelboat cargo I could turn a profit on, but in the end I got my lady. I just hope they're taking good care of her until I can get back to her."

His face glowed when he spoke of the *Missouri Belle*. Like the adoration of a man for his beloved mistress. How could a woman ever hope to compete with a rival like that? Not, she reminded herself hastily, that she had any remote intention of trying.

"You're forgetting something," she reminded him. "There's a death sentence waiting for you back there."

"There won't be," he said resolutely, "when I catch up with that brother of yours and haul him back to Missouri to clear me."

Margaret didn't argue with him. She no longer knew what to believe in regard to his guilt. She had yet to be convinced that Trace would have lied during the trial. There seemed to be no motive for it.

Whatever the truth, Archer was not, in her opinion, being very realistic about this pursuit. His chances of finding Trace and forcing him to return to Saint Joseph on his behalf struck her as remote. His relentless determination was awesome, though. As stubborn as the ambition that had driven him to acquire his steamboat, to raise himself to a better station in life.

Margaret knew she was in trouble when she found herself admiring him for that. Throwing down the razor, she handed him a dampened towel. "You're finished."

Wiping the lather from his face, which seemed to her even more angular as a result of his illness, he inspected himself in a scrap of mirror. The rest was in shards, broken during their retreat from the floor of the canyon.

"Good job," he complimented her, stroking his jaw. "Not so much as a nick."

"I'm not exactly an amateur. I shaved my father after his stroke."

He gazed at her soberly. "There was no one else by then, huh?"

She had made the mistake of telling him earlier how her life had changed when her father's investments had collapsed on him. They should never have exchanged confidences about their pasts. There was a tender look in his eyes that made her vulnerable. She was in danger again.

Feeling a sudden need to get away from him, she got to her feet and went to the edge of the ledge outside the alcove. The bottom of the canyon was no longer swollen with water.

"The creek is down," she announced. "I'm going to look for the wagon. There may be useful things I can rescue."

"Want some company?"

"Certainly not. You stay right here and work on recuperating."

"Be careful down there," he called after her.

* * *

Dragging a sack behind her, Margaret trudged up the slope. There was a mournful look on her face when she reached the overhang and dropped beside Arch.

"Not good, huh?" he asked.

She shook her head. "The wagon is around that first bend, but it's not going anywhere. It's still on its side, and a back wheel was smashed on the rocks. One of the oxen is down there. Dead, poor thing. It must have been trapped in the floodwaters. I didn't see any sign of the others."

"Maybe they made it down to the plain," he said hopefully. "What did you find to salvage?"

She sighed. "Not much. Mostly clothing that got left behind. The rest of the stores were either carried away or ruined by the waters. These are all wet and dirty, too, of course, but at least they can be washed and dried."

She began pulling garments out of the bag, inspecting each one for damage. One of them was the blue muslin dress she had worn the evening of the Fourth of July celebration. When she shook it out, something that had been tucked between its folds fell into her lap. She picked it up, turning it over in her hand.

It was the painted fan Toby had taught her to flirt with that night. But it would never serve that purpose again. Soaked in the flood, it was in tatters, its bright colors smeared and stained.

As she looked at it, knowing it was beyond repair, something infinitely sad came over Margaret. The fan was a cheap novelty. Its loss didn't deserve her tears, but they came anyway. Within seconds, she was weeping uncontrollably.

Archer was dismayed. "You're crying over a fan?

You battle a plague, a rattlesnake, a mountain lion, and a flood, all without losing your self-control, and you go to pieces over a ridiculous fan?''

"I can't help it," she blubbered, clutching tightly to the fan. "It just seems like—like the final straw."

"Yeah," he said softly, "I guess after everything that's happened you are entitled to a few tears."

The next thing she knew she was on his lap. How did she get there, and when had his arms encircled her protectively? It was a mistake to permit this. She knew that, understood the risk involved, but her need was too great to resist him.

He held her, comforted her with soothing words. "Have I told you how brave you are, precious? If I haven't, I'm telling you now. You're some woman, all right. Why, you'd walk through fire if you had to, wouldn't you?"

"You—you told me I was spoiled," she sniffed. "Spoiled and—and useless."

"I was wrong."

She shook her head. "No, you were right, but I've changed."

"I guess we've both changed," he said, his hands slowly stroking her back.

Archer Owen is an enigma, she thought. How could a man, tough and unyielding, bred in that brutal world of the keelboats, be as tender as he was in this moment? Where had he acquired such sensitivity?

It was a gentleness to which she was highly susceptible. That was why she didn't stop him when he began to kiss her. They were innocent kisses at first, lightly placed on her eyelids, nose, and cheeks. Kisses meant to dry her tears.

276

It was when his mouth settled on hers that an intimacy was ignited. The eager intimacy of his searing lips, his searching tongue, his hands on the sides of her breasts.

Margaret's senses rioted, threatening to betray her. The feelings were intensified by the images that swarmed through her head. Wanton images of their long sessions of exciting sex before she'd overcome her amnesia. He had been an unbelievable lover, and she had responded to him without restraint.

Why wasn't she blushing with shame over those memories? And how could she still want him like that? It couldn't be right, not after the way he had lied to her, used her. *It couldn't.*

There was another image, the trusting face of Enoch Rawlins back in St. Louis, that gave her the courage to draw back from Archer's intoxicating kisses.

"What we did before will not happen again," she informed him emphatically as soon as she was able to catch her breath. "I'm not Meg Carver now. You aren't my husband."

His hands, still holding her, tightened possessively against her ribs. "What the hell does it matter who we are? You love me, don't you? So why shouldn't we—"

"What did you say?" She stared at him in alarm and disbelief.

"You heard me. Why else would you have saved my neck from the rope, sacrificed your own skin to stay here in the wilderness nursing me through whatever it was I had? If that isn't love, I don't know what is."

"I can't believe your monumental conceit! I saved

you because I couldn't stand by and watch a fellow human being suffer, and that's all it was!''

''And I say you're fooling yourself. I say you are in lo—''

''Stop saying that!'' she cried.

''Aw, Meg, please. Remember how this felt, how good we were together?''

He strained his rigid arousal against her bottom, yearning for her, and she panicked.

''I'm Margaret,'' she insisted. ''Margaret Sheridan. I've promised myself to a man in St. Louis. He's waiting for me, and whenever it's possible I'm going back to him.''

''Why? And don't tell me it's because you love him. I wouldn't believe it.''

''I do care for Enoch, and he cares for me. And he—he offers something I need.''

He stared at her, his eyes narrowed. ''I see. Money, huh? The kind of material wealth a lout like me can't possibly provide. I guess you haven't changed as much as we both thought.''

Archer abruptly thrust her aside and got to his feet. This time it was his turn to walk away.

For two days they barely spoke to each other. Margaret kept busy washing and mending the clothes she had rescued and feeding their cooking fire out on the ledge.

Arch, equally restless, insisted on going down to the wagon and wrestling the damaged wheel off the axle. After carrying it back to their camp, he raided the trees for a supply of wood, then spent long hours whittling new spokes.

Where the wagon was going without oxen, even if he did succeed in repairing the wheel, Margaret couldn't imagine. Nor should he have been wearing himself out with this effort, but she didn't try to stop him. Not this time.

Both of them were unhappy, but neither of them wanted to discuss it. What was the point when there could be no future for them together? All they shared now was a past that she wanted to put behind her. But she felt unable to do that while they existed in this limbo, waiting for the arrival of the second caravan. She prayed for that relief.

By the afternoon of the second day, Margaret could no longer stand the strain between them. "I'm going down to the river," she announced.

Arch, sitting cross-legged on the ground, looked up from his carving. "What for?"

"I want to check that arrow I left by the cottonwood tree. If there were high waters down there, the stones could have washed away. And I think I need to lay a second arrow where the creek meets the river. It's an opportunity to look for the oxen."

He frowned. "I don't know that I like you wandering off on your own like this all the time."

"I did it when you were ill, didn't I? And I won't be alone. I have this." She held up the rifle.

Arch didn't argue with her. Maybe a little break from each other was what they both needed.

He watched her as she left the ledge and picked her way down the slope. Even here in this rough place, her slim figure moved with an enticing grace that made him ache with longing. It wasn't only lust he felt for her. It was something more, an emotion he was unable to define. Maybe it was just gratitude because she had saved him.

Hell, Arch didn't know. Love? He didn't know what it was to *feel* love. It was something alien in the world he'd come from, so how could he recognize it? All he knew for sure was that he had this powerful desire for her. But with a death threat hanging over him, what was the use? She was right. Even if he did clear himself, he had nothing to offer her but a battered old steamboat.

He was tired suddenly. The truth was, he had yet to recover his strength, and he had been pushing himself these past two days. Tossing down the carving knife, he stretched out on his back, upraised arm shielding his eyes against the glare. Within seconds, he was asleep.

Arch didn't know what awakened him. Maybe it was the rattle of a pebble under a heavy boot, or maybe he sensed the shadow that fell across him. Along with the danger it represented.

When he opened his eyes, there was a man gazing down at him. An unfriendly-looking brute with a cigar stuck between his teeth. There was a pistol strapped to his hip.

"Get up," he ordered Arch in a rough voice.

Arch started to obey him. But as he rolled to a sitting position, his hand flashed out for the knife he'd left on the ground. A boot clamped down painfully on his wrist before his fingers could close on the weapon.

"Try that again and I won't wait to use this." His

assailant had the pistol out of its holster and pointed at this head.

"All right, take it easy. I'll do what you ask." The boot was removed from his wrist. "See, I'm getting up."

Arch had learned a number of lessons in the days of Mickey O'Hara. One of them was the value of surprise. He used it now as he slowly picked himself up from the ground, head hanging in defeat. He was halfway to his feet when he charged like a bull.

His lowered head caught his enemy in the gut, punching the wind out of him. He went down, still clutching the gun and with Arch on top of him. The two men, cursing savagely, grappled with each other for the pistol.

Arch didn't know there was a second man. Not, anyway, until something came crashing down on the back of his skull. There was a display of fireworks before he collapsed with a grunt.

When he came to, the man with the pistol was hunkered down on the ground several paces away, puffing on a new cigar. His partner, a half-breed with a scarred face and a nasty leer, was standing beside him.

Lifting his head, Arch glowered at them. "If you're trying to rob me, you picked the wrong man. All I've got is a few supplies. Take what you want and get out of here."

The man with the cigar blew a smoke ring, his manner unhurried. "Now that's where you're wrong. You got something of real value. It's called Archer Owen."

This is no chance encounter then, Arch thought.

I'm in real trouble. "Never heard of him."

"That's funny." The man took the cigar out of his mouth and studied it. "Because the description I got fits you like a glove. Be a real coincidence if there was two men out here with parts of their left earlobes missing, wouldn't it?"

"What do you want?"

"It's not what I want, Owen. It's what Enoch Rawlins wants. He'd of come hisself, but the man's laid up in a sickbed back at Ft. Laramie. He sent me in his place. Name's Hank Shaw."

Rawlins was in Ft. Laramie? "How did you find me?"

Shaw jerked his head in the direction of the smoldering campfire. "Smoke from that was as good as a signpost. Now suppose you tell me where the woman is hiding, and we can get on with the business at hand."

"What woman? I'm alone here."

"Margaret Sheridan is with you, and Rawlins wants her back."

Hank Shaw had a mean face that reminded him of Mickey O'Hara. Arch wouldn't trust a man with a face like that, and certainly not to safely escort Meg back to her bridegroom. "Margaret Sheridan went on with the first section of the Delaney wagon train."

"Don't think those feminine drawers drying over that bush down there are yours, Owen. She's here somewheres." He got to his feet, flipping the cigar away and turning to his partner. "Find her, Black Feather, and bring her back."

Shaw chuckled as the half-breed turned and scrambled down the slope. "She's as good as here. Never saw a man that could track like that breed.''

Arch glared at him murderously. ''If he so much as touches her—''

''Black Feather would never do that. He's a real gent—when the price is right. And with Rawlins being so generous, I made sure of that.'' He fingered the pistol. ''Gonna have us an interesting session when they get back.''

Four of the oxen were safe. Margaret had spotted them grazing peacefully on her way out of the hills. That left a fifth unaccounted for. It might be anywhere.

She found the arrow near the dead cottonwood tree undisturbed. Getting to her feet, she stared across the river at the flat plain stretching to the horizon. There was no sign of a wagon train. The burned grass on that side was already sprouting a new green. Within a few weeks, there would be no sign of the fire.

Margaret wasn't really thinking about that, though. She was thinking about Archer and how hopeless their situation was. A man like him couldn't understand that you didn't build a worthwhile relationship on mutual lust.

A woman needed other things. She needed security. The kind of security Enoch offered. Margaret hadn't changed so much that she didn't still value that. Whatever skills she had learned, how could she exist without it? Poverty frightened her. But Arch didn't see that. He thought she was still being shallow.

But most of all, a woman needed love. Enoch had told her he *did* love her. All Archer had ever said was that *she* loved *him,* nothing about how *he* felt about *her.*

And, anyway, she didn't love him. How could she? He was a fugitive who had used her to get to her brother. He was all wrong for her. So she didn't love him. *She didn't.*

Her emotions were still in a turmoil when she headed back to the canyon. At the juncture of the creek and the river she stopped to build a second arrow pointing into the hills. She had collected stones and was finishing the arrow when she sensed someone behind her. Archer?

Swinging around where she knelt, she was alarmed to find that her visitor was a half-breed with a raven's feather stuck in his headband. He might not be an enemy, but then why had he been so stealthy that she'd never heard his approach? Her gaze cut to the rifle she had laid on the ground. What were her chances of reaching it?

Understanding her intention, he swooped down on the rifle before she could move. Once it was in his possession, he motioned for her to get up. Margaret rose to her feet, trembling.

Could he understand English? She tried. "I'm not alone. My husband is nearby, and he will be—"

"No use to you." He grinned at her, revealing broken teeth. "Shaw holds him."

"Shaw? Who is—"

"No talk. They're waiting."

He refused to answer any further questions, conducting her in silence back to the canyon. Margaret's fears mounted as they followed the creek into the hills. Were she and Archer about to be robbed and murdered?

A second man, with a stubble of beard on his broad face and a lethal pistol in his hand, met them when they climbed the slope to the overhang. "Good work, Black Feather."

Archer was there, but when he tried to go to her, the pistol was shoved in his face. "She ain't been harmed, Owen, so just stay where you are."

Though shaken, Margaret tried to question the man. "Who are you? What is this all about?"

"Now, ma'am, just relax, because we've come to rescue you. And just as soon as we take care of an essential little matter here, we'll be on our way back to civilization."

"What matter? I don't understand."

Shaw didn't answer her. He was busy looking out from the alcove, searching the canyon in both directions while Black Feather guarded Archer with the rifle. "Now that looks like a likely spot for it, just up there. What do you think, Owen?"

Margaret followed the direction of his gaze. The ledge that supported their camp ascended on the left toward the canyon rim and then ended abruptly, this time in a sheer drop to the canyon floor.

"He's choosing the place for my execution," Arch explained quietly. "Aren't you, Shaw?"

Shocked, Margaret stared at Archer and saw that he meant it. What was more, when her gaze flashed to Shaw's face, she read his ruthless intention. Not again. Please, God, not again.

"Let's go," Shaw said, pointing the way with the

muzzle of the pistol. "You, too, ma'am. I need me an official witness."

"Let her stay here with Black Feather," Archer appealed to him. "Don't make her watch me die. Rawlins wouldn't thank you for that."

Margaret gasped. "Enoch sent you?"

"That's right. Paid me to bring you back to him safely."

He was already leading the way up the ledge. Archer had no choice but to follow him since Black Feather had the rifle poked into his back. Margaret ran after Shaw, pleading with him.

"Enoch may have paid you to return me to him, but not to kill this man! He wouldn't want that! You musn't do it!"

Shaw spat in contempt. "He's a condemned murderer, ain't he? What would you have me do?"

"Take him back to Missouri with us! Let the law there handle it!"

"And have him try to escape every chance he gets? No, we're gonna settle it here and now."

They had reached the end of the ledge. Shaw, facing Archer, chuckled cruelly. "You oughta thank me, Owen. It's not every day a man gets to pick how he's gonna die. What'll it be? A bullet from this?" He waved the pistol, then nodded toward the yawning space off the end of the ledge. "Or a dive from there?"

Margaret couldn't bear it. She had saved Archer from a noose, sacrificed her soul to save him from a life-threatening illness. Was she to lose him now to this insanity?

"You ain't answering me, Owen," Shaw taunted his prisoner.

"I'm not going to do your dirty work for you, Shaw."

"Then I guess it's a bullet."

He leveled the pistol in the direction of Archer's heart. Margaret's insides screamed with a helpless fury.

What happened next occurred with such swiftness that she failed to comprehend it. In one second Shaw's face was livid with malicious pleasure; in the next it registered bewilderment. The pistol fell from his hand, clattering on the rock as he clutched at the arrow protruding from his chest.

The arrow had arrived without sound or motion, or so it seemed to Margaret. It was just suddenly there, buried in Shaw's chest. But she did hear the hiss of the second arrow, which rapidly followed the first. It found its mark in Black Feather's throat. He dropped without a cry.

Shaw, gasping for air, staggered back on the ledge. He was still clutching at the shaft of the arrow when he toppled from the height, his body landing with a dull thud on the rocks far below. Margaret and Archer stared at each other in consternation.

"How?" she cried. "Where?"

"They came from up there," Archer said.

They lifted their gazes, searching the canyon rim several yards above them. Hard on its edge, and off to the right, a band of Cheyenne warriors peered down at them. Mounted on their rugged ponies and with weapons drawn, they were a formidable sight.

Margaret expected another shower of arrows at any

second, and was prepared to find cover. That was before Archer raised a jubilant shout.

"It's Lone Wolf and his braves!"

Lone Wolf? And then she remembered. The son of the chief, Gray Eagle, that Archer had brought comfort to on his deathbed in the Cheyenne village.

Archer waved both arms, hailing his rescuers. "You've slain my enemies, Lone Wolf. My heart is filled with gratitude."

The Cheyenne brave saluted him, calling down solemnly, "Your Great Father must walk with you, holy man."

"Yeah, maybe He did bring you here."

"Through the spirit of a wounded buffalo we followed on our hunt," said another voice, explaining how they had come to be there. It was a young, eager voice.

Margaret's gaze shifted to the left, discovering a boy who looked back at her in earnest fascination. He was small but sturdy, and as he crowded his pony to the very lip of the canyon, craning his neck to get a better view of the white man and his woman, she saw a curious mark on the side of his thin neck. It was shaped like a crescent moon and was either a kind of tattoo or a birthmark.

There was something else about the child that struck her. His hair was as straight and black as the others, his eyes dark, his dress that of a Cheyenne, but he wasn't Cheyenne. Or at least, not entirely. Surely, there was a white bloodline in the boy. A strong one. Or was she imagining it?

No chance to find out. Lone Wolf spoke sharply to the boy in their Algonquian tongue, rebuking him for his discourteous interruption. The child, looking sheepish, backed away from the rim of the canyon, disappearing from view.

Lone Wolf raised his hand in farewell. "Safe journey, holy man. We will not meet again."

His message was plain. He and his braves had paid a debt owed to Archer for easing the chief's last hours. Nothing else was to be expected of them. They swung their ponies around and were gone as suddenly as they had arrived.

There was a silence down on the ledge. Then Archer, drawing a deep breath, observed dryly, "Looks like there's a couple of bodies to be dealt with. I suppose they at least deserve a decent burial."

Margaret, forgetting all about the boy, insisted on helping him. When they had finished covering the graves, Archer gazed at her speculatively. "You all right?"

She nodded. "I'm just tired, that's all."

But by sundown every joint in her body ached, and she was running a fever. There was no question of it. She was down with the same sickness that Archer had suffered.

He nursed her all through that night and the next day and the one following it. It was late afternoon of the third day when the Delaney caravan arrived at the cottonwood tree by the river. Arch, going down into the canyon to meet the party that came looking for them, knew he was about to face some serious questions.

Chapter Fourteen

"How is she doing?" Arch anxiously asked the couple.

Cooper, leaning against the tailboard of the Delaney wagon, which was parked slightly apart from the others in the camp beside the river, frowned at him. "She's not really your concern anymore, is she, Owen?"

Arch had expected that. They had been treating him like a leper ever since he and his patient, along with their wagon and possessions, had been moved down from the canyon. Everyone, that is, except Agatha, who interceded now on his behalf.

"I think, my love," she gently reminded her husband, "that since he has been caring for her, he is entitled to know."

Cooper made no further objection. It amazed Arch how the man seldom denied his wife whatever she asked. It must be particularly true these days, he thought, eyeing the tall woman. She was seated on a stool nursing Matthew Delaney with the same quiet dignity she demonstrated in any function she performed, her shawl preserving her modesty.

There was an expression of pride and tenderness on Delaney's face as he watched his son being fed. It gave Arch a strange feeling in his gut seeing that look, a kind of yearning he'd never experienced before.

Did Agatha sense what he was feeling? She smiled at him as she continued. "Meg—or rather, I should say Margaret now—is with Ella and Lizzie at their wagon. Trust them to care for her like a sister. She is resting comfortably and ought to be up and about in a few days."

"That's good. She was pretty sick, but nothing as bad as I was."

"Not as severe an attack, I expect. In any case, you are surely both past the contagious stage and no threat to the caravan. However"—she paused to adjust the shawl—"I should tell you that Margaret has expressed in the strongest possible terms a wish to remain attached to Lizzie and Ella's wagon."

"Yeah," Arch said glumly, "I kind of expected that. Doesn't want to be around me, huh?"

Cooper spoke up sharply. "Can you blame her after the way you used her?" He stood restlessly away from the tailboard, impatient to get on to the essentials of this confidential meeting. "It's time you favored us with an explanation, Owen. And you'd better make it a *straight* one this time."

Arch shifted his weight from one leg to the other. "You spoke to Enoch Rawlins back at Ft. Laramie, didn't you? How much did he tell you?"

"Enough to know you're up to your neck in trouble. Now suppose you give us the rest, and we'll tell you what we're going to do about you when you're finished."

Arch left nothing out of his story, starting from the beginning back at Saint Joseph and ending with the episode of Hank Shaw and Black Feather. When he was finished, it was twilight and Matthew Delaney had been transferred to his father's arms, where he slept peacefully against a broad chest.

"Look," Arch said, pleading his case to them, "if I was guilty, I wouldn't be risking my backside chasing all the way to Oregon after Trace Sheridan. I'd have run for cover back East somewhere, wouldn't I?"

Agatha, hands folded demurely in her lap, nodded. "If your argument is a reasonable one, and I grant you that it is, then why does an intelligent woman like Margaret Sheridan refuse to accept it?"

"Because I deceived her. Because I'm calling her brother a liar. And because . . . well, I suppose because she's all mixed up about me anyway."

Agatha tipped her head to one side. The light from the campfire revealed the gleam in her eye. "And what about you, Archer Owen? Are you all mixed up about *her*?"

Cooper interrupted their exchange, exasperated. "Aggie, this isn't our problem. What to do with Owen until we reach Ft. Vancouver is." He turned to Archer. "There's no way to send you back from this point and no practical way to confine you while we move on."

"Don't worry," Arch assured him. "I have no intention of running off. I want to get to Oregon same as you because that's where Trace Sheridan is."

"I'll have to trust you then. I'm not about to hang you like Frank Parker tried to do. But," he added grimly, "make no mistake about it. When we reach Ft. Vancouver, I'm turning you over to the authorities there. They'll decide what becomes of you."

"Fair enough," Arch agreed.

Archer thought the interview was ended, and started to leave. But Agatha stopped him. "There is something you might care to know, Mr. Owen."

"What's that, ma'am?"

"Enoch Rawlins will not remain at Ft. Laramie unless the gunman he hired returns with Margaret Sheridan. We know now this will not happen. Therefore, when he is sufficiently recovered, he will hire a guide and ride after us. On horseback he will overtake us long before Ft. Vancouver."

"You sure that's his intention?"

"Quite sure. He is eager to be reunited with his bride."

Cooper, rocking his son in his arms, spoke up. "We ought to send her back to him at Ft. Laramie, Aggie."

"Oh, that would never do. It will be days before Margaret is well enough to ride. Nor can we spare

293

either a horse or a man to take her all that distance. I am afraid her only option is to move on with us in the morning.''

Cooper gazed perceptively at his wife. ''Aggie, no,'' he warned her.

''My love,'' she assured him innocently, ''I am only stating the facts of the situation. But then perhaps none of this is of interest to Mr. Owen.''

She gazed at Arch, and there was a clear challenge in her eyes. What are you going to do about it? That was what she was silently asking him. And he asked it of himself: What was he going to do about Meg and him? What did he *want* to do?

He didn't have to go looking for any answer, though, because the answer was right there with him and had been for a long time. It was just that he'd been too scared of it to do anything but deny it. Until this moment when Agatha Delaney forced him to acknowledge it.

Crossing half a continent with a woman who puts fire in my veins has done things to me, he thought. Damn it all to hell, she's changed me.

And the long trail had changed him. He had created a wife and daughter for a self-serving purpose, and they had ended up sneaking into his heart. Unbelievable, but he had liked being a husband and father, caring for them, sharing with them. And now he didn't want to lose his family. That was the answer.

For the first time in his life, something more than a steamboat mattered to Archer Owen. Oh, he still wanted the *Missouri Belle,* all right, but it wasn't enough. Nothing could ever again be as important to him as Meg and Molly.

Sweet mother, *was* he in love with the woman? Yeah, he was. He could admit that now. Actually in love and out of his mind even thinking about something permanent with her. His circumstances hadn't changed. He still had nothing to offer her or Molly with his life in a mess and a death sentence staring him in the face.

That should have stopped him right there, if he'd had any sense. He guessed he didn't, however, because he intended to fight for them. Whatever it took, he was going to win Margaret Sheridan. But time was his enemy. He had only a matter of days, possibly a few weeks at most, to convince her he was exactly what she needed before Enoch Rawlins arrived to claim her.

"I'm interested all right," he assured Agatha. "But I have a question."

"Yes?"

"Does everyone on the caravan know about Enoch Rawlins?"

She shook her head. "They are aware of a gentleman convalescing at Ft. Laramie, but not his connection to the woman they knew as Meg Carver. There seemed to be no purpose in sharing this knowledge with them after Cooper and I complied with Mr. Rawlins's request to speak privately with him in his sick-room."

"Think we could keep it that way?" Arch appealed to them.

"I see no point in that," Cooper objected.

"I think, my love, Mr. Owen fears someone may inform Margaret that Mr. Rawlins is on his way."

Cooper scowled at him. "You mean she doesn't

295

know her bridegroom intends to collect her?''

Arch shrugged. "She knows Rawlins hired Shaw to bring her back, not that he's at Ft. Laramie. That, uh, never got mentioned somehow.''

"Which means she's under the impression he's waiting for her back in St. Louis,'' Cooper said. "Then she has to be told. I won't have her lied to anymore.''

"Technically,'' Agatha pointed out to him, "it is not a lie, although I suppose an argument could be made that an omission qualifies as . . . Now, husband, it is no use your looking at me in that way. There are enough complications as is. Mr. Owen deserves to settle the matter with Margaret without adding another. Soon enough for her to know Mr. Rawlins is here when he arrives. I am convinced of this.''

"I give up. You're as much a rascal as he is.''

"Yes, my love, I know.''

Thanks to Agatha, Arch had a reprieve. But he had to make that time count, which was why he was on his way to the wagon where Meg was recuperating. His self-confidence, which had been so strong in that first flush of excitement when he'd realized he loved Meg and was determined to win her, had dimmed. He was nervous, worried about what he was going to say to her.

He found her propped up with pillows on a camp cot in sight of the fire where Lizzie and Ella were busy preparing supper. She wasn't enthusiastic about his being there.

"How are you feeling?'' he asked, crouching beside the cot.

"I shouldn't speak to you," she said, her voice hoarse. "Not when you went and gave me this plague."

"I had to show my appreciation somehow for your saving me, didn't I?"

"Yes, well, you were much too generous. But I will survive." She shifted herself on the cot, her tone becoming pointed. "Thank you for your care, Archer, but as you can see, I'm in the hands of other nurses now."

"Yeah, I noticed that."

She lowered her gaze, fingering the quilt that covered her. "Did you have any luck in rounding up the oxen?"

"All five of them, and Delaney has promised me a spare one so I'll have a full team for the wagon when we roll tomorrow."

She nodded. There was an awkward pause; then her eyes lifted and met his. "I won't be returning to that wagon. Did they tell you?"

"I heard."

There was a finality in her tone. He knew she wanted no part of him now that their arduous and emotional interlude in the canyon had ended and it was no longer necessary for them to be together. He hadn't been forgiven for stealing her away from Saint Joseph, for taking advantage of her in her amnesia. But Archer refused to accept her rejection. Should he tell her he loved her? No, he'd only scare her by blurting out something as startling as that.

Taking her hand, he tried to tell her in another way. "Look, Meg, I know it's hard to believe this. Sometimes I wonder myself if I'm ever going to manage it.''

"What are you trying to say?"

"Just that somehow I am going to prove my innocence. I won't give up until I do. And when I've been cleared, when I'm a free man again, then . . . well, see, I thought maybe you and Molly and—"

She didn't give him a chance to finish. Understanding exactly where he was going, she snatched her hand away. "Let's not start that again. There is no question of anything in that direction, particularly now that Enoch has demonstrated just how much I mean to him."

He frowned at her. "How do you figure that?"

"He didn't accept my disappearance. He sent someone to find me and bring me back to him. Yes, I know. Shaw was an unfortunate choice, but I'm sure Enoch didn't realize how vicious the man was when he hired him."

Arch made a serious mistake then. He went and lost his famous Welsh temper. He couldn't help it. Her logic was so flawed that it infuriated him.

"What kind of argument is that for a marriage?" he thundered. "If a man loves a woman, *really* loves her, he goes after her himself!" Which is what Rawlins did try to do, but Meg didn't know that. "He doesn't hire a gunman to get her! Did that fever go and scramble your brain so bad you can't see that?"

She stared at him coldly. "I think you'd better leave."

"Not until I'm finished."

"You *are* finished," Ella informed him. His raised voice had alerted her, and she hurried over to the cot, waving a wooden spoon at him. "Now vamoose."

She was a tiny woman, but she had the stamina of an ox. Arch might have defied her fierce command anyway, but he realized he'd just made a prize fool of himself. Definitely not a recommended method for winning the woman you loved. Unless he wanted to lose the war altogether, a retreat now was his only choice. Getting to his feet, he stormed off into the darkness.

When he was gone, Ella turned to Margaret, plumping her pillows, fussing over her. "Big lout doesn't know when to give up, does he?" she muttered.

No, he doesn't, Margaret thought, and that worried her. She was afraid of him, afraid of the feelings he evoked in her, the confusion whenever he was near her. It seemed that it wasn't enough to have attached herself to this wagon. He was still too close.

Oh, if only she could get away from him altogether, leave the train now and go straight to St. Louis! But that was out of the question. Not just because there was no one to accompany her back east. There was Molly. She couldn't abandon Molly. She'd have to go on to Ft. Vancouver, make arrangements there for Molly and her to return home.

Would Enoch welcome Molly, agree to raise her? He would have to. Margaret would make it a condition of their marriage. Molly had been on her mind ever since she had glimpsed Agatha's baby. She longed for her own baby. Molly would be crawling by now, putting everything into her mouth she could reach. Margaret hated missing those developments.

"Supper will be ready in a few minutes," Ella said.

"Do you feel well enough to eat something?"

Margaret assured her that her appetite had improved. Ella patted her on the shoulder and returned to the fire. Both women had been protective of her since she had joined them. They would never have been concerned about her like this before Ft. Laramie. They had changed.

No, that's not right, she realized. It's *I* who have changed.

Among other things, she had shed the vanity that characterized Margaret Sheridan, had learned to care about someone besides herself. The women must have sensed this change and were responding to it.

Turning her head, she looked toward the hills where the canyon lay. She could make out their bulk against the starry sky. She had walked through fire in those hills, as well as down here on the trail, emerging with courage, resourcefulness, and values she had been unable to appreciate until now.

She would never be the same again. The old Margaret was gone forever. The problem was, she wasn't certain she fully understood the new Margaret yet or all that she wanted. She was still confused about her, and she didn't like that.

This was going to be a lot tougher than he'd figured, Arch realized. Right now Meg was mixed up about a lot of things, including him. There was only one thing she was clear about, or stubbornly convinced that she was clear about. She believed Rawlins was the right man for her. Arch had to prove to her he wasn't and that *he* was the right man for her. But how?

He thought about it as the wagon train continued

its journey across a hot, sage-covered plain. He got no answers from himself, at least none that he trusted. Deeply frustrated, he decided he needed advice.

That evening, camped at the the spot where the caravan rejoined the main trail, he went to seek the support of his only ally. He found Agatha changing her baby. She listened to him politely as he explained his problem. Then, to his surprise and disappointment, she turned him down.

"I am at a loss to help you, Mr. Owen."

He gazed at her, perplexed. "But I thought another woman . . ."

"You are making a mistake. I have no solution to offer you." Securing the diaper, she gathered Matthew into her arms and looked thoughtfully at Archer. "However, if I may make a suggestion . . ."

"What?" he asked her eagerly.

"I believe what you need is the counsel of another man. Yes, I am certain that is just the thing for you to do."

"I don't—"

"My husband, Mr. Owen. Go to my husband. Having piloted several wagon trains of women across the continent, he has an astonishing knowledge of my sex. Very useful to you, I should think, to have a man's perspective on the situation."

"Ma'am," he pointed out to her, "your husband doesn't exactly approve of me. You don't really think he'd go and gleefully share his, uh, wisdom of females with me?"

She smiled at his woebegone, helpless expression. "Everyone likes to be needed, Mr. Owen. Even gruff bears like Cooper J. Delaney."

Arch came away from Agatha grumbling about the promise she had somehow won from him to approach her husband. What was the fool woman trying to do? Get him to ask advice from a man who had been suspicious of him from the start, who didn't even like him?

He found Cooper out on the trail, examining in the twilight the marker the first section had left behind to indicate they had safely returned to the main trail. The wagon master, getting to his feet, reluctantly listened to his appeal.

"Let me get this straight," he growled when Arch had finished. "You're asking me to teach you to court Margaret Sheridan?"

"Well, yeah."

"You're out of your mind."

"I know. I guess that's what happens when a man is in love."

"It sure as hell is." He gazed at Archer for a long moment. "Owen, you are in a pitiful state. And I am about to make a serious mistake, but I never could stand to see a man suffer."

"So what do I do? Do I go and tell her I love her?"

"Sure, you could do that—if you want to lose her. You think she's going to believe a declaration like that at this point? Well, she won't. You have to *show* her you love her."

"How?"

"I don't know. Be inventive. Women respond to flowers and letters and poems, things like that. Shows them you know how to be sensitive and caring."

"I'll try those. First thing in the morning."

"No, you will not. You will hold back for a day

or two, get her to wondering. Then when you do make your move, it will be something small and simple but very attentive. And that's all you do. After that you walk away until the next time. Anything overwhelming, and she'll throw up a wall you'll never get through. You've got it take it slow, Owen. Slow and gentle. You understand me?''

Arch wasn't sure that he did, but he obeyed Cooper's advice. It drove him crazy, but for two days he carefully avoided any contact with Margaret, heightening his anticipation and, he hoped, her uncertainty.

On the third day the wagon train camped in a mountain meadow at Bear River. The place was a lush oasis. After securing his wagon, Arch went in search of wildflowers. He returned with an impressive armload of blooms that one of the women, who gave him a ribbon so he could tie them in a bouquet, told him were bellflowers.

Bouquet in hand, and carefully restraining his eagerness, he sought out Margaret. She was much stronger now. He found her helping Ella and Lizzie to prepare their evening meal. She looked startled when he presented the flowers to her.

''They're blue,'' he said.

''I can see that.''

''What I meant,'' he went on awkwardly, ''is that they're the color of your eyes.'' Damn. Was that too obvious? It probably was.

She regarded him suspiciously. ''What are they for?''

''Nothing special,'' he assured her casually. ''Just an offering to tell you I'm glad to see you on your feet again.''

She hadn't accepted the bouquet yet. She was still wary. "I'm not going to invite you to supper, Archer."

"Couldn't stay if you did. I accepted an invitation to eat with the Delaneys."

"Oh. Then in that case . . ." She took the flowers from him. "They're lovely. It was very thoughtful of you."

"Glad you're pleased. I'll say good night then."

With that he was gone, leaving Margaret to wonder what had just happened and why. When she disappeared into the wagon to look for a container for the bouquet, Ella and Lizzie examined the flowers.

"Not exactly roses in the moonlight, are they?" Ella observed.

"Well, I don't suppose they were meant to be romantic," Lizzie said.

"Uh-huh." Ella grinned at her friend, looking wise.

The following afternoon Arch went to the wagon master and handed him a sheet of paper over which he had labored for hours.

"What's this?" Cooper asked.

"A poem. Thought I'd have you look at it before I give it to her."

Cooper scanned the lines. "Lips like cherries? Skin like a ripe peach? A blush of sweet berries? She's a woman, man, not an orchard!"

"But it rhymes."

Cooper snorted and handed the paper back to him. "It's pathetic. You'd better try a love letter instead."

"I don't know what to say."

"You managed to create something for those wild

sermons of yours, didn't you? Work on it.''

Arch did, and by the time they reached Soda Springs he had written and delivered his letter to Meg. Ella and Lizzie had no qualms about sneaking a peek at its contents the moment Margaret's back was turned.

"He's no Shakespeare, is he?"

"Maybe not," Lizzie agreed, "but did you see how she sighed over it? Probably this line here about how much he admires her, even if he can never have her for his own. I don't know about *her,* Ellie, but he sure has me melting.''

"M'm, this is definitely getting interesting."

On the evening they camped at Steamboat Springs, the members of the caravan gathered around a central campfire to trade songs and stories. One of the men accompanied Arch on his mouth organ, and to Margaret's chagrin, and secret pleasure, he serenaded her with "Bonnie Bluebells," again in allusion to her eyes.

Then, knowing how much she enjoyed singing herself, even though her voice was an embarrassment, he urged her to join him in a duet of "Loch Lomond."

When they were finished, Lizzie leaned over and whispered to Ella, "Now *that's* love."

Ella nodded solemnly. "Has to be. When a man can put up with a voice like hers, there's no other explanation."

By now the whole caravan was aware that Archer Owen was steadfastly wooing Margaret Sheridan. They watched the campaign with fascination and amusement. Among the men there were wagers on how soon he would get her back into his tent.

Margaret, knowing Archer was deaf to argument, endured his siege, confident his attentions would stop when he realized she was never going to surrender to him. But on the day he gifted her with a beribboned box of taffy he'd paid one of the women to make, she realized this nonsense had gone far enough. She handed the box back to him.

"Don't you like taffy?" he asked, all innocence.

"I want you to stop playing these games with me. And don't you dare ask me *what* games. It's humiliating. The whole wagon train is laughing at us."

"It's only a box of taffy, Meg."

"And only a bouquet of flowers, or a sentimental letter, or a sweet ballad under the stars. Don't you think I know what you're trying to do? Well, it's not going to work. I'm not going to fall into your arms, because I don't—"

"Yeah, I remember. You don't love me. You love Enoch Rawlins. You're going back to Enoch Rawlins. You're going to make Enoch Rawlins a good wife."

"That's right. So you can just forget about all these little attentions you've been paying me."

"You don't care for them, huh?"

"I do not."

But the problem was, she did enjoy them. Enjoyed them far too much, and that only complicated the problem, because nothing had changed. Archer was still not right for her. He was still a condemned man without a future.

Then why did she persist in finding him so wildly alluring? And why was she beginning to seriously question his guilt? Maybe because he was so earnest about proving his innocence. He never missed an opportunity along the trail to make inquiries about her brother and his mysterious companion.

All right, she hoped he did clear himself. She was even ready to forgive him for abducting her and then taking advantage of her in her amnesia. But in all other respects they were worlds apart. Which was why she should have been nothing but relieved when he ended their exchange politely. "Well, maybe if I ever get myself out of this mess and back to Missouri, you'll invite me to your wedding."

She wasn't relieved, though. She was irritated by what suddenly seemed like indifference from him. And when he turned and walked away without another word, the box of taffy tucked under his arm, she was downright angry. And that didn't make any sense either.

Arch went straight to Cooper to report the discouraging outcome of his latest maneuver.

"I've been doing everything you suggested to wear her down, only it's not happening."

"You been careful to never argue your suit with her?"

"Not a word."

"How about mentions of any, uh, past bliss the two of you might have experienced?"

"Been silent about it."

That had been a tough one, Arch thought. Every time he encountered Meg he longed to remind her of those long, rapturous sessions they had shared. Not that he figured she could possibly forget them. They had been too good together. He sure as hell knew he'd never forget them.

That was what was killing him. Being near her all the time and not being able to touch her. Just thinking of those sweet breasts of hers in his mouth and those long, silky legs wrapped around him made him hard.

Cooper must have been aware of his deep frustration, and the reason for it. He chuckled and then cautioned him, "Patience, boy. You'll get there."

Arch hoped so. If something didn't develop soon, it could be too late. Every day he looked to the east, fearing the sight of a dust cloud on the trail that would indicate the arrival of Rawlins. If that happened before he had a chance to win Meg, he didn't know what he was going to do. Probably, to start with, change the shape of Rawlins's nose with his knuckles. Damn it, Meg belonged to *him*. Why couldn't she see that?

"So what do I try next?" Arch pleaded.

"You don't," the other man said. "You're going to relax and have a good time. You're going to enjoy yourself."

"Huh?"

"Hey, Aggie," Cooper called to his wife, who was gently patting their son's back after his current feeding, "we should be reaching Ft. Hall by tomorrow."

"Always a welcome sight."

"Think the wagon train should celebrate."

"But, my love, our arrival at Ft. Hall has never been the occasion of a celebration before."

"Think it should be this time."

Agatha eyed the two men thoughtfully, then nodded slowly. "Yes, I believe you are right. A dance in the evening, would you say?"

Cooper nodded. "Yeah, a dance would be good."

Chapter Fifteen

Margaret, wearing her blue muslin party dress, sat between Lizzie and Ella and glared at the dancers out in the broad circle formed by the wagons. Or more correctly, she glared at the tall figure of Archer Owen swinging his latest partner around the hard-packed ground that served as a floor. The woman, face flushed, eyes shining, was practically drooling as she gazed up at his rugged, smiling face.

"He sure is having hisself a good time, isn't he?" Lizzie said.

To the point of being ridiculous about it, Margaret thought sourly, but she refrained from saying so. Archer was the delight of the party, clapping his hands between steps in time to the fiddles sawing out a lively "Turkey in the Straw," then enthusiastically whirling his partner into the next measure. This was not the behavior of a glowering Deke Carver who had refused to participate in the Fourth of July dance.

"Yeah," Ella said, "and so are the women lining up to dance with him."

They were sickening, Margaret thought. Practically clawing each other in their eagerness to be his partner. I suppose it's because they know now he's a bachelor, that we were never married. She refused to believe it had anything to do with his brawny good looks or that silly frock coat that accentuated the breadth of his shoulders and the narrowness of his hips.

"Funny, though," Lizzie said to Margaret, "that he ain't come anywhere near you all evening."

Idle comment or not, Margaret knew that both women were avidly watching her, waiting for her reaction. She preserved her silence.

Oh, she knew what was happening, all right. Archer was deliberately staying away from her while he paid attention to every other woman on the caravan. It was a strategy meant to make her jealous. She had no trouble recognizing it. Not when she had used that same technique herself at the Fourth of July celebration. He was a fool if he thought it would work on her. That was what common sense told her, but her emotions didn't seem to want to listen to reason. They had her sitting there fuming. It was maddening.

There were far more women on the caravan than men, but Margaret wouldn't have lacked for partners of her own. The low-cut blue muslin alone would have guaranteed that. But she had chosen to remain with Ella and Lizzie. As much as she had always enjoyed dancing, she felt too flat this evening to make the effort.

However, she had a reason not to turn down Cooper's invitation when he urged her to join him in a waltz. She lost no time in expressing it as they wove among the other dancers.

"I am disappointed in you, wagon master."

"How's that, ma'am?"

"You've gone over to the enemy."

"Oh?"

"Not only have you gone over to him, but you are helping him."

"Is that so?"

"Yes, it is so. You're responsible for this evening, and you're responsible for the antics of Archer Owen. The two of you are a pair of rascals. Don't deny it. One of the women overheard you instructing your pupil and told Ella."

"Well, you hear all kinds of rumors on a wagon train."

"Are you laughing at me, wagon master?"

"He'd better not," warned a voice just behind her. As familiar as it was, it caught her off guard, its deep, mellow cadence like a warm caress. "I wouldn't tolerate that, Delaney."

Cooper came to a halt as Archer moved up beside them. "I meant no offense, Owen."

"Maybe, but just to make sure of that, you'd better let me finish this waltz for you."

"Think you're right," Cooper said, releasing her.

Trapped, Meg thought. I went and let these two schemers trap me out here.

Cooper turned and drifted away through the crowd, abandoning her to Archer, who faced her with open arms. She refused to step into them.

"Everybody is looking at us, Meg," he challenged her. "They're waiting to see if you're too scared to dance with me."

Damn him, he was giving her no choice. She permitted herself to be gathered into his arms and swept around the floor.

"You and that man have made a spectacle of me," she muttered.

"You're a sensation in that dress, precious."

"Did you hear me?"

"Just like you were the night of the Fourth. Remember that night?"

"I don't want to be reminded. And stop staring at me like that." His eyes were devouring her.

"You afraid to remember how it was with us that night?"

"Yes. No. I—I don't know."

"We danced just like this. Then we went back to our tent." He leaned forward until his mouth was close to her ear, his voice slow and silky. "And we made magic together in that tent. I didn't forget. You haven't, either."

"I've danced enough. I want to leave the floor."

To her surprise he obliged her. Arms still around her, he waltzed her through the other couples and off to the edge of the circle. Then she realized he hadn't returned her to Lizzie and Ella.

"Where are you taking me?" she demanded as he drew her between a pair of wagons.

She found herself in the stillness of the deep shadows cast by the fort's high stockade walls. He hadn't answered her. She tugged at his hand clasping hers. "Take me back."

"I will," he murmured.

"Now."

"In a minute." Turning her around so that she was facing him, he pulled her into his arms.

"Archer—"

"There's something I want to tell you first. And I want to be holding you when I do."

"I don't want to listen to anything you have to tell me. It's all lies, anyway."

"Only when it had to be, Meg. But tonight I'm being honest," he promised her solemnly. "More honest than I've ever been about anything in my life."

She caught her breath, sensing what he was about to say. Half of her feared to hear it, the other half welcomed it with a traitorous joy.

"What—what is it?" she whispered.

"Back in the canyon I insisted you couldn't marry Enoch Rawlins because you loved me. I'm still convinced that's true, even if you can't admit it. What I didn't know then, was maybe too scared to know, was how much *I* loved *you*. I'm not scared now, Meg. I'm here with my arms around you, and I'm saying it slowly and carefully so that whatever happens, you won't forget it. Because I want you to remember this for the rest of your life. *I am in love with you, Meg Sheridan, and I expect to go to my grave loving you.*"

313

There was a tense silence between them. She was only dimly conscious of the fiddles playing another waltz. The music and the dancers seemed very far away. It was too dark for her to see Archer's face. She couldn't read his expression to know if he meant what he was saying. But then she didn't have to search those amber eyes of his. Not when she could feel his every emotion in the way he held her so earnestly. She could almost hear the eager thumping of his heart in that powerful chest.

"Meg?" There was concern in his voice. She hadn't responded. Her silence must have him fearing the worst.

"Let me go," she commanded.

With a long sigh of disappointment, he released her. She was free now. Free to lift her hands to frame his lean face on either side. Stretching up to meet him, she drew his mouth down to her own, and she kissed him. Whatever the consequences, she kissed him deeply and recklessly as he responded with surprise and delight.

All sanity vanished, defeated by pure emotion. Her senses had control now, gorging themselves on the heat and hardness of his rangy body, the clean, masculine scent of him, the flavor of his tongue and breath blending with her own. There was sound, too. The sound of a lusty growl low in his throat as he took charge of the kiss, his arms winding around her again, his mouth tender and forceful at the same time.

Margaret rejoiced in his embrace, submerged herself in his need that matched her own. She made no objection when, still kissing her, he lifted her up into his arms and carried her off into the darkness.

"Where are we going?" she asked him as his mouth finally permitted her a breathless pause.

"To the tent. I set it up behind the fort where we could be private."

"Sure of yourself, weren't you?"

"Hopeful."

She knew that where they were going and what they would do when they got there would be no secret to the rest of the caravan once it was realized they had disappeared into the shadows. She didn't care. Not tonight. Not after Archer's compelling confession to her.

Freshly laundered bedding was waiting for them inside the snugness of the tent. Yes, she thought as he placed her on it, he was very sure of himself. And she didn't mind that, either. She was glad of his confidence as he helped her to shed her clothes, then guided her hands into helping him remove his own.

When they were both naked, they stretched out on the pallet side by side. With eager hands they reached for each other in a feverish exchange of intimate caresses.

The darkness of the tent made them blind. Margaret had to touch him everywhere in her need to discover his superb body all over again. Her fingers renewed their familiarity with the planes and angles of his face, then moved downward over his hard shoulders and hair-roughened chest, learning the heat and textures of him. She remembered all of his sensitive places and how, when she made contact with them, he would emit little groans of satisfaction.

"There," he rasped when her hand trailed across his quivering belly.

"That's it," he gasped when she stroked his muscular thighs.

"And here," he pleaded, carrying her hand to his engorged shaft.

He went a little wild when she squeezed him there, and suddenly he was all over her with wet kisses and skillful hands that sent tremors coursing through every part of her body. His mouth settled finally on her breasts, where he inhaled her rigid buds, tongue swirling around them, tasting and taunting.

Margaret heaved against him, her tormented flesh begging for their union. She thought this was his intention when he parted her legs, and was mystified when he slid down her body until his head was level with her thighs.

"What's happening?" she whispered.

"Something you'll like," he promised.

She was shocked when he buried his face in the downy mound between her thighs. This had never happened before!

Nor this! she thought, jolted by the sensation of his tongue seeking and finding the nub that governed her pleasure. What happened next was both torture and delight as his probing tongue lifted her into a mindless state of rapture.

Her fingers raked through his thick lion's mane, her body bucking and twisting as if to throw him off. And all the while there was a roaring in her ears that built to a scream until finally, sobbing aloud, she was carried over the edge.

The exquisite spasms were still rocking her body when Archer, levering himself over her, entered her with with one long, deep thrust. The experience of being joined to him at such a powerful moment was incredible.

"You all right?" he murmured, a smile in his voice as he rested inside her.

She couldn't find a breath to answer him. All she could manage was to pull his face down to her own. Her mouth found his in the blackness, lavishing him with grateful kisses.

The restraint must have been awful for him. But he permitted her as long an interval of recovery as he could endure. Then, inflamed by the tightness that gripped him, he began to move, his rhythms slow and measured at first, then increasing in tempo and potency.

In disbelief Margaret found herself climbing the pinnacle with him. Was it possible for her to peak again so soon? But this man was teaching her what her own body was capable of, secrets she'd never learned about herself before. And here was another wondrous lesson from him, because within seconds she was soaring again. Archer was right behind her, winning his own long-denied release.

Afterwards, content in his arms, she listened to the muted sound of the fiddles on the other side of the fort. They were playing "Greensleeves." In the distance a coyote barked.

She and Archer were silent. He had expressed his love for her tonight. He hadn't asked for any answer from her, though he must be hoping for one. Margaret couldn't provide him with what he wanted to hear. She was still struggling with uncertainty.

And why, she wondered restlessly, had she never

realized before how sad a melody "Greensleeves" was?

Ft. Hall was several days behind them when the caravan camped beside the Raft River. It was a warm afternoon. Many of the women were busy doing laundry on the banks of the stream. Most of the men, including Archer and Cooper, were in the hills cutting trees. To Margaret the river was aptly named. They were going to have to build rafts to carry the wagons across it.

She was on her way to join the other women with her basket of wash when one of the young guards, always alert for an attack, raised a cry.

"Riders coming in on the trail from the east!"

Shading her eyes, Margaret gazed in the direction he indicated. She couldn't make out much more than a cloud of dust. Was this trouble on the way?

"It's all right," the guard said, lowering his rifle but keeping it ready. "Just two of 'em, and they ain't Indians."

Which didn't mean anything, she thought. The Indians weren't always unfriendly, and there were plenty of white men who could be hostile. But she was prepared to accept his assurance and continue on her way to the river. Then, as the two men on horseback approached, she stopped. There was something distinctly familiar about one of them.

She waited until they rode into camp. The younger one, with the long hair and buckskins of a mountain man, swiftly dismounted. As he went to help his companion, who was almost falling off his horse in his weariness, Margaret gave a little cry of stunned recognition. Dropping the basket, she ran forward.

By the time she reached them, Enoch had managed to slide off his mount and was being supported by the young mountain man. He looked ready to collapse, but he summoned a smile for her.

"I hate for your first sight of me to be this," he apologized.

Margaret had a score of questions to ask, but they would have to wait. "You're unwell!"

He shook his head. "I'll recover, my dear. This isn't the first time the wilderness has disagreed with me."

She turned appealingly to the younger man. "Can you help him to the wagon over there? He needs to lie down."

She raced on ahead, explaining her need to Lizzie, who had just returned from the river. Together the two women quickly prepared a bed in the shade. The mountain man lowered Enoch onto it, explaining to Margaret, "He weren't that strong when we left Ft. Laramie, and time we got to Ft. Hall, it was all he could do to sit his saddle. But he would push on. Guess I never should've agreed to guide him, exceptin' he paid so well. Ma'am, would you have something to eat? It's been a long day."

"I'll feed him," Lizzie offered.

The two of them went off to the fire, leaving Margaret kneeling beside Enoch. His eyes had been closed, but he opened them when she leaned over to check on him.

"Don't look so worried, my dear. This is only temporary. I'll be on my feet again by tomorrow, and we'll celebrate our reunion."

319

"Enoch, what are you doing here?"

He reached for her hand, squeezing it. "I suppose I should have stayed at Ft. Laramie, but when Hank Shaw failed to return with you, I couldn't wait. I had to come myself. I had to be with you."

"I don't understand any of this. I thought you were back in St. Louis."

He looked astonished. "But the Delaneys knew I was at Ft. Laramie and why. Didn't they tell you?"

He struggled to sit up, and Margaret gently pushed him back down on the pallet. "It doesn't matter. We'll sort it out later. You just rest."

She stayed with him until he fell asleep. Then, getting to her feet, she asked Lizzie to keep an eye on him. Her mind was churning as she marched off to the Delaney wagon. She found Agatha putting her son down for a nap.

"Yes, I have already heard," she said before Margaret could speak. "Mr. Rawlins has arrived. How is he faring?"

"He's exhausted. At least I hope that's all he's suffering. He told me you and the wagon master knew he was at Ft. Laramie."

"Yes, that is correct."

"But why did you keep that knowledge from me?"

"There were—reasons."

Margaret stared at her with a sudden suspicion. "Who else on the caravan knew Enoch was at Ft. Laramie? Did you tell Archer?"

Agatha shook her head. "He already knew."

"How?"

"The late Mr. Shaw mentioned it to him."

"And all this time he kept it from me." Margaret

was beginning to understand, and she was furious. "Archer asked you not to tell me, and you and Cooper agreed. That's what happened, isn't it?"

"Yes."

"You were wrong to do that! *Very* wrong!"

Agatha sighed. "I am afraid that is just what we were. But he was so very anxious for an opportunity to prove to you how worthy he is that—"

"He isn't worthy of anything but the noose that's waiting for him! He's a lying devil!"

Refusing to discuss it any further, Margaret went back to her own wagon. Enoch was awake again and eagerly waiting for her. He wanted to know what had happened to Shaw, and was shocked when she told him about the events in the canyon.

"But that's monstrous! I hired the man to rescue you, not to harm Owen. I never cared about anything except your welfare, Margaret."

She believed him. "And you crossed a continent to prove it."

"My dear, you mean everything to me. You must know that."

"I do now, Enoch."

She sat by his side the rest of the afternoon. He was asleep again just before sundown when she went out to meet the men returning from the hills. Her face must have registered her seething emotions because Arch, shouldering an axe and covered with wood chips and sweat, took one look at her and said grimly, "He's here, isn't he?"

She lifted her chin, her voice frigid. "Enoch and his guide rode into camp a few hours ago."

"And you're mad as hell. Meg, listen to me—"

"No! There will be no discussion about it. I've had enough of your dishonesty."

"I wasn't being dishonest with you that night at Ft. Hall. Doesn't that count for something?"

"Ft. Hall was just another lie to get me into bed with you. I can see that now."

Arch was suddenly angry, too. "What's it going to take to convince you I meant every word of that night? Do I have to take out my heart and let it bleed for you? Would that be enough?"

"I—I don't want to hear this. All I came to tell you is to stay away from me from now on. I don't want you anywhere near me or my wagon."

His eyes narrowed dangerously. "Is that so? Well, if you won't talk to me, maybe Rawlins will. Yeah, I think it's time he and I met. Where is he? At your wagon?"

Before she could stop him, Arch headed in the direction of her wagon. She ran after him, dragging at his sleeve. "I won't have Enoch bothered! He's not well!"

"What are you afraid of, Meg? That the two of us will end up slugging it out to see who gets you? Could be that's not a bad idea." Shaking her off, he strode on.

He hadn't understood what she tried to tell him. He was being stupidly possessive and jealous, listening only to that mean temper of his. If he hurt Enoch in his blind rage, she would see to it that he never went back to Saint Joseph. She would hang him herself here and now.

Margaret was close behind him when he reached the wagon. "Rawlins, where are you?" he roared.

Enoch lifted his head from the pallet, startled by the sight of the lean-faced man towering above him. Margaret went to him, murmuring quickly, "Archer Owen."

"Ah," Enoch said, and she heard his immediate understanding in that simple expression. "What can I do for you, Mr. Owen?"

She noticed that Arch, too, was surprised when he looked down and discovered the slight, dark-haired figure on the pallet. This fragile man was not the viper he had expected to confront. He suddenly didn't know what to say.

"What is it, Mr. Owen?" Enoch encouraged him. He struggled to sit up on the pallet.

Margaret, kneeling at his side, could see the effort it was costing him. Her eyes blazed at Archer. "I told you he wasn't well! Why can't you let him be?"

"It's all right, my dear," Enoch reassured her, then addressed himself again to Archer. "I think I know why you're here, Mr. Owen. It's because of Margaret, isn't it?"

Arch, awkward about the situation now but still determined, nodded. "I figure it's a subject that deserves to be settled, yeah."

"I see. Well, if you will be so good as to give me a day or so to recover my strength, then I will be happy to meet with you regarding the future of my bride."

Margaret was incensed by this typically masculine exchange. "I am not a territory for you to battle over! *I* will decide my future! Now go away, Archer Owen!"

He was left without a choice. She watched him

storm off in the direction of his own wagon. Then she turned her attention back to the man on the pallet. "I forbid you to meet with him, Enoch. There is nothing to settle about my future. I have done that already."

She hadn't until this moment. Since Ft. Hall she had been struggling with indecision, wondering to whom she really belonged. Archer, who claimed to love her? Enoch, who represented security? Her emotions had been in turmoil over that question. Archer confused her, tormented her senses by his very existence. But now she knew. Whatever longings he aroused in her, whatever unacknowledged feelings she might have for him, she couldn't trust Archer Owen.

She had made her choice. And was irritated that she was close to tears over it.

Enoch recuperated on a bed inside the wagon when the caravan moved on. As a rule, no one rode or slept inside the wagons. The space, crammed with supplies and gear, was too precious to permit it. But Margaret insisted on making room for his bedding.

She spent all of her spare time caring for him. And every day she renewed her conviction that he was right for her. He had traveled hundreds of miles to find her, risked his health and his business back in St. Louis to be with her. He must love her very deeply. And didn't he prove it with the discussions they had as he slowly recovered his strength?

"My dear," he assured her, "you don't have to try to explain Owen to me. I don't care to know what might have been between you. It's all in the past. *We* are all that matter now."

She was touched by his trust in her. There were other demonstrations of his caring.

"We've come too far to turn back," he said to her one morning. "Much better to go on to Ft. Vancouver with the caravan. I was talking to the wagon master. He told me there are often ships at the fort. I think we should arrange to sail home. The voyage would be a long one, but I don't care to struggle with the overland trail again."

That was when she told him about Molly and how she couldn't bear to leave her behind in Oregon. "I came to love her, Enoch. I can't give her up. I *won't* give her up."

She was relieved when he smiled and patted her hand. "Then I will love her, too. We'll arrange to adopt her, raise her as our daughter."

On another occasion he spoke longingly of St. Louis and their future there. "Once we're home we'll be married and resume our lives. You'll be able to put this whole ordeal behind you."

There was something about his confident plan that alarmed her. She had to make him understand. "Enoch, I can't go back and simply pick up where I left off. If I'm to be your wife, there will have to be changes in what you expect of me because *I've* changed."

He looked puzzled. "What changes, my dear?"

"I—I'm not certain about that yet." It was frustrating. Everything had been so clear and straightforward before Archer had abducted her and put them on this wagon train. All she had desired was a traditional marriage to Enoch Rawlins and lifelong security. She still wanted those, but they were no longer enough.

"I just know," she told Enoch, "that I have to be more now than an ornamental wife. I need to be useful, to matter. I haven't decided in what capacity, but I think I'll recognize it when it comes to me. Does any of this make sense?"

"Of course it does, and you know you'll have my support."

She wasn't sure that he did understand, but it didn't matter. The important thing was he didn't argue with her. He agreed with everything she proposed. Enoch would make her a perfect husband. So perfect she was convinced she would learn not to care that he didn't excite her senses.

It killed him watching the two of them together, but Archer stayed away from them. Meg was so fiercely protective of Rawlins that, even if he had dared to approach the man again, she would probably accuse him of assault. And with his past, the Delaneys might decide to physically restrain him until Ft. Vancouver.

Arch would have risked it anyway, had he figured he stood a chance of still winning her. But how could he challenge a man who was frail because he'd sacrificed his health for Meg, traveled halfway across a continent to get her back? Arch was the villain now, Rawlins the hero. Her sympathies were all for Rawlins, and Arch had the feeling that the little bastard wasn't wasting an opportunity to play on every one of them.

Yeah, there was something not altogether genuine about Rawlins, but Meg wouldn't have listened to any warning from Arch. She didn't want him anywhere near her. Arch had gambled to make her his, and he had lost. He was miserable.

But neither he, nor any other member of the caravan, had time to worry about anything but survival after they crossed the Snake River. The rigors of the trek demanded the full attentions and efforts of every man and woman, for they had reached the most brutal portion of the trail. As the summer waned, they traveled over a scorched wasteland where water was scarce and the only vegetation was the endless sage.

The only thing that heartened them on this long, punishing crossing was the regular signs along the trail that the first section of the train had safely passed this way.

There was little relief once the dry badlands were behind them, because now they dealt with a grueling climb through the rugged Blue Mountains where the aspens were turning to gold.

It was with joy that the emigrants sighted the Columbia River many weeks later. They were in the Oregon now that they had all heard about, a lush, green land of towering firs and majestic mountains. The terminus of the trail at Ft. Vancouver was almost theirs. For most of them it meant the hope of a new beginning. For Archer it meant either that or the end of everything.

Chapter Sixteen

"A steamboat! A steamboat right here in the wilderness!"

Archer couldn't believe his eyes. The sleek little stern-wheeler was berthed in an inlet within sight of Ft. Vancouver. He eyed it with excitement from the bow of the flatboat that led a flotilla of similar craft carrying the emigrants and their wagons. With a trail yet to be cut through the difficult terrain east of the fort, it was necessary to travel by commercial ferries down the Columbia River on the last leg of their journey.

Nothing but the sight of a steamboat could seize

Arch's emotions in this moment when he was so near to what he had been seeking for months. He thought longingly of his cherished *Missouri Belle* back in Saint Joseph as they glided past the inlet.

Cooper, who stood beside him, chuckled at Arch's astonished discovery of the stern-wheeler. "No, it's not a mirage. She's the *Genevieve*. The Hudson's Bay Company sent her over from London. McLoughlin despises her." Arch had already been told that Dr. John McLoughlin was the chief factor of Ft. Vancouver. "Doesn't know what to do with a steamboat, so he just lets the *Genevieve* ride there in the inlet. She's nothing more than a storehouse for his collection of Indian artifacts."

"But that's criminal! She could be serving the settlements!"

"Tell McLoughlin that." Cooper's voice sobered. "I'll have to turn you over to him when we land, Owen. You know I have no choice about that."

"But not before I speak to Trace Sheridan," Archer pleaded. He'd learned from one of the ferryman that Meg's brother and his traveling companion had been delivered to the fort and, as far as the man knew, were still there. "Promise me that much, Delaney."

"The factor will have to decide that. Don't worry. He's a reasonable man, and I'll do what I can on your behalf."

That was all Archer could hope for. He turned his attention back to their approaching destination. Ft. Vancouver was a thriving place, its economy dependent on the profitable fur trade. The stockaded walls embraced a number of log buildings, but there were even more structures scattered outside the walls. The sprawling community was perched on the banks of the broad Columbia River opposite the mouth of the Willamette River, whose fertile valley was the lure that brought Eastern settlers to the region in increasing numbers.

But Arch wasn't interested in that, or the two oceangoing sailing ships moored to the wharf, as they neared the landing. His whole focus was on what waited for him inside the fort. This was it! He either cleared himself today, or he faced the gallows again.

He did spare one glance for the flatboat just behind their own boat. Meg and Rawlins were on that craft. She was still avoiding Arch, and made certain that, whenever possible, they traveled apart. He could see her dark hair, remembered how he had sifted his fingers through its silky mass. The image made him ache. But what was the use of yearning for what he couldn't have?

Cooper nudged him. "McLoughlin," he said, indicating a commanding figure with a tall frame and flowing white hair.

The chief factor had emerged from the fort to meet the arriving emigrants. Archer, his gaze fastened on him as their flatboat pulled to the landing, found himself praying that Dr. John McLoughlin would listen to him. It was all he had.

Enoch stayed behind at the flatboat to supervise the unloading of their belongings and to make inquiries about the ships. Margaret, eager to be reunited with Molly, went on into the fort.

As she passed through its open gates, she had a glimpse of Archer's tall figure on the other side of the immense, open rectangle. He was speaking earnestly to the two men who accompanied him, Cooper Delaney and the chief factor. Then the three of them disappeared into one of the many buildings.

Archer's fate was in the hands of other people now. She refused to think about him. She would go out of her mind if she started to think about him.

Molly. Where would she find Molly? There were all sorts of people, most of them male, bustling around the quadrangle, but she recognized no one from the first section of the wagon train. She was about to question a logger headed for the gate when she was startled by a loud whoop of joy.

A gaunt, awkward scarecrow burst from the doorway of a long, low building at the side of the yard. He wore an oversized apron that exploded with color, and waved a wooden spoon with a flourish. They raced toward each other, and met in a fierce embrace.

"Love, love," Toby squealed, "I was giving you one more day to get here, and then I was starting back east to look for you. Let me see me what the trail has done to you." He held her at arm's length, his long head tipped to one side as he considered her. "My, my, we have changed some, haven't we?"

Margaret laughed. "I know, blisters and freckles."

"No, it's not that. You've become—dare I say it?—your own woman."

"Have I?"

"You have. I can see it in your eyes. And what do we have to thank for that?" One of his eyebrows quirked. "Or should I say who?"

She knew he was referring to Archer, and she didn't want to go into that. "Toby, it's a long story, and I'll tell you everything later. But right now I'd like to see Molly. Is she well? Where is she?''

''Blooming, and she's in my kitchen.''

''*Your* kitchen?'' she asked him as he led her toward the building from which he had emerged.

''Temporarily, anyway. Would you believe it, love? I'm cooking for Dr. McLoughlin's staff, wages and everything, and my meals have been a sensation. They all swear to it. I shall miss it when the regular cook returns. The wretch has gone up the Willamette somewhere to get married. This way.''

They entered the building, passed through a dining hall, and reached a spacious kitchen equipped with a great black cookstove. A blanket was spread on the scrubbed pine floor. Seated cross-legged on it was a slim Indian girl playing with Molly. The girl smiled shyly at her as Margaret knelt beside the baby.

''She's gotten so big!'' Margaret exclaimed, marveling at how much Molly had changed.

''They do that, love. Has two teeth now, she does.''

''And I missed sharing them.''

''Not to weep. She hasn't taken her first steps yet, so you shan't miss that.''

''I'm afraid she doesn't remember me. It's Mama, darling.'' Margaret held her arms out to the baby and waited. Molly hesitated for a moment, then crawled into them. Margaret scooped her up into her arms and held her joyfully. ''Mama missed you so much, sweetheart.''

The Indian girl watched their reunion with interest. Margaret smiled at her over Molly's head. ''Thank you for looking after her. Both of you.''

Toby introduced them. ''This is Little Alice. An

angel who assists me in the kitchen. I'm teaching her how to make exquisite pastries.''

Little Alice got to her feet. ''Shall I set the tables now, love?'' she asked.

''If you would, love.''

Margaret was amused as Little Alice went off to the dining hall. ''Learning some other things from you, too, isn't she?''

''She's a Chinook,'' he explained. His rawboned figure had moved to the stove, where he stirred something with the wooden spoon he still brandished. ''They paint their canoes in the most gorgeous colors. I adore the Chinook people.'' He frowned. ''With the exception, that is, of Geoduck and his woman, Big Alice.''

''Another Alice?''

''Mm, Little Alice's sister, and you wouldn't fancy they could be cut out of the same piece of cloth. Nothing sweet-tempered about Big Alice or Geoduck.'' He paused, glancing at Margaret as she rocked Molly gently. ''The two of them have gotten friendly with your brother and his partner.''

Margaret's head came up. ''Trace?'' In her concern for Molly she had forgotten about Trace being at Ft. Vancouver. ''Are he and his partner still here?''

''Little Alice told me this partner hired her sister and Geoduck to take him somewhere in their canoe, but your brother stayed behind. He's laid up with a bad leg in a little cabin outside the gates.''

Margaret suddenly felt guilty about Trace. ''I'd better see him.''

Toby took Molly from her and gave her directions to the cabin. The door behind which Archer and the other two men had disappeared remained closed as she crossed the quadrangle. She had no idea whether they were still behind it or already on their way to the cabin. She knew that Archer would make every effort to get to Trace.

Enoch was nowhere in sight when she came through the gates. She assumed he was still busy making arrangements about their passage on one of the ships. Following a path around the side of the fort, she reached the cabin Toby had described.

Its door was open to the sun and air. She stood on the threshold, gazing at the occupant of an armchair. He was alone in the room, his bandaged leg propped on a stool, his head on his chest as he dozed.

This was her twin. They had the same blue eyes, dark hair, and slender build. They shared similar features, though on Trace that full mouth and clefted chin were somehow softer, weaker. Maybe because they suited a woman more than a man. What they did not share were the same interests. They had never been close, never loved each other as brother and sister were supposed to love. Margaret knew this was her fault as much as Trace's. Was it too late to change all that?

Stirring on the chair, he opened his eyes and lifted his head. His gaze met hers. "Look who's here," he said softly. There was no surprise in his voice. She knew he must have heard, either from Toby or other members of the first section of the train, that she was coming.

"It's been a long time, Trace."

"It has at that." He studied her for a moment. There was the same expression on his face that Toby had worn earlier and almost the same words of discovery. "You've changed, Margaret. Grown up, haven't you?"

She feared that *he* hadn't. There was something in his careless smile that told her he was still immature, still self-centered. "I've been through a lot," she said.

"So I was told." He leaned sideways in the chair, trying to look behind her. There was anxiety on his face now.

He's wondering if Archer is with me, she thought. He's worried about that. Maybe even frightened. "I'm alone," she assured him. She didn't add that Archer Owen had come two thousand miles to catch up with him and wouldn't give up until he'd confronted him. But Trace might have already been told that.

"Come in," he invited her. "There's another chair here somewhere. I'd get up and look for it myself, but as you can see . . ." He indicated his injured leg.

Margaret found the chair in the shadows behind him. She dragged it up to the side of his armchair and perched on it. "What happened to your leg?"

"Just an accident. Heavy box toppled from a pile and fell against it when we were arriving on the flatboat. One of us, either Austin or me, bumped into it in our eagerness to get a glimpse of the fort."

"Austin?"

"My partner, Austin Pine. We came out to Oregon together."

"If he's your partner, why isn't he here taking care of you?"

"He didn't want to leave," Trace said, defending him. "But if he had stayed, we would have missed an opportunity to transact business with this Chinook village downriver that our contact, Geoduck, knows about.''

"To make your fortune?''

"That's right. Austin went to bargain with the village to supply us with furs in exchange for goods we'll bring them. There's a big profit to be made in furs.''

"Providing you can afford the goods to trade for them.''

"Oh, Austin is financing that part of it.''

Then why, Margaret wondered, does he need *you* as his partner? But she didn't say that. "And meanwhile your leg—''

"Will be just fine. It's already mending. A few days more, and I'll be walking instead of hobbling. Don't worry about me, Margaret. I've got a woman who comes in to take care of me, and there's a doctor at the fort who stops by to make sure the wound doesn't become infected.''

"All arranged for by the generous Mr. Pine, I presume.''

"Well, yes. He's my friend, isn't he?''

"I'm glad you have such a good friend, Trace. But there are other people who care about you. Do you realize you haven't asked me one question about your wife and son.''

He shifted in the chair, looking uncomfortable. "How are Hester and William?''

"They were fine when I last saw them, though probably missing you dreadfully by now.''

"Well, I do plan on going back to them, just as soon as—''

"Yes, I know. Just as soon as you make your fortune."

"Maybe you shouldn't wait for that, Sheridan," interrupted a familiar deep voice from the open doorway. "I'm kind of anxious that you go back now. Only this time, I'd like you to tell the truth to that court in Saint Joseph."

Trace's startled gaze swung in the direction of the doorway. Archer was standing there, Dr. McLoughlin and Cooper just behind him. The three men came on into the room and stood in front of the armchair. Trace eyed them nervously.

"Does that interest you, Sheridan?" Archer said. "Because it sure as hell interests me."

Margaret might not have been there. Archer didn't trouble to glance at her. His entire focus was on Trace. His face was as hard as his voice.

Trace, collecting himself, looked defiant. "I don't have to talk to this man. He's already had his trial and was convicted."

"And you wish like anything that I hadn't gotten away from that noose, that I was dead and buried so you could forget about me. Only I'm here instead, and I'm not going away until—"

"That's enough, Owen," the chief factor ordered him in his authoritative voice. "We agreed I would conduct this dialogue. Mr. Sheridan." He turned to Trace. "Mr. Delaney and I are here to bear witness to what is said."

Trace's expression became surly. "I have nothing to say. I said it all back in Saint Joseph. Why are you bothering me?"

"Because Mr. Owen has made a serious charge

337

against you, and he's crossed two thousand miles of wilderness to do it. I confess I am impressed enough by that to investigate the matter.''

Trace was indignant. "So now you're on his side?''

"I am impartial," McLoughlin insisted, "and you'd all do well to remember that. But in the interest of justice—''

"Why are we wasting all this time?" Archer said, interrupting him impatiently. "Ask him! Ask him what really happened that night at the hotel when Willis Hadley was murdered and robbed! Now that he doesn't have a whole town to cower behind, maybe he'll give us the truth!''

The chief factor scowled at him. "Owen, either you remain quiet or we don't proceed." He turned back to Trace. "Mr. Sheridan, I must ask you to search your conscience before you answer. Did you bear false witness against this man at his trial?''

Trace didn't hesitate with his reply, though Margaret noticed he refused to meet McLoughlin's direct gaze. "No, certainly not. I testified Archer Owen killed Willis Hadley, and I stick with it.''

Archer couldn't keep silent. "He's lying again! What about the little farm-implement salesman in the checkered pants, Sheridan? He was one of the players in the card game where Hadley won all that money from us. I hear he's your friend and partner now, that you came west with him. Where was Austin Pine that night?''

"I am not going to caution you again, Owen," the chief factor warned him. "Either you curb your tongue or I will ask the guard outside to step in here

338

and remove you." Again he addressed himself to Trace. "Is Austin Pine involved in this affair?"

"No. He never came anywhere near Willis Hadley that night."

"Then I will ask you one final time. Was your testimony at the trial an honest, complete one?"

"I said so, didn't I? Why would I have lied? What could I have possibly gained by it?"

Archer, unable to control himself, burst out, "That's the big question here, isn't it? Just how *did* you benefit?"

Trace's voice was almost a whine. "I won't tolerate any more of this. I've given you what you came for. Now go away. I'm a sick man. You can see I'm a sick man."

Archer, in his desperation, was dangerously angry at this point. "I'm not going to let you hide behind that either, Sheridan. You either tell the truth or—"

"Owen, no." It was Cooper this time who quietly intervened. "There's nothing more we can do. Come away."

"You're just going to let him get away with this?"

"Delaney is right," the chief factor said. "I am sorry, Owen, but unless something more develops, I must regard this matter as settled."

Archer exploded. "If you won't get the truth out of this lying little bastard, I will!"

Before either of the two men could stop him, he launched himself at Trace. The armchair in which Trace was seated overturned with the impact of the attack, clattering to the floor. Margaret, shocked by Arch's blind rage, watched in horror as he landed on top of her sprawled brother. His hands closed around

Trace's throat, ready to choke the truth out of him.

The struggle was a brief one. Cooper sprang forward, broke Archer's hold on Trace, and hauled him to his feet. "You fool! You've gone and made it worse for yourself!"

Trace sat up, rubbing his throat. "You can see for yourselves what he is! The man has a murderous temper! What other evidence do you need to lock him up?"

The chief factor, who had called in the armed guard who'd accompanied them, made his decision. "You leave me no choice, Owen. I order you confined to the Ft. Vancouver jail until arrangements can be made to have you transported back to Missouri."

Archer, subdued now, said nothing. This time he spared a single, fleeting glance for Margaret, a look she was unable to define. Regret? Remorse? Or simply an empty bitterness? Whatever it was, it made her heart ache as she watched him being led out of the cabin, Dr. McLoughlin and the guard on either side of him.

Only Cooper remained. He expressed his concern for Trace. "Are you all right, Sheridan?"

"Just go away."

Margaret, meeting Cooper's gaze, nodded. Cooper understood and left the cabin. She righted the chair and knelt on the floor to help her brother up.

"Your leg. Did he make it worse?"

Trace pushed her away. "I don't need you, either." He managed to get to his feet and ease himself back into the armchair. "The damn leg is all right."

"Trace—"

"You, too. Go away. I've had enough." There was a brooding look on his face.

"I'll come by later."

He didn't answer her. Margaret left the cabin, feeling sick over what had happened there. She knew she ought to go and find Enoch, take him to meet Molly. But her steps turned in another direction.

She had a sudden need to be in the company of another female. A woman who would understand that, less than an hour ago, she'd been clear and certain about her intentions, had known exactly what she wanted for herself and Molly, and now was nothing but confused. There was only one woman who could provide her with the sympathy and gentle advice she longed for in this moment. That was why she was on her way to see Agatha Delaney.

The Delaney log cabin sat in a grove of tall hemlocks beside the river. Someone on the flatboat had pointed it out to Margaret just before their arrival at the landing. She had no trouble finding it. The track along the riverbank brought her straight to its front door.

The place had a cozy, friendly look. There were flowers in the yard and shutters at the windows painted a soft, cheerful blue.

Agatha answered her knock with a smile of welcome. "Margaret! What a nice surprise."

"I was just admiring your home. You and Cooper have made it very special."

"Thank you, but this is not our regular home, you know. Our headquarters are at our ranch up the Willamette. But we seemed to spend so much time coming and going from Ft. Vancouver that Cooper finally

341

built us this cabin. We are very fortunate to have it. With so many new arrivals in the area, it is difficult to secure comfortable accommodations at the fort, and after months on the trail . . ." She broke off, sensing Margaret was troubled. "But this is not a social call, is it? You would not be here so soon after our arrival if it were."

Agatha stepped aside in the doorway, inviting her to enter. Margaret found herself in a simply furnished but attractive room. There was a stone fireplace, and a cradle sat near its hearth. A young half-breed woman seated beside it was leaning over to admire its sleeping occupant, Matthew Delaney. There was a wistful smile on her mouth. But when she looked up, Margaret was startled to see that she had been weeping. Margaret felt she was intruding on something obviously emotional.

"You already have a visitor," she apologized. "I shouldn't have come."

"Nonsense," Agatha reassured her. "Magpie does not mind."

The young woman wiped her eyes and smiled at Margaret. "We all come to Miss Agatha with our cares."

Agatha chuckled. "I seem to have a gift for listening." She introduced the two women, explaining to Margaret, "Our friend Magpie came west with us on our first crossing."

"And now you live here at the settlement?" Margaret inquired politely.

Magpie shook her head. "My husband and I have a farm across the river. But when the flatboats appeared with your wagons, I came at once in the canoe.''

"Magpie was anxious for news," Agatha said. "Just as she is whenever we return to Oregon. And unhappily, though I make inquiries everywhere during our crossings, once again I was unable to tell her what she longs to hear."

Magpie explained for a puzzled Margaret. "I have a son out there somewhere. At least I pray he is still alive. Daniel was three years old when his father took him away and hid him from me."

"An awful man," Agatha added, "who died without telling us to whom he entrusted Daniel. That was several years ago, and since then we have searched everywhere without result."

"Do you have children?" Magpie asked Margaret.

"A baby girl whose parents died, but I love her as though she were my own."

Magpie nodded solemnly. "Then you understand what I feel."

Agatha put her arm around the young woman. "I made Magpie a promise long ago that I would not rest until Daniel was returned to her. Nor will I."

Magpie patted the older woman's hand with gratitude, then squared her shoulders. "And I don't give up hope. It's all I have. I must go now. My dear husband is patient, but he'll wonder what's keeping me."

Agatha started to see her to the door, and then stopped. "Wait. I nearly forgot to give it to you."

"What?"

"Something I had a clever artist paint for you before we left Independence." She disappeared into the bedroom, and returned a moment later bearing a miniature. "He executed two of them. I am keeping one to aid us in our search. But this one is yours."

Magpie accepted the small portrait, gasping with excitement and pleasure as she examined it. "It is Daniel! Daniel as I last saw him! But how could the artist paint his likeness?"

"I gave him a careful description, all the details you shared with me, and he worked his magic."

"*Wonderful* magic." Magpie proudly displayed the miniature for Margaret's approval. "You see? My son."

Margaret glanced at the portrait. "He's a very handsome little boy."

Magpie glowed over her compliment. She started to withdraw the miniature, but Margaret checked her. Something had just triggered her memory. "May I see it again?" Magpie obliged her, and this time Margaret looked at it carefully. "Yes, it is there. A mark on the side of his neck shaped like a crescent moon."

Magpie nodded. "Daniel's birthmark. Even this the artist included."

It was the insightful Agatha, gazing at Margaret's face, who realized that her comment about the birthmark was more than just a casual observation. "What is it, Margaret? What have you remembered?"

"I think," she said slowly, "that it's possible I may have seen your little boy."

Magpie, eyes wide, stared at her. "Where? When?"

Margaret described for them the episode in the canyon when the Cheyenne hunting party had saved Archer's life by killing the brutal Hank Shaw and his companion. "The child who was with the band was living like a Cheyenne," she said, "but he wasn't Cheyenne. He was more white than anything."

"And he resembled the portrait here?" Agatha pressed her.

"I think so. The same coloring, anyway, and probably the same basic features. It's hard to be sure because, of course, he was older than this likeness."

Agatha nodded. "And therefore changed some."

"But not the crescent-moon birthmark!" a trembling Magpie reminded them.

"Yes," Margaret said, "the boy in the canyon carried that identical mark on the side of his neck."

"Then it *was* Daniel!" the young woman cried, overcome with emotion. "I know it was Daniel! And he is with these fierce people!"

"He looked healthy and happy," Margaret tried to reassure her. "I had the impression Lone Wolf was fond of him, like a stern father looking out for his son. But other than to tell you that someone on the first section of the train remarked that this Cheyenne band was out of its usual territory, which means they may have moved on by now, this is all I know. I'm sorry. If only I'd realized . . ."

Magpie was shedding tears again, but they were joyful ones this time. "Oh, but you've already given me a beautiful gift! Just to know he's alive and well . . ."

Agatha added her own appreciation after Magpie departed a few minutes later. "You have made her a very happy woman, Margaret. Now that we have actual evidence of Daniel's survival, it renews the hope that one day our search will produce results so that

345

mother and son can be reunited.'' She angled her head in the familiar manner that meant she was being perceptive again. ''But I forget that you yourself are not a happy woman at this moment.''

Margaret's laugh was a painful one. ''Oh, Agatha, you must be so weary of all of us flocking to you with our woes.''

''When that happens, I will not hesitate to let you know. Now sit and speak.''

Margaret took the chair Agatha indicated, and told her what had happened in Trace's cabin.

''Which explains,'' Agatha said when she'd finished, ''why my husband is not yet here. He must still be with Dr. McLoughlin. But your brother . . . do you feel he could be lying?''

''I just don't know. Trace's ugly mood could be explained by guilt, I suppose. If somehow this is the chance he's always wanted to get rich, but it means he has to send a man to the gallows and he's dealing with that—'' She broke off, shaking her head. ''Only none of it makes sense.''

''And why is that?''

''Because there doesn't seem to be a reason for Trace to lie. He can't have profited in some way from the winnings that were taken from Willis Hadley when he was murdered. That can't be what's financing this fur venture. Archer himself admitted, when he shared the whole story with me back at the canyon, that the money had been planted in his room, and when he was arrested the court confiscated it.''

''No,'' Agatha agreed softly, ''it does not seem to make sense. Nor, I imagine, do your feelings make sense to you. Would I be wrong in thinking that you are deeply confused about Archer Owen?''

"I've promised myself to Enoch," Margaret insisted. "Anything else would be impossible. I *know* it would, but the thought of Archer and that noose waiting for him in Missouri . . .''

"Yes, it must all seem very hopeless to him now. He must be suffering greatly. Probably is sorely in need of comfort.''

Margaret stared at her. "You're not suggesting that I . . . no, I couldn't possbily visit him at the jail.''

"No, I suppose not. Still, it would be an opportunity for you to make absolutely certain that you have chosen the right man.''

"I can't go there! I just can't!''

She met Enoch on her way back to the fort.

"You had me worried, my dear. I couldn't imagine where you'd gotten to. Good news. I've settled our passage, but it means we have to sail this evening. Were you able to see your brother?''

"Yes, I saw Trace.''

He noticed the expression on her face. "What is it? Is something wrong?''

She repeated her story of what had happened at Trace's cabin. Enoch shook his head. "Unfortunate, but not surprising considering the man's temper.''

"Even so, I find it very hard now to believe Archer is capable of murder. And if he is guilty, why would he risk everything to prove he isn't?''

Enoch shrugged. "I suppose it's possible he was out of his mind with rage when he killed Hadley, perhaps doesn't remember the episode and therefore is convinced of his innocence.''

347

"Or that Trace *is* lying, and if my family is responsible for his false conviction—"

"My dear, you are hardly responsible for your brother's testimony, whatever it was."

"All the same, I'd feel much better if we could leave Archer with some shred of hope before we sail tonight. Enoch, you have so much influence back in Missouri. Couldn't you use it on Archer's behalf when we get home? You could urge the governor to— what is the word?—*commute* his execution to a prison sentence. If we could promise him that much . . ."

"Is it so important to you, Margaret? Is this man more to you than you led me to believe?"

"I'm marrying you, Enoch. I chose you for many reasons, not the least of which is your decency and sense of humanity."

He sighed. "Very well. You may inform Mr. Owen that I'll do what I can."

"Thank you, Enoch."

"By sending a message to him," he added. "I forbid you to try to go him in that jail."

"*Forbid* me, Enoch?"

He couldn't know it, but his unfortunate choice of word was a challenge she couldn't ignore.

Chapter Seventeen

He was locked in a cramped, dark cell in a building at one side of the fort's quadrangle. It reeked of its last occupant, a sour odor that seemed to emphasize the hopelessness of his situation.

The only light came from the small, barred window in the thick door reinforced with iron bands. It was from this opening that he heard his name whispered. Lifting his head from the cot on which he was stretched, he stared at the grille.

She called to him again. "Archer."

He rose from the cot and went to the door, gripping the stout bars of its window. She stood outside in the corridor, and the sight of her perfect face so close to his filled him with despair.

He'd been certain he had glimpsed her for the last time in Trace's cabin. To see her once more only made it worse. Now he would have the anguish of parting from her all over again.

"How did you get permission to come here? Did Cooper arrange—"

"No, it was Toby who managed it for me. He's on friendly terms with the jailer. The jailer is in love with his cooking. But I have to speak to you from out here, and I can only stay a few minutes."

"Why did you come? What do you want?" His tone was deliberately surly. He wanted her to go away. He couldn't bear it. Her presence was torture, a painful reminder that he would never realize his dream of being a husband and father, of running the *Missouri Belle* again on the free, sweetly flowing rivers.

"I—well, there's something I had to tell you. Something encouraging."

"What is it? Did your brother decide to—"

"No." She shook her head regretfully. "It's nothing to do with Trace. It's something Enoch has agreed to do on your behalf."

He listened while she told him about Rawlins's promise to urge the governor of Missouri to commute his execution to life imprisonment. He could see the disappointment on her face when he failed to express his relief.

"Very generous of your bridegroom," he said dryly, "but tell him to forget about it."

She was shocked. "You're choosing the noose over survival?"

"That's just what I'm doing," he said bitterly. "Do you think I want to spend the rest of my days rotting away in some filthy cell like this one? I'd rather die a sudden death than a slow one."

"You can't mean it!"

"Yes, I do mean it. But there is something you can do for me."

"What?"

"Get out of here. Take Molly and go back to St. Louis with Rawlins. Marry him and get on with the life you planned before I came along to spoil everything."

She didn't move. She stood there staring at him, and he could feel his insides turning over.

"What are you waiting for?" he said impatiently, eager for her to be gone before he did something foolish like breaking down in front of her.

"I have something to ask you," she said quietly.

"Well?"

"That night you said you loved me ... were you telling me the truth, or was it just another lie to get me into bed with you?"

Oh, sweet mother, she would ask him this! And though it killed him to deny her his love, though it was the hardest thing he would ever do, Arch knew he had to send her away believing he wasn't worth her grief. He didn't want her spending the rest of her life being haunted by something neither of them could ever have.

"It was a lie," he told her in a voice he hoped was convincingly cold and calculating. "Not just so you'd

351

sleep with me. I figured if I could make you fall in love with me, you'd be on my side when it came time to face your brother.''

"You were using me again?"

"Yeah, that's right."

"Then you were never in love with me."

"I never loved anything in my whole life except the *Missouri Belle*. Satisfied?"

"Yes."

The expression on her face was destroying him. He couldn't stand it. "What are you waiting for now?" he demanded.

"Archer—"

"Just go, damn it!"

She turned and walked slowly away down the corridor. Clutching the bars so tightly his knuckles ached, he watched her vanish around a corner. *Be happy back there in St. Louis, precious,* he called out to her silently. *Just be happy, will you?*

It had been a mistake to see him, Margaret thought, emerging onto the quadrangle. A foolish thing to do.

She could feel the tears threatening to slide down her cheeks, and she didn't know why. It wasn't as though she were in love with Archer Owen, even though she did care about him. This was just injured vanity, that's all.

But the thought of his death . . . she couldn't bear it!

Enoch was waiting for her when she came through the gates. He looked irritated. "Where did you disappear to this time? With so much to arrange for before we sail—" He stopped, gazing suspiciously into her face. "You went to visit Owen, didn't you?"

"Yes."

"And after I expressly—"

"You were right, Enoch. I shouldn't have gone. It did no good. He doesn't want to be saved from the rope. I'm sorry I didn't listen to you."

Softened by her apology, he was ready to forgive her. "Well, you tried. All you can do now, my dear, is to try to put it all behind you. A long voyage should help. I spoke to the ship's captain again. He is ready to marry us once we're at sea."

She was dismayed by his haste. "And not wait for a wedding in St. Louis?"

"I see no reason for delay. This offers us the opportunity to honeymoon on the voyage."

Yes, he was right. The sooner she was Enoch's wife, the safer she would be from regretting Archer Owen. She started to answer him, but she felt her gaze pulled in the direction of the inlet upriver where the little steamboat belonging to the fort was berthed. It reminded her of another steamboat, and though she knew her sudden intention was wildly impractical, she felt she had to attempt it.

"Enoch, I'll let the captain marry us, but may I ask for a wedding gift when we're back in Missouri?"

"My dear, of course I plan to present you with a wedding gift. What will it be? A piece of jewelry perhaps? A ring of your choice?"

She shook her head. "Nothing like that." She told him about the *Missouri Belle* waiting in Saint Joseph for its owner and captain who would never see it again. "That little stern-wheeler is the only thing Archer Owen has ever been able to call his own. It's all

353

he's ever trusted or loved. Enoch, if he could be assured that the *Missouri Belle* would be preserved by people who cared about it, I think when the time came for him to—'' She couldn't bring herself to name it. ''Well, I just think it would make it easier for him to face what's waiting for him.''

Enoch stared at her as though she'd taken leave of her senses. ''You're asking me to buy this—this steamboat of his from the authorities who've impounded it?''

''Is it so very unreasonable a request?''

''It is out of the question. What would you do with the thing?''

''Hire someone responsible to operate it. Keep it as a legacy for Molly. I think he'd like that.''

''No.''

''Enoch, please. I've parted from him, I'll never see him again. And if you'll just do this one last thing, I promise never to mention his name to you again.''

''Even if I were inclined to grant you your request, it isn't possible.''

''But why?''

He hesitated, then told her. ''Because the *Missouri Belle* no longer exists.''

She stared at him, feeling a little sick. ''Enoch, what have you done?''

''You might as well hear it now. You would probably have learned about it anyway once we're back home. I purchased the stern-wheeler from the people who had impounded it when I came to Saint Joseph looking for you. Purchased it and ordered it burned in the river. It's done. It can't be reversed.''

''How could you?'' she whispered.

"Why is it so hard to believe?" he said bitterly. "Archer Owen had taken from me what was mine. He deserved to be repaid for that."

"So you took what was his and destroyed it."

"Yes, and wished him destroyed along with it. It's a pity Shaw didn't manage to kill the devil when he had the chance."

"You assured me you'd hired that vicious brute only to rescue me, not to harm Archer. But that was a lie, wasn't it? All along you wanted him to kill Archer. That's what you intended, just as you did *not* intend to help Archer when we got back to Missouri, because that had to be another lie."

She looked at him, and she realized she had never known Enoch Rawlins. She had believed him to be gentle and kind, a man of ethics. Believed he had followed her west because he'd loved her, couldn't bear to lose her, when all along he'd been driven by nothing more than a vow to recover a possession that had been stolen from him. Ultimately, that was all she was to Enoch—a possession.

"Margaret, there is no time for this. We can discuss it in detail once we've sailed. There will be the opportunity then for me to convince you—"

"Of nothing. I won't be on that ship with you, Enoch, because I regard you as much more than a serious mistake. I regard you as a vindictive, mean-spirited man who would have made my life a misery if I had married him."

"You're being a fool, Margaret. How will you and the child live without me to support you?"

"Yes, there was a time when I needed your money, when I was frightened at the prospect of a future without it. Not anymore. I have all that's necessary now to make my own security.''

''How?'' he sneered.

''By relying on myself.''

''You'll fail!''

''I don't think so. I think I'll manage a very good living for myself and Molly. All I ever really lacked was confidence, and I acquired that on the trail. I wish you a good voyage, Enoch.''

Without a morsel of hesitation or regret, she turned her back on him and walked back through the gates of the fort. Once in the quadrangle again she stopped, jolted by a realization so powerful that her legs suddenly felt too weak to support her. Knowing she would collapse if she didn't sit down, she found a bench over against one wall. She settled on it, oblivious to all the individuals coming and going in the quadrangle as her mind seethed with a fresh discovery.

Dear God, how she could she have been so blind? As blind as when she had suffered amnesia. Because all along it had been right here in her heart, and she had refused to see it. Had been too anxious to safeguard a future with Enoch to acknowledge it. But now that she had shed that false promise of security, was no longer frightened of an existence without wealth, the truth was there like a glowing beacon. She was deeply, passionately in love with Archer Owen. What's more, whatever his self-sacrificing denials of a few moments ago, she was confident now that he genuinely loved her.

It terrified her to think that she had almost left this place without him. If she had sailed with Enoch, there was the certainty that sooner or later she would have realized her terrible error, but by then it would have been too late. She would have lost Archer, and the emptiness of her life without him would have haunted her the rest of her days.

Lose him? Oh, God, she *would* lose him if they sent him to the gallows for a murder he'd never committed. That she had ever questioned his innocence was unthinkable to her now, for of course he hadn't killed Willis Hadley. Not her Archer, with his loving nature under that tough exterior, his basic goodness that was incapable of taking a life. No, not even when his temper got the best of him. Never! But those in charge were convinced he was guilty, and unless she found a way to save him . . .

Trace. Trace was the key to everything. Whatever it took, she had to convince her brother to tell her the truth. He was her one hope. Her *only* hope. She had to go to Trace.

Margaret found him as she had left him earlier, seated in the armchair with his injured leg propped on a stool. This time he had a book in his lap. He had to be immensely bored if he was reading, she thought, because Trace seldom found entertainment in books.

He lifted his dark head from the pages when she entered the cabin, asking warily, "Come to say goodbye?"

"No." She told him about Enoch and how he was sailing without her.

"You're a fool, Margaret. You're giving up a man with a name and a fortune. People like us don't get along in this world without money and comfort."

"I'm not that kind of people anymore, Trace."

"No? Then why are you here?"

"Because I need you."

"For what?"

"To tell me the truth about that night Willis Hadley was killed."

He closed the book with a loud, impatient slap. "You're not going to start that again."

"I have to, Trace. It's the only way I can clear Archer Owen." He didn't answer her. She moved close to his chair and stood over him. "There's something about this partnership you have with your friend, Austin Pine, that's very odd. I've been thinking about it. How you left your wife and son and risked your life traveling hundreds of miles across the wilderness to trade for furs. How you claim the two of you are going to make a fortune in furs, even though neither one of you has any experience in the trade and even though the Hudson's Bay Company largely controls the fur traffic in this region. Don't you think that's odd, Trace?"

"I don't want to talk to you anymore, Margaret. I want you to leave."

"It's much bigger than furs, isn't it, Trace? It's something neither you nor Austin Pine could resist, something connected with Willis Hadley's death."

"Go away!"

"Whatever it is, your partner has gone to get it, hasn't he? Only, he's left you behind. Maybe he won't return when he has it. Maybe he'll keep it all for himself and disappear without you."

"No!"

She leaned over him. "If it was Austin Pine who

murdered Hadley, then you can't trust him, Trace. He'll betray you. It could be that he already has. Did you ever stop to consider that your leg wasn't an accident? That Pine deliberately knocked that box into you because you'd served your purpose, whatever it was, and he no longer needed you? That if you were laid up with an injury you couldn't accompany him?''

There was a wild, anguished look in Trace's eyes. "I didn't lie! I told the truth!''

"No, Trace, you did lie in court. You did it for some promise of wealth." She crouched down beside his chair and took his hand. "Twins or not, we were never alike, were we? Except in one way. You said it yourself. We wanted money, the luxuries we'd had and lost, only we didn't have what it took to earn them for ourselves.''

"That's not so!''

"It is so. But Trace, if I could find the way to believe in my own courage and abilities, so can you. I'll help you. I'll do whatever I can to enable you to reach inside yourself and make your own success. You have to, Trace, because I can see that what you did to Archer is eating you up inside. You won't be able to live with it.''

"Oh, God, let me alone, can't you?''

He tried to snatch his hand away, but she clung to it. "We're sister and brother, but we were never close. Twins who were like strangers. I'm to blame for that as much as you. But if you care for me at all, you'll help me. I love him, Trace. Archer means everything to me, and I can't bear to lose him. That's why I'm here on my knees. That's why I'm pleading with you. . . .''

Her session with Trace wrung every last bit of energy out of her. She was exhausted when she came away from the cabin a half hour later. Exhausted but on fire with excitement as she hurried back to the fort.

"If you'll forgive me saying so, love, you look a proper mess. Here. Dab."

Toby sympathetically handed her a clean dish towel, and Margaret applied it to her eyes. She knew they must be red and swollen from the tears that had had been streaming from them.

They were seated on high stools at the worktable in Toby's kitchen. Little Alice was in the next room putting Molly to bed for the evening. It was long after sundown. Margaret supposed the ship carrying Enoch must have sailed by now. Not that this in any way mattered to her. Even if it had, she would have been too busy dealing with her anger and frustration to think about it.

"You haven't swallowed so much as a morsel all day, have you?" Rolling his eyes, Toby tried again to urge a plate of food on her.

She shook her head. "Can't."

"It's not that hopeless."

"It is," she insisted, flinging down the dish towel in disgust. "Dr. McLoughlin is even more stubborn than Trace was. No matter how much I argued and pleaded with him, he refuses to release Archer. He doesn't trust him after witnessing his rage in the cabin. He says that Trace's confession now may be nothing more than an elaborate fiction to accommodate a desperate sister."

"Well, love," Toby observed, having already listened to the story she had poured out to him after she'd left the chief factor's quarters, "it is a fantastic tale."

"Not you, too!"

He held up both hands defensively. "Peace. Toby Snow is in your camp, remember?"

"But if *you* refuse to believe it, what chance do I have of—"

"Hold, hold. I am prepared to believe every incredible syllable of your brother's story. I only point out to you why the good doctor is unwilling to do so."

"When Austin Pine returns, he says. Then he'll look into the matter again, he says. Not before that, he says. But that's the infuriating part. If Trace is right about his knowledge, I'm convinced Pine won't come back here. Not once he's got his hands on what he came for."

"Yes," Toby sniffed, "a real pickle, isn't it?"

"Meanwhile, Archer has to remain in jail. He doesn't even know what's happening. Dr. McLoughlin won't let me see him again or send a message to him. He found out that I already visited Archer without his permission, and he's annoyed about that."

Toby sighed, got to his feet, and stretched his gangly frame. "Which, I fancy, leaves us with but one choice. We will have to go after this Pine chap ourselves and bring him back."

Margaret stared at him. "I would say you're joking, except I know that whenever you're this casual about a subject it means you're serious."

"Very true."

"But it isn't possible to catch up with him. Austin Pine left here—"

"Yesterday morning, I believe. Recall, however, that he is traveling by canoe, and it is a long way to the destination you described. And with any luck his progress is being slowed by the reluctance of Geoduck and Big Alice, who must not be anxious to go there since this is a forbidden place to Chinooks. That is what you said, isn't it?"

"Yes, but if we have to go by canoe ourselves—"

"Be sensible, love. Can you picture me paddling a canoe? We will be using a much faster object of transportation than that, which is precisely why we must break Archer out of jail. Not to mention that he has the strength to haul Pine back here to face the chief factor."

Margaret's head was swimming. "Toby, you're talking in riddles. What transportation? And how can we get Archer out of that cell?"

"You're not paying attention, love. The *Genevieve,* of course. And with the help of a late-night snack . . ."

Margaret and Toby huddled in the thick shadows in a corner of the deserted quadrangle. The fort was silent, all of its occupants asleep except for a lone sentry at the main gate.

It was an hour or so before daybreak. The sky was still black, without a hint of light, the air raw. Margaret shivered and hugged the shawl around her more tightly.

She suspected her chilled state had more to do with her nerves than the temperature. It was all this tense waiting. It felt as if they had been standing there for-ever, their gazes fixed on the dark building that housed the jail.

There was a risk in breaking the silence between them. Voices carried, and they didn't want to alert the sentry. But in the end Margaret could no longer stand it.

"What if he didn't eat them?" she whispered.

Toby was insulted. "*My* muffins?" he hissed back. "You're joking, of course. There is absolutely no way he could have resisted them."

"Yes, but . . ." She paused to get a better grip on the cumbersome rolled quilt she carried. "What if he decided to save them for his breakfast?"

"Impossible. He could hardly wait to get his chubby little fingers on them when I brought the plate to him. I promise you the greedy gut would have gob-bled every last crumb before crawling into bed."

"Then why is there no result yet? That was hours ago."

"Patience, love. This sort of thing takes time to work."

She made an effort to have patience. They went on watching the building where the jailer slept in the front room, behind which was Archer's cell. Margaret and Toby had themselves managed to catch a few hours of sleep in Toby's quarters, knowing they needed to be rested for the long ordeal ahead of them. Molly and Little Alice were still fast asleep in the kitchen building behind them. The young woman had promised to safeguard the child until they returned.

Margaret, eyeing the sky, was unable to hold her worried silence. "It's going to start getting light before long,'' she whispered again, ''and if something doesn't happen soon, it will be too late. Are you sure you put enough of those seeds into the batter?''

Toby made a sound of exasperation, which she felt sure was accompanied by the familiar rolling of his eyes. ''Love, I tell you again just what Gentle Wind told me when she shared her supply of goodies with me,'' he said, referring to the Lakota medicine woman he had met back at Ft. Laramie. ''A few of the seeds add a safe, lovely flavor. Too many of them, and there will be an unpleasant reaction involving a—ahem—lengthy session in the privy. Well, I dumped in the whole lot. Satisfied?''

''But if they made the muffins taste odd to him—''

''There!''

Toby clutched her arm in excitement. A light had flared in the window of the jail. Seconds later the door burst open, and the rotund figure of the jailer emerged bearing a lantern. Without pause he raced across the quadrangle in the direction of the privies on the other side, his nightshirt flapping around his bare legs.

Toby, unable to help himself, giggled. ''Oh, dear, such a terribly urgent look on his face.''

''Poor man. You should be ashamed of yourself. Which you can be later, because right now we need to move.''

The door to one of the privies had slammed behind the jailer. Margaret and Toby, hugging the shadows, sped around the perimeter of the quadrangle. She feared a challenge from the direction of the gates, but the sentry was more interested in checking the scene outside the stockade than the yard behind him.

Reaching the jailhouse door, they slipped inside. The jailer had left a candle burning. Toby used it to light a second candle, which he handed to Margaret.

"My, my," he said, lifting a key off its hook, "look what else he left behind in his haste. How very careless of him." He gave her the key and took up a post at the window. "You'll have to hurry, love. No telling how long his plump little backside will be parked on that seat over there."

Juggling the key, the candle, and the quilt, Margaret rushed along the corridor. She was relieved when she reached Archer's cell to find his lean face pressed against the grille of the door. She wouldn't have to waste precious seconds rousing him. He was astonished at the sight of her.

"Sweet mother, it's you! What's going on out there?"

"Your release," she said, managing to fit the key into the lock.

"Meg, no. There's nowhere for me to run, and when they find out you—"

"You're not escaping. You're coming back here with Willis Hadley's murderer."

"What in—"

"That's all you have to know. I'll explain the rest when we're out of the fort and on our way. Now stand back."

Though totally bemused, he obeyed her, backing away from the door. Turning the lock, she pushed into the cell. She gave him the candle to hold, and began to arrange the rolled-up quilt on the cot.

"Where's my keeper?" he asked.

"Busy in one of the privies." She drew the cover

on the cot over the quilt. "Unless he comes into the cell itself to check, this should satisfy him you're asleep in here. And by the time they bring you a breakfast tray, we'll be far away."

"You're getting pretty good at this, Meg," he said, following her out of the cell.

"At what?" she asked, closing and locking the door.

"Helping me to break out of jails."

"Well, you do keep getting arrested."

Snatching the key out of the lock, she led the way back to the front room, where she replaced the key on its hook and blew out the second candle.

Toby, still at the window, reported, "It's clear out there. Let's scoot before he—" He broke off with a sharp exclamation. "Too late! The privy door is opening! He's on his way back!"

Margaret edged to the side of the window to look. The jailer was crossing the quadrangle. "Is there another way out of here through the back?"

"Don't think so," Archer answered, "but if we have to, we'll lock him up in one of his own cells. This should help."

She turned her head to see that he had seized a loaded pistol from a gun rack high on the wall.

Toby chuckled. "Not necessary. He's about to be occupied again. Oh, mercy!"

Margaret sneaked another look through the glass. The jailer had come to a halt in the middle of the quadrangle, an expression of renewed panic on his round face. Swinging around, he fled back to the privy. The moment he scuttled inside, they went into action.

Checking the room to be sure everything was as they found it, except for the pistol, which was now in Archer's belt and hopefully wouldn't be missed for sometime, they slipped out into the quadrangle. Toby knew the way to an unguarded postern at the back side of the fort. They reached it without incident, unbarred it, and stole out into the pre-dawn darkness.

There was an autumn mist cloaking the river. It helped to conceal them as they gained the riverbank and followed it upstream toward the inlet. Once silence was no longer necessary, Margaret breathlessly filled Archer in on all the essentials without going into any of the background Trace had shared with her earlier. That story would have to wait until they were under way on the river.

When she was finished, he stopped her on the path. "You've told me everything but why you let Rawlins sail without you. Why you stayed behind to help me."

"I know now that you're innocent."

"Not good enough. *Why*, Meg?"

An impatient Toby was waiting for them to catch up with him. "Archer, there is no time for this."

"I don't move another step until I hear."

"It—it's complicated."

"No, it's simple. Say it!"

"Because I'm in love with you, you fool! Now will you move?"

"Oh, yeah," he said, and she could feel him charged with a sudden energy and decisiveness that matched her own exhilaration. "I can move, all right! Mountains, if I have to! Hauling Austin Pine back here ought to be a cinch!" He threw an arm around her waist. "Remind me when this is all over, precious, that I owe you about fifty years of hot kisses!"

Chapter Eighteen

"Ooo," Toby squealed, "look at all the lovely toys in there, and wouldn't I just love to play with them!"

He held the lantern high so that Margaret, squeezed beside him at the window, could peer into the steamboat's locked saloon at Dr. McLoughlin's collection of Indian artifacts. The walls and tables were crowded with rattles, ropes of beads and shells, feathered headdresses, and ceremonial masks of every description.

"Fascinating," Archer said dryly from behind them on the deck. "But if you're through admiring, let's get busy and demonstrate that the *Genevieve* is worth more than just a warehouse for the chief factor's curiosities. Because if he did value her, he'd keep a guard posted on board.''

Reminded of why they were there, Margaret turned around to face him. ''We're lucky he doesn't, and please tell me you know how to operate her.''

''Precious, there isn't a steamboat made that won't perform for me, and this sweet little lady is no exception.''

Taking charge, he led them away from the saloon to that part of the vessel where the engine and boiler were located. The firebox that fed the boiler, facing forward in order to catch the draft, was almost hidden behind a mountain of cordwood that was stacked everywhere on the deck.

''Plenty of fuel, anyway, but I'll need a fireman to handle it. Toby, this is your chance to prove your manhood.''

Toby responded, injured, ''I *am* a man, and I don't need to prove it.''

''Sorry, Toby, you're right. How about proving you're a hero then?''

''That I can attempt. How different can it be shoving wood into a firebox instead of a cookstove?''

''I'll help him,'' Margaret offered.

''No, you won't, precious, because I'll need you with me as navigator up in the pilothouse. Uh, you do know—''

''Oh, yes, I know just where we have to go. Trace is familiar with the map Austin Pine carries, and he described it all to me.''

''We're in business then.'' Archer showed Toby how to check the gauge to be sure the pressure was maintained but never dangerously high.

The sky was getting light by the time the boiler was adequately fired. The fort would be stirring soon. Worried about discovery, Margaret was relieved when they finally raised the hinged gangplank to its boom and cast off the lines. She followed Archer up into the glass-enclosed pilothouse, and stood beside him as the paddle wheel began to turn. The spoon-shaped bow backed away from the bank, and once they were clear, Archer swung the *Genevieve* about and headed them out into the open river.

"Still got the mist with us," he said. "That's good. We can hide in it as we slip past the fort."

"But we can't hide the throb of the engine," she pointed out.

"No, but we can soften it a lot with distance. That's why I'm steering a course for the other side. Her draft is shallow, so we can hug the south bank as we pass the fort. The Columbia is wide enough here that they shouldn't easily hear us. And even if they do, they have nothing fast enough to catch us."

Nevertheless, Margaret was tense with anxiety as they chugged through the mist. She expected at any second to hear the stillness out on the waters shattered by the blast of a cannon. At the same time, she couldn't help but be aware of Archer beside her. Whatever the threat to them, there was an expression of contentment on his lean face. He was at the wheel of a steamboat again.

It's like he's come home, she thought.

The long minutes crawled by as she waited for some outraged challenge from the direction of the fort. None came, and after a time she was aware that they were in the main current once more.

"We're in the clear now," he reported.

With the mist still on the waters she didn't know how he could tell, but then he had an uncanny skill with rivers and steamboats.

"All right," he said, "we're on our way downriver, but where to?"

"Beyond the mouth of the Columbia."

He whistled in surprise. "That's a long way off. Even with the current in our favor, it will take most of the day."

"Archer, we'll need to go right out into the ocean itself. Is the *Genevieve* capable of that?"

"She shouldn't mind the open sea. She's a honey of a boat, with a rugged hull built to take punishment. So what's out in the ocean?"

"A little island the Chinooks call Aku."

And as the sun rose, burning the mist off the river, and Toby went on feeding the firebox below, she told Archer the incredible story her brother had shared with her.

"About a year ago, Willis Hadley, the man you were accused of murdering, rescued one of the Chinooks. He'd been captured by an enemy tribe and eventually traded east to a band of Comanches."

"That's not hard to believe," Archer said. "Hadley mentioned he'd been involved in trade on the Santa Fe Trail, which is Comanche territory, and the tribes have been known to hold slaves. The Comanches are a fierce people, so this fellow wouldn't have had an easy existence with them."

"Apparently so, because in gratitude the Chinook gave Hadley an earring he'd managed to hang on to. It was very old, solid gold, and originally came from

Mexico. Hadley was excited about it. How had a Chinook from the Oregon coast gotten a thing like this?"

"And the Chinook told him."

"He did, and this is where the story becomes more legend than fact. But Hadley believed it, and so did Austin Pine and Trace after him."

"Go on."

"A long time ago, and we may be talking generations here, a Spanish ship on a voyage of exploration was wrecked off the Oregon coast. Some of its crew survived and lived with the Chinook in one of their villages, but two of their stronger members headed south on foot. Months later they managed to reach Mexico. The viceroy's brother was one of the officers of that marooned crew. The viceroy didn't hesitate to order the only ship in port on a rescue mission."

"Which was carrying?"

"Aztec gold. The ship would recover the survivors and then continue on its voyage to the Orient. It never reached the Chinook village. It, too, was wrecked off the Oregon coast in a wild storm. Its crew was lost, and none of those first survivors ever made it back to Mexico."

"So the gold earring came from that wreck?"

"On Atu Island, yes. The Chinook that Willis Hadley saved inherited it from an ancestor, who had helped himself to a few of the golden ornaments. But Atu Island already had a bad reputation with the Chinook, and when this ancestor died a violent death following his visit to the wreck, they were convinced the island was a cursed place haunted by evil spirits. It was forbidden to go there after that or even speak of it."

"And Hadley was convinced the treasure is still there."

Margaret nodded. "The Chinook refused to take him there, but he was persuaded to help him draw a detailed map."

"Then why didn't Hadley head straight to the site?"

"Because it was halfway across the continent and he was broke. He needed funds to pay for a journey like that. He hoped to get them back in Saint Joseph."

Archer, his eyes on the river, was silently thoughtful for a few seconds. "I think," he finally said, "I'm beginning to see what happened next. Hadley fell in with the little farm-implement salesman and made the mistake of thinking he's as meek as he looks."

"Exactly. Austin Pine agreed to finance the trek for half of the treasure. And then came that card game you were all involved in."

"And Hadley had big winnings," Arch remembered. "So big that I suppose he no longer needed Austin Pine."

"They quarreled about it late that night at the hotel," Margaret continued. "When Hadley refused to have anything more to do with him, Austin Pine stabbed him to death and helped himself to the map and the earring. But Trace caught him at it."

"So Pine promised your weak-willed brother a share of the fortune if he would tell another story about what he'd witnessed, and I became the scapegoat."

"You were convenient. Everyone knew you had a hot temper, that you'd accused Willis Hadley of cheating at the card game. And you were staying just down the hall. Pine was able to sneak into your room and hide Hadley's winnings where the sheriff would find them.''

''That brother of yours has a lot to answer for.''

''I think he already has, Archer. I think he's been suffering his own private hell for months now. He just didn't know how to let go of an impossible dream.''

''Yeah, I hear the lure of gold can make a man give up his own soul.''

''I wonder if the treasure *is* actually there.''

''Does it matter, as long as we catch the bastard who's convinced it is?''

''No, I guess it doesn't.''

The sun climbed into the sky as the *Genevieve* steamed onward. Hour after hour the paddle wheel churned the waters while miles of wooded banks slid by. It was just before noon when Archer's sharp eye spotted a wisp of smoke rising in a small clearing off the starboard bow.

''What are you doing?'' Margaret asked him as he turned them toward the riverbank.

''I want to have a look at that smoke, and Toby needs a rest. He must be exhausted by now. Besides, it's an opportunity to take on more wood.''

The three of them went ashore after the *Genevieve* was secured. The source of the smoke proved to be the smoldering end of a log inside a circle of stones.

''Just as I figured,'' Arch said, examining the remains of the fire. ''What do you want to bet Pine and his two friends camped here last night? Which means he won't have reached the island yet, not in a canoe. We've still got time.''

There was plenty of dry wood lying around, and

while Toby stretched out in the clearing, Margaret and Archer collected armfuls and carried them on board the steamboat, adding to the diminished fuel. Then the three of them ate a cold, hasty meal from the provisions Toby had stored in a locker last night. They were under way again within an hour.

It was late afternoon when the shores on either side of the river, which had been steadily widening, seemed to disappear over the horizon. They had reached the open sea.

"We go north now," Margaret directed Archer.

He turned the vessel, and they followed the distant coastline off to their right.

"How far to the island?" he asked.

"Several miles. We should see it soon."

He searched the horizon ahead of them for the first signs of Aku or the glimpse of a canoe. Neither appeared. She noticed he was wearing a worried frown.

"I don't like the looks of that sky up there," he said.

He was right. There were dark clouds massing over the northern horizon. Margaret found the sight of them alarming.

"A storm?" She thought of those other violent gales that long ago had smashed two ships against the rocks of Aku, and she shuddered.

"Could be."

They were already encountering swells, which she found uncomfortable after the smoothness of the river. She had believed them to be the normal action of the ocean, but maybe they were the forerunners of a rough sea. The *Genevieve* didn't care for them either. She was wallowing drunkenly.

"I think I see it," Arch said, nodding at a green smudge on the horizon. "Will there be a safe place to land?"

"The wreck is located on the other side of the island. It's a wild shore there, but there's supposed to be a sheltered cove on this side."

They were rolling rather badly now. Water was slopping over the decks. Margaret kept her eyes on the elusive island and prayed.

"We've got a problem!" Archer said, looking out his side of the pilothouse.

Startled, Margaret followed the direction of his gaze. Toby was down there, hanging over the rail and retching miserably.

"He's seasick," Archer said. "There's no way he can go on feeding the boiler, which means we're going to lose pressure here, and without it we're helpless. You're going to have to take the wheel, Meg, while I go down there and keep us steaming."

She stared at him in a panic. "No! Why can't I handle the fueling myself?"

"Because we're tossing too much now. You wouldn't be able to stay on your feet down there, but I'm used to it. Meg, you can do this. Just keep the wheel steady, and trust the *Genevieve* to do the rest. And as soon as we're in the lee of the island, I'll be back to land her."

And with that, he placed her hands on the wheel and was gone. She could suddenly feel the power of the vessel in her control, and it was awesome and at the same time absolutely daunting.

You can do this. Archer trusts you to do it. You have to do it.

377

She clung to the wheel while the seas grew choppier under a rising wind. The *Genevieve*, suffering the punishment of the waters that battered her, seemed to groan in every seam, but she plowed gallantly onward through the waves while Margaret fought to keep her steady.

The bump that was Aku grew larger, taking on a definite shape. Margaret could make out the forest that covered it. There was still no sign of a canoe. If it had capsized in the heavy seas, drowning its three occupants, or if Pine had already left the island, their voyage would be for nothing. Without the real killer, Archer couldn't be vindicated.

The sky grew even blacker in the north. Either they reached the island before it broke, or—But she dared not think of that prospect.

The *Genevieve* crawled toward its destination, the paddle wheel biting into the dark, angry seas. Slowly, but surely, it made progress, and at last they gained the lee of the island and quieter waters. Margaret could see the opening into the promised cove directly ahead. But where was Archer? She could never bring the steamboat safely through that gap, never mind landing her on the shore.

And then, as suddenly as he disappeared, he was beside her again in the wheelhouse. She sagged in relief.

"All right," he said breathlessly, "I'll take her now. Good job, Meg."

She gratefully turned the wheel over to him, and within minutes he had berthed them in the cove. An excited Toby, already recovering from his bout of seasickness, met them on the engine deck.

"Good news, love! Their canoe is there on the beach!"

Margaret could see it now, one of the brightly painted and elaborately carved cedar canoes of the Chinooks drawn up on the sand. Austin Pine was here on the island with Geoduck and Big Alice!

"We're going after them," Archer said, checking the pistol he still carried. "Toby, you stay here with the *Genevieve*."

"But my innards are behaving themselves now."

"I need you to keep the *Genevieve* safe. I'd leave Meg with you, but she knows the way."

Arch gave him no chance to argue. Grabbing Margaret by the hand, he hurried the two of them ashore. She loved this man, but he could be exasperating, and she told him so as they headed up the beach.

"Did you have to hurt him like that? He wanted to come with us, and now he feels left out and useless."

"He's been plenty useful, and I'll make sure he knows it. But those yellow pantaloons of his would have shouted we were coming. Which way?"

"There's supposed to be an old path here that cuts through the island to the other side."

They found it, and though it was overgrown from long disuse, it could still be traveled. The thick evergreen forest swallowed them as they plunged into the interior of the small island. It was dark under the trees, and the rumble of thunder reminded them of the advancing storm.

Archer led the way, the pistol ready in his hand. They moved swiftly along the trail, not speaking. Margaret could feel them climbing, and wasn't surprised when, after a mile or so, they emerged abruptly from the forest on the edge of a sheer cliff over-hanging the ocean. The path turned to the right here, taking them around a shoulder of rock and within sight of the rugged north shore of the island.

"This is it!" Margaret said, dragging at his arm.

They found themselves looking down into a wide, exposed bay. The strong wind carried long rollers in from the ocean, driving them past spikes of rock that rose from the wild waters like rows of wicked teeth. The largest of them, an immense black monolith, was connected to the island by a long arc of hard sand that formed a natural causeway on the far side of the bay.

"The wreck is supposed to be hung up on that," Margaret said, indicating the mountain of black rock.

"Don't see any sign of it."

"Trace said the rock is split, and the broken ship was flung up into the cleft and wedged there."

"No wonder it went undetected except for a few daring Chinook. With the dangerous currents that must be out there, no boat, not even a canoe, could get anywhere near it from this side of the island. But where are Pine and his two friends? I don't see any sign of them either."

They had the answer to his question a moment later when they advanced cautiously along the path several more yards. From behind them, without warning, a pair of rifles were shoved into their backs.

Margaret, stifling a cry, turned her head to discover two faces grinning at her maliciously. The man and woman wearing them had been so cunning that she and Archer had neither heard them nor detected a movement. The couple must have been concealed in the woods just around the bend in the path.

The man grunted a command to Archer. "Throw down gun, or my woman kill your woman."

Archer lowered the pistol and dropped it to the ground. It was swiftly appropriated. The muzzles of the rifles retreated from their backs as the couple backed away a few paces. Another order was barked at them.

"Now you turn."

Geoduck and Big Alice, Margaret thought fearfully as she swung around to face them. Big Alice had been aptly named. She was a mountain of a woman with an expression as mean as her sister's was sweet. Geoduck, with his long black hair and sly gaze, looked just as dangerous.

"Where's Pine?" Archer demanded.

"Wait," Geoduck growled, and that's all he would say.

He and Big Alice kept the rifles trained on them. Long minutes passed as the four of them went on standing there on the cliff under the shoulder of rock. The wind had increased, spitting drops of rain at them. There were lightning and thunder as well, but the storm had yet to release its fury. Margaret could sense that Archer was on fire with frustration, his mind searching for a method of escape.

After a time she became aware that Geoduck and Big Alice were casting anxious glances in the direction of the cliff face on the far side of the bay. They were looking for something, and they must have sighted it finally, because their expressions became tense.

Then Margaret saw it, too. A small figure had

emerged from the woods over there and was beginning a descent down to the causeway. It had to be Austin Pine on his way to the treasure. The cliff on that side was not as precipitous, but Pine was obviously not athletic either. He picked his way from rock to rock with slow, laborious care.

She knew Archer was seething with the need to go after him, but their captors were experiencing another mood. They're nervous, Margaret realized. It isn't just the storm on its way or Pine clinging to that cliff. It's the island itself. It's being here in this haunted, forbidden place. That's why they aren't accompanying Pine to the site of the wreck itself. That's why they dare not come any farther than this.

Margaret herself felt it was a scene where any unearthly horror could strike. Which was why seconds later her heart leaped into her throat when, along with a flash of lightning, there came the fiendish howl of a demon over their heads.

All four of them lifted startled eyes to discover an apparition looming above them up on the shoulder of rock. It was a towering, hideous thing, its outstretched arms dripping with tangled seaweed, its writhing body clad in ropes of shells, its face a distorted nightmare. An evil that had materialized from the depths of the ocean.

The wind wailed, the lightning flared again. And Geoduck and Big Alice, with shrieks of terror, turned and crashed through the forest, fleeing to the cove and their canoe. Margaret would have been tempted to escape with them, had it not been for the outrageous yellow pantaloons.

The specter above them, cackling with laughter,

scrambled down the rock. "Costume, effective lightning, correct timing! One couldn't ask for better theater!"

"Couldn't resist breaking into the saloon and helping yourself to the collection, could you?" Archer challenged him.

"*Borrowing*, love," Toby corrected him, removing the ceremonial mask from his bony face. "And aren't you grateful I did, because it did just occur to me when you were gone so long that you might be in a spot of trouble."

"Toby, my man, I will be indebted to you for the rest of my days."

"A pity they took all the firearms with them, though."

"At this point," Archer promised them, "my fists are going to be enough. Let's go."

With no further delay, he turned and raced along the path that led to the other side of the bay. Margaret and Toby sped after him. But Archer's long legs, together with his urgency, brought him to the place where Pine had descended well ahead of them. By the time they reached the scene, he was already sliding and leaping from level to level down the cliff. He shouted for them to remain on top.

They hung back, watching the chase, ready to help Archer if he needed them. Austin Pine had gained the causeway and was trotting toward the huge spur of black rock where the surf was boiling. Rollers were beginning to break and run over the long strand of curving sand.

"The tide is coming in," Margaret said. "The causeway is going to be covered."

But Pine, wild with the fever of gold, was oblivious to both the threat of the tide and his pursuer. Nor did Archer count the risks as he landed on the causeway and tore after him. Pine was more than halfway along the ridge of sand when Archer caught up with him.

Margaret, clinging to Toby, found the tension unbearable as she watched the desperate struggle below. The waters were around the ankles of the two men now, rising fast toward their knees, as they locked in combat.

"They'll be trapped!"

"No, love, it's all right! He has him!"

Austin Pine was no match for Archer. One solid blow, and the little farm-implement salesman collapsed. Slinging the limp body over his shoulder, Archer sloshed back over the causeway and began to scale the cliff. Eager hands hurried to help him raise his load.

The storm broke with sheets of driving rain before they were able to regain the cove. But it didn't matter. They had what they had come for.

Chapter Nineteen

The Delaneys were hosting an afternoon party to celebrate Archer's acquittal. The chief factor of Ft. Vancouver, after questioning Austin Pine at length in his cell, had determined exactly who was responsible for Willis Hadley's murder. Archer was a free man, and though Dr. McLoughlin wasn't happy about the theft of the *Genevieve,* he was ready to forgive the perpetrators. After all, the *Genevieve,* having managed to ride out the violent storm in the snug cove at Aku Island, had returned to the fort in calm seas with no damage either to the steamboat or its contents.

The parlor of the Delaney log cabin was small,

which made it seem very crowded, but Margaret felt this just added to everyone's enjoyment.

Magpie and her husband had crossed the river in their canoe to join them. A gregarious man, her husband was giving them an account of the treasure seekers who had rushed to Aku after hearing the story of its gold.

"They was swarming all over the island but didn't find a thing up on that rock, excepting a few broken timbers. Guess the kind of roaring storm that threw the ship up there years ago carried the wreck out to sea again and the treasure along with it."

"If there ever was a treasure to begin with," Toby said. "One can only wonder now whether it was a reality or just the stuff dreams are made of. Ah, well . . ."

Margaret and Archer exchanged contented smiles. She knew that neither one of them had any regrets about a lost treasure. They had their own riches, and it didn't involve gold. Molly for one, she thought. The child was crowing with laughter as Archer rode her on his knee. It gave Margaret a sweet ache inside watching the two of them together. A father with his daughter. Her love for them swelled to new heights, and then was suddenly tempered when Cooper turned the conversation to a subject that had been worrying her since their return from Aku Island.

"So, what are your plans now, Owen?"

"We haven't discussed it, but as soon as it can be arranged, Meg and I will be heading back to Missouri. I may have cleared myself with the chief factor here, but it means nothing until the court in Saint Joseph exonerates me."

"I don't see that it's necessary for you to do that in person," Cooper said. "I imagine that Dr. McLoughlin will make certain a letter of explanation accompanies Pine when he's transported to Missouri."

"And I'll do my part to make things right with the court when I get home," Trace added. Margaret's remorseful brother had already promised her he was prepared to return to his family and responsibilities in Saint Joseph. She would miss him now that they had learned to appreciate each other.

"You see," Cooper said. "No need for you to leave. You might even consider making your home right here in Oregon. We'd welcome you if the two of you decided to stay on."

Archer shook his head. "No future in it. You forget I'm a riverman with the *Missouri Belle* waiting for me in Saint Joseph. I need my steamboat."

Margaret and Toby exchanged swift, concerned glances.

"You could be a riverman right here," Cooper argued. "The way McLoughlin feels about the *Genevieve*, I don't have any trouble believing he could be persuaded to sell her. You could run the *Genevieve* on the Columbia and the Willamette wherever they're navigable. Time we had a regular service to haul supplies to the settlements and carry out our products. What do you say, Owen?"

Archer laughed. "The *Genevieve* is a sweet little boat, but what do you suggest I buy her with? The *Missouri Belle* is all I've got in the world, and she isn't worth a lot, except to me."

"Oh, Aggie will loan you whatever you need. You wouldn't know it to look at her, but she's richer than that legendary treasure that got away. And she's always ready to finance new ventures that will make her even richer.'' He grinned at Agatha, who was moving around the room offering more cake and coffee. ''Aren't you, Aggie?''

''My love, you make me sound dreadfully mercenary. The truth is I am investing in Oregon and its settlers. I have little interest in swelling my purse, and yes, we do need a steamboat service on the rivers. Will you have another slice of cake, Mr. Owen, or a loan?''

''Neither one, ma'am, thank you. You see, the *Missouri Belle* is very special to me. She's more than just my future. She's . . . well, she's been my home.''

Margaret could no longer stand this. Setting down her cup and saucer, she got to her feet. ''Archer, let's go outside. I'd like to take a little walk.''

He looked up at her in surprise. ''Now?''

''Yes, please.''

She could see he was bewildered, but he offered no further objection. He stood, placing Molly in Cooper's lap. ''Here, introduce her to your son.''

''Excuse us,'' Margaret murmured to the gathering, taking Archer by the hand and leading him to the door.

The company was moving on to a new topic when they left, a speculation of whether Geoduck and Big Alice had perished in their canoe or had managed to flee somewhere into the wilderness.

Margaret drew Archer down to the river path. They strolled side by side in the direction of the inlet where the *Genevieve* was moored. Once out of sight of the cabin, he asked her, "Now what was that all about back there?"

She stopped and turned to him. "We've had no chance to discuss it, but do you intend for us to be married? Or am I assuming too much?"

"Do I want us to be married? Only as soon as possible, that's all. Right here at the fort if we can arrange it. And if this is all you're worried about . . ."

He looked relieved and started to take her in his arms. She held him off. "There's something else."

"Then let's hear it, because I've got to tell you, precious, the solemn look you're wearing is scaring me."

"Archer, I want to be a wife to you and a mother to Molly. Those will always come first with me, but they aren't enough. Not anymore. I need to do more. Do you understand?"

"I think so. You're saying you have a dream now of your own to realize. And that's fine with me. What is it?"

"I want to open an inn." She went on rapidly telling him the rest, knowing if she paused her courage would fail her. "It was Agatha who gave me the idea when she mentioned how more and more people are arriving in the area, visitors as well as new settlers, only there are no proper accommodations for them. And since it was Agatha who inspired my intention, I'm sure she wouldn't hesitate to help me build an inn. I'd serve regular meals, of course. Toby would be in charge of the kitchen. You know he cooks like a dream, and I think I can convince Little Alice to—"

"Meg, no. Do you realize what you're saying? It would mean staying here in Oregon."

"Yes, that's just what I want us to do."

He shook his head stubbornly. "You can have your inn back in Missouri. Maybe not right away, because I'll have to go to work to get the *Belle* repaired, but as soon as she's running and earning profits again—"

Unable to bear any more, she put her hand against his mouth to silence him. "Archer, you can't have the *Missouri Belle*."

He stared at her, frowning. Then he slowly removed her hand from his mouth. "There's something you haven't told me. What is it?"

There was no way to avoid it. The time had come to hurt him. "The *Belle* isn't waiting for you back in Saint Joseph. Archer, she no longer exists." And as gently as possible, she told him how Enoch Rawlins had destroyed his cherished steamboat.

She understood the anguish in his eyes, shared in it. There was a long, awful silence when she was finished.

"Darling, I'm so sorry," she whispered. "I know what she meant to you."

Still, he said nothing. She anxiously searched his face, knowing if he couldn't accept his misfortune, terrible though it was, she would lose him. There would be no wonderful dream for them to share.

In the end, he drew a deep breath and released it slowly. "You know what?"

"What, dearest?"

"I mind that the *Belle* is gone, and I'm going to miss her. But it's Rawlins who lost, not me. I won because I have all that really matters, you and Molly. That's right, isn't it?"

Margaret could feel the tears of relief slide down

her cheeks, together with her joyous laughter. "Yes, sweetheart! Oh, yes, it is!"

She went eagerly into his waiting arms. His mouth found hers in a slow, thorough kiss that expressed the promise of a long life together. A life that would be secure, not because of the dreams they would share, the obstacles they would manage to overcome, or even the children they might bear, but because of their deep, lasting love for each other.

When Archer finally released her, he turned his head, his gaze seeking the *Genevieve* at rest in the inlet. "Wonder how much McLoughlin will ask for her?"

"We'll have to find out."

"Later. Right now I'd like to go and see how much cargo she'll hold, and afterwards . . ."

"Yes?"

"Well, I noticed there's a wide bunk in the saloon just waiting to be used." His meaning was clear.

"I have no objections to that," Margaret said. "None at all."

Throwing an arm around her waist, he hurried her toward the inlet and their future.

DELANEY'S CROSSING

JEAN BARRETT

Virile, womanizing Cooper J. Delaney is Agatha Pennington's only hope to help lead a group of destitute women to Oregon, where the promise of a new life awaits them. He is a man as harsh and hostile as the vast wilderness—but Agatha senses a gentleness behind his hard-muscled exterior, a tenderness lurking beneath his gruff facade. Though the group battles rainstorms, renegade Indians, and raging rivers, the tall beauty's tenacity never wavers. And with each passing mile, Cooper realizes he is struggling against a maddening attraction for her and that he would journey to the ends of the earth if only to claim her untouched heart.

_4200-2 $5.50 US/$6.50 CAN

MADELINE BAKER

Beneath A Midnight Moon

Winner Of The *Romantic Times* Reviewers Choice Award!

He comes to her in visions—the hard-muscled stranger who promises to save her from certain death. She never dares hope that her fantasy love will hold her in his arms until the virile and magnificent dream appears in the flesh.

A warrior valiant and true, he can overcome any obstacle, yet his yearning for the virginal beauty he's rescued overwhelms him. But no matter how his fevered body aches for her, he is betrothed to another.

Bound together by destiny, yet kept apart by circumstances, they brave untold perils and ruthless enemies—and find a passion that can never be rent asunder.

___3649-5 $4.99 US/$5.99 CAN

LOVE FOREVERMORE

MADELINE BAKER

The West—it has been Loralee's dream for as long as she could remember, and Indians are the most fascinating part of the wildly beautiful frontier she imagines. But when Loralee arrives at Fort Apache as the new schoolmarm, she has some hard realities to learn...and a harsh taskmaster to teach her. Shad Zuniga is fiercely proud, aloof, a renegade Apache who wants no part of the white man's world, not even its women. Yet Loralee is driven to seek him out, compelled to join him in a forbidden union, forced to become an outcast for one slim chance at love forevermore.

___4267-3 $5.99 US/$6.99 CAN

SAVAGE SPIRIT

CASSIE EDWARDS

**Winner of the *Romantic Times*
Lifetime Achievement Award for Best Indian Series!**

Life in the Arizona Territory has prepared Alicia Cline to expect the unexpected. Brash and reckless, she dares to take on renegades and bandidos. But the warm caresses and soft words of an Apache chieftain threaten her vulnerable heart more than any burning lance.

Chief Cloud Eagle has tamed the wild beasts of his land, yet one glimpse of Alicia makes him a slave to desire. Her snow-white skin makes him tremble with longing; her flame-red hair sets his senses ablaze. Cloud Eagle wants nothing more than to lie with her in his tepee, nothing less than to lose himself in her unending beauty. But to claim Alicia, the mighty warrior will first have to capture her bold savage spirit.

_3639-8 $4.99 US/$5.99 CAN

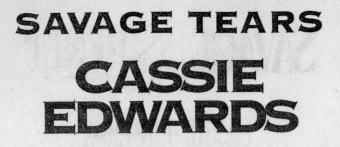

SAVAGE TEARS

CASSIE EDWARDS

Bestselling author of *Savage Longings*

Long has Marjorie Zimmerman been fascinated by the Dakota Indians of the Minnesota Territory—especially their hot-blooded chieftain. With the merest glance from his smoldering eyes, Spotted Horse can spark a firestorm of desire in the spirited settler's heart. Then he steals like a shadow in the night to rescue Marjorie from her hated stepfather, and she aches to surrender to the proud warrior body and soul. But even as they ride to safety, enemies— both Indian and white—prepare to make their passion as fleeting as the moonlight shining down from the heavens. Soon Marjorie and Spotted Horse realize that they will have to fight with all their cunning, strength, and valor, or they will end up with nothing more than savage tears.

___4281-9 $5.99 US/$6.99 CAN

Dorchester Publishing Co., Inc.
P.O. Box 6640
Wayne, PA 19087-8640

SAVAGE LONGINGS

CASSIE EDWARDS

"Cassie Edwards is a shining talent!"
—*Romantic Times*

Having been kidnapped by vicious trappers, Snow Deer despairs of ever seeing her people again. Then, from out of the Kansas wilderness comes Charles Cline to rescue the Indian maiden. Strong yet gentle, brave yet tenderhearted, the virile blacksmith is everything Snow Deer desires in a man. And beneath the fierce sun, she burns to succumb to the sweet temptation of his kiss. But the strong-willed Cheyenne princess is torn between the duty that demands she stay with her tribesmen and the passion that promises her unending happiness among white settlers. Only the love in her heart and the courage in her soul can convince Snow Deer that her destiny lies with Charles—and the blissful fulfillment of their savage longings.

_4176-6 $5.99 US/$6.99 CAN

Forever Gold

CATHERINE HART

**"Catherine Hart writes thrilling adventure...
beautiful and memorable romance!"**
—*Romantic Times*

From the moment Blake Montgomery holds up the westward-bound stagecoach carrying lovely Megan Coulston to her adoring fiance, she hates everything about the virile outlaw. How dare he drag her off to an isolated mountain cabin and hold her ransom? How dare he steal her innocence with his practiced caresses? How dare he kidnap her heart when all he can offer is forbidden moments of burning, trembling esctasy?

__3895-1 $5.99 US/$7.99 CAN

Flames of Rapture

Lark Eden

"Great reading!"—*Romantic Times*

When Lyric Solei flees the bustling city for her summer retreat in Salem, Massachusetts, it is a chance for the lovely young psychic to escape the pain so often associated with her special sight. Investigating a mysterious seaside house whose ancient secrets have long beckoned to her, Lyric stumbles upon David Langston, the house's virile new owner, whose strong arms offer her an irresistible temptation. And it is there that Lyric discovers a dusty red coat, which from the time she first lays her gifted hands on it unravels to her its tragic history—and lets her relive the timeless passion that brought it into being.

_52078-8 $4.99 US/$6.99 CAN